HE WHO
LIFTS THE
Skies

HE WHO LIFTS THE *Skies*

KACY BARNETT-GRAMCKOW

MOODY PUBLISHERS
CHICAGO

ISBN: 0-8024-1368-4

1 3 5 7 9 10 8 6 4 2

Printed in the United States of America

Library of Congress Cataloging-in-Publication Data

Barnett-Gramckow, Kacy, 1960-
  He who lifts the skies/Kacy Barnett-Gramckow.
      p.cm.—(Genesis trilogy; #2)
  ISBN 0-8024-1368-4
  1. Noah (Biblical figure)—Fiction. 2. Bible. O.T. Genesis—History of
Biblical events—Fiction. 3. Noah's ark—Fiction. 4. Deluge—Fiction. I. Title.
  PS3602.A8343H4 2004
  813'.6—dc22

                                                              2004005169

To my wonderful brothers, Bob, John, Jim, and Joe,
who could conquer any wilderness.
And to Kerrin, Lynn, Debbie, and Janine, my perfect and beautiful
sisters-in-law, who conquered my brothers.
Thank you for the joy and blessings you've brought to our lives.

Acknowledgments

THANKS TO Moody Publishers editors Amy Schmidt and Dave DeWit; I appreciate your hard work. Also to Michele Straubel, blessings! Amy Peterson—Author Relations Manager and fellow author—you are a jewel for being so patient while answering my last-minute questions. Special recognition to Lori Wenzinger, Becky Armstrong, and Carolyn McDaniel for sending files on short notice, and to LB Norton for her perfect critique—and all the fun questions.

Mary Busha, my agent, thanks for all you do—and for your gracious, timely advice. Regards to Seth Bartels/ Solidstate Interactive, for all the dialogue while creating our Web site, www.gram-co-ink.com. In addition, gratitude to John Barnett and Janine Barnett for their inspirational bow-and-arrow experiences—you didn't know you were doing research for me, did you? I owe you each a dinner "out." Special thanks to Chris Seeley and the Falcon 1644 Crew for all the work, fun, and support. And to Rosanne Fahrenbruch for the coaching in Hebrew; you've added to my family's lore. I just wish I'd inherited sturdier vocal cords.

Barbara LeVan Fisher, your artwork is amazing!

I would also like to recognize Tim Wallace at www.trueorigin.org. Thanks for your courtesy and for your informative Web site. To the staff at Triple R Ranch in Chesapeake, Virginia, thank you for your eternal lessons and for teaching this coward to enjoy riding years ago! Also, to my local critic crew: Jennifer, Natalie, Celeste, Diane—I'm typing as fast as I can. To my dear husband and the whole Barnett-Gramckow clan, I love you all.

Prologue

IN THE FIRST AGE beneath the blue heavens, before the times of nations, all the kindred tribes of the earth yielded to the Most High as their judge.

But from among all the kindred tribes of the earth came those who contended against the Most High in the darkness of their souls. Longing after their own desires, these rebellious ones bowed to a man of many names: the Hunter, the Grand One, the Mighty Assembler. And he became their Great King of the earth.

Delighting in his own power, this Great King encouraged his rebels to scorn the Most High and seek other ways to ease their guilt-stricken souls. Now, because the Great King so gladly lifted the burdens of their hearts and shouldered the weight of the very heavens for their sakes, the rebellious ones gave to him a new name: He-Who-Lifts-the-Skies.

*The earth's leaders are plotting together
against Adonai
and his Anointed.
"Let us break their bonds," they cry,
"and cast off their restraints!"
The One enthroned in heaven laughs;
Adonai looks upon them with scorn.*

(Adapted from Psalm 2:2–4)

One

STEPPING OUT OF HER lodge, Annah breathed in the soft spring air as she studied the evening skies. Dawn and dusk were her favorite times—if it was not raining—for then she could see the colors she had loved from the heavens of her childhood. The first faint tinges of rose and violet soothed her now, as always.

Have I stopped mourning for the skies of my youth? she wondered. *I think I will change my mind every day of my life. Today yes, tomorrow no.*

As she stared up at the sky, Annah felt thick, heavy woolen folds descend upon her tunic-clad shoulders. Her husband, Shem, was wrapping her in her gray wool shawl. He scolded her gently, his voice soft against her ear. "You're as careless as the children of our children. It's too cold for you to be outside without your shawl."

Annah smiled, patting her husband's long brown hands

as he wrapped his arms around her. "After all these years, beloved, you should be tired of following me around and fretting about me."

"I'll never grow tired of following you," Shem murmured teasingly. "As long as you know where you're going."

"I'm going for a walk."

"Then I will follow you."

Almost as one, they turned and went down a well-trampled path, traversing the sloping fields surrounding their lodge. As they walked, Annah looked up at her husband. Shem smiled at her, his warm brown eyes glinting in his darkly bearded face, as irrepressible as a little boy.

Your smile is more wonderful than all the skies of my childhood, Annah thought. *Why should I mourn for them? As lovely as they were, they covered nothing but violence and hatred.* "You almost look younger than your own sons," she told him.

He became somber, as if troubled by the truth of her words. "Annah, beloved, I've been thinking about our children. . . ." He stopped.

Wondering, Annah turned to see what had caught his attention. A young man's cheerful voice echoed up to them from the forest-hedged slopes below.

"Father of my Fathers! Are you leaving because we've arrived?"

"That depends upon how many people you're bringing with you," Shem called back, laughing. "Come greet your Ma'adannah."

"Who is it?" Annah whispered to Shem as they watched the dark outlines of the woods. Almost as soon as she asked the question, Annah saw a lanky young man emerge from the shadows of the trees. He was clad in leather and fleece, burdened with a thick bentwood-and-

12

leather traveling pack and armed with a flint-tipped hunting spear and a knife of stone. The young man's cheerful face, his smooth, deep brown skin, lustrous dark eyes, and straight black hair all marked him as one of Annah's own descendants: Eliyshama, the youngest son of her grandson Meshek.

Delighted, Annah called out, "Eliyshama! Is your father with you?" She had not seen Meshek and his family for nearly three years.

"Ma'adannah." Eliyshama waved a greeting, then pointed his hunting spear toward the shadowed trees. "My father and my I'ma are coming. And we've brought Metiyl, son of your son Asshur."

"Metiyl?" Annah gasped. She hadn't seen Metiyl in more than ten years. Almost dancing, she hugged Eliyshama, accepting his hearty kiss. "It's so good to see you again. You've grown! And thank you for bringing Metiyl."

Shem greeted Eliyshama with a fond hug, then caught his arm eagerly, asking, "Is our Asshur coming to visit us too?"

"Only Metiyl, not his father." Eliyshama sighed heavily. But his dark eyes sparkled, betraying his joy. "Are you grieved, Father of my Fathers? Should I go to your Asshur and beg his presence here?"

"No, because then my Asshur would keep you with him for ten years," Shem answered, his tone half laughing, half serious.

By now, Annah could see her grandsons—the tall, black-haired Meshek, and the shorter, stockier, wild-haired Metiyl—both armed with stone knives and flint-tipped hunting spears. Just behind the two men, Annah glimpsed a blue-shawled head: Meshek's wife, Chaciydah, walking slowly, her head bowed. Immediately, she grew concerned. Glancing up at Eliyshama, Annah asked, "Is your mother ill?"

"My I'ma is worried," Eliyshama answered, the light fading from his dark eyes. "Ma'adannah, she's had a daughter; we've hoped the child would improve."

"Improve?" Annah clasped Eliyshama's wrist. "The child is ill?"

Eliyshama shrugged. "We don't know. We're praying that you and our First Father Shem can tell us what to believe. My I'ma has been half crazed with fear."

Chaciydah has always allowed her fears to rule her mind, Annah thought, trying to soothe herself. *Perhaps the child's illness is Chaciydah's own nothing-whim.* Quickly, she descended the slope to meet her grandchildren.

As the elder grandson, Metiyl claimed the privilege of kissing Annah first. Laughing, he jarred her with an enthusiastic hug, scratching her with his coarse beard and almost rapping her head with his spear. "Ma'adannah! You're as young as ever. Here's a kiss from my father, with his most respectful greetings; he misses you."

"Then where is your father, if he misses us so much?" Shem demanded, his genial question echoing Annah's own feelings of quiet disappointment.

"He couldn't leave his lands or his flocks." Metiyl curled his hands around his hunting spear reflexively, his brown face suddenly grim. "They need his protection."

Annah frowned. "His *lands* need protection? From what? The wild animals?"

"No, Ma'adannah. My father protects his lands and belongings from the sons of his cousins."

Metiyl's growling hostility made Annah shiver.

Glancing from Annah to Shem, Metiyl said, "I'll tell you everything at the evening fire. Here are Meshek and

Chaciydah. And . . ." he whispered, "their youngest child."

Annah's heart thudded. If Metiyl was concerned, then obviously there *was* something wrong with this infant girl.

Annah kissed the tall, silent, black-bearded Meshek. Then she turned to Chaciydah. The younger woman's large, tender brown eyes were shadowed with fatigue, and her slender, tawny face lacked its usual ruddy glow. Before Annah could greet her, Chaciydah dropped her leather supply pouch, babbling like a frightened child.

"Ma'adannah, after seven healthy sons, the Most High finally grants me a daughter—then He allows her this affliction. Look at her, Ma'adannah! I'm in despair!" Chaciydah pushed aside the light blue folds of her woolen shawl, revealing a small bundle nestled against her chest in a soft leather carrying pouch.

Gently Annah lifted the small bundle from its carrying pouch and opened the gray folds of the outermost blanket to reveal the sleeping child's face. Annah could not prevent herself from gasping in shock. *This child has no color. O Most High, what does this mean?*

Even in the growing dusk, Annah could see the pale translucency of the infant girl's skin and the extraordinary noncolor of her hair. Shem was beside Annah now, his long brown fingers holding back the gray woolen blanket. Lifting her gaze to his, Annah questioned her husband silently: *What do you think?*

His lips faintly puckered, Shem lifted one dark eyebrow, cautioning Annah without words: *I don't like this.* He spoke to Chaciydah and the others soothingly. "Come, let's go visit with my father and my mother. They'll want to welcome you. We'll present your daughter to them and ask their opinion. Don't look so worried, Chaciydah; I'm sure your daughter will live."

Still carrying the infant, Annah followed Shem up to the path traversing the hillside. By the set of his shoulders and his brisk pace, Annah knew that her husband was profoundly disturbed by the sight of this child. As if in response, the tiny girl emitted a thin, angry squeal of protest, her cry becoming louder and more shrill as Annah carried her up the path.

Annah's discomfort grew with the child's cry.

As she warmed herself near the glowing, crackling fire in the stone-lined hearth in the lodge, Annah studied the colorless infant girl. The tiny child was alert in her mother's arms, her young eyes wide, flickering here and there in apparent wonderment.

"I believe she's perfectly healthy," Annah told Chaciydah. "She sleeps well, she cries loudly, she feeds well, and she's watching everything. You shouldn't worry, Chaciydah."

"But her lack of color is dreadful," Chaciydah mourned. "And look at her eyes. They aren't even brown. They're smoke gray!"

"Let me hold her," Shem's mother, Naomi, urged Chaciydah. "It's always good to hold an infant." Her silver hair gleaming in the firelight, Naomi crooned to the child. "I agree with your Ma'adannah, little one; your mother shouldn't worry about you. Even now, your little mind is busy."

As Naomi whispered to the child, Annah glanced at the men, who had gathered on the opposite side of the hearth. Her father-in-law, Noakh, was sitting on a comfortable heap of mats and fleeces with Shem, Meshek, and Eliyshama. They were facing Metiyl, whose deep voice was rising with anger as he lifted his broad, work-roughened hands in the firelight.

"Now my horsemen-cousins ride through my father's lands and threaten his tribes with new weapons they've made. Everyone's afraid to oppose them. And," Metiyl added ferociously, "their 'Great King,' Nimr-Rada, encourages them to take whatever or whomever they please!"

Annah felt her stomach churn at this news. Raising her voice, she asked Metiyl, "They take whomever they please to serve them?"

"To serve their Great King, Nimr-Rada—the Subduer of Leopards," Metiyl snorted, nodding to Annah. "That Nimr-Rada has made himself ruler of us all, whether we want him or not."

Annah shut her eyes, heartsick. She remembered Nimr-Rada as a young boy, dark, powerful, full of courage. He had always led his brothers and cousins during their games, and later, during their hunts. Even Noakh and Shem had been astonished by his physical abilities.

Now, however, Noakh shook his gleaming silver-curled head sorrowfully. "Nimr-Rada abuses the gifts of the Most High. No man should set himself above his brothers and use them for his own will."

"But, Father of my Fathers, how can we stop him?" Metiyl pleaded, leaning toward Noakh, seeming almost desperate. "You or one of your sons should come and reason with him; perhaps he will listen to you and quit tormenting us."

When Noakh remained silent, Shem answered Metiyl quietly. "Nimr-Rada has heard our words from the first days of his life. He knows the stories of the Great Destruction and of the heavens that existed before this new earth. He knows the truth of the Most High, the Word. But he has chosen his own will above the Most High's. Our words won't change his rebelliousness."

"Then listen, O Shem, Father of my Father; I haven't told you everything." Metiyl straightened, still indignant, his dark eyes kindling in the firelight. "Our Nimr-Rada has been given a new name. As if he doesn't have enough names already! The young men who follow him are calling him 'He-Who-Lifts-the-Skies,' because they claim he protects them from the judgment of the Most High. Some are even saying that he's the Promised One, who will free us from the curse brought upon us by our Adversary, the Serpent, in the Garden of Adan. Worse, Nimr-Rada allows them to say this. They even put their noses to the ground and all but worship him!"

Annah pressed her hands to her face, feeling as if she had been slapped. Unable to breathe, she looked at her husband and his father. Shem's eyes had widened in shock.

Equally affected, Noakh groaned, "O Most High, how should we deal with this Nimr-Rada, son of Kuwsh?"

From her place beside Annah, Naomi huffed audibly. Her lined, brown face stern, she lifted an eyebrow at Metiyl. "Kuwsh *knows* his son can't be the Promised One, because the Most High revealed to my Noakh that the Promised One would be a son of our Shem's son, Arpakshad. We have no choice in the matter. What does Kuwsh say about his 'Great King' son?"

Metiyl lowered his head, obviously unwilling to speak. At last, he said, "I'ma-Naomi, you won't be pleased; Kuwsh rejoices in his son's power. He encourages this adoration —though he knows it is wrong."

Clearly disgusted, Naomi handed the colorless infant girl back to the anxious Chaciydah. Then she looked past the crackling flames of the hearth toward her husband, Noakh. "My dear one," Naomi said stiffly, "we should send a message to warn Kuwsh and his 'Great King' son. They cannot be allowed to set themselves against the Most High; they invite another Destruction to pour down upon us all."

"You are right, beloved," Noakh agreed, his eyes distant, lost in thought. Quite suddenly, Noakh stood and, with a hint of an ancient limp, went outside.

Shem followed him, casting a sidelong glance at Annah, silently encouraging her with his eloquent eyes: *Wait for me.*

Annah knew that her husband and father-in-law were troubled beyond words. Shem and Noakh would consider the situation and pray at length before giving an answer. They had to be alone. To prevent Metiyl, Meshek, and Eliyshama from following them, Annah lifted her hands in a cautioning gesture. The men relaxed and waited, facing her. She was one of the First Mothers of all the tribes. They would listen to her.

Sighing, Annah spoke to Metiyl. "Your father, my own son Asshur, was like a brother to Kuwsh, and like a second father to Nimr-Rada. Why haven't they discussed these matters? Why does Kuwsh allow his son to torment your father's tribes?"

"Because, Ma'adannah," Metiyl answered respectfully, "Kuwsh bows before that Great King, Nimr-Rada."

"Ugh!" Naomi cried, outraged. "Since when does a father bow to his own son? I'm glad my Noakh left before he could hear such words!"

Annah steadied herself before speaking again. She

looked at Meshek. Keeping her voice low, she said, "You're too quiet, Meshek. Has Nimr-Rada threatened your family, or the lands of your father?"

Meshek's eyes flashed; Annah saw his rage and pain. Lifting his tapering brown hands, Meshek dropped them again, limp upon his knees. "Ma'adannah . . . my father too has bowed to Nimr-Rada."

Annah swallowed hard. Meshek's father was her youngest child, her last son, her baby Aram. *No*, she thought to Aram, unable to believe it was true. *Aram, why should you bow to another man? Didn't your father and I teach you that the Most High alone is worthy of adoration? How can you bow to Nimr-Rada?*

Meshek spoke again, disrupting her thoughts. "My brothers also follow Nimr-Rada. And their sons and *my* sons and their wives and children. They all follow him."

"Eliyshama is the only son we have left," Chaciydah added, tremulous. "Nimr-Rada has claimed the loyalty of all our others. That's why I begged the Most High to give me only daughters from this time on. At least my daughters will stay near me. But then, look how this one's afflicted!" Grieving, Chaciydah rocked the tiny girl.

Clearing his throat, Meshek said, "This is the reason for our visit, O Mothers of my Fathers." Meshek faced Annah and Naomi, carefully enunciating each word. "I won't give homage to Nimr-Rada. He's taken enough from me. I'm bringing those who are left in my family back into the highlands to live."

"We'll be less than a morning's walk from here," Chaciydah added, as if trying to comfort herself with the thought.

"I'm sorry," Annah whispered to Chaciydah, Meshek, and the others. She was unable to say any more. She longed to scream and tear at her hair. Their news was like hearing of an impending death. Her sons, her grandsons, their wives, and their children were embracing other ways, shunning all wisdom and freedom itself. The peace and tranquility of six generations were being crushed by the will of one man.

Nimr-Rada, she thought, wailing inwardly, *why are you doing this? Why do you accept the homage of others? You've been loved and admired from the first day of your life. Why wasn't it enough for you?*

Naomi's voice shook. "I prayed I would not live long enough to see the children of my children hating each other. Now it will be as it was before the Great Destruction. All the violence, the hatred, the killing . . . My dear one, my Noakh, must be ill at the thought of it." She began to cry, wiping away her tears with her aged brown hands. As Annah comforted her, Naomi patted her daughter-in-law's hand.

Their silence was broken by the sound of footsteps. Noakh entered the lodge, followed by Shem. Annah turned, surprised to see them so soon. Shem met her gaze, calm and quiet, his dark eyebrows lifted, questioning: *Are you well?*

Annah shrugged, looking away: *I don't know. Beloved, how can I tell you that our youngest son, our own Aram, bows to Nimr-Rada? And our other sons and daughters are following him as well. . . .* Annah bit her lip hard, composing herself. If she thought about her children now, she would cry. She didn't want to add to her husband's distress—not in the presence of the others.

As if realizing that Annah could not bear his scrutiny, Shem spoke to Chaciydah reluctantly. "Daughter, have you named your little one yet?"

Chaciydah blinked, apparently shocked by his question.

"Father of my Fathers, how could we give her a name before presenting her to you and our Ancient Ones? And of course we couldn't think of a name, fearing that she might die."

"She won't die," Shem answered firmly. He approached Chaciydah, reaching for the infant.

In his comforting, reasonable voice, Noakh said, "We have inquired of the Most High. He is silent concerning Nimr-Rada. But this little one will live, and she has a name." Lifting one long, aged hand, Noakh gestured to Shem, who stood apart from him. Holding the infant easily in both hands, Shem lifted her high, presenting her to them all, making the ceremony brief but formal.

"Sharah. She will be above all other women. She will cause great cities to be built. She will be lifted high." Turning the infant to face him, Shem continued, "Sharah, you will be like a fortress, high and strong. This is what the Most High has revealed."

As Shem spoke, Annah heard Chaciydah gasp in delighted disbelief. Even the somber Meshek smiled. Tenderly, Meshek took his daughter from Shem and gave her to Chaciydah. "Now, beloved, you won't worry so much."

But I will worry, Annah thought, eyeing Shem. Her husband usually enjoyed holding infant children and naming them. This girl-child was an exception. Sharah troubled him, imposing upon him an unnatural formality. *Why?*

Shem looked away, clearly avoiding Annah's silent question, just as she had avoided his earlier. Irritable now, as if complaining, Sharah began to cry.

Sharah tensed in Annah's arms. Her small, almost-three-year-old body resisted her great-grandmother's every move as Annah wrapped her in a warm blanket and carried her outside the stone-and-timber lodge to study the dawn. "It's too early in the morning for you to be running loose," Annah whispered to the restless child. "But look at the sky, lovely . . ."

Seeming persuaded by the note of wonderment in Annah's voice, Sharah followed Annah's gaze. Gradually her childish squirming subsided. Encouraged, Annah whispered, "Look, my Sharah. See how the Most High makes the sky beautiful for our sakes? See how He brings our servant Shemesh higher and higher in the heavens, until the stars fade away?"

As they gazed at the dawn, Annah continued softly. "Listen to the birds, now, my Sharah. They are singing for joy because it's spring."

"There . . . birds," Sharah whispered in response, pointing one delicate, pale finger toward the nearby treetops, where birdsongs of every pitch and type emanated from every available branch.

Pleased that Sharah had appreciated something beyond her own wants, Annah kissed the little girl's soft, translucent cheek and breathed in the sweetness of her shining noncolored curls. Sharah squirmed, impatient again. Annah carried her inside and released her from the blanket. "We should go wake your mother and your baby sister."

Sharah pressed her small pink lips together. "I do it," she told Annah firmly.

Before Annah could stop her, Sharah charged across the woven grass mats toward the thick leather draperies shielding the sleeping area. Alarmed, Annah hurried after her. The sleeping area was warm and dark. Annah was unable to see immediately, but she heard the thudding impact of Sharah's small body against the low bed. Annah also heard Chaciydah whispering to Sharah, her soft voice drowsy. "There you are, my little one. Come to I'ma. Be careful of the baby."

As Sharah scrambled into the bed, Annah lifted the red deerskin covering away from the one small, squared window in the far wall. Daylight illuminated the snug, orderly room. Collections of intricately woven baskets, tanned hides, thick furs, and mats lined the walls. Garlands of sweet herbs hung above the low bed, lending a dry, soothing scent to the air. Chaciydah was nestled in the bed beneath layers of woolen covers and fleeces, nose to nose now with Sharah. The baby, a tiny one-month-old daughter, was safely tucked against the pillow behind Chaciydah, away from Sharah.

"Good morning," Annah said, pleased to see fresh color in Chaciydah's slender brown face.

"Ma'adannah," Chaciydah sighed, stretching and yawning. "The baby and I both slept well. I feel much better today. I've already fed her and changed her wrappings. If I may ask, will you watch her while I bathe and dress?"

"How can I refuse?" Annah lifted the blanket-swathed infant from the pillow behind Chaciydah. The baby gazed up at Annah mistily, like a blissful dreamer, her tiny ruddy face fringed with soft brown hints of curls. Annah loved the child's contented and pleasing expression. "We'll have a good visit together," she cooed. "And we'll watch over your sister, you and I, because she's so busy!"

"At least this baby seems easy to please," Chaciydah sighed, lapsing into an attitude of helpless regret. "And she has color in her skin and her hair. Though I'm afraid her eyes will be even more pale than her sister's."

"You shouldn't be concerned with your daughters'

looks, Chaciydah," Annah said, wondering how much of the conversation Sharah would absorb. "You must see beyond their color, or lack of color. They *are* beautiful."

"As you say." Chaciydah sounded doubtful.

To urge Chaciydah out of her fretfulness, Annah said, "I'm sure your husband and son will return today, bringing my husband with them. You should get up now. Bathe yourself, put on your favorite clothes and your ornaments, then braid your hair. Take your time. I'll feed Sharah, then do some cleaning."

Chaciydah's eyes shone. "Ma'adannah, thank you."

"No, I thank you for giving me time with your little ones." Annah nuzzled the warm infant in her arms. It felt good to hold a baby, particularly one so sweet. *What will we name you?* Annah asked the infant silently. *You're such a joy that no name will be quite enough to describe you. My Shem will be happy to see you. And I'll be happy to see him.*

Annah smiled, thinking of Shem. They had been apart for much of the past five weeks, since Annah had come to tend Chaciydah during and after the birth of this child. Sharah, too, needed care, though the little girl didn't seem to think so.

Now Sharah was crawling across the bed, restless. Chaciydah frowned and reached for one of Sharah's bare feet. "Little one, where are your leggings?"

"They ugly," Sharah muttered.

"I've had her wrapped in a blanket," Annah explained to Chaciydah. "But I'll put her leggings on before we eat."

"No!" Sharah lifted her chin defiantly, scowling at Annah.

Immediately, Chaciydah began to plead with Sharah. "You need them, little one. Leggings keep your feet warm and—"

25

"They ugly!" Sharah interrupted, her words and expression truculent, daring her mother to argue with her.

To Annah's astonishment, Chaciydah humbly agreed. "You're right. They are ugly. I'll find some way to make them pretty for you."

Chaciydah, Annah thought, dismayed, *why do you always give in to the child?* The little girl's refusal to wear leggings was a trivial thing. But her consistent stubbornness and arrogance toward her mother—and Annah—were serious. Why didn't Chaciydah recognize the importance of teaching her daughter to respect others?

"Don't frown at your mother," Annah reprimanded Sharah quietly. "Or at me." Sharah's lower lip went out stubbornly. Annah stared at her hard, willing the child to yield. At last Sharah looked away, still pouting.

"Don't worry, I'll be sure she wears her leggings," Annah told Chaciydah. "Go make yourself ready for visitors, and for your husband, while you have time."

"But Sharah might fuss," Chaciydah murmured, hesitating. "She seems so fragile compared to my sons."

"She's a fortress," Annah said dryly. "Don't let her noncolor deceive you, Chaciydah. She's no different from any other child."

"I'm sure you are right." Chaciydah sighed again.

Trying to bolster Chaciydah's courage, Annah whispered, "Be a mother to your daughters, not a servant; don't let them rule you."

"I won't, Ma'adannah."

But by midafternoon, Chaciydah was kneeling beside the bed, knotting decorative fringes around Sharah's leggings—placing each knot exactly where Sharah's imperious little finger designated and apologizing if Sharah wasn't pleased.

Chaciydah, Annah thought, *you are acting like her servant!*
It's not good for her.

Pondering the situation, Annah went into the main
room of the lodge, checked the baby—safe in her basket—then slapped a puffy heap of dough into a kneading
trough. It calmed Annah to pound, fold, and push at the
dough until it became a smooth, resilient grain-speckled
mass. She would shape it into flat, chewy cakes for their
evening meal. The cakes, accompanied by simmered
dried fruit, a thick stew of preserved meat and grains, and
early spring greens, would be enough for six—if the men
returned tonight.

After cleaning the dough off her fingers, Annah caressed Chaciydah's infant daughter. From her seat in the
carrying basket, the baby studied Annah solemnly, her
gray eyes wide and delicately fringed with dark lashes.

"You're wonderful," Annah told the child, in a light
speaking-to-an-infant voice. "How glad I am to see you!
And my beloved will be glad to see you too, yes he will.
And I'll be glad to see him!"

A smile played about the baby's mouth, and she
kicked within her robes and blankets, seeming to urge
Annah to pick her up. Unable to resist, Annah lifted the
infant from her basket and rocked her. She was kissing
the child's tenderly rounded chin when a shadow fell
across the doorway. A small pebble clattered onto the
mats before Annah. Smiling, she looked at the one who
threw it: Shem.

He grinned. "Now I see why you've stayed away from
me for so long, beloved. Am I dull by comparison?"

"Never." Annah carried the infant to him, delighted.
"Here she is. I dare you to resist her."

Shem cuddled the infant expertly. "Little one, I was

27

amazed when your father told me he had another daughter."

Annah stared at her husband, bewildered. "Why are you amazed? Does it matter that she's a girl?"

"Not at all. It's just that I had supposed she would be a son when I learned her name. But we know the Most High's thoughts are perfect even when we can't understand them." Shem's mouth twitched as if enjoying an incomparable joke. "How tiny you are!" he exclaimed to the infant. His voice softening, he added, "Such little hands. It doesn't seem possible that you should receive the name given to you by the Most High . . . Karan."

Annah blinked, startled. *Karan. To push. To gore.* It was hardly a proper name, particularly for a girl. "Why should she have such a name?" Annah demanded.

"This little one will push her enemies until they can't escape," Shem answered, smiling down at the infant. "The Most High, the Word, gave her this name. Perhaps it's a harsh name for a girl, but she is Karan."

How could you ever have enemies? Annah wondered, studying the tender-eyed infant girl. *And why?*

"Karan?" Aghast, Chaciydah took her infant daughter from Shem. *No,* she thought, staring down at her baby, who was drifting off to sleep. *Karan is too harsh a name for a woman. No, you'll be Keren. Like a ray of light. That's a woman's name, and similar to Karan. Yes, I'll call you Keren.*

Two

"I HOPE THERE ARE no newcomers at Eliyshama's wedding feast," twelve-year-old Keren murmured to Sharah as they wound long skeins of fine blue-gray wool onto carved wooden shuttles. "I hate how they jump and stare the first time I look at them. It makes me think I'm a bad dream come to life."

A ray of sunlight slanted through the open door of the lodge, illuminating Sharah's pale curls and her defiant adolescent scowl. "Let them stare at you. I don't care when they stare at me. It pleases me that I'm unlike other people."

"You *are* unique, O-Girl-of-No-Color," Keren agreed, twitting her sister gently. "Newcomers wonder at you. But when they see my brown skin and my brown hair, they expect to see brown eyes. Instead, they see no-color eyes, and they jump as if I'm a fright."

Sharah sniffed, yanking more thread from her blue-gray skein. "Most of the time you *are* a fright, with your hair and clothes all wild. I'm ashamed to be seen with you."

Keren glanced down at her rumpled brown woolen overtunic and her smudged, mismatched leather under-tunic. Clothes weren't as import to her as they were to Sharah—who was neatly clad in matched red and blue wool. Keren defended herself. "But I always comb my hair when we have visitors. And at the harvest, didn't I wear my new robe the very first day, when only the Father of my Fathers and I'ma-Annah were here?"

"I wish you wouldn't call her that; she's Ma'adannah. You sound like an infant, calling her I'ma-Annah."

"She likes being called I'ma-Annah," Keren argued, keeping her voice low in deference to their mother, who was working just outside the lodge. Quarrels always distressed Chaciydah. "Anyway," Keren persisted softly, "I wish you wouldn't be so formal with I'ma-Annah all the time. You hurt her feelings."

Rolling her eyes upward, Sharah sighed impatiently. "I suppose now you're going to tell me that I've hurt the feelings of the Father of my Fathers too."

"Actually, you have hurt him. I see his sorrow whenever you behave as if you can't wait to escape his presence."

"He's dull. Always so solemn."

"Not always," Keren answered beneath her breath. It was useless to argue. Sharah hated visiting Shem and I'ma-Annah, but Keren adored them. At the end of each day, when all the work was done, her great-grandparents would sit by the evening fire with the Ancient Ones, Noakh and Naomi, and tell wonderful stories of the Most High, the Creation, the Great Destruction, and of their many adventures beneath the blue heavens. As they talked, they would laugh, feed Keren from their own bowls, kiss her, and fuss over her. Then Shem would play his flute and they would dance.

I love to dance, Keren thought, lapsing into a daydream. *And I love watching I'ma-Annah and the Father of my Fathers. They are so beautiful together. When I marry, my husband and I will love each other in exactly the same way.*

Her daydream was interrupted by a shove from Sharah. "Hurry with your work! I want to go outside."

"It's cold outside; you hate the cold," Keren said, whipping row upon row of the fine, light thread onto the long wooden shuttle. "You just want to see if Eliyshama has finished polishing that piece of red stone he's been carving. He never said he would give it to you. For all you know, it's for his beloved."

Sharah tossed her pale curls confidently. "Eliyshama has already given Tsereth a stone carving—and it was a much larger stone. She won't want this one."

"But what if he plans to give it to our I'ma? Or to I'ma-Annah, or I'ma-Naomi?"

Sharah answered Keren with a threatening, tight-lipped glare. Keren ducked her head submissively and focused on the long wooden shuttle. Finished at last, she tucked her shuttle, and Sharah's, into a lidded basket beside their mother's floor loom.

Slapping the basket lid shut, Sharah said, "You're too slow! Come on." She seized Keren's arm and dragged her outside the lodge.

Their mother was stirring an acrid-smelling mixture of dye in a large, blackened clay pot at the hearth. Chaciydah straightened wearily and pushed a brown curl away from her forehead. Lifting one finely arched, skeptical eyebrow, she asked, "Have you finished winding the shuttles?"

"Yes, I'ma," Keren answered, as Sharah pulled her toward their brother.

Bundled in a thick gray open-fronted leather robe and a warm brown-furred tunic, Eliyshama was sitting cross-legged on a woven grass mat near the smoking hearth. He was knotting a dark leather cord between his long brown fingers and didn't look up as they approached.

Keren smiled secretly. *You know we're coming,* she thought to her brother. *But you're ignoring us because you know Sharah wants your stone carving.*

Sharah pulled Keren to a stop in front of Eliyshama. "Are you finished? Let me see it."

"See what?" Eliyshama pretended surprise. He lifted the leather cord and displayed his carving, a smooth, polished circle of bright red stone, pierced through the center. "It's just a cord with a shiny rock that I'm using as a balance for my spear."

"Liar," Sharah accused, making Keren cringe.

Eliyshama gave Sharah a long, even look. "Watch," he commanded. Quickly, he knotted the leather cord with the bright red stone to the middle of his long ashwood spear. Then he stood, balancing the spear, preparing to throw it into the field beyond the lodge. Keren glanced at Sharah. Hot pink tinged Sharah's face, though her lips were pressed tight, furious and pale.

Eliyshama ignored them both, concentrating as if his aim were critical. He took several running steps and, raising his left arm for balance, gave a mighty throw. "There," he said, watching his spear slice through the cool autumn air and then land, quivering, in the short-grazed field. "It works. But then again, I might give that shiny red stone to the first person who reaches my spear."

Impulsively, Keren ran for the weapon. She loved to run. It was the one way she could win against Sharah, who hated running. This time, however, Sharah actually kept pace with her as they charged across the cold, damp field. With a frantic burst of energy, Keren flung herself ahead. Seizing the spear with both hands, she wrested it from the moist earth, only to have Sharah knock her to the ground. Still gripping the spear, Keren huddled above it protectively, laughing as Sharah struggled to push her away from the coveted red stone.

"Let me have it!" Sharah screamed.

I can't, Keren thought, still laughing, hysterical, unable to explain. *You're leaning on me, I'm kneeling on the spear, and my fingers are stuck beneath it.* At last, gasping, she yelled, "Get up; I'll give it to you!"

"Your word!"

"My word, truly." Keren's shins and fingers were hurting, pressed hard against the spear. "Ow! Just get off me, Sharah."

All at once, Sharah's weight lifted from Keren's back. Sighing in relief, Keren sat up. "I was going to give it to you anyway, since you want it so much."

"But you won the race," Eliyshama said, startling her. She hadn't realized that he was behind them. He sounded cold, harsh—unusual for Eliyshama. "You won the carving, Keren."

Keren looked over her shoulder at her brother. Eliyshama seemed irritated. Sharah sat on the ground beside him, sulking. Obviously Eliyshama had yanked Sharah aside to free Keren.

He meant for me to win this thing, Keren thought, surprised. *But if I take it, Sharah will be angry.*

Smiling at him, willing him to understand, Keren said, "The stone is so pretty, Eliyshama, and you've cut and polished it so beautifully that Sharah is certain she can't live without it. So she'd get it from me somehow. I only wanted to win the race against her. Here, Sharah." Keren unwound the leather corded stone from Eliyshama's spear and looped it over Sharah's gleaming head. "Are you happy?"

"Eliyshama," Chaciydah called from behind them. They turned toward her; Chaciydah was furious, her thin brown cheeks were flushed, her eyes narrowed. "Why have you set your sisters against each other? You knew Sharah was expecting the stone carving. Why didn't you just give it to her?"

"Too much is given to her, I'ma," Eliyshama argued. "I found the stone, I cut it, I polished it, and I corded it. But Sharah insists it must be hers, and you and Keren simply agree to let her take it—as if it was never mine to give as I please. I wish I'd saved it for Tsereth. But if *Sharah* is pleased, then never mind."

Snatching up his spear, he said, "I'm finished resting. I'll go help Father with the herd." He started to walk away. But then he looked back at them, his eyes actually fierce. "Quit giving in to Sharah, both of you!"

I've never seen him so angry, Keren thought, watching her brother. *He's never been rude to I'ma.* Anxious, Keren cast a sidelong glance at her mother.

Chaciydah watched Eliyshama, stricken, blinking hard, obviously forcing back tears. At last she silently lowered her head and went back to work at the hearth.

Seeing her mother's distress, Keren felt her stomach tighten miserably.

Still sitting on the ground beside her, Sharah gave

Keren a swift kick to her fleece-booted ankle. "If you intended for me to have the stone carving, then you shouldn't have challenged me by running for the spear. Now you've made Eliyshama and our I'ma very unhappy. You should go apologize to I'ma."

"I will. But you should go with me."

Sharah looked away, fingering the red stone, unmoving.

~ⴰⴰ ⴰⴰ~

Keren eyed her father nervously. As tired as he was, she could tell he was furious. He led her and Sharah outside to the cool, starry darkness. Stopping at the glowing-embered hearth, he said, "Sit."

Almost as one, Keren and Sharah sat on the hard ground. Keren shivered, staring at her toes as her father paced. She knew he was choosing his words carefully because I'ma was listening from just inside the doorway of the lodge.

At last he said, "Look at me."

Keren lifted her head and looked up at her father. But Meshek was staring at Sharah; she had ignored him. Meshek slammed the butt of his herding staff into the earth directly in front of Sharah, making her jump as he snarled, "Look at me!"

Sharah looked.

Meshek leaned down toward Sharah, seeming barely able to control himself, though he spoke just above a whisper. "Every day, there are new problems! New foolishness! Fights, tantrums, rebellion, and doing as little as you can to help your mother! As if she doesn't have enough to bear." Taking a quick breath, Meshek eyed Keren now, as well as Sharah.

"Have either of you noticed that your mother is not strong? She doesn't need further distress from you—nor do I. Life is hard enough here without all these scenes from my daughters. Listen to me—and don't roll your eyes, Sharah! After we've celebrated Eliyshama's marriage, you'll spend the winter with the Ancient Ones, and the Father of my Father, and his Ma'adannah. You will *work* for them. And if I hear of any shirking or rebellion from either of you, I'll beat you with my herding stick—never mind what your mother says! Do you understand me?"

"Yes, Father," Keren whispered. Beside her, Sharah nodded, her lips a thin, colorless line. Meshek stared hard at her. At last, Sharah lowered her eyes and fidgeted with the edge of her blue overtunic.

Sighing, Meshek straightened wearily. "Stay here beside the hearth until I call you. Don't move and don't fight, do you understand?"

This time, Sharah answered with Keren, their voices in unison. "Yes, Father."

Keren thought, *An entire winter with I'ma-Annah, the Father of my Fathers, and the Ancient Ones, Noakh and I'ma-Naomi!* She smiled, delighted. Sharah gave her a furtive shove. Keren ignored her, focusing her attention instead on the high, glittering stars. In her heart, she wanted to dance.

There are no newcomers, Keren realized happily, as she followed Meshek, Shem, Eliyshama, and I'ma-Annah through the temporary encampment. She recognized everyone. Most were from her mother's tribe, among them Chaciydah's brother, the rough-voiced, full-bearded

Ashkenaz, and his son Azaz, Tsereth's father. But Meshek's stocky cousin Metiyl was also waiting to greet them. He winked at Keren, making her want to laugh. Two of Metiyl's adolescent sons, Yeiysh and Khawrawsh, were studying Sharah, who was walking beside Keren.

Sharah's expression was remote, as if she were completely unaware of Yeiysh and Khawrawsh, and all the other young men who were staring at her.

But you'll keep me awake tonight, telling me exactly what you think about each of them, Keren thought, glancing at her sister. *You're laughing inside. You love all this attention. Even so, it's not your wedding day; it's Eliyshama's, and you can't take this joy from him.*

Keren smiled at Eliyshama. He was splendid, clothed in new deerskin boots and a robe of deep red wool, beautifully seamed and belted with trimmings of brilliant blue. But Eliyshama's fine new garments were nothing compared to his expression; he was beaming with happiness. *I'ma,* Keren thought to the absent Chaciydah, *I wish you hadn't been too ill to come to the wedding. I wish the Ancient Ones, Noakh and Naomi, were here too. How they'd enjoy seeing Eliyshama today.*

The other young, unmarried men in the encampment were gathering around Eliyshama, exuberant, laughing, punching his arms, slapping him on the shoulders, and praising his composure. Eliyshama grinned, jostled his more boisterous relatives, and thanked the others for their compliments. Raising his voice, he called out, "How can I be married if I have no bride? Where have you hidden her?"

Still laughing and teasing, the young men led Eliyshama through the center of the encampment. Following Meshek, Shem, I'ma-Annah, and Sharah, Keren ducked behind I'ma-Annah's arm, content to watch the festivities from the shadows. I'ma-Annah hugged her, smoothing her hair as they watched and waited for the bride. Keren peeked up at I'ma-Annah, pleased by her attention. I'ma-Annah looked perfect today, as graceful as ever, her sleek black hair clasped with gold talismans, her pale blue garments delicately edged with white wool, impressive gold cuffs on her wrists.

You're so beautiful, Keren thought to her. *I wish I could be like you.*

Women's voices echoed through the encampment now in a trilling, singsong melody, followed by squeals of laughter and the sounds of whistles, drums, bells, and clapping hands. Tsereth was coming, surrounded by her sisters, her mother, her aunts, and all her maiden cousins, who sang and danced around her as they led her through the maze of gray and tawny felted tents in the encampment. Keren clutched I'ma-Annah's hand, forcing herself not to rush out and dance with Tsereth's family.

"It's hard for little feet to be still," I'ma-Annah murmured, hugging Keren once more. "But look at your new sister, child. Isn't she beautiful?"

Tall and imposing, her soft brown hair streaming down to her knees, Tsereth was radiant in a flowing, gracefully fashioned cream-and-red gown and brightly fringed boots. Eliyshama's carved red stone rested at the base of her smooth brown throat, and her big, dark eyes sparkled as she met Eliyshama's gaze. Eliyshama simply stared at her, obviously delighted and incapable of speech.

Keren laughed, enjoying the spectacle, until someone nudged her sharply in the ribs. She glanced over at the offender, Sharah, who rolled her eyes and pantomimed her boredom. *You won't spoil my happiness,* Keren thought to her sister. *If I have to, I'll run over to Tsereth's family and stay with them instead of you.* Swiftly, Keren looked away from Sharah to Shem.

Father of my Fathers, Keren thought to Shem, *one day you'll bless my husband and me as you are blessing Eliyshama and Tsereth today.* She watched Eliyshama clasp Tsereth's hands as Shem praised the Most High and pronounced blessings and approval upon their marriage. As soon as Shem stepped back, Eliyshama kissed Tsereth, almost lifting her off her feet as he embraced her.

Tsereth's family laughed and clapped, uttering tongue-rattling cries of jubilation. I'ma-Annah leaned down, whispering to Keren, "Go kiss your new sister!"

Keren didn't need to be urged a second time. She ran to Tsereth, ducking around some of her cousins to reach her.

"There you are, my little bird," Tsereth cried, bending to hug Keren. "I'm so glad to see you! I wish you could have come to visit me as soon as you arrived last night; we would have fed you sweet cakes and meat until you were so full you couldn't move. Come, give me a kiss, then kiss your brother."

Obediently Keren hugged Tsereth and planted a happy kiss on her cheek, then turned to Eliyshama. He was smiling at her fondly, and he rumpled her curls before sweeping her up in a quick, tight hug. "Now," he whispered, "you can visit my wife's sisters and enjoy yourself."

Before Keren could reply, Eliyshama put her down and turned to greet Tsereth's father, Azaz, who was tapping him on the shoulder, demanding his attention. Suddenly unsure of herself, Keren hesitated amid the crowd. A firm pair of hands descended upon her shoulders. Her father smiled down at her. "Go play," he urged, nudging Keren toward the unmarried girls at the edge of the crowd.

Shyly, slowly, Keren walked toward them. One of the tallest girls, Tsereth's sister Khuldah, saw her and beckoned, her voice loud enough to make heads turn. "Pale Eyes! Why are you dragging your feet? Come here. We're going to eat soon, and you have to sit with us. Where's your no-color sister?"

"She's coming, I'm sure," Keren said, hurrying to meet Khuldah, so she wouldn't yell again. Keren really didn't mind being called "Pale Eyes." It was Khuldah's way of accepting her. But Khuldah's loud, carrying voice made Keren want to run away to the shadows where she could hide from the frowns and lifted eyebrows of the adults, who were watching them.

"The food's all prepared," Khuldah said, licking her lips. She was a sturdy girl, confident and unconcerned, the leader of all the maiden cousins her age. Even Sharah couldn't intimidate her. Now Khuldah lowered her voice to Keren, her brown eyes roguish, "When I saw your brother, I almost couldn't breathe! I'd forgotten how handsome he is. No wonder Tsereth has been gabbing on about him. There's your no-color sister. Is she going to talk to us, or is she going to be a nose-in-the-air again?"

"She didn't like the way you ordered her around the last time we were here," Keren confided, remembering their previous visit two years past. Sharah had been furious with Khuldah throughout their stay. "Sharah hates being told what to do."

"Oh," Khuldah said, clearly unconcerned. "Poor Sharah. Well, if she doesn't like playing our games by our rules, then she can play with the little ones and tell them what to do." She turned to Sharah. "Girl-of-No-Color! Are you going to sit and visit with us, or are you going to ignore us again? We're sisters, after all."

"As you say," Sharah answered coolly. She frowned at Keren. "You were supposed to stay with me."

"Father told me to stay with Tsereth's sisters. Eliyshama said so too."

"I heard no such thing," Sharah snapped, looking away.

"Let's go help set out the mats and dishes for the feast," Khuldah said, grabbing Keren's hand and pushing one of her cousins ahead of her. "The sooner we finish, the sooner we eat."

Keren heard Sharah mutter very softly behind them, "Cow!"

Shocked, Keren held her breath fearfully, but Khuldah had either not heard Sharah or graciously chose to ignore the slur.

They followed Khuldah to another open area of the encampment, where the earth had been plowed and trampled to allow for an enormous cooking hearth. The scent of roasting meat made Keren swallow hard. She hadn't realized that she was so hungry. Sharah was apparently hungry too; she unrolled the long woven grass mats without argument. But she stayed away from Khuldah when they ate, seeming too engrossed in her food to talk to anyone. Khuldah, meanwhile, knelt beside Keren, who gladly listened to her easy, friendly chatter.

Encouraged by Khuldah, Keren ate until she felt she was bursting. Chunks of roasted mutton, crisp flat breads, dried cherries, savory vegetables with barley, hard-boiled eggs, and most delicious of all, a tender roasted quail. "I think I won't eat for a few days," Keren sighed, tossing the quail bones into the crackling fire.

"Wait until we've finished dancing; you'll be ready to eat by then," Khuldah assured her. They stood by the fire, warming their hands against the early evening chill. Khuldah gave a full-throated chuckle. "When I get married, we're going to feast and dance for two weeks!"

"You'll have to find a husband first," Sharah said airily, as she came to toss the remains of her quail into the fire.

Khuldah scowled, but before she could answer, Metiyl's sons, Yeiysh and Khawrawsh, came running into the encampment, their eyes wide and tense, their voices roughened by alarm. "Horsemen! Coming straight toward us from the west! Horsemen of Nimr-Rada!"

Instantly the adults leaped to their feet, the men calling to each other, the women gasping, snatching up the youngest children, then hastily retreating to the edges of the open area, with the older children following.

Keren turned to search for her father, but Sharah grabbed her wrist. "We'll hide in the tents!"

"As if that'll do any good, fool!" Khuldah cried. "They have horses; we don't. If they've come to demand tributes and aren't satisfied, they'll burn the tents with you inside. All you can do is wait with the others and try to stay out of their path."

Another hand touched Keren's arm now, making her jump and gasp, frightened. I'ma-Annah said, "Come with me, all of you. Quietly."

Three

AS KHULDAH SCURRIED off to stand with her mother and sisters, I'ma-Annah guided Keren and Sharah through the encampment to stand with Shem, Meshek, Eliyshama, and the wide-eyed Tsereth. Metiyl, flanked by Yeiysh and Khawrawsh, stomped up to Shem and Meshek.

"Why are they so far from their own territories?" Metiyl demanded, furious, his broad nostrils flaring. "We come this way to escape them, and they follow us here. There are only a few of them. We should fight!"

I'ma-Annah spoke, quietly distressed. "Son of my son, why should we destroy our time of joy with rage and violence?"

Metiyl snorted. "*We* aren't the violent ones, Ma'ad-annah; they are. And I say we shouldn't allow them to just come in here as they please. We must resist them!"

"I wish to hear what these followers of Nimr-Rada

have to say," Shem announced firmly, quelling the angry Metiyl. But Shem exchanged a cautioning look with I'ma-Annah, who pulled Keren closer, reaching for Sharah as well.

The horsemen were riding into the encampment now. Gaping, Keren clung to I'ma-Annah's waist. To see men actually riding horses was almost an unimaginable thing. But they were real, and they were approaching. Five horsemen, their dusky coloring deepened by the sun, all similarly clad in leather tunics, broad leather bands on their forearms, and leather leggings, with short cloaks of rough-edged fleece. Each man wore his dark hair tightly bound into a severe plait at the nape of the neck. Keren stared at their backs, wondering about the odd narrow pouches of leather slung from their shoulders. Sticks of wood—straight, bare, polished, and notched and feathered at the ends—were sticking out of the pouches.

"See their weapons," Metiyl growled to Shem, his rage still visible. "They've blades on the tips of those feathered sticks, and they propel them from a distance using those tight-strung wands of wood. Cowardly weapons!"

Shem stared at the horsemen, his expressive eyes widening in astonishment. And I'ma-Annah stiffened, clearly surprised. Trembling, Keren glanced over at her father. Meshek looked like a figure of clay, unmoving, glaring at the horsemen. From her left, Keren heard Eliyshama mutter to Tsereth, "My brothers, three of them at least, have come to our wedding."

Three of my brothers, Keren thought, dizzied by the realization. *Which three?* Names ran through her mind. Names that had always been whispered by Chaciydah in tones of mourning: *Miyka, Ra-Anan, Mattan, Kana, Bachan. . . .* There was another, but she couldn't remember his name now. *Who are you?* She stared at the horsemen, trying to choose her brothers from among them.

The lead horseman swung one long leg over the neck of his black-and-tawny horse and dropped lightly to the ground, a swift, showy movement. The other four horsemen followed his example silently. Now, the lead horseman approached Shem and Meshek, stopping a short distance before them, folding his brown hands respectfully and lowering his head in a reverent nod. "Father of my Fathers, I hoped you would be here. Your son Aram, the father of my own father, sends you his greetings." Glancing at Meshek, the young horseman said, "He also sends you greetings, Father."

Meshek answered with a tight, hard-eyed nod, and one curt word. "Neshar."

Neshar, Keren thought, gazing at the lead horseman, remembering his name, and seeing his resemblance to Eliyshama. *You're my brother Neshar.* As she was thinking this, Keren felt I'ma-Annah take a quick breath.

"My Aram is well?"

Neshar seemed grateful to I'ma-Annah for her question. "Your Aram thrives, Ma'adannah. Truly, he heard of my brother's wedding and sent us to convey his love to you." Almost too quickly, Neshar added, "He regrets that he can't come here himself."

"My youngest son is too busy," I'ma-Annah said, her tone a stiff mingling of disapproval and disappointment.

Shem spoke loudly enough for everyone to hear. "Do you intend to stay here for the night?"

"Are we welcomed, O Father of my Fathers?" Neshar's question was clearly directed at everyone in the encampment. "If not, then we'll continue our journey."

"To where?" Metiyl challenged him harshly. "These

lands haven't been claimed by your Nimr-Rada."

Neshar remained calm. "My brothers and I promised to take our friends into the mountains to hunt for a few days. Then we'll go down to the steppes to rest until spring."

"So you say." Metiyl turned away, showing his scorn and disbelief. A hum of discontented voices arose throughout the encampment. Keren shivered, feeling the animosity of the others toward the horsemen. Moving forward, Shem lifted his hands. Everyone hushed, restrained by their love and respect for their First Father.

"Listen to me," Shem called out. "You are all the children of my children. And the sons and daughters of my brothers, whom I love. We have come here—in peace— to share our joy at the marriage of Eliyshama and Tsereth." He swept one arm toward the horsemen in an embracing, almost pleading gesture. "These are also the children of my children, and the sons of my brothers. I wish to speak to them and hear what they have to say." His eloquent face hardening, Shem said, "As I live, they will move among you in peace. You will not provoke them, and they will not provoke you! Do not bring the judgment of the Most High down upon yourselves with your anger; you cannot stand against Him."

Hearing his undeniable authority, Keren's anxiety diminished. Glancing around, she saw that the others would receive their visitors in reluctant peace. Even Metiyl lowered his wild-curled head.

Neshar motioned to his fellow horsemen. Immediately, they removed their fleece cloaks and draped them over the black-and-tawny backs of their horses. By unspoken agreement, two of the young men gathered the dangling leather straps fastened about the horses' heads and guided the animals to an open field just outside the encampment. Neshar and the two remaining horsemen looked expectantly at Eliyshama and Tsereth, who were obligated to welcome them formally.

Clearing his throat, Eliyshama said, "Beloved, you may remember my own brothers Neshar, Mattan, and Bachan."

"Welcome." Tsereth said nothing more.

Breaking the awkward silence, I'ma-Annah said, "Come, let's sit and finish our meal. Sons of my son, we will bring you water and food."

They returned to their feast, rearranging the grass mats to accommodate the newcomers. Shem sat on the mat with Keren's three horsemen-brothers, watching them. As her horsemen-brothers rinsed their hands and faces in water grudgingly provided by Tsereth's sisters, Keren noticed the others in the encampment watching them as well. Feeling anxious again, she knelt between I'ma-Annah and Sharah, keeping her eyes lowered to hide her distress. I'ma-Annah nudged Sharah and Keren, gently urging them to pass food to their brothers.

Neshar stared at Sharah. "Child-of-No-Color, you lived. We were sure you would die."

Frowning, Sharah pushed a wheat cake at Neshar. "Well, the way our I'ma has been mourning for you, my brothers, you all should have died."

Keren marveled at Sharah's audacity, but no one scolded her; Meshek was actually nodding in agreement.

"Our I'ma isn't here?" Mattan looked around, seeming genuinely concerned.

Seated across from him, Meshek straightened. "Your mother is ill. She stayed in the mountains with the Ancient Ones." Eyeing his sons severely, Meshek said, "Her ill health was caused by her mourning for you since you abandoned us."

Neshar, Mattan, and Bachan ducked their heads and picked at their food, accepting their father's reprimand. When Meshek said nothing more, I'ma-Annah took Keren's hand. "Now, you three, you haven't met your second sister. This is Karan."

But our mother calls me Keren, Keren thought to her brothers.

Startled, Bachan gulped and swatted Neshar's chest with the back of his callused brown hand. "Look at her eyes! They're the color of pale metal! Who will believe us when we speak of her?"

Pausing between bites of bread, Neshar stared at Keren, then at Sharah. "We shouldn't speak of either of them."

"He's right," Mattan agreed, watching Sharah. "No one will believe us. They'll say we've gone mad." He grimaced, his slim brown face amazingly like Chaciydah's. Keren was fascinated by the resemblance. Neshar looked very much like Meshek and Eliyshama, while Bachan had hints of both his parents: Chaciydah's dark brown curls, her big brown eyes, and Meshek's long limbs.

"Will you continue to serve that Nimr-Rada?" Meshek demanded suddenly.

Neshar cleared his throat uneasily. "The Great King will send others to search for us if we don't return at the appointed time. And if we don't return, he will require compensation from our families."

Enraged, Meshek snarled, "Compensation from me for *my* sons, who should have never gone with him at all? I owe Nimr-Rada nothing for taking my wayward, thankless sons! You've brought me nothing but grief!"

"Father." Neshar passed a hand over his face, as if wearied. Then, looking straight into Meshek's eyes, he pleaded, "We regret your suffering, believe us. Listen, I beg you. We were glad to hear of Eliyshama and Tsereth's wedding. We've looked forward to seeing all of you, including our I'ma. But you know that if we hadn't agreed to go with the Great King, he would have considered us—and you—his enemies."

"But you went with him gladly," Meshek said, thrusting his outspread fingers toward his sons to emphasize his point. "All six of you! You were so eager for adventure and gain! Now, you three, tell me, where are your other brothers? Where's Miyka? And Ra-Anan? And Kana? Are they too ashamed to present themselves here today?"

Neshar answered, subdued, "The Great King wouldn't excuse them from their duties. They also feared you'd be angry."

"But you three don't care that I'm angry?" Meshek cried. Keren saw veins pulsing in her father's forehead. His rage was so horrible that she longed to run away.

Mattan leaned forward, his face—so like Chaciydah's—intense. "Father, whether you believe us or not, we care. Otherwise we wouldn't have been willing to endure the hatred of everyone in this encampment."

"They have reason to hate you!"

Defensive, Bachan said, "We've taken no tributes or compensation from our own tribes, Father. No one in this encampment has a claim against us."

"But you *have* taken compensation from other tribes," Shem interposed calmly, raising his dark eyebrows. "And they—all of them—are kindred tribes. They are your own cousins, the children of my brothers."

Unable to argue with him, Neshar, Mattan, and Bachan

lowered their eyes. Meshek stood and marched off, as if he couldn't endure the company of his horsemen-sons. Exchanging a look with I'ma-Annah, Shem said, "We'll discuss these matters tomorrow. Eat. I'll reason with your father later, for your mother's sake."

As Keren's brothers finished their food, one of their companions returned from the edge of the encampment. He moved quietly, his expression wary, reserved. His dark brown eyes flicked here and there, missing nothing, not even Keren's eyes. He didn't blink or jump, but he studied her and Sharah solemnly, then turned to Neshar, who introduced him to Shem. "Father of my Fathers, this is Zehker, one of our friends."

"Zehker." Shem smiled. "Which tribe are you from?"

Zehker lowered his head. "My father . . . is of the sons of Yepheth."

His answer was as wary as his demeanor. *He didn't say his father's name, as most men do,* Keren thought, baffled, watching Zehker as he bowed and retreated slightly. *And he looks like some wild creature, ready to run away.*

"That's the most I've heard Zehker say in three days," Neshar told Shem, amused.

"He *is* like my brother Yepheth," Shem said, looking as mystified as Keren felt.

"When Yepheth decides to speak, you can be sure he means every word that falls from his lips," I'ma-Annah added, smiling, obviously remembering her brother-in-law fondly. "Does anyone have news of him, and his beloved Ghinnah?"

"They're visiting the tribes of their children in the mountains to the distant west," Bachan informed I'ma-Annah. "We've heard rumors that they will eventually come down to the plains to live, but then, we hear many rumors."

As they talked, Meshek returned. With an apologetic glance toward Shem and I'ma-Annah, he sat down again. Keren held her breath; her brothers fell silent.

Meshek spoke tersely. "We won't discuss that Nimr-Rada. And I won't disown you if you'll come with us to greet your mother." Glaring at his sons, his eyes reddening, Meshek said, "You can't begin to comprehend the sorrow you've inflicted upon us. Even so, if you come with us for a few days . . ."

"We'll come," Neshar agreed hastily, without consulting the others. "I give you my word." Mattan and Bachan nodded, relaxing suddenly. I'ma-Annah sighed. Everyone looked relieved.

Watching them, Keren felt like singing for joy. Her lost brothers—three of them at least—were returning to the mountains to visit their mother. *Perhaps they'll live with us*, Keren thought, gleefully hugging herself, trying to imagine the look on Chaciydah's face when they returned.

Unexpectedly, Tsereth spoke with perfect teasing lightness. "Well, I thought I'd dance on my wedding day, but everyone looks as if it's the end of a terrible hunting trip. I should feel insulted."

"I'll dance with you!" Keren burst out, unthinking. Instantly, everyone looked at her. Embarrassed, she covered her mouth. Everyone laughed except the silent Zehker. He looked away.

Finished with his evening meal, Zehker watched Neshar, Mattan, Bachan, and the others as they danced to the rhythms of the flutes, chimes, and drums. Their earlier animosity seemed to evaporate as they moved through an intricate stepping dance around the fire. *They've forgotten I exist,* Zehker decided, satisfied. He preferred to remain unnoticed and unheard, hidden by the shadows. Even with the assurances of Shem, their First Father, Zehker didn't feel safe in the encampment. He felt like prey.

I'll insist that we keep watch tonight, he thought. *Even if I'm the only one alert enough to keep it.*

Cautiously, Zehker reached for some soft wheat cakes, dried fruits, and a generous helping of roasted meat. He wasn't taking food for himself, but for his friend, Lawkham, who had stayed at the edge of the encampment to tend the horses. By now, Lawkham was probably digging through their supplies, searching for some hidden packet of dried meat and parched grain cakes, certain he'd been forgotten.

Heaping Lawkham's food in a red-and-black glazed clay bowl, Zehker glanced at the dancers, watching the two young sisters of Neshar, Mattan, and Bachan. The older child was extraordinary, with her no-color skin and hair. She danced with all the poise and grace of an adult. But the younger girl surpassed her remarkable no-color sister by the pure joy revealed in her every step, her smile, and her shockingly pale eyes. She was full of life. Even from his place in the shadows, Zehker heard her laughing.

She's a truly happy child, Zehker thought, watching the girl until the other dancers obscured her. *Was I as happy when I was young? I don't remember. But it doesn't matter.*

Brooding, Zehker strode to the western edge of the encampment, where Lawkham had started a small, neatly banked fire.

"There you are!" Lawkham exclaimed, his eyes and teeth gleaming in the firelight. Holding up a barklike chunk of dried meat, he said, "I was bracing myself to eat one of these rocks, but forget that now. What did you find?"

Taking refuge in his usual silence, Zehker thrust the bowl at Lawkham and sat beside the fire. Lawkham grinned and plopped down next to him, shoving the despised chunk of dried meat into a leather pouch. Tearing into a soft wheat cake, then a slice of roast, Lawkham talked between bites.

"Now, if you were a more sociable person, Zehker, you would tell me that the others are all dancing and singing and enjoying themselves. The bride is lovely, of course, but her family is less than pleased to see us. In fact, you're sure that they'd like to beat us bloody and roast our horses for the next feast tomorrow. Am I right?"

"Perhaps."

Lawkham chuckled. "Did Neshar or Mattan or Bachan —any of them—think to tell their relatives that we brought gifts to celebrate the wedding?"

"No."

"Of course not," Lawkham agreed placidly. "Why should the four of you remember your manners if I'm not there to prompt you? Did *you* say anything at all?"

"Eight words."

Lawkham blinked, looking startled. "Eight? Who managed to pour oil down your throat? Some pretty girl?"

"No."

"I forgot," Lawkham sighed. "How foolish of me. You consider it too dangerous to flirt. I pity your future wife, whoever she is. She's simply going to have to read your mind." Picking at the dried berries, he asked, "How long are we going to stay?"

"We're going to visit their mother," said Zehker, allowing Lawkham to draw his own conclusions.

"Ah." Lawkham rocked backward slightly, chewing the berries. "So much for hunting. We'll be chopping wood instead. At least that's what I'd expect to do if I were visiting my mother in the mountains. Hearing all this from you now, Zehker, am I to believe that our three comrades weren't disowned completely?"

"Not completely."

"Hmph. It might have been easier if they'd been disowned." Lawkham gnawed at the roasted meat. "Their family will grieve over their separation in the spring."

"Perhaps," Zehker agreed. *But at least they have a family to return to.*

Finished with his food, Lawkham stared at the black-and-red-patterned clay bowl and raised his eyebrows approvingly, expertly, for he was the son of a potter. "Beautiful bowl. Very well made. Your choice?"

"It was there."

"Of course. It was simply there, so you snatched it. You could care less that it's wonderfully made. You're the sort who should only use unbreakable wooden dishes that are just *there.* I'll have to warn your poor wife—if you ever find one." Lawkham laughed, seeming amused by the idea of Zehker's eventual marriage.

Zehker ignored his teasing. The thought of marrying and having a family chilled Zehker. *No,* he told himself firmly. *It's safer to be alone.*

"You aren't actually going to speak to them," Khuldah scoffed, daring Sharah as they made their way toward the western edge of the encampment. Keren followed them, quivering inwardly. It was very bold of Sharah to challenge Khuldah to go on this unapproved visit to their horsemen-brothers. None of the other girls would go, fearing their parents would be angry.

Defiant, sweeping her glistening, colorless hair away from her face, Sharah said, "They're my brothers. Why shouldn't I visit them?"

"Because even a brother can become a husband!" Khuldah snapped. "You know that. And our parents won't be happy to hear that we've been visiting them on our own."

"Then why are you coming with us if you're so worried?" Sharah stared at Khuldah, her pale eyes shining, hardening.

Through past experience, Keren knew that Sharah was glorying in this little triumph over Khuldah. Neither girl would retreat, but Khuldah was definitely following Sharah against her will.

"I am worried," Khuldah admitted, lifting her squared chin, returning Sharah's stare. "But I'm not a coward. And I want to hear your reply when your brothers ask why you've come visiting."

Sharah merely smiled, never missing a step. Keren shivered, thinking, *I shouldn't go with them. Father will be angry, and I don't want him to be angry with me.* She hesitated, but Sharah grabbed her arm.

Tossing her head and looking down her nose at the indignant Khuldah, Sharah said, "I'm glad my little sister isn't some silly fret-over-nothing girl."

Hearing this, Keren felt trapped. If she ran back to the encampment, Sharah would punish her severely. It would be safer to face her father's wrath later. By now they were at the edge of the encampment, approaching the hearth used by the horsemen. Their brothers and the other two young men were tending their horses, combing their black-and-tawny coats and rubbing a thick yellow salve into their black hooves.

Bachan saw Sharah first and grinned, leaning over to backhand Neshar. The instant Neshar saw Sharah, Keren, and Khuldah, he raised an eyebrow.

You aren't happy to see us, Keren thought, dismayed. *You look just like Father when he's angry.*

Neshar ran one hand over his long, straight black hair, which was loose and damp from being scrubbed. The other four young men were also freshly scrubbed and shaved, for they had spent the morning hunting. I'ma-Annah and Tsereth's mother were already cleaning, trussing, and seasoning the fat partridges and hares the young horsemen had caught for their evening meal. And Neshar clearly believed that Sharah and Keren and Khuldah should be in the encampment helping them.

"Why are you here?" Neshar was so rude that one of his friends, a lean man with heavy black curls and a wonderfully expressive face, rolled his dark eyes in mock disgust. But the other young man, Zehker, simply watched them, unmoving as a piece of carved wood.

Sharah answered Neshar lightly, smiling. "We didn't think you'd mind. It's just that our little sister wanted very much to see your horses, but she's too shy to ask." As she spoke, Sharah dug her fingers into Keren's arm, warning her to be silent.

Neshar eyed Keren, displeased. Keren's palms were sweating. She longed to hide but kept still. Leaning down, Neshar compelled her to look at him. "Is this true, my sister?"

Keren nodded, swallowing hard, unable to speak. The black-curled young man sidled up to Neshar and murmured something to him. Neshar glanced at him, then back at Keren, as if making a decision. "Come then." He beckoned Keren, lifting his chin. "I doubt my horse will bite you if we're careful."

The horse is going to bite me, Keren thought, *because I've lied. Then Father will be angry, and I'll be punished. I hate you, Sharah!* Ducking her head, she followed Neshar to his handsome, round-bellied horse, which was tethered to a stout peg half buried in the ground. The horse was even larger than Keren had believed. *Perhaps I'll be sick and die before I'm trampled,* she thought, shaking.

Neshar stopped a short distance from the horse, turning his back against it. "I don't want him to see this yet," Neshar told Keren quietly. "Hold your hands out and together, like a cup." She held out her hands, scared but obedient. Reaching into a leather bag slung at his waist, Neshar removed a fistful of flaked barley and poured it into her hands. "My horse's favorite treat," Neshar explained. He backed away. "Now, wait there. And whatever you do, don't drop the grain."

Keren waited fearfully. For an instant, she thought the creature would ignore her. But then it approached, snorting out its breath. Keren shut her eyes and held out the grain. She heard the horse, then felt it snuffling at her hands. Just as Keren thought she might scream, the horse began to eat the grain with amazing delicacy. Its muzzle was soft against the palms of her hands, its tongue moist when the oats were completely gone. Keren opened her eyes, relieved and oddly elated. The black-and-tawny creature pulled away, then stood still, watching her, its big brown eyes alert and peaceable.

"It didn't even try to bite me," she told Neshar as he returned.

"But you thought it would," Neshar observed wryly.

"And I thought you'd faint from pure terror. Admit it: You only did this because Sharah coerced you."

When Keren nodded, Neshar sighed, his mouth twisting, revealing his disgust. "Let me give you some advice, my pale-eyed little sister. Sharah may be clever and unique, but she isn't wise. Don't follow her. She will lead you to grief. Also, if I were you, I'd go to our father immediately and confess this visit to him. He will be more lenient with you if he hears the truth from your own lips. Agreed?"

"Agreed." Keren smiled at her brother shyly. "I know you're right about Sharah. But this once, I'm glad I followed her. I think your horses are wonderful."

Neshar's answering smile was genuine. "Thank you, little one. Now, go straight to our father as we agreed. Run."

"I will!" She ran, passing the openmouthed Khuldah and the startled Sharah. To her great delight, they ran after her, calling for her to stop. Laughing, she refused, making them chase her.

Peering through the dusky encampment, Keren trotted toward the impressively large and crackling evening fire. She was eager to reach her father, who was sitting near I'ma-Annah, listening as Shem played a restful night song on his carved wooden flute. Most likely, Shem would tell stories at the end of his song, and Keren wanted to sit where she could hear every word. She also wanted to be near her father.

With all the confidence of a youngest born, truly forgiven and much loved, Keren scooted between I'ma-Annah and her father, nudging herself comfortably beneath

Meshek's arm. "Little mischief," he grumbled kindly, hugging her to his side. Keren sighed, pleased that he wasn't angry with her. Leaning against her father, she smiled at I'ma-Annah, who reached over to stroke her hair.

"Have you argued with your sister and Khuldah?" Meshek asked, lowering his head so she would hear his voice.

"No," Keren murmured. "I just wanted to be with you and I'ma-Annah."

"I should have punished Sharah this afternoon. She led you and Khuldah out of the encampment. You confessed and protected her to avoid a scene, didn't you?"

Unable to disagree with the truth, Keren nodded reluctantly, studying the shadows that were flickering across the woven grass mat before her. Meshek hugged her again. "Don't worry. I understand. But, from now on, don't protect Sharah. If she deserves to be punished, then let her be punished."

Meshek said nothing more, for the last melancholy sweet notes of Shem's night song faded into an expectant silence.

Pretending consternation, Shem looked around. "What, my children? You're not asleep yet?" Everyone laughed at his mock teasing, and Shem grinned like a boy. To Keren, he almost looked younger than Eliyshama.

"She wants a story, beloved," I'ma-Annah murmured to Shem, while tilting her head gracefully toward Keren.

"Why not? It's early yet," Shem answered agreeably, straightening as he tucked his flute into the broad woolen belt at his waist. "But to be sure everyone remembers the truth, I will start as always." Raising his voice, causing everyone to look at him, he said, "In the beginning, by the Word of the Most High, the heavens and the earth were created. The earth was without form and void. . . ."

Hearing these familiar words, Keren relaxed and watched the others. Some of the men were silently mouthing the words. They had memorized these stories, Keren realized. Her father had memorized them as well. Determined to learn the stories for herself, Keren watched Shem again. His voice rose and fell in pleasing cadence, coaxing everyone to learn of the past. To learn that the Most High, by His Word and His love, spoke the light into separate existence from the darkness. That by His Word, He brought all plants and creatures into being. Of Himself, the Lord gave the first breath of life into His own likeness that He had wrought from the earth—and this likeness was Adam, who was the Father of all her Fathers. And Adam lived in the luxuriant Garden of Adan, from which flowed the mighty river that separated into four smaller rivers (the first river, the Pishon, Keren remembered, curved about the land of Khawvilah where I'ma-Annah was born years upon years later). While Adam was in the Garden of Adan, it pleased the Most High to create a companion for Adam from Adam's own rib. This companion was Adam's beloved, later named Havah.

"Now," Shem hissed, chilling Keren by his words, "The serpent was more crafty than any animal. . . ." Beside Keren, I'ma-Annah exhaled audibly as Shem continued to recite, for she despised the serpent, their Adversary.

Keren listened, remembering that the Most High condemned the deception of the serpent and pronounced by His Word that a man would descend from the woman, a Promised One who would crush the head of the serpent.

Shem paused, departing from his usual recitation.

Turning toward their five horsemen-visitors, he said, "Understand me, all of you: We don't know who our Promised One will be. The Most High alone knows him. I can only tell you that I am not he. Nor is my son Arpakshad—though the Most High has indicated to our Noakh that Arpakshad will be a father of the Promised One."

The five young horsemen listened without reacting as Shem sternly reiterated, "No man—no matter how powerful he is—can claim to be the Promised One unless the Most High names him from the sons of Arpakshad."

He continued the ancient story, his voice rising and falling in restful tones. Expelled from their beautiful Garden of Adan, Adam and his Havah mourned the curse they had brought upon the earth. Years later, they also mourned the death of their son Hevel by the hand of his brother Kayin. Then came the first city—built by that murderer Kayin. Following these verses, Shem related first inventions, histories, and the spiritual origins of tyrannical *nephiylim*: giants who inspired further evil upon the earth. Then he told of the Most High's call to Noakh, father of Shem, Khawm, and Yepheth.

"Then you met I'ma-Annah," Keren said softly, but not softly enough. Shem heard her and smiled, his brilliant eyes flashing in the glow of the fire.

"Yes, then I met your Ma'adannah." He glanced at I'ma-Annah, as if silently urging her to speak.

I'ma-Annah spoke gently but clearly enough to be heard by everyone. "In those days beneath the first heavens, all of mankind resisted the love of the Most High. They would not hear His Word. They despised His gifts and in their hatred, they turned upon the world of that time—which He loved, and which was beautiful beyond anything that any of you could imagine beneath these blue heavens." She sighed, apparently remembering the beauties of the previous world with regret. "Even so, this world has never known such evils as existed then."

Neshar and his horsemen-companions were listening, half hidden in the darkness. I'ma-Annah looked at them, the oval of her beautiful face shadowed with sadness. "I have always prayed that the children of my children would never turn upon each other in this new world. And yet . . . now I see that they will, in time."

Hastily, as if it was too painful to endure, she continued. "As a child, I saw my eldest brother crush the life breath from my dear father, who was the only person in my family who truly loved me. Then my brother choked me and threatened to kill me if I said anything. For the remainder of my childhood, I didn't utter a single word—not one—because I was so afraid of my eldest brother. But how I longed for justice! Eventually, every person in our settlement knew that my brother had murdered my father. Yet no one cared. My father's life was worth nothing to anyone." I'ma-Annah shut her eyes briefly, then looked up at the distant heavens.

"Every night, my dreams were haunted by my father's murder. Each day, I longed to scream out words that would have provoked my immediate death. To protect myself, I covered my face with a veil; I pretended to be a madwoman." She glanced around now, studying the faces of her children's children, her expression softening fondly.

"What would you have done?" she asked. "I question myself sometimes: 'What else could I have done?' I thought I would go mad. I was scorned, beaten, humiliated, bitten, kicked, scratched, spat upon, utterly despised. Who could love a nonspeaking woman? A nothing?" Quietly, she stretched one small hand toward her beloved,

Shem; the gold on her wrists flashed wonderfully in the firelight. He took her hand and kissed it, silently urging her to continue her story. I'ma-Annah smiled at him, her love so evident that Keren sighed.

"One day, my eldest brother beat me yet again. Then his wife and my own mother scolded me. They didn't care that I was in pain. No one cared. No one loved me. I was in such despair I longed to die! I ran to the river, crying, seeking death. But before I could throw myself into the river, someone threw a rock into the water at me. One rock, then another!"

Teasingly she swiped a hand at Shem, and everyone laughed at his expression, a lovingly guilty plea for understanding.

"What else could I do?" he demanded, lifting his hands, echoing I'ma-Annah's words. "I had to stop her."

"You just wanted to throw rocks at the pretty girl," Metiyl called out, full of raucous good humor.

Chuckling, I'ma-Annah continued. "So there I was, water dripping off my face, a crying, nonspeaking, miserable creature—and this strange young man is throwing rocks at me, begging me without words to not kill myself. Why should he have cared? No one else in my family cared. But he did. And so I knew I had to continue living."

Her eyes darkened then, remembering some sorrow. "My family was fighting, all of them; they hated each other so much. Not one person in my settlement truly loved another. My eldest brother's wife, Iltani, hated my eldest brother, but she still wanted to have a child. Therefore, she turned to the Adversary, to the Serpent worshipers. A foolish thing to do. The Nachash—the leader of the Serpent worshipers—demanded the death of another to 'give' Iltani the child she requested. At the time, my mother

63

was bearing a child. Iltani fed my mother poison and killed her, then took my mother's dead child to the Nachash. I was grieving and so angry that I didn't care what happened. I followed Iltani through the darkness—for it was night—and I spied upon the lodge of the Nachash, hating the Nachash for demanding the life of my stillborn brother."

I'ma-Annah paused, and everyone listened in silence. "Evil is clever. And perceptive. The Nachash sensed that I was watching, and she screamed at me, asking if I would accuse her before the Most High. Iltani grabbed a knife of stone and ran to find whoever was spying on her. I knew she would find me and kill me. I ran. As I ran, I spoke for the first time since my father's murder. I cried to the Most High, begging Him to save me. And do you know what He did?"

Some of the younger children shook their heads, gaping at I'ma-Annah. She widened her eyes at them, saying, "He let me fall! By His mercy, I was hidden in deep grass. Iltani didn't find me, and so I was saved." Lowering her voice, I'ma-Annah said, "Iltani found one of my brothers and killed him instead—they'd been fighting earlier, and she blamed him. But everyone in the settlement turned on Iltani and killed her for the pleasure of killing her, not for justice. Truly, they didn't care for my dead brother any more than they cared for my father.

"I hid in a tree that night, terrified. And yet, I felt the presence of the Most High—surrounding me as completely as the love of any devoted father." She swallowed; Keren could see tears glistening in her eyes. "The Most High became my own Father that night. The most perfect Father.

"When I knew that Iltani and my brother were dead, I

went to the river. Shem found me there and was so distressed by my grief that he sent his mother, our I'ma-Naomi, to pay my eldest brother to release me from his household—which was an unheard-of thing. My greedy brother accepted I'ma-Naomi's offer. The next day, I married my beloved, not realizing that by this marriage, the Most High would save my life yet again. I didn't know of the Great Destruction to come."

"And I was afraid to tell her," Shem confessed, surprising everyone. It was difficult to imagine that the eloquent, persuasive Shem could ever fear speaking. "I was afraid she would run away. How could I have said the words? 'Beloved, now that we are married, I must tell you that the earth beneath our feet is going to tear itself apart and be utterly destroyed by water from beneath and above. And the Most High, by His Word, will allow this to happen.' I was sure she would say I was a madman."

"He forgets that he married a madwoman," I'ma-Annah replied, provoking quiet smiles. "Our Ancient One, Noakh, told me the next day. I didn't want to believe that this Great Destruction could happen. And yet, I knew it was true. The earth itself was as full of tremors of violence as the creatures who lived upon it. And the Most High, whom I love, was utterly scorned by everyone but those in the Lodge of Noakh.

"Later, I tried to warn my sisters of the coming destruction—as Father Noakh had been warning everyone he met for years upon years. But like everyone else, my sisters thought I was a fool, as our Noakh was considered a fool." I'ma-Annah sighed. "I often think of my sisters. I wish they had listened to our warnings. But they were like everyone else alive at that time—full of scorn and malice: *evil*. And when the waters poured over the broken earth, they were swept away. They wouldn't listen. They did not believe."

"Believe us now," Shem urged them all, including Keren's horsemen-brothers and their companions. "Believe us when we say that if there is a next Great Destruction, then according to the Most High, it will not be by water. I fear it will be by fire, and I pray it will never come to the children of my children. I beg you and the generations to follow: Remember the love of the Most High! He longs for the companionship of His children, which you are—all of you! Be faithful to Him, and He will protect you as He protected the Father of your Fathers, our Noakh, and everyone in the Lodge of Noakh."

Somberly, Keren waited to hear more, but Shem reminded everyone that they were at a wedding; they must dance and celebrate their lives before the Most High. To encourage them, he pulled out his flute to play, promising them more stories later.

Much later, when everyone was tired and preparing for sleep, Keren hugged I'ma-Annah and Shem, saying, "When I'm very old, I pray I'll be able to tell stories to the children of my children as wonderfully as you do."

To Keren's dismay, Shem flinched visibly, and an endless sorrow seemed to drop upon him like the largest stone in the world. He glanced at I'ma-Annah, as if he longed to say something to her, but she turned away quickly, as if she couldn't endure what she might hear.

Why did my words cause them such grief? Keren was afraid to ask.

Four

"YOU ALWAYS GET TO sit in front," Sharah grumbled to Keren as they rode astride Neshar's horse. "You can't say that Neshar doesn't favor you; he does and it's unfair!"

Keren hesitated, watching the horse's alert dark ears flick back toward her. *You're listening,* Keren thought to the horse, combing her fingers through its rough, dark mane. *I hope Neshar isn't listening; he'd be angry.* She waited, but Neshar continued ahead on foot, the leather reins of the horse looped through his lean fingers.

Glancing back at Sharah, Keren whispered, "If you weren't so unhappy all the time, and if you'd think of others before yourself, then perhaps they'd like you more. Anyway, Neshar lets me sit in front because I'm shorter. He told you so."

"That's his excuse," Sharah sniffed. "You're not that

much shorter; he just likes you more. Everyone does." As an afterthought—or an insult—Sharah added, "Even the horses like you more."

Exasperated, Keren hushed. Trying to reason with Sharah was like talking to a stone carving. She looked ahead at the others. Shem, Meshek, and Eliyshama were leading the way up the cold, rocky slopes, with I'ma-Annah and Tsereth following, all of them well wrapped in layers of leather, wool, and fur. They were purposeful and eager despite their bulky clothes and traveling packs, for they expected to reach the Lodge of the Ancient Ones this evening. *And I get to stay there for the winter*, Keren thought, satisfied. *I hope my I'ma is feeling better. She will be so glad to seen Neshar and Mattan and Bachan, though the other two may frighten her at first. Especially Zehker.*

Keren would have turned to look back at Zehker, but Sharah was blocking her view. *I haven't seen you smile once these past two weeks*, Keren told Zehker in her thoughts. *Even my father smiles at least once a day. Are you always sad? Or do you dislike everything so much that you find no reason to smile?*

Keren gasped, startled by Sharah's fingers suddenly digging into her ribs.

"Now we'll have to endure the whole winter, working for the Ancient Ones," Sharah said, aggrieved. "I should have begged to stay with our I'ma's cousins."

They wouldn't have you, Keren thought. Aloud, she said, "But you were always arguing with Khuldah. You should be more friendly."

"Don't lecture me, stupid!" Sharah gouged Keren's ribs again. "You don't understand anything."

Then you shouldn't talk to me, if I'm so stupid, Keren decided, pressing her lips together hard. *How I wish you could be happy, Sharah. My life would be so much easier.*

She maintained a near-perfect silence toward her sister throughout the afternoon. Gradually the terrain became familiar, and she saw two thin columns of gray-blue smoke rising from beyond the next thickly forested slope. "We're almost there," she said aloud.

Looking over his shoulder at her, Neshar said, "So I see. You've missed this place?"

"Very much," she answered, smiling.

"I suppose you would; it's been your only home."

Wounded by his apparent disdain, Keren said, "I've always been happy here. I love visiting the Ancient Ones."

Neshar answered with a shrug. Seated behind her, Sharah cackled softly. "See? You're the only person beneath the blue heavens who loves to visit here."

Keren lowered her head, refusing to speak. Her elation—and her secret hope that her brothers would stay beyond winter—vanished. *I'ma will be so sad when my brothers leave us again.*

They rode up the final incline toward the lodge of the Ancient Ones, then Neshar brought the horse to a standstill in front of the dwelling. Noakh and Naomi had already emerged to welcome them, but Chaciydah stood quietly in the doorway. Until she spied Neshar. Laughing, she ran to hug him. Then, seeing Mattan and Bachan, she covered her face with her hands and wept.

Distressed by her mother's tears, Keren swiped the tears from her own face and prepared to descend from the horse. Sharah was already scrambling down, seeming unaffected by their mother's emotional turmoil.

How can you not cry? Keren wondered to Sharah, amazed and indignant. Distracted, she slid off the horse and tumbled flat on her face against the cold, damp earth, giving a yelp of pain. Pressing her hands to her face, she struggled to sit up. Someone grabbed her arms to steady her. I'ma-Annah. And Tsereth was pulling her hands away from her bleeding mouth. Lawkham crouched beside them, obviously concerned.

"Little one, let me see," Tsereth pleaded.

"Ow! I bit my tongue."

"Is that all?" Lawkham's cheerful, teasing voice lifted over Keren's pain. "Why, that's nothing; you have to bite your tongue every time you to talk to your sister."

Keren laughed, then winced. She covered her mouth with her hand again, hating the acrid taste of the blood.

"Here." One low, abrupt word made Keren turn and look up. Zehker leaned toward Keren, his smooth brown face expressionless as he offered her a small, clean piece of soft leather. She stared at him, bewildered.

Tsereth, practical as always, took it and pressed it to Keren's bleeding mouth, thanking him. Zehker nodded silently, returning to the horses as if nothing had happened.

"You have no other injuries?" I'ma-Annah was asking.

Now the ancient I'ma-Naomi was beside them, peering down at Keren with a worried look. "Can you walk, Karan-child?"

"Her tongue is bleeding, and her chin is scraped, but they'll heal quickly," Tsereth told them. "Now, little one, let's see if you can walk. We need to go clean the dirt off your face."

Holding the soft piece of leather to her mouth, Keren stood. Her mother was now hugging Mattan and crying, while her other sons and her husband hovered about her uneasily. They hadn't noticed Keren's fall. Sighing, Keren turned to go into the lodge with Tsereth, Sharah, I'ma-Annah, and I'ma-Naomi. At the doorway, she glanced at

Zehker again, wishing she had thanked him for his help. She caught his eye for an instant, but he looked away. *As if he doesn't want to see me,* Keren thought, feeling his rejection even more acutely than the wound in her mouth.

"I don't think that Zehker likes you very much," Sharah told Keren as they sat down inside the lodge. She sounded pleased.

Zehker unstrapped the thick leather bundles from his horse and piled them on the ground quickly, his nerves on edge. Everything about this place unsettled him.

No. He forced himself to be honest. *I've been uneasy ever since we entered the encampment. This First Father, this Shem, his presence, his kindness—he's not what I expected. This entire family is more than I expected. More than I should consider. I think I'll ask Nesh-ar to allow me to leave before the snows set in. If I stay here—with them—until spring, I'll go mad.* Grimacing inwardly, he thought, *I might even join the Ancient Ones in offering sacrifices to their Most High. What would our Ra-Anan say then? He'd say I've regressed. As if Ra-Anan's way is any easier to bear.*

With an effort, Zehker pushed his dangerous thoughts into the darkest, most hidden portion of his mind, where they had hovered for twenty years. It was safer to ignore their existence. Swiftly he unloaded all the horses, covering each animal with a protective layer of fleece. Soon Lawkham was working beside him, rubbing the horses with a thick swatch of soft leather, crooning to them, irritating Zehker with his unending, good-natured noise.

All at once Lawkham slapped Zehker with the horse-scented swatch of leather, saying, "See there? You worried for nothing. The child's perfectly fine—happy as ever."

71

Suppressing a scowl, Zehker glanced toward the lodge. The youngest girl, Karan, or Keren—they called her both —had emerged from the doorway to visit her parents and brothers, who were still talking. The child's face was clean; a reddened abrasion on her chin was the only evidence that she had fallen at all. Her expression was contented as usual—a sweet daydreamer's face, untouched by fear or grief. And when her brother Eliyshama began to tease her, threatening to tickle her, she laughed and skittered away, coltishly thin and joyful.

I'm glad you aren't hurt, Zehker thought unwillingly, looking away from the child. *But how I envy you your joy.* With an effort he pushed away his renewed doubts, telling himself, *I'll leave this place soon and never return.*

"Our reunion has gone better than I expected," Neshar sighed into the darkness as he, his brothers, and their friends left the evening fire in the lodge to tend their horses.

"It has," Bachan agreed, sounding pleased. "But I keep staring at the little ones. Who will believe we have such sisters?"

"We tell no one," Neshar commanded firmly. "Not Kana or Miyka or Ra-Anan."

"But they're our own brothers," Bachan argued, halting, his obstinate expression visible in the moonlight. "How can we not tell them?"

"And Ra-Anan will know soon enough whether we say anything to him or not," Mattan objected, clearly defiant. "Nothing remains hidden from him for long."

Comprehending the extent of Mattan's loyalties to

Ra-Anan, Neshar bit down the traitorous, dangerous words that sprang to his lips. What Mattan had said was true: Ra-Anan, with his growing influence and his wealth of informants, would eventually hear of Sharah and Keren. And knowing Ra-Anan, he would find some way to benefit from his sisters' unique attributes. They would be like weapons to him. Or pawns.

"Ra-Anan must not hear of our sisters from us. He will demand their presence in his courts, and our parents would never agree to part with them. It's too dangerous, and our sisters are too young to serve in Ra-Anan's schemes to please He-Who-Lifts-the-Skies. Therefore, I say that we let them spend their childhood in peace. We tell no one."

Neshar glared at his brothers and friends, willing them to obey. Mattan and Bachan agreed grudgingly, and Zehker nodded somberly. But Lawkham grinned, as if thoroughly amused, his teeth shining in the darkness. Neshar scowled at him.

His grin fading, Lawkham raised his hands in protest. "I agree! Trust me."

But do I trust you? Neshar wondered, staring at Lawkham. *Do I trust anyone these days? No, I'm not a fool. I'll be watching you all.*

Fine

IT SEEMED FRIGHTFUL to Keren that she was twenty-five years old. Particularly now, as she slouched self-consciously, standing beside I'ma-Annah, who was shorter.

"Usually, I would tell you to stand straight," I'ma-Annah scolded gently. "But with working the gold, you'll slouch anyway." I'ma-Annah knelt and used blackened metal tongs to slowly nudge a small clay dish filled with beaten gold toward the ruddy, glowing center of her fire pit. When she was satisfied that the clay dish had heated evenly and would not crack in the fire, she said, "Now, Karan, your job is to force air onto the coals. Here are the foot bellows."

"Thank you, I'ma-Annah." Keren slipped her foot into the strap atop the leather bellows and went to work. This was the second year I'ma-Annah had allowed her to work the gold. In previous years she had learned to make baskets, clay pots, garments of leather, garments of wool, powders for paints, and carvings of stone. But gold working was now Keren's favorite task. Stomping vigorously, she had the coals burning in an eye-hurting glow when the Ancient Noakh came from a nearby field to sit, rest, and watch.

"Ah, little one," Noakh teased—he loved calling her "little one" now that she was so tall—"where's our Sharah? Isn't this her gold that you're working?"

"Here I am, Ancient One," Sharah said, coming out of the lodge, carrying a clay basin of coarse river sand. Deferential, she knelt opposite I'ma-Annah. In the past few years, Sharah had trained herself to move and behave with a peculiar grace, which commanded the attention and esteem of everyone outside her own lodge. Sharah's unique looks and deceptive charm had attracted numerous admirers. At the last encampment during the previous autumn, she had finally agreed to marry her most persistent suitor, Bezeq. Striking and powerful, Bezeq was a leader of one of the northern tribes and adored by all the unmarried women—a triumph for Sharah.

I pray Bezeq will provide the status you crave, my sister, Keren thought, glancing at Sharah's beautiful face. Her sister's gray-blue eyes were fixed upon the gold—a gift from Bezeq.

"Perhaps it should be a band to wear about my throat," Sharah said, looking at I'ma-Annah almost humbly, as if she were seeking her opinion.

I'ma-Annah nodded, sorting through a number of clay and stone molds at her side. "There should be enough gold for a band. Here's the perfect mold." She held up a graceful stone crescent for Sharah's approval.

In silent agreement, Sharah took the crescent rim of

stone, pressed it into the dish of sand, then set it near the coals to warm. She would gradually turn the bowl and nudge it into the fire to heat the sand and the stone rim, so that the rim would not crack when exposed to the purified molten gold.

Glancing up at the clouded, end-of-winter sky, Noakh said, "We'll have rain tonight. It's a good thing that you've started this today." Watching Sharah, he mused aloud, "In three weeks you'll leave to join Bezeq and his people. Then, I suppose, our Karan will marry within a few years."

"We pray she will, Ancient One," Sharah answered politely, her gaze fixed on the gold. "But my sister behaves as if she doesn't care for any of the young men."

That's because I haven't met a man who would prefer to look at me rather than at you, thought Keren, still working the bellows. *The men are all so fascinated with you that I don't exist when you're nearby. And the ones who do notice me are frightened by my no-color eyes.*

"The Most High will send your sister's beloved to her in the proper time," Noakh murmured. He patted the folds of his thick gray overtunic absently, finally producing a dark leather pouch containing his treasured and aged iron carving blade, and the piece of antler he had been shaping to use as a retouching tool. After a comfortable silence, Noakh spoke again, pausing on occasion to study his work. "The first time I saw you, Sharah, I knew you were a sign to us. The Most High is preparing to divide the tribes and scatter them over the entire earth."

Confounded, Keren stood on the bellows, unmoving. I'ma-Annah nudged her to work again.

Undisturbed, Noakh continued, "The children of my children have not been faithful to the will of the Most High. They do as they please. They huddle together and ignore His presence instead of spreading out to subdue the earth. And although the Most High is patient, He won't endure their rebellion forever."

Keren glimpsed a flash of impatience in Sharah's elegant, noncolor features.

"But the Most High won't destroy the earth again," Sharah protested.

"Not with water," Noakh reminded her amiably. "But this earth—like the earth before the Great Destruction—could perish. I fear, as Shem does, that it might burn away like the impurities within your gold."

Looking down at the now-molten gold, Sharah said, "I will remember the Most High, O Ancient One."

But you've already forgotten Him, Keren thought, watching her sister's face, undeceived. *You're thinking of the gold you will wear. And when you've forgotten the gold, you'll think of some other object or desire. How I pray you'll be happy with Bezeq. You've never been truly satisfied in life, and that has affected us all.*

Pondering Sharah's situation, Keren continued to force air against the coals until I'ma-Annah motioned for her to stop. Sounding pleased, I'ma-Annah said, "See how the gold is like a mirror? And the stone form is ready. Step back now, Karan-child."

Keren watched, admiring I'ma-Annah's skill as she grasped the tongs, seized the dish of molten gold, and poured it smoothly into the crescent stone mold, which rested securely in the dish of heated sand. The gold flowed throughout the graceful rim, glowing, warm, and beautiful. Even Sharah looked pleased by the results. She smiled as I'ma-Annah said, "We'll let it cool until evening, then we will incise a pattern and—"

A man's echoing call of greeting stopped I'ma-Annah's plans. Wondering, Keren looked down the slopes, toward the woods. Eliyshama, Neshar, and Bachan were climbing the slope, leading two well-laden horses. Eliyshama looked grim, Neshar stoic, and Bachan amused.

Seeing them, Keren's heart thudded uncomfortably. Obviously, her horseman brothers had been visiting their family again, after an absence of three years. "Mattan didn't come this time," Keren thought aloud. "Perhaps they've quarreled again. I hope our I'ma isn't upset."

"I suppose we'll go to our own lodge in the morning," Sharah muttered, one pale eyebrow lifted in poorly concealed disgust. She only wanted to stay in the lodge of the Ancient Ones, Keren knew, because I'ma-Annah was working the gold for her wedding.

"We'll finish your gold this evening," I'ma-Annah told her. "Unless you want it to be very elaborate."

"I want it to be beautiful, Ma'adannah. I will wait the three weeks if need be."

Eliyshama bent to greet Noakh, then turned to kiss I'ma-Annah.

After binding his horse's reins to an aged, battered stump, Neshar also formally greeted Noakh and I'ma-Annah, bowing his head slightly as he spoke. "Ancient One. Ma'adannah. It's good to see you both."

"Welcome," I'ma-Annah murmured, her beautiful eyes shining. "If you will excuse me, I'll go tell your I'ma-Naomi that you're here. Karan, Sharah, be sure no one jostles the gold while it's cooling." I'ma-Annah hurried into the lodge, her steps swift and eager as a young girl's.

"My sisters," Bachan greeted Keren and Sharah, forgetting to acknowledge the ancient Noakh first, "I expect you to cry when I tell you that we cannot stay. Neshar and I have been commanded to return to the Great City before summer."

"I weep," said Sharah, clearly unmoved.

"I'm sorry we missed your visit," Keren told her brothers, meaning every word. "How is our I'ma?"

"Probably still crying," Eliyshama answered quietly, as Neshar nodded in mute agreement and Bachan rolled his eyes. "Tsereth and the children are with her."

"They'll cheer her up; they always do." Keren smiled, thinking of her energetic, bright-eyed young nephews, Meysha and Darak, and their toddler-sister, Yelalah.

"At least stay until my son Shem returns with our herd," Noakh urged. "What's one more evening?"

"Ancient One, we're bound by our pledge to return," said Neshar, glancing at Noakh, fond, but not wholly regretful. "Perhaps we'll meet the Father of my Fathers on our way down through the hills."

Eliyshama cleared his throat and smiled at Noakh. "I, however, will stay for the night, Ancient One, if you aren't bored with me."

"Who can be bored with you, son of my sons? You must tell us about your children—and give us your word that you will bring them to visit next time." Noakh heaved himself to his feet and gestured toward Neshar and Bachan to follow him into the lodge.

Keren started after them, then changed her mind and returned to sit with Sharah, who was waiting for the gold to cool.

"Do you like it?" Keren asked, peeking down at the gleaming rivulet of gold.

"It will be the first of many gold ornaments." Sharah sat back on her heels and studied Keren. "In spite of all our quarrels, my sister, it will be strange to not see you for years at a time."

"You'll miss me?" Keren blinked, surprised.

"Somewhat." Sharah stared at the gold once more. "It's just that you've always been so near to me—lurking like an irritating shadow."

"Thank you," Keren said, refusing to be stung.

Bachan was coming out of the lodge again, his dark eyes glittering, one corner of his mouth turning sardonically. "I've heard you're to marry that Bezeq of the northern tribes, my sister."

"Are you angry?" Sharah's disdain was unmistakable.

Bachan stared at her, then smiled. "I pity Bezeq. Even so . . ." With amazing swiftness, he caught a long curling strand of Sharah's hair, whipped it around his brown fingers, and lopped it off just below her jawline, wielding the sharp blade of his obsidian knife so unexpectedly that Keren gasped.

Sharah screeched. "Bachan! Why did you *do* that?"

"A token, my sister," Bachan said, returning to the horses. "Proof that the unnatural exists."

"I could beat him!" Sharah breathed to Keren, wrathful, as she clawed at her mutilated lock of hair. "How can I possibly hide this?"

Keren shrugged. "Why hide it if you can't? Braid it and flaunt it as if you meant to wear it that way. The other young girls will imitate you."

Sharah gaped at Keren, then laughed. "You're right. That's what I'll do. My dear shadow-sister, I believe I will almost miss you after all."

❦ ❧

"Ra-Anan commands your presence," the huge guardsman told Bachan, his silhouette dark against the moonlight, his stance fierce, compelling Bachan to obey.

"Why should the great Ra-Anan care to see me?" Bachan demanded, irritated at being roused from a sound sleep in the middle of the night. "Since when does he trouble himself with one of his unworthy brothers?"

"Come at once or I'll bind you," the guardsman answered, tensing.

Unnerved now, and wide-awake, Bachan left the cramped, clay-bricked soldiers' quarters and followed his hostile escort through the midsummer night's quiet of the slumbering Great City. Feeling the hardened clay of the main road beneath his feet, Bachan wished he had not been too intimidated to lace on his sandals. It galled him that he would appear before Ra-Anan disheveled and barefoot, like a mere farmer.

Ra-Anan's residence was at the edge of the Great City, a low, sprawling, nondescript brick home, surrounded by a scrupulously tended, wall-enclosed courtyard garden. Despite his growing power, Ra-Anan was careful to cultivate the appearance of simplicity. Too great a display of influence and wealth would annoy He-Who-Lifts-the-Skies and jeopardize Ra-Anan's position amid the growing hierarchy of the kingdom.

Thoroughly respectful of his brother's abilities, Bachan felt his stomach tighten as he was led through a narrow gate that opened into the torchlit garden.

"There," the guard muttered, pointing toward a pair of mats arranged near a glowing clay brazier. "Sit."

Knowing his place, Bachan chose the less elaborate, thinly cushioned mat, and sat cross-legged upon it, contriving to appear at ease. A serving boy appeared, dressed in a simple leather tunic with a cord of leather at his throat bearing an amulet of pure white stone, marking him as one of the household of Ra-Anan. Furtively, the boy cast a dishful of spices and fragrant wood into the brazier, then slipped away before Bachan could question him.

Sweet, sharp smoke arose from the brazier, a deterrent to the mosquitoes that flitted through the darkness seeking flesh. *And blood, like Ra-Anan,* Bachan thought, swiping a mosquito from his forearm.

At that instant, Ra-Anan emerged from his house, tall, reed thin, and clean shaven, though he was married. Even Ra-Anan's head was shorn and oiled—giving him an odd, vulturelike appearance, which Bachan secretly despised. Because it was the middle of the night, Ra-Anan wore only a simple wrap of untrimmed white fleece. As Ra-Anan approached him, Bachan stood and folded his hands properly, bowing his head with only the exact measure of respect required, nothing more.

His narrow upper lip curling faintly, Ra-Anan sat down, then nodded to Bachan, indicating that he should sit as well. Silently Ra-Anan reached into his white fleece wrap and pulled out a gleaming, braided coil, which he showed to Bachan in the torchlight.

The instant he recognized the braided coil, Bachan gulped for air. It was the lock of hair he had cut from Sharah's head four months past. *How did you get hold of that?* Bachan wondered to Ra-Anan, shocked.

"This was found in your gear," Ra-Anan informed him coldly, enunciating every word. "Did you think you could hide her existence from me forever?"

Bachan stiffened defensively. "Neshar demanded my word that I say nothing."

"Who else has said 'nothing' to me after all these years?"

Bachan was about to argue when he saw Mattan emerge from the shadows of Ra-Anan's house. *Traitor-brother,* Bachan thought, sneering at Mattan. *Thief. I should never have shown you that lock of hair.* Grudgingly, knowing that Ra-Anan already knew everything, Bachan said, "Lawkham and Zehker, guardsmen of the Great King. They've seen her. But they deserve no punishment, Ra-Anan. They merely honored Neshar's command, because he was their leader at that time. You know it's true. Even so, it's too late for you to do anything; our no-color sister is now married."

"What about the younger one with the pale eyes?" Ra-Anan queried softly, narrowing his own eyes until they were hooded and full of menace. "Is she married?"

Thinking of the sensitive, daydreaming Keren, then glancing at Mattan, Bachan rasped out the truth, hating himself. "No. She's not married, or betrothed."

Ra-Anan's dark, hooded eyes gleamed. Silent once more, he waved both Bachan and Mattan away. As soon as they were outside the gate, and a safe distance from the guard, Bachan struck Mattan's jaw with one clenched fist. Mattan accepted Bachan's blow, staggering but not falling.

"Traitor!" Bachan hissed. "You're no brother to me! Why did you tell Ra-Anan about Keren? She's done you no harm, but he will destroy her with all his schemes!"

"Better her than us," Mattan muttered stiffly, holding his jaw. "And you told Ra-Anan she wasn't betrothed, I didn't. You're just as guilty."

Chilled by his own sweat, Bachan asked, "What's Ra-Anan going to do?"

Mattan looked away. "He's going to tell He-Who-Lifts-the-Skies. They'll punish Neshar for hiding this. Beyond that, I don't know. They may punish us too, though I think he might excuse Zehker and Lawkham."

Looking at Bachan, he said, "I'm sorry. I heard a rumor

here, in these very streets, that one of the northern tribal leaders had married a beautiful woman with no-color skin and hair. I knew it was Sharah, and I knew Ra-Anan would hear of it before too long. And when Ra-Anan is angry . . ."

"I know." Bachan shuddered, wishing he could warn Neshar. And Keren.

Six

KEREN BREATHED IN the last hints of scent drifting down from the sacrificial altar tended by Noakh, Shem, and Meshek. Pressing her hands to her face, she prayed, *Guard us, O Most High. I ask Your protection for my family, for Sharah, for myself, for us all. Though I'm not afraid*, she thought at last, looking up into the autumn-blue heavens. It would be an adventure to visit the tribe of Bezeq, and to stay with Sharah while she awaited the birth of her child. *Why do I have such difficulty thinking of Sharah as a mother?*

"You don't have to go," Chaciydah whispered, plucking at Keren's sleeve. "Actually, I wish you wouldn't. Tsereth's also expecting another child; she needs you here. *I* need you here."

Smiling, Keren kissed her mother's thin cheek, then hugged her tight, willing her to be strong. "Yesterday, my I'ma, you wanted me to go to Sharah because you remembered what it was like to bear children in a strange place, surrounded by people you didn't know. Today you say that you and Tsereth need me. What should I do?"

"I know I'm being selfish. But you've always been such a comfort to me and such a joy to your father; I can't bear to see you go," said Chaciydah, in a flow of emotion that brought tears to her eyes. "Not that I love you more than I love Sharah, but since she's been gone, life is so peaceful. I detest the thought of changing anything."

"Our Karan will return to us," said I'ma-Annah, comfortingly tranquil as she smoothed Keren's shawl of blue-gray edged with crimson, tucking its ends around Keren's throat.

"Certainly, she will return to us," I'ma-Naomi agreed, hugging Keren fiercely. "But Khuldah and her beloved are waiting, as is that Yithran and his mother. It would be rude to delay any longer. Give me a kiss, Karan, then go kiss your father and his fathers."

Obediently Keren leaned down and kissed I'ma-Annah and I'ma-Naomi, closer to tears now than she had been when she kissed her mother. Meshek was coming down the hillside from the altar, followed by Shem and Noakh. Somber faced, he hugged Keren and kissed her forehead lightly. For a brief instant, Keren saw his dark brown eyes flicker. *He doesn't want me to go,* she realized, saddened.

Taking her hands, Meshek said, "Give me your word, daughter, that if you meet some young man who wishes to marry you, and you are certain that you desire to marry him, then you'll send him to me before pledging yourselves to each other."

"I give you my word, Father. I'd never marry without your permission," Keren promised—though marriage seemed so unlikely that she couldn't take the possibility to heart. "Truly, if I meet such a man, I'll send him to you at once."

"May the Most High bless you," Shem told Keren, his dark eyes fathomless. "Remember Him, child."

"Always," Keren promised, marveling at his intensity. One glance from Shem could overpower a torrent of words from any other man. It was difficult to look away from him.

"Our prayers are with you, little one," Noakh said, smiling fondly. "Keep that Sharah safe from her own impulses."

"If anyone can, O Ancient One," Keren agreed.

Khuldah was coming to fetch her, clearly under orders from the others in her group. By her marriage, less than two years past, Khuldah was a member of the tribe of Bezeq. Shortly after her marriage, Khuldah had convinced her husband and his people to join her family at the encampments, thus unwittingly introducing Bezeq to Sharah. Khuldah had also decided that the restless Sharah needed Keren's calming presence.

"Pale Eyes!" Khuldah approached Keren. "My husband and the others are eager to leave. Are you coming?"

"I'm ready." Keren retrieved the heavy leather traveling pack she had borrowed from Tsereth. *I wish I could say good-bye to you again,* Keren thought to Tsereth and Eliyshama, who had stayed behind with their children. *I'm going to miss you all.*

Controlling her pang of regret, Keren struggled with the traveling pack, distributing its weight across her shoulders. Khuldah pulled Keren's hair away from the straps to prevent it from snagging, then grabbed Keren's arm. She cast one last smile of farewell toward her family and hurried down the slope, away from the lodge of the Ancient Ones, to join the others.

"I'm so glad you've agreed to come with us," Khuldah

whispered. "I've missed talking with you. But look: Yithran's staring at you again, never mind that his mother is displeased."

Keren flushed. The dusky, tousle-haired Yithran—as physically attractive and impressive as his brother Bezeq —was indeed staring at her. But his mother, the dignified matriarch Nihyah, had averted her narrow, decorous face, her finely curved mouth suddenly a tight line.

You don't like Sharah, Keren realized, hastily looking away from the disapproving Nihyah. *And it irritates you that your second son is now watching me. I wish I could tell you not to worry. If you dislike my sister so much, then I wouldn't dare encourage your son.*

Determined to avoid Nihyah and Yithran, Keren walked behind Khuldah and her husband, Merowm, who was nut-brown, vigorous, and easily amused—a perfect match for Khuldah. As the day progressed, however, Keren noticed that Yithran was gradually closing the distance between them.

As they were sitting down for their midday meal, Yithran stopped directly in front of Keren, stared into her eyes, and smiled. His admiration was so unmistakable and so disturbingly pleasant that Keren looked down at her leather-clad feet, blushing hotly. *This is going to be a difficult journey*, she thought. *Unless I act now.*

Snatching her leather traveling pack, she hurried to sit beside the startled Nihyah. Yithran wouldn't dare to flirt with her in front of his own mother. To make certain that Nihyah understood her completely, Keren appealed to her, "Mother of Bezeq, please, let me keep company with you."

Nihyah's shocked expression eased into a grudging smile. "Stay with me for as long as you like, child. I'm glad you asked."

"Nothing I do pleases her," Sharah hissed to Keren, flinging a bitter glance toward Nihyah's proud back. "How I wish her husband hadn't gone to pay tribute to the Great King! She never has enough work to keep her from antagonizing me."

"The mother of your husband has a good heart," Keren murmured. She dropped her traveling pack, then edged into the shadows of Bezeq's stone-and-timber lodge, drawing Sharah along with her, praying Nihyah couldn't hear her. "But Nihyah is as strong willed as you are, my sister, and you must talk to each other and work together if you are to live in peace. Even more important: You must permit yourself to lose an occasional contest."

"To her?" Sharah puckered her lips in distaste.

"Yes, *lose* to her once in a while. Use those manners you pretend to have."

"You sound like your I'ma-Annah."

"Thank you. That's the kindest thing you've ever said to me."

"I didn't mean it kindly, and you know it," Sharah said.

Nihyah was listening, Keren was sure, so she changed the subject. "You look beautiful! I'll be so glad to see your child."

"I'm huge," Sharah complained, sliding her hands over her rounded abdomen.

"You carry a child better than any woman I've ever seen," Nihyah told her, approaching with a thick, puffy bale of furs.

Noticing Sharah's stunned expression, Keren suspected that this was the first compliment Nihyah had ever given her daughter-in-law. To encourage the pleasantries,

Keren asked, "What do you think, O mother of Bezeq: Does my sister carry a son or a daughter?"

"A son," Nihyah answered, lifting her chin proudly. "See how high she carries him? And she felt him moving quite early."

"I agree," Sharah said, her attitude neutral. "This child's a boy; he's so busy."

Khuldah came into the lodge now, shaking off her damp cloak. Seeing Sharah, Khuldah hooted with laughter. "You look wonderful! You've probably done nothing except eat and grow in all the weeks we've been gone. But listen: The men are all eating and talking in my husband's lodge, and I said we'd be visiting and feasting with all the other women for the evening. Though I might fall asleep early. Aren't you tired, Pale Eyes—I mean, Keren?"

Keren tried not to laugh. Khuldah's habit of calling her "Pale Eyes" had irritated Nihyah on their journey.

Now Nihyah raised one thin, arched eyebrow. "I was just making a place for her to sleep. Come, Keren, we'll help you to settle in, then we should eat. After so many weeks of travel, it will be good to sleep beneath a solid roof."

"She likes you," Sharah muttered, watching Nihyah smooth the furs over a clean, dried heap of straw, neatly tucked into a corner. "How did you manage that?"

"Healthy fear," Keren answered softly, thinking of the bold, staring Yithran. "I don't want her to be angry with me."

"Coward."

Other women were coming in now to welcome Keren. As Sharah and Nihyah greeted them, Khuldah whispered, "Now that we're home, Pale Eyes, I'll tell you my secret: I'm with child too! I've known since before our journey, but I didn't want my Merowm and that Nihyah to fuss about taking me along. Merowm nearly fainted tonight when I told him—although I'm so round he should have noticed weeks ago. But forget that. Listen: What do you think of Yithran?"

"I'm not thinking of him."

You are perfect, Keren thought, gazing down at Gib-bawr, Sharah's dark-haired infant son. He was sleeping, nestled against her chest in a carrying pouch of supple leather. *You've been the brightest part of this winter for me. If you'd only sleep during the night as you do during the daytime. Your mother would be so much happier.*

Keren grimaced. At least Sharah was sleeping now. Perhaps she would be less irritable when she awoke. Overwhelmed by the fatigue of caring for an infant, Sharah regarded her tiny son as mere work to be handed off to the nearest woman—usually Keren.

But I don't mind, Keren thought, smiling at her sleeping nephew's chubby face.

Shivering in an errant draft, Keren pulled an untrimmed deerskin coverlet around her shoulders, then settled down near the fire to pick through some pounded barley. As she worked, she rocked Gibbawr. *I wish you were mine,* she thought, admiring the dark forelock of his feather-soft hair. *Whenever I hold you, I desperately want a child of my own. I want many children. Perhaps I should marry Yithran after all.*

Nihyah hurried in just then, her arms full of coarsely split pieces of dried wood. Her narrow brown face was alight, smiling. "Bezeq and Yithran have returned from their hunting trip; they'll be coming in soon. What can we give them to eat?"

"Soup," Keren answered, hastily looking down to prevent Nihyah from noticing her embarrassment at the mention of Yithran. "And wheat cakes and dried olives." As she spoke, she donned a leather mitt and uncovered a wide-shouldered clay pot, steaming at the hearth. Bits of venison in the broth would enhance the barley, and she would add dried herbs and some salt to season it. That would satisfy the hungry Bezeq and Yithran for a while. Shielding Gibbawr with one arm, Keren dumped the barley into the pot, stirred it, and recovered the pot.

"I'll tend this," Nihyah told Keren, edging her away from the hearth. "You take Gibbawr to his mother. He will be hungry soon."

"Thank you. I'm sure you're right." Keren stood, then hesitated. Bezeq was coming into the lodge, heavily clad in furs. His angular, handsomely bearded face brightened as he caught sight of her holding Gibbawr.

Lifting one big, sinewy hand, he beckoned eagerly. "Let me see my son. Has he grown while I've been away?"

"You've been gone for only two days, my brother," Keren reminded him, smiling. Gibbawr was stretching within the confines of his carrying pouch, apparently recognizing his father's deep voice. Keren eased the strap of the pouch off her shoulders and presented the now-awake Gibbawr to his father.

"Aha!" Bezeq lifted his infant son, holding him face-to-face. "Have you missed me, my son? Well, when you're old enough, you'll come hunting with me. Then you'll miss your mother instead. Am I right?"

Gibbawr squawked plaintively—his usual prelude to a full-throated wail. Bezeq grinned and quickly handed him to Keren. "I'll let you hold him again, my sister. When he's happy, bring him to me."

"As you say." Keren started to turn from Bezeq, but he lifted one hand, silently asking her to wait. Wondering, she glanced up at him. Bezeq's smile was gone.

Emphatically, he said, "Stay with us, Keren. Marry my brother. He desires you as his wife—more than he has ever desired any other woman."

How like you, Keren thought, watching her brother-in-law steadily. *You are so bold, you and Yithran; you aren't even trying to enlist your mother to speak to me as proper men should. And yet, that's part of your charm.*

Gibbawr was crying now. Keren lifted him to her shoulder and patted his small, sturdy back soothingly. "Give me a while to consider your request. I'll make my reply to your mother; it would be terrible if this should take her by surprise."

"I'll speak to her," Bezeq assured Keren, not the least bit shamed by her indirect rebuke. "Will you tell my Sharah that I've returned?"

"I'll tell her." *He looks so happy,* Keren thought, turning from Bezeq. *Despite all of Sharah's tantrums, he's still infatuated with her.*

Her heart thudding in an odd mixture of distress and elation, Keren hurried into the small sleeping area to face Sharah. Gibbawr was squalling, frantic for nourishment.

Even as she entered the dimly lit sleeping area, Keren heard Sharah's sleep-roughened voice. "He's crying already? It seems I just fell asleep. Did I hear Bezeq talking?"

"He's returned from his hunting trip," Keren answered above the baby's angry wail. She crouched beside the low bed, handing Gibbawr to Sharah. Sighing heavily, Sharah took the infant in her arms.

As Gibbawr hushed and settled in to nurse, Sharah

grumbled, "I'm so tired, and this child is always hungry. Now Bezeq will want my attention as well. I suppose he's brought us venison again?"

"I suppose," Keren murmured, not daring to say more.

Sharah exhaled her disgust. "I'm sick of venison. I'm sick of everything. Nothing is as I expected it would be. I had more freedom in the lodge of our father. Though I despised that place too.

"Listen, Keren, you must help me to persuade my husband to lead us out of these hills this year. I want to visit the plains and see the cities where our brothers live."

"Why should you care to visit our brothers? You've always been so rude to them that they'd hardly welcome our company."

"It would be a change!" Suddenly ferocious, Sharah snatched Keren's hair. "Say that you'll help me. Bezeq will listen to us if we're united in this."

"You're presuming I'll stay," Keren answered through gritted teeth. She didn't dare to pull away. The roots of her scalp were tingling, burning as Sharah twisted her hair even tighter. "But yes, Sharah, you have my word. I'll speak to Bezeq for your sake—and for his. Now, let me go before we fight and upset your son."

"Thank you." Sharah released Keren's hair, polite now, as if they'd just finished a peaceable visit. "And I think you should stay and marry Yithran."

"The way you behave toward me, my sister, I'm sure I'll refuse."

"It's the lack of sleep." Sharah actually sounded remorseful, exhausted. "I'm so tired I can't even think clearly. Sometimes I think I'll go mad. You must forgive me."

"I forgive you," Keren muttered, willing the obligatory words past her lips. "But I won't stay here if you continue to treat me so rudely, Sharah. I don't care if I have to walk all the way back to our father's lodge by myself."

"Yithran will follow you. He won't give up, Keren." Disgusted again, Sharah said, "He's just like his brother."

Keren stared at her sister's exquisite profile, which was barely discernable in the dim light filtering in from the hearth of the main room. *You don't love your husband,* she thought to Sharah. *But he does love you. How I pity you both.*

Nihyah had left the doorway of the lodge open, and the fresh spring air and the clear sunlight made Keren long to run outside. *Later,* she told herself. *When my work is done.* She had promised Nihyah that she would finish the grain cakes for their evening meal, so Nihyah could mend a leather tunic.

"Yithran hopes you will consider him as a husband," Nihyah told Keren, as she seated herself nearby and began to pick through an assortment of bone needles. "So I'm asking, Keren: What do you say to my Yithran?"

Keren put a small log on the lowering hearth flames, then spoke reluctantly. "If you don't approve, Mother of Bezeq, then I'll refuse to marry Yithran. I won't be the cause of distress between you and your second son." As she waited for Nihyah's answer, Keren pinched a lump of dough from the wooden kneading trough and pressed it between her fingers, working it into a small cake, praying her nervousness didn't show.

Do I want to marry Yithran? If she didn't, then how could she refuse him without offending his entire tribe? But if Nihyah was against the match, then her own fears meant nothing either way.

"I approve," Nihyah said, allowing Keren a smile. "But you hesitate, Keren. And I don't want you to marry my son if you aren't sure of your feelings for him. Don't let Yithran—or Bezeq—coerce you into this marriage."

"Thank you for understanding." Keren sighed, deeply relieved. She frowned at the dough; it was sticking to her fingers because she had forgotten to grease her hands. "I'll give you my answer in a few weeks."

Kneeling in the grass beside Keren, Yithran spoke quietly, "It's been a month now. I've allowed you more time than you requested."

Keren smiled and picked through the basket of crisp green shoots she had gathered to extend their evening meal. "I've noticed. And I didn't think you could ever be so patient." Yithran's behavior these past few weeks had been a source of wonder to Keren, and to everyone in the tribe. He was thoughtful now, guarding his temper, seeking advice from the older men, working hard in the lower fields, then doing endless chores for his mother, and behaving with perfect courtesy toward Keren. Even as Yithran spoke to her, Nihyah and the hugely pregnant Khuldah were watching them from the nearby stream, for Yithran was careful never to approach Keren when she was alone.

He sighed gustily. "I've been thinking that you won't want to live so close to your sister for all your life. And you'd miss your parents and the Ancient Ones. I've been thinking, too, that if you become my wife, eventually we might lead our own tribe nearer to your parents."

"You don't need to say these things to please me."

Keren stripped the tough outer layer off a shoot. "I don't long to be the matriarch of a tribe."

"All the more reason for you to be one," Yithran answered, urging her to reconsider. "You'd never use your status to please yourself. You would think of others instead. Look how you've been able to strike a balance between my mother and your sister. Some of the older women tried to negotiate peace between them before you arrived, and they failed. But you've managed them both without offending either one."

"I happen to understand Sharah and your mother," Keren pointed out. "Perhaps the other women simply weren't close enough to either of them to have any real effect on their opinions." She reached for another shoot, but Yithran covered the basket with one wide brown hand, making her look at him.

"Marry me," he pleaded, actually humble.

You love me, Keren thought, secretly admiring his smooth, even features. *And if I don't love you now, I will eventually. I know we'd be happy together, and have children together.* She looked away, trying to compose herself. "When I left the Lodge of the Ancient Ones, I gave my word to my father that I would not pledge myself to any young man, unless I first sent that young man to speak with him. So I'm asking that you honor my father's request: Go to my father. Tell him that I've sent you and ask for his blessing on our marriage. If he agrees, then I'll agree."

"I'm leaving now!" His eyes shining, full of fire, Yithran jumped to his feet, started back toward the stone-and-timber lodges, then stopped, as if he had forgotten something. He returned quickly and knelt beside her again. "If your father agrees, then should we plan to meet him at an encampment after the harvest?"

"Will you actually return before then?" Keren asked, unable to resist teasing him.

Yithran grinned. "I'll run all the way. Here . . . I almost forgot to give you this. I found the stone years ago. And I traded other stones like it to have this made on my last hunting trip." Reaching into the leather pouch slung at his waist, Yithran produced a slender cuff bracelet of gold, hardened and tinted pink by the addition of copper. A clear oval crystal gleamed from the band's smooth, polished center. Keren gasped at the sight of it but immediately shook her head. "It's beautiful, Yithran, but I can't accept it. Not yet."

"It's not a token of betrothal," Yithran argued. "Only a remembrance. I don't want you to forget me while I'm gone." He set the bracelet on the pile of shoots and stood, leaving her no choice but to accept his gift. Slowly Keren took the bracelet and slipped it onto her wrist. It fit perfectly.

Aware of Nihyah and Khuldah watching them, Keren said, "Perhaps you should go tell your mother and take leave of her properly."

"I'm going." But he leaned toward her again and whispered, "In my thoughts, I am kissing you." Keren blushed uncomfortably. Grinning, Yithran strode over to his mother and spoke to her. When Nihyah laughed and clapped her hands enthusiastically, Yithran kissed her. Then he hurried away, calling other young, unmarried men from their lodges, demanding volunteers as companions for his journey.

"I can't believe she's mine," Khuldah said as Keren knelt beside the bed to admire the tiny, fuzzy-haired newborn in Khuldah's arms. "And Merowm is so happy. He actually thinks she might marry Gibbawr one day."

"Who can say what will happen?" Keren tucked a finger into the infant's tiny hand and smiled as the perfect fingers curled, gripping her finger. "What are you going to name her?"

"The mother of my husband said we should consider Meleah."

Merowm's mother, Kebuwddah, was a domineering woman, fragile seeming as a dried twig and shrill as a bird when excited.

"Where is Kebuwddah?" Keren asked, suddenly aware of the hush within the lodge.

"She's gone to the stream to fetch water, then probably to gossip with the other women," Khuldah murmured, caressing Meleah's downy head.

A sudden, high, trilling sound cut through the quiet evening air. Some of the women were calling out a welcoming warning cry to alert the tribe that visitors were approaching. The outcry suddenly intensified. As Keren and Khuldah listened, Keren could hear someone calling her in the rising din. Sharah. Wondering, Keren hurried to the doorway of Merowm's lodge. The women of the village were milling about, chattering and staring at a fleece-draped horse, its reins tethered to a log in the woodpile beside the lodge of Bezeq. *That horse belongs to a follower of Nimr-Rada,* Keren realized, stunned.

"There you are!" Sharah cried. She marched across the trampled pathway separating Merowm's lodge from the lodge of Bezeq. "Stop staring at the horse. That overbearing father of my husband has just returned from the Great City. Nihyah's giving out orders right and left, and . . ."

Sharah's complaints faded. More horsemen were riding into the village now, all clad in the same pale leather tunics and short fleece cloaks, all armed with knives of flint, and with their bows and arrows. The young horsemen were all strangers, except for two. She remembered them from Eliyshama's wedding: Zehker and Lawkham.

"He's still rude," Sharah said, frowning at Zehker, who avoided looking at them. "And now, even that know-everything Lawkham doesn't look at us. Why should my husband endure them?"

As Sharah complained, Keren became aware of another horse stopping so close beside them that Keren could have easily touched the horse's tawny-and-black side. Wondering, she stared up at its rider.

Adorned with broad, lavish bands of gold, and clad in a striking leopard-skin robe—fashioned with the slain leopard's head covering his heart—this horseman seemed to be the very embodiment of absolute power. Tall and heavily muscled, his black hair was braided severely away from his broad, high-boned, dark brown face, and his full, wide mouth was drawn up at one corner, arrogant and compelling.

But it was his eyes that drew and held Keren's attention. Heavy-lidded obsidian eyes, revealing nothing and commanding everything. Keren was too fascinated by this stranger to be frightened. But she felt the blood drain from her face as some of the women whispered loudly among themselves, "The Great King! Nimr-Rada's here! Where's our Bezeq? He-Who-Lifts-the-Skies has come."

Seven

"SINCE WHEN DOES a son marry without consulting his father?" Bezeq's father, Ramah, demanded amid the crowded Lodge of Bezeq. Keren almost cringed at his hostility, glancing at Bezeq and Sharah to see their reactions.

They sat together on a heap of furs near the glowing hearth, seemingly unmoved. Bezeq merely lifted one dark eyebrow and said, "When a father leaves his son for years on end, then the son must decide certain matters for himself. As I have done—with my mother's agreement."

Kneeling just behind Bezeq and Sharah, Nihyah lifted her chin, clearly challenging her husband to argue with her before all their guests. Ramah glared at Nihyah, then turned toward Keren, his bearded face harsh. Keren sat perfectly straight, resolving to not appear fainthearted before Yithran's father.

"And what of this one?" Ramah demanded, waving one raw-boned hand toward Keren in a gesture of dismissal. "Should I allow my Yithran to marry such an oddity?"

Keren stared into the fire. Everyone was watching her, including the enemy of her father, that Nimr-Rada, who sat in the place of honor before the hearth. *I am an "oddity," a freak. O Most High, will this Ramah turn Yithran against me?*

"It seems I have kept you from your family too long, Ramah," the great Nimr-Rada interrupted, his voice deep, resonant.

Despite herself, Keren looked up at him, enthralled by his aura of power.

Impatient, Nimr-Rada leaned forward on his seat of furs and tapped the haft of his intricately carved wood-and-leather flail against the woven floor mats. "Because your family's affairs concern you so much, Ramah, you will stay here for the next five years and tend them. As for your second son marrying this one . . ." Nimr-Rada stared at Keren now, an unending, unknowable look. "Does it matter what he has decided? They are not yet betrothed. You can tell your son that this marriage will not take place, if you do not approve."

There was not a sound in the lodge. Everyone stared at Ramah, who looked shaken. "My lord and king, what is my family to me if I am denied your presence for five years? Forgive me."

"Do you believe I am offended?" Nimr-Rada asked, one corner of his full mouth curling, not quite mocking. "No, this matter is not my concern. It is, however, your concern, Ramah. You made it so by protesting your sons' decisions. Stay with your family. In five years you will have matters arranged to your satisfaction. Then you may present yourself in my courts, with your mind at ease."

It's more than that, Keren thought, undeceived. *The mighty Nimr-Rada does not respect Ramah and wants to be rid of him.* Clenching her jaw, she thought, *If my father says I should marry Yithran, then I will. But Yithran and I would have to live with the Ancient Ones in the highlands, because Ramah is now my enemy.*

Already Ramah was scowling at Keren, obviously blaming her for his exile. Sharah and Bezeq watched Ramah, displeased. Nihyah in particular was fuming at her husband.

Keren was grateful that Nihyah was eager to defend her, but she didn't want to have any part in a quarrel. *I'm leaving this lodge tonight,* Keren decided. *I'll stay with Khuldah and help her until Yithran returns.*

Keren fingered the slender red-gold bracelet on her wrist, remembering Yithran and trying to console herself. Instead, she felt only despair. And fear. Nimr-Rada was watching her relentlessly, making her want to fidget. Keren didn't look at him again. Sharah, however, glanced from Keren to Nimr-Rada and back to Keren, silently reproaching Keren for ignoring the "Great King."

Why should I acknowledge him? Keren thought, defiant. *He's rude to stare!*

Obviously discomfited by the prolonged silence, the women of the tribe of Bezeq took refuge in a ritual of courtesy. Hurriedly, they offered the evening meal: roasted venison, seasoned greens, tender root vegetables, salt-smoked fish, broad wheat cakes, preserved honeycombs, lentils, curdled goat milk, dried cherries, and toasted nut meats. The women also passed around watered wine in drinking vessels of clay, horn, and wood. Tensions eased, and everyone began to talk, even to laugh, as they ate.

The food tasted dust dry and bitter as metal to Keren, but she ate anyway to prove that she wasn't humiliated. She was just reaching for a piece of salty smoked fish when she heard rustling behind her.

A man's voice, hushed but amused, said, "The joyous child has become a woman of silence. I miss your laughter, Karan-Keren, but even so, I'm pleased."

Surprised, Keren looked over her shoulder. Lawkham. The irrepressible young horseman smiled at her. She lowered her head, hoping to discourage him by not responding.

Undaunted, Lawkham spoke in a teasing, lulling whisper. "I thought I would never see you again, little sister of Neshar. But here you are. And that foolish Ramah is your would-be father-in-law. Are you sure you want to marry his son? I would hesitate, Keren-Pale-Eyes. Particularly now, when our Great King seems interested in you. He has not yet taken a wife, though many have been offered to him—beautiful, intelligent, truly desirable women. And yet"—Lawkham's voice became even softer, edged with irony—"the Keren-child I remember had a sense of honor. You'd never accept our Great King as a husband when you've almost promised yourself to another, would you?"

"No." Keren shivered at the very thought of marrying Nimr-Rada.

"Of course not," Lawkham murmured, seeming pleased to be correct. "But your pale and beautiful sister would answer differently, given the same choice."

Keren glanced at Sharah and realized Lawkham was right. Sharah would choose the mighty Nimr-Rada instantly. As if sensing that she was the subject of their conversation, Sharah excused herself from her husband and circled the hearth to visit Keren. Tossing her pale, braid-bound head proudly, Sharah stared at Lawkham.

"You're that rascal-horseman we met at the marriage of my brother Eliyshama. How did you manage to become a guardsman to the Great King?"

Unaffected by Sharah's hauteur, Lawkham answered easily. "I am the son of the son of a brother of the Great King. I am also one of the Great King's best marksmen, as is my adopted brother, Zehker. We've earned our places of honor." Straightening, Lawkham said, "Speaking of Zehker, he apparently has a word or two for me—a rare thing. Forgive me; I must depart."

They watched Lawkham pick his way through the crowded lodge toward the somber, watchful Zehker, who had positioned himself just inside the door. Zehker spoke briefly to Lawkham, tipping his head stiffly toward Keren and Sharah.

"That Zehker is a stupid piece of wood," Sharah muttered to Keren. "Even now, he can't be bothered to be polite. He always did despise you, Keren, remember?"

Remembering that Zehker never displayed emotion beyond his natural grimness, Keren said, "You exaggerate."

"I think not," Sharah said, pleased. "Look, I'm sure he's told that Lawkham not to go near you again. You're a creature to be shunned."

"Thank you, my sister." To her deep humiliation, Keren could not prevent tremors of pain from breaking into her voice. "Now that I've been shamed before the entire tribe, I'm going to stay with Khuldah. I leave you to deal with your husband and his family. By the way, it must be time for you to feed Gibbawr. I think I hear him crying."

Garbed in a leather tunic and leggings, Keren edged along a branch of the willow tree, satisfied with her morning's harvest. The fresh willow-branch cuttings would make a fine sleeping basket for Khuldah's little Meleah. *I'll make it big enough to last through the autumn, and I'll pad it well*, Keren decided. *Though I'd better hurry, or Meleah will outgrow it before I'm finished, the hungry little bird.*

Moving easily, Keren dropped her bale of cuttings to the ground, then jumped down after them. The instant she straightened, she saw sunlight gleam against a flint arrowhead poised in the bushes less than a stone's throw away. One of the mighty Nimr-Rada's huntsmen had apparently turned an arrow toward her.

She froze, uncertain whether she should move or call out a warning. But then the flint arrow was lowered. A laugh echoed from the bushes, and Lawkham emerged from his hiding place, followed by the wary Zehker. "Keren Pale Eyes!" Lawkham called to her happily. "Make a less animal-like noise next time. Though I wouldn't mind catching one such as you."

Before Lawkham could say anything further, Zehker gave him a silencing, warning shove. Lawkham grinned, shoved Zehker in response, and turned away from Keren, apparently bent on continuing their hunt. As they departed, Zehker glanced back over his shoulder at her.

Keren tried to see hatred in his glance or loathing or even mere indifference. But Zehker revealed nothing beyond a quiet sense of watching. *You are a confusing man,* she told him in her thoughts. *I don't believe you hate me, as Sharah claims. And yet you behave so oddly. I don't understand you at all.* Yithran's boldness, as discomfiting as it could be, was preferable to that Zehker's unmoving, horseman-hunter's face.

"Keren-child!" A woman's voice called to her, high and shrill. Keren turned to see Merowm's mother, the pretty, fragile-seeming Kebuwddah, scurrying to meet her. "What did he say to you?" Kebuwddah demanded. "Did he insult you? If he did, I'll . . ."

Laughing, Keren shook her head and patted Kebuwddah's slender arm, knowing that Lawkham and Zehker might still be within earshot. "No, I'ma-Kebuwddah. He simply warned me that I should sound less like an animal and more like a human if there are hunters about—which there apparently are."

Obviously reassured, Kebuwddah sighed as if disgusted. "Even so, this whole situation is disgraceful; you've done nothing to deserve such wretched treatment from that Ramah. Which reminds me: I came looking for you because Sharah is waiting for you in the lodge of my son."

Keren frowned. She hadn't seen Sharah for the past three days. "Why would Sharah visit me and risk angering Ramah?"

"I don't know, Keren-child." Kebuwddah waved her small hands as if the whole matter were too much to consider. "But I do know that Sharah came visiting without her son. Which is another thing I don't understand. Most new mothers are proud of their infants and refuse to be separated from them. It makes me wonder if she even loves her son."

"Let me gather my things," Keren murmured, wanting to avoid any discussion of Sharah's shortcomings as a mother. "Is Khuldah still sleeping?"

"Can anyone sleep if Sharah is upset? No, when I left, Khuldah was feeding Meleah and listening to Sharah.

Perhaps you should listen to her too, Keren-child. If I were your mother, I would say that you should take her advice."

But Sharah's advice has never been in my own best interests, Keren thought, darkly amused. She retrieved her bundle of willow cuttings, her stone knife, and her red-edged gray-blue shawl from the base of the willow tree. Frustrated at the prospect of facing Sharah, Keren thought, *I'll return to the Ancient Ones.*

She hurried after Kebuwddah, who walked with amazing speed for one who seemed so fragile. Ignoring the curious glances of the Great King's loitering guardsmen, Keren followed Kebuwddah through the tribal village and into the Lodge of Merowm. Sharah was seated near Khuldah, but she sprang to her feet the instant she saw her sister.

Sharah's mouth was a colorless line, and veins showed blue in her forehead and throat. "Where have you been?" She snatched Keren's arm, digging her fingers in hard, making Keren drop her bundle of willow cuttings.

Determined to be polite for Khuldah's sake, Keren smiled at Sharah and—with her free arm—indicated the mats near the hearth. "Please, my sister, sit down and rest with me while we talk. Have you had something to eat?"

"Khuldah gave me a grain cake," Sharah said dismissively. "Anyway, it's taken you so long to return that I don't have much time. I wanted to warn you that Ramah won't accept you as Yithran's wife."

"And what if Yithran manages to persuade his father to accept me? You know he won't give up easily."

"Yithran will listen to his father," Sharah insisted. "Especially now. Listen to me: the Great King has asked about you. Stupid as you are, he's *interested* in you. Ramah knows this and will reject your marriage to Yithran for that reason. Now, this is our chance to have all that we deserve! I say you must marry the Great King."

Incredulous, Keren rocked back on her heels. "You're insane. Marry that Nimr-Rada? The same Nimr-Rada who has caused our father and mother such pain?" She shook her head. "No, Sharah. I'd never marry him, even if I were free of Yithran."

"Forget Yithran! He's lost to you. Your best choice now—the most incredible choice—is to marry the Great King."

Leaning forward, putting her face directly in front of Sharah's, Keren deliberately emphasized each barely controlled word. "I don't want to marry that Great-and-Mighty-He-Who-Lifts-the-Skies-King! Our father would never accept him, Sharah. Never."

"It doesn't matter if our father won't accept him!" Sharah retorted. Her eyes glittered like a wild creature's. "Our father has no authority over him. Think of it, Keren —you'd have power over all other women—and over all men but one."

"I don't want such power, Sharah, and I won't discuss this matter any further, except to say this: For any man to have such authority—to have all the mighty names held by Nimr-Rada—it should frighten you, Sharah. It frightens me. Nimr-Rada's power and his names are like a challenge against the Most High."

"Despite that, he lives," Sharah pointed out, smugly. "And his power grows. Perhaps you should consider that the Most High has chosen to bless the Great King. Perhaps you should—"

"I've given you my answer," Keren said, digging her fingers clawlike into the woven mats between them. "I will *never* marry that Nimr-Rada."

"You are quite certain?" Sharah asked, suddenly cool, dispassionate.

"Quite certain."

"As you say, my sister."

Sharah stood, turned on her leather-clad heel, and stomped out of the lodge without taking proper leave of Khuldah and her mother-in-law, Kebuwddah.

Keren lowered her head into her hands and shuddered, heartsick, almost crying. "She won't give up! O Most High, how do I manage such a sister?"

"You're quite sure this is what you want to do, Keren-child?" Kebuwddah asked, her shrill voice actually timid. "If Yithran is lost to you . . ."

"Don't say it, please!" Keren cried. "I won't marry that Nimr-Rada. He's torn my family apart with his ambition." Softening her tone, she said, "I'm sorry, Kebuwddah. I shouldn't have raised my voice to you."

"I understand, Keren-child," Kebuwddah assured her. "I only pray you've made the right choice."

Khuldah shifted the tiny, sleeping Meleah in her arms, chuckling softly. "Well, I'll say that I've never seen you so angry as you were with Sharah. I was so amazed I couldn't speak! And now I can say that I have a kinswoman who refused the Great Nimr-Rada. I'm honored."

Torn between frustration and mirth, Keren chose to laugh.

"We have to talk, Keren," Sharah insisted, stubbornly planting her feet just outside the doorway of the Lodge of Merowm. "You can't ignore me forever."

Keren shut her eyes, wearied. Sharah was a pain that would not go away. "Come inside then, and eat with us. Merowm should be here soon for his midday meal. Where is Bezeq?"

"Finishing his meal. Then he said he would take a nap with Gibbawr. It's good to be rid of all those horsemen and to have the lodge to ourselves again—except for that Ramah and his Nihyah." Glancing inside the lodge at the staring Khuldah and Kebuwddah, Sharah muttered, "Actually, I'd rather stay outside. Come walk with me. No one can listen to us that way, and I need some time away from the others. I'm sick of all the quarrelling."

"Then you don't plan to quarrel with me?" Keren couldn't believe it was the truth.

"As I said, I'm sick of quarrelling. Will you walk with me or not?" Sharah sounded almost dejected.

Thinking of what it must be like to live in the same lodge as Ramah, day after day, Keren felt pity for her sister. Ramah's displays of temper had increased with the departure of Nimr-Rada two days before. Keren had actually heard him screaming at Nihyah this morning.

"I'll get my shawl," she agreed, her reluctance fading. She retrieved her shawl from beside the basket she had been working for Meleah. "I'm going for a walk with Sharah," she told Khuldah.

"We'll save some food for you," Khuldah promised, as Kebuwddah nodded from her sleeping pallet. She was rocking Meleah, hoping to get her to sleep before the mealtime so they could eat in peace.

"Why did you bring your shawl?" Sharah asked as they walked through the village toward the warm, green meadows. "It's a beautiful day. You won't need it."

Keren shrugged, glancing down at her treasured gray-blue, red-edged woolen shawl, the work of her mother's hands. "I suppose it's a habit to take it with me. Anyway, I can use it to gather shoots or herbs."

Sharah sniffed contemptuously. "I let Nihyah do the gathering."

"You let Nihyah do everything. I'm amazed that she and Bezeq let you get away with your laziness."

"I gave Bezeq his son. That's enough for him, and for Nihyah. But Ramah is becoming too arrogant. I can't endure him much longer, Keren. The thought of dealing with him for five years is too much. Nothing is as I expected it would be here. Nothing! I hate it, I hate it!"

Alarmed, Keren stared at her sister. Sharah's face had a bright, fevered flush. There were even tears in her eyes—and Sharah never cried. Feeling wretched, Keren said, "I'm sorry you're so unhappy. Perhaps Ramah will take Nihyah and go visiting elsewhere for a while. Then you and Bezeq and Gibbawr could have some peace."

"Even that wouldn't help." Sharah swiped her tears angrily. "I want to leave these hills. I'm sick of them. I want to go visiting and see our brothers and escape this place. If you had married the Great King, you could have taken me with you for a while. But it's too late for that now."

Keren sighed, exasperated. "Will you never forgive me for refusing that Nimr-Rada?"

"I should have known you'd refuse, you coward. Let's talk about something else, or I'll become furious with you again." Sniffling delicately, Sharah asked, "Did Merowm really say that his Meleah should marry my Gibbawr?"

"I never heard him say so," Keren answered truthfully. "But who can say what will happen? And Meleah is a pretty baby."

"Unlike her mother," Sharah said, with a dry, humorless laugh.

"You exaggerate, as always," Keren murmured. "Khuldah is attractive in her own way."

They were beyond the limits of the village now, moving through densely shaded woods, then into an open field. Her face bathed by sunlight, Keren shut her eyes and listened to the multitudes of birds singing, quarrelling, and fluttering about in the trees. A beautiful day. She glanced over the field, spying a sprouting mound of earth. "Tubers!"

Ignoring Sharah's scornful glance, Keren found a stick, knelt down, and began to loosen the earth around the tubers. She was just lifting a clump of damp soil away from the tubers when a horseman rode out of the trees on the opposite side of the clearing. Another horseman followed him. Then another. Nimr-Rada's men. Startled, Keren looked up at Sharah. "They've come back. Why?"

"They never left," Sharah said, perfectly calm, her eyes gleaming.

"What do you mean? They left two days ago." Keren stood, clutching a tuber. Nimr-Rada's horsemen were forming an efficient, orderly line. Now Nimr-Rada himself came riding out of the trees, his eyes fixed on Keren and Sharah, his powerful, broad-boned face actually reflecting pleasure.

"They've returned for us," Sharah informed Keren. "I told him we'd be here."

"Sharah, how could you? I told you I'll never marry that Nimr-Rada!"

"You won't," Sharah answered, flinging Keren a proud, defiant look. "But I will. And you're coming with me."

"No." Keren started to retreat, shaking, appalled. Sharah snatched her arm. Keren wrenched herself free, then ran, dropping her digging stick, the tuber, and her shawl.

"Keren!" Sharah screeched. Keren glanced back, just in time to see Nimr-Rada motion for the guardsmen to follow Keren. Terrified, she ran into the dense, sheltering woods, praying for the protection of the Most High.

Eight

KEREN CHARGED INTO the woods, scraped past some coarse shrubs, then scrambled up the nearest tree. As she huddled in the crook of a branch, she fought hysteria, thinking, *This is a fruit tree. I can't hide here, it's too small. But if I get down now, I'll be seen. I hear them searching for me....*

She could also hear her own breathing, ragged and harsh. Trying to muffle the sound, she covered her face with her hands. But her fingers and palms were coated with damp soil; the taste of the dirt filled her mouth and her nostrils, gagging her, making her eyes water.

Be calm, she told herself, hearing a rustling noise. *This tree may be small compared to some, but it's leafed, and it's surrounded by shrubs and evergreens. If I keep still, then I'm only a shadow, if those guardsmen don't look too hard.*

Even as she thought this, a young guardsman—on foot—neared her tree. Lowering his dark-braided head, he poked through the shrubs with a flint-tipped arrow. Keren trembled as he passed. He didn't look up. She drooped, relieved. A memory arose in her mind, I'ma-Annah saying, "I hid in a tree that night, terrified. And yet, I felt the presence of the Most High surrounding me. . . ."

O Most High, please save me now, as You saved I'ma-Annah. Tearful, Keren wiped her eyes against her arms, then stiffened. Another man was passing the shrubs surrounding her tree. Lawkham. He was looking upward, but in the wrong direction. No doubt he remembered seeing her jump out of the willow tree when she was gathering cuttings for Meleah's basket.

Why did you have to see that? Keren groaned inwardly. She watched until Lawkham moved away, then shifted her gaze to a thin ray of sunlight flickering over the shrubs below. Surely Nimr-Rada and his men would give up searching soon.

Now, from the shadows below, a young guardsman's toughened brown hand slowly reached toward the thin ray of sunlight. Keren watched the man's hand, perplexed. What was he reaching for?

His fingers outstretched, the young guardsman pinched at a leaf, and—with the utmost delicacy—drew away one very long, curling, almost invisible hair. *One of mine*, Keren thought, horrified. For an instant, she saw no one. Then Zehker waded into the shrubs and grasped the lowest branch of her tree.

Expressionless, he looked up at Keren and motioned for her to descend.

Keren shook her head, tears welling in her eyes as she begged him beneath her breath, "No, *please.*" All her fears were in those two words. If she said anything more, she would cry. Zehker's eyes flickered, deciding. He answered with an almost imperceptible nod. But before he could re-move his hand from the tree, a voice called to him.

"Zehker, you've found her!" Another young man hur-ried into view, looked up at Keren, and laughed, his teeth white in his ferretlike brown face. "I'll tell He-Who-Lifts-the-Skies—he will reward us both." He darted away, call-ing to the others, "Stay with Zehker! Don't let her escape."

Other young guardsmen crowded about the wary Zehker now, hacking away the bushes with their flails and axes. Some of the young men were grinning, watch-ing her speculatively. Keren shut her eyes, humiliated.

I'm merely a creature they've snared. Just listen to them, laughing and congratulating each other over a successful hunt! But I won't let them win, she thought fiercely. *They'll have to drag me out of this tree; I'm going to climb higher.*

She heard others approaching. Then Nimr-Rada's rich, strong, unmistakable voice said, "Come down, my sister. You have no reason to be afraid."

I won't answer you, Keren thought, enraged. She stood on her branch, preparing to climb higher.

Nimr-Rada's voice hardened. "Do you think you will save yourself? You are mistaken! And if you defy me any further, that Yithran will pay for your disobedience."

Yithran. Keren froze.

Nimr-Rada continued, "How many days has your Yithran been gone? Eight? Nine? Think of him, my sister. He and his two companions are on foot. Perhaps they have stopped to hunt along the way. My horsemen could easily overtake them before they reach the Lodge of the Ancient Ones."

Unable to believe what she was hearing, Keren looked down at Nimr-Rada.

He actually smiled. "His mother won't even have the

comfort of burying his corpse."

Keren shut her eyes, aghast, imagining Yithran surrounded by the soldier-horsemen of Nimr-Rada, their arrows aimed at his heart. The blood seemed to stop in her
veins; her face, her hands, her feet, all went cold.

"Come down, my sister," Nimr-Rada urged. "If you are
obedient, then you—and your Yithran—have nothing to
fear."

He will do as he said, Keren realized. Yithran and his two
companions would be dead within days. Nauseated, she
crouched on her supporting branch, set one foot on a
lower limb, and slowly descended toward the base of the
tree. As she scooted onto the lowest branch, Nimr-Rada
put out one large hand to steady her. Scorning his help,
Keren shied away from his hand and dropped to the
ground. She straightened and glared at him. "I've obeyed
you. Now you must keep your word."

"I will keep my word," Nimr-Rada answered. His eyes
incomprehensible, he added, "And you will keep my word
as well."

Turning, he called to his men, "Listen to me, all of
you. This woman is like poison! The instant any man
touches her—including me—his penalty is death. And
this is how we handle such a one." Using his elaborate
wood-and-leather flail, he prodded Keren through the
mutilated shrubs and onto the path. Striking her shoulders, legs, and rump, he goaded her toward the clearing
as if she were an animal.

Seething, Keren thought, *This is your revenge because I've
refused your attentions!* How could Sharah admire such an
arrogant, spiteful being? But of course, her sister was just
like him at heart.

Sharah was waiting for them at the edge of the trees.

Her pale eyes glinting, she shoved Keren. "You're so stupid that I can't believe you're my sister! Look at you; you've got dirt all over your face."

"I'd rather have a soiled face than a filthy spirit, my sister," Keren muttered.

Before Sharah could answer, Nimr-Rada grabbed her. Compelling her to step into his linked hands, he lifted her onto a horse tethered nearby. When he looked back at Keren, she shrugged, unwilling to move. "If I'm like poison, Mighty One, then how can I get on that horse? I can't mount it by myself."

Instantly she regretted her sarcasm. Nimr-Rada was obviously not used to such defiance. He tensed, seeming ready to thrash her, but then he restrained himself. "A way will be found."

Lawkham approached. Inclining his head respectfully toward Nimr-Rada, he said, "As you command, Great King."

Quickly, Lawkham took two unfinished, unstrung wooden bow staves from a nearby horse and stood beside Sharah's horse. Zehker followed him, silent as always. Lawkham aligned the two staves, and he and Zehker held the ends, forming a narrow, branchlike step between them. Nimr-Rada grunted approvingly and swatted Keren toward the horse with his flail.

"Don't touch us," Lawkham warned Keren. "Place your hands on the horse for balance."

Infuriated by Lawkham's inventiveness, Keren obeyed. She mounted the horse behind Sharah, struggling with the long skirt of her tunic, thinking, *It's a shame I can't be like poison to my sister.*

Sharah was smiling at Nimr-Rada, her pale profile alight with pleasure. Nimr-Rada lifted his dark eyebrows, obviously satisfied as any hunter who has caught a prize. Moving easily, he vaulted onto his horse, snatched the reins of Sharah and Keren's horse, and motioned for his waiting horsemen to follow them.

I won't cry, Keren thought, as they rode away from the lands of the tribe of Bezeq. *Somehow, I'll escape. If I can keep my mind clear, if I can throw Sharah off this horse. . . .*

Despite being jounced by the movements of the horse, Sharah managed to pick the slender, carved wooden pins from her braided hair. Flinging the pins away, she rapidly finger combed her long, pale hair until it fluttered in Keren's face.

Irritated, Keren swiped at Sharah's hair. "What are you doing?"

"I'm declaring myself free of Bezeq. I'm no longer his wife."

"Are you also no longer Gibbawr's mother?"

"He's better off without me." Sharah actually sounded lighthearted. She shrugged and changed the subject. "Really, now that we're grown, it looks so indelicate for us to sit astride like this."

"If you can think of a better way to ride a horse without falling off, then do so!"

Keren longed to slap her. In one breath Sharah had abandoned her baby and then fretted about looking indelicate. How could she be so unnatural? Digging her fingers hard into Sharah's upper arms, Keren hissed, "You are monstrous! Why have you done this to me?"

"Let go of my arms."

"No! Why have you done this to me?"

"Because," Sharah whispered viciously, "the Great King said that your presence is necessary."

"Why should I be necessary to *him?*" Keren leaned into

Sharah, feeling as if she were on the edge of an uncontrolled, raving fit. "Doesn't he know that I despise him for tearing our family apart?"

"I've said no such thing to him." Sharah jerked her arms free. "And you'd better keep those angry thoughts to yourself if you want to live. The Great King won't endure your contempt, Keren."

"I don't care! No woman beneath these blue heavens has ever abandoned her husband—not to mention an infant son. And what about our parents? They'll be devastated by this shame."

Stiffening, Sharah said, "It's too late for me to change anything now. But why should you care? You've always said to me 'Be happy.' Well, now I am happy, and you're angry with me."

"I meant that you should be happy with what you have! Instead, you always want what you shouldn't have. You have kicked your blessings in the teeth."

"Don't you dare lecture me." Turning, Sharah snatched Keren's hair, almost knocking her off balance. Then, just as suddenly, Sharah gasped and released her. Keren flinched. Nimr-Rada was jabbing Sharah, then Keren with the haft of his flail.

"I punish my men when they fight," he snarled. "Believe me, my sisters, I treasure you both, but you will suffer agonies if you don't behave."

I believe you, Keren thought, lowering her eyes hastily. Nimr-Rada's men, as proud and courageous as they were, feared him and respected his every word.

Trying to calm herself, Keren focused upon Yithran's delicate gold-and-crystal bracelet, still gleaming on her wrist. *Yithran, I wish I could believe you're safe. But I'm sure that no matter where I am, Nimr-Rada will always be able to send his men to kill you if I try to escape. He's contemptible.* In despair, Keren looked up at the cloud-dappled heavens, wailing in her heart, *O Most High, I don't understand! I prayed to You with all my might. Why didn't You save me, as You saved I'ma-Annah? Why?*

Wearily, Keren braced her hands on either side of the horse's black-and-tawny neck, stretching as much as she dared. Three days of sharing this horse with Sharah had consumed most of her patience, as well as her physical endurance. She stared up at the reddened dusk, aching miserably from head to toe. Soon Nimr-Rada would allow them to stop for the night. Not that it mattered to Sharah, who was behind her, leaning against her in a dead-weighted sleep. Keren longed to push her sister and watch her fall in a graceless heap onto the ground. Even asleep, Sharah was a burden. *She's probably drooling in my hair.*

Grimacing, Keren looked ahead. Lawkham was leading her horse—a task Nimr-Rada had abandoned after the first day of their journey, to Sharah's disgust.

As if sensing Keren's weariness, Lawkham looked over his shoulder, giving her a sly grin of encouragement, then turning away, straight-backed and dignified, as if he had never noticed her at all.

You're a prankster and a flirt, she thought to Lawkham, liking him. *But as for your "adopted" brother, Zehker, he's strict enough to be someone's father.*

Keren watched, irritated, as Zehker brought his horse alongside Lawkham's and spoke to him, nodding toward Nimr-Rada, who had apparently commanded them to change places. At once Lawkham handed the lead reins of

Keren's horse to Zehker.

That Zehker is arrogant, Keren decided. *But Lawkham does-n't even care. Don't they ever fight?*

Lawkham was talking quietly, his hands gesturing in sweeping motions, his eyes shining as he spoke. Zehker merely responded with nods, shrugs, and an occasional word or two of agreement. Studying them, Keren realized that they understood each other completely. *My own brothers aren't such friends with each other.*

Her stomach tightened at the thought, and she wondered when she would see her brothers. The previous night, as they sat near the evening fire, Nimr-Rada had implied that Sharah and Keren would see their brothers soon. But there had been a reproachful note in his voice, making Keren reluctant to question him further. And Sharah, seated beside Keren, had elbowed her hard, signaling her to be silent.

Stretching now, Sharah yawned, "Who's leading us? Ugh, it's that stupid Zehker. He's made himself our guard."

"As your Great King commanded," Keren murmured.

"Well, I want to be rid of him as soon as possible; I'll tell my beloved so."

Beloved. Keren clenched her jaw. Sharah was behaving as if she had never been married at all—as if Nimr-Rada would be her first and only husband. She was about to remind Sharah that she was truly married to Bezeq, but the high echoing call of a distant horn stopped her. Keren looked up.

Nimr-Rada was leading them out of the hills and onto the vast grass-covered plains. A proud, sun-darkened horseman rode toward them, brandishing a hollowed, curving, polished ram's horn in a triumphant gesture of greeting. Other horsemen rode up to join the first horseman, forming orderly, well-trained lines.

"Look at all the horsemen!" Sharah exclaimed. "There are more than a hundred."

At once Nimr-Rada took the lead reins of Keren's horse from Zehker. Waving his free hand dismissively, he said, "Move to either side; guard my sisters."

Zehker and Lawkham bowed their heads and drew their horses back to ride with Keren and Sharah.

Keren shivered, grateful for their protection. She knew that Nimr-Rada had trained a large army, but she had never translated this knowledge into multitudes of real living horsemen. Seeing so many of them together was overwhelming—and this was only one portion of Nimr-Rada's supremely confident, forbiddingly armed followers. Now Keren understood why all the tribes of the earth regarded them with such fear. She hunched her shoulders, wishing she could hide.

"Straighten up," Sharah hissed, thumping Keren's back with her fist. "Don't be such a coward. Really, as fearful as you are, I should be sitting ahead of you now."

"You wanted me to sit in front so you could rest," Keren reminded Sharah, her fear negated by a fresh surge of anger. "Don't worry, O Woman-of-No-Color. Those horsemen will see you wherever you are." As she spoke, Keren heard the disdain and rage in her own voice. *I sound like Sharah,* she realized, hating the thought. *O Most High, help me; I do not wish to become like my sister.*

Lifting her chin, Keren studied Nimr-Rada's broad, leopard-skin-cloaked back. The instant she looked at him, Keren was unable to look away; now Nimr-Rada radiated a boundless charisma that commanded the admiration of his followers.

The Great King's horsemen were stopping, dividing

their ranks so he could ride in among them. Lifting the lead reins of Keren and Sharah's horse, Nimr-Rada called out to his men, "I have done what I said I would do! I have brought my sisters—who are like no others—to dwell among my people!"

Hearing this, Keren longed to shrink down into nothingness so she would not have to endure the scrutiny of countless avid eyes. But she kept her gaze fixed on Nimr-Rada. They were riding in among the horsemen, who responded in a high, unified, tongue-rattling cry of triumph. The piercing sound chilled Keren, making the hair tingle and crawl in her scalp. Sharah seemed equally affected and tightened her arms about Keren until Keren couldn't draw in a full breath.

Using his free arm, Nimr-Rada lifted his elaborately carved flail, silencing his men. "Tonight, we celebrate the arrival of my two sisters. Go ahead of us to prepare our places!" Grandly he waved his flail toward their encampment, which was already set up in the distance amid the flowing, flowering grasses of the plains.

Yowling enthusiastically, Nimr-Rada's horsemen broke their formations and kicked their horses into a full gallop. Unnerved, feeling her own horse start to move after them, Keren dug her knees hard into the creature's sides, while pulling on its mane, causing it to balk. Ahead of them, still holding the reins, Nimr-Rada was jolted backward by Keren's action but swiftly released his hold on the reins of Keren's horse to prevent himself from falling off his own horse.

"Why did you do that?" Sharah screeched in Keren's ear. "You're mindless!"

Before Keren could stammer a response, Nimr-Rada turned his horse about and faced her. His dark eyes glittered, and his voice was scathing. "I will choose to believe that you acted in pure ignorance, my sister. This time. Next time, I will beat you bloody."

Without waiting for Keren to reply, Nimr-Rada snatched the lead reins once more and urged his own horse ahead. Glancing to her left, Keren caught a tight-lipped, sidelong look from Zehker, while Lawkham—at her right—said, "If you had been anyone else, He-Who-Lifts-the-Skies would have knocked you senseless and left you for the vultures."

"You must learn," Zehker muttered, his tone as cryptic as his words.

Their words wounded Keren more than Sharah's furious pinches and digs to her ribs. No one spoke to her as they rode into the huge encampment—a series of smaller leather-tented camps, all encircling the most spectacular painted-leather tent, which obviously belonged to Nimr-Rada.

As Nimr-Rada's horsemen were tending their horses and building small hearths for their evening fires, Keren noticed his guardsmen scurrying throughout the encampment, whispering to their newly met companions, gesturing toward Keren emphatically.

These new horsemen are learning that I'm like death to them, Keren realized, feeling ill. *They're telling each other that I must be managed like the most poisonous creature alive.*

"You will sleep here tonight," Nimr-Rada told Keren and Sharah, as he drew their horse to a standstill in front of a circular leather tent, set up within a stone's throw of his own. He dismounted and helped Sharah down, ignoring Keren completely. "This tent will be your dwelling until we reach the Great City. There, you will each have your own household."

"Will I be separated from you?" Sharah asked, seeming alarmed, touching Nimr-Rada's leopard-skin-clad chest to make him answer her. Smiling, he enfolded Sharah's colorless hand with one large, brown fist.

"You, my Sharah, will not discard me as easily as you discarded that Bezeq."

His words sounded more like a warning than an endearment.

Stiff and sore, Keren managed to slide off her horse. As she entered the tent with Sharah, she said, "Such possessiveness from any man would frighten me, Sharah. Aren't you afraid?"

"No." Pushing her hair back in an airy gesture, Sharah said, "I'll have the most powerful man on earth as my husband. What more could I want? You, however, will never have a husband. You will never be touched by any man. And you have only yourself to blame."

I blame you, Keren thought, fuming. But it would be useless to say so. Yet it wasn't just her fear of angering Sharah that restrained her. She realized that she did not mourn for Yithran as intensely as she should. Perhaps her regard for him would never have equaled the deeply rooted love she had recognized between her I'ma-Annah and the Father of her Fathers, Shem.

Keren's thoughts of Yithran were dashed as two heavy bundles of furs hurtled through the tent's entry flap.

Jumping up, Sharah screeched, "I won't endure this! When we arrive in the Great City, no one will throw my belongings around like rubbish!"

"I'm grateful they've thought to give us sleeping furs at all," Keren said. As she picked up the bundles and untied them, another bundle bounced through the entry flap, surprising Keren into a burst of laughter. Peering out the entry, she saw Lawkham sauntering away, obviously pleased with himself.

You're a rascal, she thought, smiling. Her amusement faded when she saw Zehker. Armed with a spear, he stood just outside the tent. He gave her one impenetrable look, then deliberately turned the other way. Behind her, Sharah gave Keren a sharp nudge.

"See, he despises you. But forget him. Let's prepare for the evening meal."

One of the bundles, so rudely presented by Lawkham, contained a carved wooden comb, which Sharah immediately claimed for herself. Grudgingly, she shared the comb with Keren before the evening meal. Keren longed for a bath, but that was out of the question in this encampment of men. She used some drinking water to rinse her hands and face—a poor alternative to a refreshing scrub, or a swim in the river.

At dusk, they joined Nimr-Rada in a place of honor before the great hearth near his tent. Seated on the edge of the mat farthest from Nimr-Rada and Sharah, Keren gaped at the many foods offered for the evening meal. Tiny roasted birds—glazed and golden—presented on skewers, fragrant simmered grains, steaming root vegetables glistening with oil, pungent mixtures of fruit and wine, flat herb bread, and slices of venison so hotly spiced that she half choked.

Nimr-Rada laughed at her, obviously enjoying the sight of her sniffling and mopping her face. After their meal, however, he vanished into the darkness without a word.

Keren stood, planning to return to her tent, but Zehker detained her with a wave of his spear. "Stay," he commanded, the word terse and toneless.

Beside Keren, Sharah sputtered contemptuously. "You, Zehker, are so . . ."

Her words were drowned out by the sudden thunder of drums and the blaring of horns, which instantly melded into a heartbeatlike rhythm accented by flutes and innumerable chimes. A herd of animals charged toward the fire from the fringes of darkness. No, not animals, Keren realized, but men clothed in the whole hides of a multitude of creatures: deer, lions, bulls, bears, and some creatures she had never seen.

The pulse of the music quickened, drawing Keren into the scene before her. A hunter, tall and powerfully muscled, burst in upon the portrayed herd with such speed that she pulled back, genuinely startled. The weapons in the hand of this hunter were more than mere weapons; they were instruments of balance, cadence, and astonishing grace. Keren had never seen such spectacular dancing before. This was not simply a celebration of joy before the Most High. It wasn't a celebration for the Most High at all; it was a celebration of the power of one man —Nimr-Rada, the hunter.

As she recognized the hunter-dancer, he turned to her and to Sharah, his eyes fiery, his presence wholly captivating. Keren was so stunned that she couldn't move, not even when he whipped his weapons toward her face, keeping time with the rhythm of his dancing. She swallowed hard, attracted despite her revulsion.

Now I understand why all the people of the earth long to follow you. I understand why they think you must be the Promised One sent by the Most High.

From the shadows, Zehker watched Keren. She was

staring at Nimr-Rada, obviously captivated as a child in a dream. *I am responsible for placing her in such danger,* he thought, crushed by his sense of guilt. *I should have helped her to escape while there was time. But that chance is gone.*

The most he could do now would be to keep Nimr-Rada and his believers from destroying Keren with all their schemes. *You must learn to outwit Nimr-Rada and his fanatics,* he thought to Keren. *I will be sure you do.*

Nine

KEREN SHIFTED uncomfortably in her designated kneeling place on a mat shaded by a pale, rough-edged leather canopy. Sharah knelt at her right, and beyond Sharah sat Nimr-Rada, wearing all his gold and emanating power. They had arrived at this settlement only last night, but already Nimr-Rada was formally meeting settlement leaders and the leaders of nearby tribes.

The leaders sat on rough grass mats before the Great King, unprotected from the midday sun. The leaders' families stood behind them, listening and staring at Keren, Sharah, and Nimr-Rada. Keren wondered how they could endure the heat. She was sweating and becoming parched. The rough-clothed men, however, talked endlessly with Nimr-Rada about harvests, gatherings, metalworking, water sources, and tribal disputes. And they begged Nimr-Rada's permission to present some gifts he had previously requested of them.

Gifts? Keren stiffened, disgusted. Nimr-Rada had obviously demanded tributes from these people as protection against harassment from his horsemen. Even so, the people seemed glad to pay tributes—and to give Nimr-Rada authority over them.

As others retrieved the promised gifts, the energetic leader of the settlement crouched beside Nimr-Rada, murmuring explanations and descriptions.

Listening briefly, Nimr-Rada raised one dark eyebrow at Keren and spoke formally. "Lady, these are yours."

Five leather-clad young women knelt before Keren. Eyes lowered, they presented her with a highly polished obsidian hand mirror; round gleaming copper trays; furs of fox, beaver, and marten; finely carved wooden bowls; and a lavish necklace of copper-hardened gold, set with striking bloodred stones.

The instant the necklace was presented, Keren felt her sister's furious, jabbing nudges in her ribs. *You may have the necklace,* Keren thought, refusing to acknowledge the envious Sharah. Instead, she looked over at Nimr-Rada, who was staring at her hard.

"Why should I accept these gifts?" she demanded, suspicious.

Nimr-Rada seemed offended. "These young women will be your attendants," he informed her coldly, ignoring her question. "They will be with you constantly from this time forward. Never come into my presence unless they are with you. Never go anywhere, or speak to anyone, unless they are with you."

Appalled, Keren looked at the pretty young women, who were obviously terrified. Two trembled visibly; the other three bowed their dark heads, clasping their hands tightly in their laps.

"They are as frightened and unwilling to leave their families as I was, O King," Keren pointed out, too angry to be cowed by Nimr-Rada's glare. "How can you justify taking them from their loved ones?"

"You will not question me!" Nimr-Rada snapped. "You will simply obey. As for you, my Sharah, these attendants will be yours." Waving a broad hand, he indicated another group—some of them wearing their hair braided and bound in the manner of married women.

Sharah leaned forward eagerly, staring at the gifts in the hands of her would-be attendants: shimmering furs, trays of beaten copper, folds of light cloth, darkly glazed bowls and pitchers, gold necklaces and bracelets set with crystals, and a collection of gleaming stones as pale as the moon. She pouted coaxingly. "These stones are so pale, Mighty One; red stones would actually show best against my complexion."

"The red stones are for your sister," Nimr-Rada said, tapping his flail, plainly forbidding her to argue. "You will have the stones resembling the full moon. Later, you will have stones as golden as the sun and as blue as the sky— but those will be brought to you from other lands."

Placated, Sharah gave Nimr-Rada a beguiling smile and avidly inspected the tribesmen's gifts. Keren wondered how Sharah could possibly ignore the women themselves, who seemed so unhappy with their new roles. Determined to speak for the silent attendants, Keren asked loudly, "Will all these women be taken from their families to do nothing but wait upon us?"

Nimr-Rada struck Keren's chest and left shoulder with his flail, stopping the very breath in her lungs. As she recoiled in pain, Sharah and the women surrounding them shrieked, terrified.

Nimr-Rada snarled. "One more word from you, my sister, and I will flay your skin to bloody strips! You will be an example to everyone here—do not doubt me!"

"Lady," the young woman nearest Keren begged timidly, "please, don't trouble yourself for us. We'll go with you gladly."

Catching her breath, Keren recognized the sincerity in the girl's huge dark eyes. All five of the young women were silently imploring Keren to agree. Rebellion against Nimr-Rada was out of the question. Struggling against the impulse to put her hands to her burning shoulder and chest, Keren nodded to her would-be attendants, and they relaxed.

Nimr-Rada gouged Keren with the haft of his flail. "Go with them before I lose patience with you altogether—ungrateful she-cat."

As Keren joined the young women, she noticed Sharah's look of satisfaction, and the way she leaned toward Nimr-Rada, clearly inviting his touch. Revolted, she turned on her heel and marched toward her tent. She had gone perhaps seven paces when she realized that everyone was staring at her, openmouthed, and none of her young attendants were following her. Looking back, she saw that the girls had stopped to gather Keren's gifts and to bow to Nimr-Rada. His dark eyes flashed from their humbly prostrated forms to the defiantly upright Keren.

I'd rather die than fall at your feet, Keren thought, looking Nimr-Rada in the eyes. *You're not the Promised One, and you are certainly not the Most High!*

Controlling herself, she waited for her attendants. When Nimr-Rada dismissed them with a growl and a wave of his flail, the five girls scuttled toward Keren like frightened rabbits. She led them to her tent, pausing to look over her shoulder before going inside. Nimr-Rada was still glaring at her.

The young women introduced themselves to Keren: Na'ah, Alatah, Gebuwrah, Tsinnah, and Revakhaw. Then they set down her gifts and confronted her.

"How can you defy the Great King?" Alatah demanded, her thin, brown face scared, her voice sweet and childish. "When you refused to bow, Lady, I was sure he would kill you."

"I was certain he would," Gebuwrah agreed. She was the biggest and sturdiest of the five girls, reminding Keren of her cousin Khuldah, without her kindness. "You shouldn't have defied the Great King, Lady. But perhaps because you challenged him, he will regard you as one of his cats to be tamed and subdued."

The other four girls nodded in agreement.

"What cats?" Keren asked, curious. Nimr-Rada had indeed called her "she-cat."

"As the name of Nimr-Rada declares, our Great King subdues leopards for sport," Tsinnah told her. Tsinnah, diminutive and rosy brown, was the girl who had pleaded with her before Nimr-Rada. "My father took me to see these leopards once. They are kept in cages and hate their guard-keepers, but I'm told that they love the Great King and rest in his presence."

"They have gold collars with jewels," Revakhaw added, as if the gold collars were most important. She was apparently the youngest of the attendants. Her glossy black curls and her eyes were dancing merrily now that her fear was fading.

"But, Lady . . . ," Na'ah hesitated, glancing uneasily toward the open entryway of the tent, her round face somber. "If one of the leopards refuses to be tamed within a reasonable amount of time, then the Great King kills it and wears its hide. We've seen that he won't spare you. Please, be careful."

Remembering Nimr-Rada's spectacular leopard-skin mantle, Keren shivered. "Thank you for your concern. I'll remember what you've said. Also, you shouldn't be so formal with me. My name is Keren."

"But we are commanded to serve and respect you, Lady," Revakhaw explained, her hands fluttering. "We must call you Lady, particularly when we arrive in the Great City, because they are so much more formal there and pay great attention to manners—which I dread. Even so, I'm glad that we're tending you, Lady, and not the Pale One. I can see that *she* wouldn't care what happens to us as long as she's happy."

"Shhh!" Na'ah put a finger to her lips, again glancing toward the tent's open entryway. "I was told that the Pale One will marry He-Who-Lifts-the-Skies. I'm sure you'd be whipped for speaking against her."

"The Pale One would be sure of it," Keren muttered dryly, still enraged that Sharah had abandoned Bezeq and Gibbawr for Nimr-Rada. Keren was equally sure that she herself would be severely punished if she revealed that Sharah was already married, and a mother.

Nimr-Rada's own guards had been sworn to silence in this matter with death threats, which made Keren nervous. Would Nimr-Rada kill Bezeq and Gibbawr to hide Sharah's past? Sharah certainly wouldn't care. Sickened, Keren lowered her head into her hands, murmuring, "O

Most High, save us from my greedy sister."

"You still pray to the Most High?" Gebuwrah asked, sounding as if Keren was afflicted with a childish superstition. Keren eyed Gebuwrah and the others.

"You *don't* pray to the Most High?"

They all shook their heads or grimaced in denial. Tsinnah spoke gently. "We have no need for such prayers. He-Who-Lifts-the-Skies has said that we should be free of our fears of the Most High."

"Which is why you bow and tremble before that same He-Who-Lifts-the-Skies *man*," Keren scoffed. "One who leaves marks like this upon your flesh." Keren lifted the left sleeve of her tunic, showing them the still-burning weal of blood-tinged flesh left by Nimr-Rada's flail. Revakhaw, Na'ah, and Tsinnah winced, but Gebuwrah and Alatah looked away uneasily.

"I'll get some water for you, Lady," Na'ah told Keren, snatching a clay pitcher from its matching basin.

By unspoken agreement, the other four girls began to tidy up the tent and arrange their sleeping pallets for the night. Obviously they were determined to avoid any discussion of the Most High, or of Nimr-Rada's cruelty. Aggrieved, Keren remade her own pallet. As she worked, she realized that all of Sharah's belongings had been removed from the tent during the meeting.

So you will go to Nimr-Rada tonight, pretending to be his wife, Keren thought to Sharah, flushing, mortified. *How will I be able to endure all this in the Great City? I dread it. I'd rather submit to a beating—though my skin still burns from Nimr-Rada's whip, and I can't imagine having wounds like this all over my arms and back. O Most High, what should I do?*

Na'ah approached now, her eyes lowered. Keren took the basin of cool water from her, saying, "Thank you, but next time, I'll get my own water. Don't wait on me."

"We *will* wait on you, Lady," Gebuwrah answered severely, before Na'ah could speak. "If we don't fulfill our duties, we'll be sent home in disgrace, and our parents will be too ashamed to receive us. We are bound, as you are bound."

"But why should we be bound?" Keren asked, almost crying. "We should be left in peace with our families— with those who love us!" Humiliated, she set the basin on a grass mat and knelt beside it, splashing the cool water over her face to hide her tears.

Tsinnah offered Keren a swatch of leather to wipe her face. Tears brimmed in the girl's eyes. "Lady, don't be ashamed to cry. We've all been crying. But we accept what's happened to us. Perhaps we will love our new lives in the Great City."

"You don't sound convinced," Keren told her. A flicker in the light of the open entryway alerted them all to the presence of another: Sharah.

She was smiling graciously, as if she were already the preeminent lady of the Great City, deigning to visit lowly creatures. "My sister," she said coolly, "your temper will be your death. The Great King is furious with you."

Keren stiffened, loathing the very sight of Sharah. "Why are you here?"

"Only to be sure you're well. And to admire your new possessions." Sharah picked her way around the pallets and mats on the floor, moving toward the heap of tributes the other girls had given Keren. "These furs are lovely. And the trays are wonderfully crafted. Ma'adannah would be proud of the maker. She would be doubly proud of the one who made this."

Lifting Keren's showy gold necklace with the red

stones, Sharah asked, "May I?" Without waiting for permission, she fastened the necklace around her pale throat, then picked up Keren's beautifully polished obsidian hand mirror, shifting it this way and that, admiring herself.

"Take the necklace and go," Keren snapped, eager to be rid of her. "Wear it at your 'wedding' tonight."

Sharah lifted her pale eyebrows in surprise. "You've guessed that already? I was only told this morning that the ceremony would take place this evening. I would have preferred a celebration in the Great City, but my beloved says otherwise." She fingered the ornate necklace and said, "You'll be there, of course, my own shadow-sister. And you'll wear your new ornament to honor me."

"Didn't you come to take it for yourself?" Keren stared in disbelief as Sharah removed the coveted necklace and set it gently on a pile of furs.

"I wish I could, but He-Who-Lifts-the-Skies won't permit it. And you've worked him into such a temper already. . . ."

Sharah straightened, her pretended graciousness replaced by her usual irritability. "Really, your first name, *Karan*, is more fitting for you, Keren. You push the Great King too much. I'll tell you: I didn't want you to come with us to the Great City. You'll be a nuisance. But He-Who-Lifts-the-Skies insisted, and our brother Ra-Anan has humbly requested the joy of meeting you. The Great King esteems our eldest brother, though he detests the others." Sharah moved toward the open door of the tent, adding, "Remember what I've said. If you push the Great King too far, I won't intercede for you."

"You've already done enough for me, thank you, sister," Keren answered, clenching her hands, feeling her nails digging into her palms.

As if she sensed Keren's readiness to attack her, Sharah bent, preparing to step outside the tent. But she turned first, smiling. "By the way, your guards are here."

Following Sharah to the entryway, Keren glanced outside. Lawkham and the forbidding Zehker were standing on either side of the entry, each holding a spear. Lawkham gave her a sidelong look and a trace of a grin, but Zehker stared straight ahead as if she didn't exist.

Furious, Keren picked at the ties of the entry cover, wanting to block the two guardsmen from her sight. The other girls, silent and gaping the whole time Sharah was in the tent, hurried to help her now.

As soon as they had closed themselves inside, Revakhaw whispered, "I think I've seen more excitement in this one day than I have in all my life! Does your sister love anyone but herself?"

Before Keren could answer, Gebuwrah said, "She's right to call you 'shadow-sister,' Lady. You look exactly like her except for your coloring."

"You do, Lady," Alatah agreed. "It's obvious you were born of the same mother."

"Speaking of looks," Revakhaw whispered, her dark eyes dancing naughtily in the dimness, "did you notice our guards? I won't mind having them follow us everywhere!"

Despite themselves, the other girls giggled. Their laughter grew, becoming hysterical, releasing them from the strains of the day. Keren allowed herself to smile. If she didn't smile, she would cry.

As the others chattered and rested in the sultry warmth, Keren remembered Sharah's comment about Ra-Anan. *Why should you request the joy of meeting me?* Keren wondered to her eldest brother. *And why should that "Mighty*

One" hold you in such esteem? It makes me anxious. May the Most High protect me from you. And from Nimr-Rada.

Relaxing against a battered stump just outside the Lodge of Noakh, Annah smoothed the sides of a large wooden bowl with fine sand. Later, she would polish the bowl with beeswax to enhance the beautiful grain of the wood. Shem had cut and shaped the bowl for her after noticing that her favorite mixing bowl was becoming worn, but Annah was finishing it to allow Shem time to help Noakh in the fields. The early summer weather promised good crops, which meant that they could stay in the highlands for the winter. They wouldn't need to move down to the warmer lowlands to shelter and search for food.

Annah hummed, contented. This past month, Keren's would-be husband, Yithran, had visited to introduce himself. And he promised that he would bring Keren to stay with them this winter after their marriage following the harvest. Yithran was a bold and forward young man—not at all the sort of husband Annah had envisioned for Keren. But he seemed to love Keren deeply. He spoke of her tenderly and had been delighted by even the smallest story of her childhood. Perhaps the fact that Yithran was the brother of Sharah's husband, Bezeq, would bring Sharah closer to Keren over time. Sharah needed Keren's softening influence. *Or should I fear that Sharah's boundless self-love and greed might harden Keren over time?*

Pondering this, Annah set down the bowl, then stretched and glanced up at the sun. Near midday. She needed to go inside and help Naomi with the meal. A sudden burst of noise made Annah look toward the western fields. A covey of quail—small, plump brown birds—had taken flight. *Shem and Noakh can't have frightened the birds,* Annah told herself. *They're in the south fields this morning. Perhaps a wild animal is approaching.*

She grabbed a rush-and-resin taper, lighting it at the smoldering outdoor hearth. *Where are you?* she wondered to the unknown cause of disturbance. *Leave us alone, as you know you should, by the will of the Most High.*

Since the Great Destruction, wild animals usually avoided humans. But once in a while, a renegade creature would stalk humans and terrorize settlements. Certainly mankind's growing fear of miscreant wild animals had played a part in the rise of that would-be-king, Nimr-Rada. No man alive could match Nimr-Rada for killing or taming wild animals. His power over the creatures of this new earth had seemed almost spiritual, which Annah shuddered to consider. She tensed, waiting.

But no animals appeared. Instead, two men emerged from the trees fringing the western field. One was Yithran. The other Annah quickly recognized as Bezeq. Annah studied them. They weren't walking quickly, as two vigorous young men should. And their dark heads were lowered, as if they dreaded seeing the Ancient Ones.

O Most High, Annah thought, her stomach suddenly churning, *what has happened? Did Keren—or Sharah, or her little Gibbawr—suffer some terrible accident?* Neither Bezeq or Yithran had raised a hand to greet her, though they had undoubtedly seen her. Annah extinguished the burning torch in a pile of dirt, tamping it carefully. Then she watched as the two young men climbed the slope to the lodge.

"Ma'adannah." Bezeq greeted her quietly, unable to meet her gaze.

The big, usually confident young man looked broken to Annah, haggard, unkempt, and emotionally wounded. His large brown hands clutched his long spear, as if it could save him from further pain. Yithran looked less unkempt, but just as shaken. When Bezeq remained silent, Yithran spoke, his voice almost breaking.

"Ma'adannah . . . Nimr-Rada has taken Sharah and Keren . . . for his own."

"What?" Annah stared at them, certain she hadn't heard Yithran aright.

"Keren was taken," Bezeq corrected his brother roughly. "But my *wife* went willingly." Tears came to his dark eyes, and he choked out his story in a voice just above a whisper. "She was so infatuated with him! With his power and his gold—and the promise of living in his Great City on the plains. She's been begging me all winter to take her there, and I refused. So she left. With him."

Confounded, Annah shook her head. "But Sharah couldn't . . . How could she leave you? And what of Gibbawr, her own son?"

Tears spilled down Bezeq's coarse-bearded cheeks, but his eyes glittered with a growing rage. "She left him! She left my son—*my son!*—with as much ease as she left me. I had to give Gibbawr to Merowm and his Khuldah to be raised with Merowm's daughter—so my son could live, Ma'adannah! So he wouldn't starve!"

Uttering a growling, maddened cry, Bezeq slammed his long spear to the ground, then passed his big hands over his face and clawed at his straggling hair. Annah wanted to comfort him, but he was too hurt and angry to allow anyone to approach him. She turned to Yithran, touching his arm. He refused to look at her.

At last, wiping his cheeks with the back of one hand, Bezeq said, "The day they left, Sharah insisted that Keren should walk alone with her. None of my tribe saw them again. When we searched, we found hoofprints and horse dung in one of the surrounding fields. They must have chased Keren; we found her shawl and a digging stick and tubers all abandoned, her footprints heading into the trees. There, the ground was trodden. She must have been hiding in a tree. There were bushes chopped away. . . ."

His eyes red, but filled with a desperate hope, Yithran said, "Keren's father is going to the Great City to demand that Keren be returned. I'm going with him."

"No!" Bezeq cried, leaning toward his brother, adamant, as if continuing an earlier quarrel. "You can't go! Our father forbids it. That Nimr-Rada would kill you instantly. Our father left me in no doubt of your fate. Even Keren's own father will be risking his life by demanding her return. And our father *forbids* you to marry her."

Listening, Annah realized that they were speaking as if Keren was the only one Meshek could attempt to rescue. "What of Sharah?" she demanded as Yithran stalked away in anger. "You're giving your wife to that Nimr-Rada?"

"She gave me up for him," Bezeq answered curtly. "Why should I want her? If I see her again, I might kill her. But, Ma'adannah, pray for Keren's father. I fear he will die when he goes to the Great City. Nimr-Rada will cut him to pieces."

Horrified, Annah shut her eyes, breathing a wordless prayer for Meshek.

Ten

"HOW COULD ANYONE long to live there?" Keren asked, gaping at the Great City, which was endlessly out-lined against the ruddy, dusky sky. The buildings looked heaped together, all squared, many enclosed by walls. She was oppressed just looking at them. *O Most High, save me from this place.*

She unconsciously tugged her horse to a standstill, overwhelmed. Lawkham rode up and rapped her horse's rump with the butt of his spear, goading it onward. She grimaced at Lawkham, but he laughed. Sighing, she looked at the Great City again. "It can't be real."

"Indeed, it's very real, Lady," Revakhaw answered, leaning around Keren to see the Great City for herself. Revakhaw had been sharing rides on Keren's horse for days; her companionship during this long journey had been like a balm to Keren. Playful as always, Revakhaw said, "Just tell yourself that it's one huge lodge. Aren't we all family? Though I thank the heavens that *some* people will reside beneath other roofs!"

"You refer to me, O talkative one?" Lawkham asked, not bothering to hide the fact that he had been listening to every word. He and Revakhaw had been trading gibes ever since they had departed from Revakhaw's home settlement.

"Why should you think that?" she asked, sounding almost demure. "But, of course, O great Lawkham, you think that all women talk of none but yourself."

"As they should."

"As they laugh!"

"Stop," Zehker commanded them quietly, looking forward. "He waits for us."

He. Nimr-Rada. Keren followed Zehker's gaze and saw that Nimr-Rada had reined his horse to a standstill. He was frowning at Revakhaw and Lawkham.

As they approached, Nimr-Rada said, "You will conduct yourselves with dignity when we ride through the streets of the Great City. If you do not, I will put you to work in the mud and slime with the other wretches who dare to disobey me."

Nimr-Rada cast a baleful look at Keren, as if blaming her for some misdeed. Keren lowered her eyes so he wouldn't see her indignation. *Don't worry, Mighty One,* she thought. *I won't enjoy riding through the streets of your Great City.*

As commanded, they rode into the city in stately silence. Keren's depression grew. The buildings in the Great City were all uniformly squared and so precisely coated with the same shade of pale mud wash that they were devoid of warmth and character. By now, the citizens of the Great City were pouring out of their homes to stand in the hard-tamped clay streets and cheer their Great King.

Nimr-Rada rode proudly, nodding and occasionally lifting his elaborate flail, saluting those who praised his unequalled might. With some difficulty Keren looked away, reminding herself not to become like Nimr-Rada's citizens, captivated by his physical and emotional attractions. By chance, she looked a citizen-matron directly in the eyes. The matron recoiled, jerking back her dark-braided head in shock.

"Look!" Keren heard the woman cry to someone. "Her eyes are the color of a mist rising from the river!"

"Impossible," a man snorted.

Hearing this snatch of conversation, Keren focused on the tawny flickering ears and black mane of her horse. She would always be strange and frightful, never a normal woman.

In the street ahead, others were gasping aloud, evidently amazed by Sharah's lack of color. Aware of the impact her unworthy sister was making, and embarrassed by her own looks, Keren lowered her head. This ride through Nimr-Rada's city was a nightmarish torture.

"Keren!" a man's voice cried to her right, his tone shocked.

Neshar, she thought, almost before she saw his face. For a fleeting instant she was delighted, eager to see one of her own brothers. Until she saw that his black hair was disgracefully cropped, his leather tunic worn out, and his arms and legs all scraped bloody and spattered with mud. He was no longer one of the handsomely attired, much-honored horsemen of Nimr-Rada. Instead he looked scraggly, hungry, and filthy. The lowest of the low.

Four other men were with him, all similarly shorn,

scraped, and humbled. In a dawning horror, Keren recognized Mattan and Bachan. And the two men with them had to be her own brothers Kana and Miyka. Their resemblance to her father was so strong that Keren was jolted as if she had received a blow to the chest. Catching her breath, she cried, "Neshar!"

But Neshar shook his head and swiftly led his four attending brothers in a desperate scramble to get away. Keren almost fell off her horse as she twisted around to look back at them.

Revakhaw whispered at her frantically, "Lady, who are they? How do you know such men?"

"They're my own brothers," Keren said, miserable.

"Your horsemen-brothers? Oh, but . . . how terrible . . ." Her words trailed away as she apparently realized that Keren's brothers were despised men who wanted nothing to do with her.

Swallowing, Keren lowered her head until her hair fell about her face, hiding her from the curious stares of others. She wanted to scream. She sobbed instead.

"No, Lady, please," Revakhaw begged distressfully, patting her back. "Don't cry yet. We'll be away from all these people soon, I'm sure. Then you can cry. I'm sorry about your brothers—so sorry! Whatever I can do to help you, I will do. By the heavens, I give you my word. . . ."

Keren forced herself to listen to Revakhaw's sympathetic promises. Otherwise, she would begin to rage at Nimr-Rada. She saw no one else in this Great City with such scrapes, or so filthy and disgracefully shorn. Who could bring her brothers so low and inspire such fear in them? Only that Nimr-Rada. He was destroying their lives. How could she fight him?

She cried quietly until they came to a less crowded

area of the city. Sensing a change in her surroundings, she lifted her head. There were fewer people on the streets here. And without exception, all the houses had high, pale walls enclosing trees within, promising calm seclusion. Ahead of her, Nimr-Rada waved his flail toward a broad reed gate, which opened as if swept by an invisible wind.

Looking back at her, Nimr-Rada said, "Lady, this is your dwelling place." Then, noticing her tear-streaked face, he growled, "Go wash yourself! You disgrace me with such a show of misery. You will be in my courts in the morning. You and your attendants."

"As you say, O King." Keren suppressed a moist sniffle. If she behaved rudely toward Nimr-Rada, he might inflict some heavier punishment on her brothers.

Maintaining her respectful facade, Keren watched Nimr-Rada depart with the impatient Sharah. Since her "wedding" to the Great King, Sharah had visited Keren only during evening meals, which Keren regarded as a blessing. Sharah was now disgustingly haughty toward everyone except Nimr-Rada, whom she flattered, caressed, and teased audaciously. She didn't even look back at Keren now to offer a parting nod. Instead, she urged her horse ahead, clearly anticipating the glories of her new home.

Farewell, Keren thought, silently offering the reluctant courtesy her sister had neglected. *At least I'll have my evening to myself*. She was grateful for the respite. She had to find her brothers and learn the cause of their disgrace and their fear. Who could help her? She could think of only one person: their brother Ra-Anan.

As she slid off her horse, in the center of the private, brick-and-tree-lined courtyard, she beckoned to Lawkham, who was turning to leave. "I must see Ra-Anan tonight."

"I can guess why, Lady," said Lawkham without mockery. "Zehker saw Neshar and the others."

Glancing at Zehker, Keren realized that he and Lawkham were angered by Neshar's obvious humiliation and wanted to help him. Keren shut her eyes briefly, thanking the Most High for giving her allies in this strange place. Already, Revakhaw was saying, "I'll go with you, Lady."

"Tsinnah and I will go too, Lady," Gebuwrah told her, hovering behind Keren. "Na'ah and Alatah can also go, or they can stay here to arrange things for your comfort."

"Whatever pleases you. Truly. Whoever wishes to stay here and rest, I will understand." Keren pushed her wildly rumpled hair off her face. "But for those who are going with me, let's be sure we are presentable. I need to find some water."

With Lawkham and Zehker carrying reed-and-resin torches to light her way, Keren slowly approached Ra-Anan's courtyard gate. Though Ra-Anan's dwelling was reasonably close to her own, preparations for this visit had taken longer than she had expected. All of her attendants had insisted upon going with her. And to spare the weary horses, they had come on foot.

The muscular, spear-wielding guard at Ra-Anan's gate was rude. "Move on!" he bellowed, waving Keren off with his burly free arm—which was garnished with a clattering assortment of animal's teeth and claws, all large, all dangling from thin strips of leather. Hunting trophies meant to impress onlookers. Or to intimidate them. As Keren stepped out of the guard's reach, Lawkham strode forward, surprisingly aggressive.

"You will call her Lady," he told the guard. "And by the command of the Great King, if you so much as *accidentally* touch a hair on her head, you'll die at once. Also, you will not flap your hand toward her as if she's a no one to be ignored. She is Ra-Anan's own sister. Greet her with respect."

The guard looked at Keren, flinched when he noticed her eyes, then ducked his head submissively. Almost fawning, he said, "I apologize for offending you, Lady. Please, wait in the courtyard. I'll tell my master you're here."

"Master?" Keren whispered to Lawkham and Zehker, as the guard led them into the courtyard, then scurried into Ra-Anan's low, sprawling residence. "He calls my brother 'master'?"

"Dear Lady, after all we've told you, even now, you don't understand the power your brother holds over us," Lawkham murmured. "Only Nimr-Rada rules him here."

Zehker nodded in agreement, his wary gaze fixed on the doorway, clearly anticipating the guard's return. As Zehker and the others kept watch, Keren looked around. The courtyard—its borders beautifully softened with lush green plants and trees—was quiet and deserted. Keren suddenly felt guilty for disturbing Ra-Anan after dark. To her surprise, they were not kept waiting. The guard hurried back, less than eager to give them Ra-Anan's reply.

"He cannot see you tonight, Lady. He is meeting with certain men who are planning . . . a building important to He-Who-Lifts-the-Skies."

They all looked at Keren, awaiting her answer. Dispirited, she looked down at the brick-paved yard. She was so tired. It would be easy to agree that she would return later. But remembering Neshar's desperation, and the disgrace of her other brothers, her strength returned. "I'll be patient," she told the guard firmly. "The matter is of great importance. If I must, I will sit here all night."

Hearing this, the guard clutched his spear convulsively and looked back at the residence, obviously alarmed at the prospect of conveying her decision to Ra-Anan.

Keren felt a rush compassion for his sake. Was Ra-Anan such a terrible person that this brawny, rude guard cowered before him? "Never mind. I'll tell him myself." She circled around the unhappy guard, giving him a protective boundary, afraid he would try to stop her with his own hands.

He lifted his spear to block her way, but Zehker approached forbiddingly.

Before matters worsened, a man's cool, commanding voice filled the darkened courtyard. "Perek, return to the gate. I will speak to my sister."

Ra-Anan, Keren thought, suddenly nervous, knowing that he had seen and heard everything. Immediately, the guard, Zehker, Lawkham, Revakhaw, and all four of Keren's other attendants bowed their heads and folded their free hands before themselves respectfully. The guard humbly retreated as Ra-Anan approached. Keren refused to bow but watched Ra-Anan emerge from the shadows.

Tall and thin, he moved in a leisurely, self-important manner, his hooded dark eyes fixed on Keren alone. She did not like him, and this realization unnerved her. He was clad in a long, one-shouldered robe of white cloth, and—to Keren's astonishment—he was completely smooth shaven. His brown skin and hairless head gleamed in the torchlight. There was no warmth or kindness in his expression or his voice.

"You were commanded to present yourself in the

courts of the Great King tomorrow morning. I did not expect to meet you until then."

"Forgive me," Keren answered, not begging but not too proud either. "I'll be brief. Today, when I entered the Great City, I saw our own brothers, Neshar, Mattan, Bachan, Miyka, and Kana. It's obvious that they're suffering some sort of punishment. They are miserable—covered with scrapes and filth. I hope you will ask the Great King to forgive them and to end their punishment."

"They are being punished for deceit," Ra-Anan told her. "And when it pleases He-Who-Lifts-the-Skies, then they will be restored to their former places. Until then, they will be common laborers, as they deserve. They must learn to appreciate the Great King's kindness toward them."

Ra-Anan's lack of concern rankled Keren. He sounded so much like Sharah. *I won't intercede for you.* Trying to remain composed, she said, "If you can't be troubled with your own brothers, Ra-Anan, then I will speak to the Great King tomorrow. Whatever our brothers have done, they don't deserve such punishment."

To her great frustration, her voice quavered, weakening. How could this hateful Ra-Anan possibly be her brother—the firstborn son of her quiet father and fearful mother? And yet, hints of her father's most stern expressions flickered about Ra-Anan's mouth. Worse, the way his eyebrows lifted as he spoke mirrored their own mother's in the most eerie, horrid way. Keren knew that the sight of their oily, smooth-shaven eldest son would appall Meshek and Chaciydah.

As if discerning her thoughts, Ra-Anan lowered his chin, menacing as a snake about to strike. "You, my young sister, will say nothing to our Great King! You have already provoked him beyond measure. You have yet to bow to him or to thank him for any of his gifts. You scorn his provisions for your comfort, and you question him at every turn. Beyond doubt, you deserved more than one blow from his flail two weeks ago. And tonight you rode into his Great City sobbing like a child, shaming him. He was merciful to you, my sister, and you had best not anger him again. When he is ready, he will restore our brothers to their former places, but not before."

Keren listened, confounded. How had Ra-Anan learned so much about her actions in the short time since her arrival? Who had been watching her and telling him everything? Just within her field of vision, Zehker shifted subtly, turning the torch in his hand. He never wasted words or motions. She interpreted his gesture as a warning that she should be cautious.

"I apologize, my brother," she said, turning to leave. "And I regret disturbing you tonight. Perhaps I will see you in the morning."

"Perhaps? You will see me more often than you realize," Ra-Anan spat, his viciousness halting her instantly. "You will be my student for years to come. Therefore, you must learn your place. Beginning now, you will never leave until I dismiss you. You will never come here unless I summon you. You will also learn some manners. In addition, you must dominate your impulsiveness and think before you speak. You will have great significance here. The lives of others will depend upon your actions, which is unfortunate, because you are obviously incapable of self-control."

Contemptuously, he said, "Now, I command you to return to your residence and contemplate your absurd, inconsiderate behavior. Tomorrow we begin your lessons. Go."

Instantly, her attendants and Lawkham and Zehker all bowed their heads and stepped back. Ra-Anan glared at her once more, then turned abruptly, going into his house without another word.

Keren's heart seemed to shrink within her. Ra-Anan deserved the name "Master." He knew just how to talk to make her feel like a stupid know-nothing girl. Even so, she pretended to be calm, following Lawkham and Zehker out of the courtyard. Her attendants trailed her, absolutely silent. Eyeing them, Keren wondered, *Who is telling Ra-Anan everything that I do and say?*

"Can I trust anyone?" she wondered aloud. "What sneaking wretch revealed so many things to Master Ra-Anan?"

"I've never said anything to anyone," Alatah protested, her girlish voice rising as if Keren had accused her personally.

"Nor have I," said Na'ah, with less assurance than Alatah.

Hearing this, Keren suppressed a smile. Though Na'ah was walking behind her, Keren could almost see her looking around furtively as she spoke. Na'ah was suspicious of everyone and afraid of everything.

"Lady, you know I would never say a word of you to anyone," Tsinnah told Keren earnestly, hurrying forward to look Keren in the eyes.

"And you should never doubt me," Revakhaw added, sounding fierce. Then, as if she had been seething for quite a while, she said, "That Master Ra-Anan has the same soul as our pale Great Lady Sharah. He cares for nothing and no one beyond himself."

"Shh!" Lawkham warned. Barely whispering, he said, "In this Great City you are always watched. Always. Whatever you say and do will be seen or suspected and reported to Ra-Anan. Or to the Great King."

"Conceal your souls," Zehker added quietly. To Keren's surprise, Zehker actually looked at them, though his lean, shadowed face was enigmatic as ever. Then, without elaborating on his cryptic warning, Zehker changed the subject. "You will see the leopards tomorrow."

"In other words," Lawkham teased, "tomorrow morning, when we are summoned to the courts of our Great King, you must not act like leopard's food."

Keren's attendants giggled nervously. But as she contemplated the meeting to come, Keren shivered. *O Most High, give me strength. Even with my new friends, I'm alone. They don't trust You or think of You as they should. Why?*

An image of I'ma-Annah appeared in her mind then. Keren could almost hear her gently telling Keren of the horrors of her past in the previous world. *Karan-child, I was quite alone among my family. If I had even once spoken aloud, I would have been killed. I had to hide my eyes and my soul from theirs. It was terrible. I had no one to trust for many years. Truly, the Most High saved me from madness.*

Remembering this, Keren looked up at the stars glittering in the darkness. Surely the Most High had brought her here for a reason. He would protect her as He had protected I'ma-Annah. But she would have to conceal her soul, as Zehker had advised.

She looked over at Zehker now. He was always so vigilant. And obviously he trusted no one; his soul was concealed. *What has caused you to hide?* she wondered, looking at him. Instantly he glanced at her, seeming impassive, though he was studying her carefully. She looked away, walking on through the dark streets, embarrassed that he had caught her staring.

Kneeling on the dais, just to Nimr-Rada's left, Ra-Anan willed himself not to lean forward. Keren—her plain, whitened-leather tunic gleaming in the morning light—was entering the hushed, open ceremonial courtyard, followed by her reluctant attendants. Doubtless someone had warned Keren's attendants that Nimr-Rada would be enjoying the companionship of his cherished gold-and-jewel-collared leopards this morning, for the girls were all clasping their hands tightly before themselves, obviously afraid. Keren held her hands more easily, but she moved slowly.

Almost shivering, Ra-Anan studied Keren's eyes, so pale that one could not help feeling a kind of spiritual awe. Delightful. Yes, Keren would be most effective in the role he had planned for her. And he was pleased by her remoteness. He had scolded her unfairly last night. Keren possessed a natural dignity that Sharah lacked.

Despite her uniqueness and pretensions of grandeur, Sharah could be perused like a token of impressed clay. She was too forward with the Great King. Too accessible. If she wanted to maintain Nimr-Rada's interest, she would have to be more mysterious and unobtainable, like Keren.

A sidelong glance at Nimr-Rada and Sharah confirmed Ra-Anan's opinion. Sharah sat close to Nimr-Rada—her feet tucked away from his lolling, drowsing leopards—while Nimr-Rada stared at Keren, his dark fingers tapping soundlessly against the gold-lashed haft of the flail in his lap. Both Nimr-Rada and Sharah were splendidly garbed in rare white cloth and dazzling gold collars, cuffs, and rings. Their elevated ceremonial seat was covered with light fleeces that showed Nimr-Rada's powerfully muscled dark skin to great advantage, while flaunting the marvelous, dizzying patterns of the tamed leopards lounging at his feet. Keren seemed untouched by Nimr-Rada's magnificence—which Ra-Anan knew would provoke the proud Great King.

Nimr-Rada never shifted his gaze from Keren. She knelt on her designated mat without bowing—which caused Nimr-Rada's dark nostrils to flare angrily. Ra-Anan longed to laugh like a wild man. And to praise Keren aloud for her show of tranquil defiance. Nimr-Rada, the Great King, Mighty Hunter, He-Who-Lifts-the-Skies, was becoming ensnared in a trap of his own making. No doubt he longed to snatch Keren off her mat and beat her into reverence. Instead, he clenched his flail hard and waved it toward a timid group of tradesmen who were waiting, huddled against the left inner wall of the court-yard.

As instructed, the tradesmen approached Keren in an orderly line. Halting, the lead tradesman bowed to her. Presenting Keren with numerous swatches of beaten leather, thin leather cords, a blade of obsidian, and a piece of brownish-orange ochre, the tradesman requested that she use the ochre to trace the outlines of her hands and feet on separate swatches of leather. Then she must allow her attendants to measure her throat, her head, her arms, her ankles, her wrists, and her height with the slen-der leather cords, cutting each cord to the appropriate length.

Keren blinked at the tradesman's request. Looking up at Nimr-Rada, she asked, "Please, why am I being mea-sured?"

"You are like poison, Lady," Nimr-Rada answered, pleasantly vindictive. "Therefore we must make your apparel conspicuous."

Keren looked down. Her measurements were obtained with minimal whispers of advice from the tradesmen and from her nervous attendants. Ra-Anan leaned back on his heels, satisfied by the discipline of the entire procedure. Nimr-Rada, too, seemed somewhat pacified.

When the tradesmen had gathered all their swatches, cords, and gear, Nimr-Rada dismissed them with a wave of his hand. Raising his voice, he told Keren, "You and your household may go, Lady. You will receive other instructions later today."

Immediately, all the members of Keren's household folded their hands before themselves in the properly respectful manner and bowed. All except Keren. Her spirit was admirable, Ra-Anan decided, but she had been defiant enough for the day. He leaned toward his young sister, glaring at her, willing her to bow.

Perfectly calm, she lifted her chin at him and flung an unmistakable look at Nimr-Rada: *You will have to kill me.*

With silent, breathtaking audacity, she turned and walked out of the courtyard. Her attendants and guards hurried after her, unsettled. Ra-Anan exhaled heavily. Was she incredibly foolish, or exceptionally brave? Aloud he said, "She should be punished for such rudeness. Shall I send for her again and insist that she bow?"

"No," Nimr-Rada growled. Clearly incensed, he rested one bare, gold-ankleted dark foot atop Tselem, a particularly favored leopard who dominated the others. "Let her believe she has won for now. We will find ways to control her behavior."

"She is such a fool," Sharah complained. "How can she be my sister?"

Nimr-Rada smiled absently and flicked at Sharah's

gleaming, pale braids. "I have heard that she voices the same question when she speaks of you, my Sharah. She is not as loyal to you as she is toward your deceitful brothers." Before Sharah could respond, Nimr-Rada looked at Ra-Anan, one black eyebrow raised. "Will you beg leniency for your unworthy brothers? I believe your sister asked this of you last night."

Ra-Anan shrugged, refusing to be surprised. Nimr-Rada had planted informant-servants among Ra-Anan's household—a fact that Ra-Anan sometimes used to his own advantage. "My Lord, I told my foolish young sister that—perhaps—when my brothers appreciate your kindness toward them, you might restore them to their former places. But that is entirely subject to your will. Why should I plead for their sakes when they betrayed us? My sisters could have been brought to the Great City years ago, for your benefit."

"Which would have made me perfectly happy," Sharah crooned, tracing one colorless finger down the sinewy contours of Nimr-Rada's arm. Shifting, Nimr-Rada caught Sharah's wandering fingertips and held them firmly. Sharah straightened, flushing, watching Nimr-Rada. He still seemed preoccupied with Keren.

"Let us consider her weaknesses," he said, grazing a foot across Tselem's spotted hide, causing Tselem to stretch languidly. "How is she most vulnerable?"

"She's devoted to those Ancient Ones," Sharah said disdainfully, her gray eyes following the movements of Nimr-Rada's foot over the leopard's wonderfully speckled hide. "She will hear nothing against them. *They* are why she won't bow to anyone."

"Then we must not speak against the Ancient Ones directly," Nimr-Rada decided. "Rather, we should let time erase the superstitious influences of those old story-tellers."

"You are wise, my Lord," Ra-Anan agreed, pleased because Nimr-Rada's decision reflected his own thoughts. "To say anything against those old people would merely prolong her rebellion. However, if she rebels further, we should punish others to gain her submission—her attendants, for example; they already seem devoted to her. What of her guards?"

"Zehker and Lawkham?" Nimr-Rada pursed his full lips thoughtfully. "They have been in my own household almost continually since they were children. I have tested them time and again; except for their secrecy in obedience to their commander, Neshar, they have always proven themselves loyal to me."

"That Zehker is more strict than our father," Sharah grumbled. "Also, he has never liked Keren. Or anyone."

"He is one of my best guardsmen," Nimr-Rada said, as if to forestall any further complaints from Sharah regarding Zehker. "He will stay in her household. And Lawkham is the son of one of my brother's sons. He will stay, provided he does not forget his place. At times, he takes too much upon himself."

"Perhaps we should add new members to her household," Ra-Anan suggested. "Ones who are loyal only to you, my Lord."

"Good," Nimr-Rada agreed. "I want to know everything she says and does. Her every breath. And, of course, I will unsettle her at every turn. . . ."

Ra-Anan was pleased by Nimr-Rada's reaction. And he noticed that Sharah was now smoldering, her glistening lashes lowered. She was jealous of Keren. Perfect. He could use that jealousy against both sisters to crush and reform their spirits. Then they would become everything he envisioned. No other women alive would compare to them—particularly where Nimr-Rada was concerned. *Let my sisters be his weakness.*

Eleven

BEWILDERED, KEREN stared at the heap of gear that Lawkham and Zehker had piled in her courtyard. Oddly shortened wooden combs, tough grass cordage, blades of obsidian and flint, retouching tools, a clay pot of resin, sinew, feathers, ointments, a collection of soft swatches of leather, and a long ashwood spear. In addition, she saw the unmistakable makings of their favored weapons—their bows and arrows—consisting of a handful of slender wooden rods, unstrung bow staves made of yew, and a long, thin pouch of leather stiffened by slim rods stitched along its sides. "What is all this?"

"Orders," Zehker said. "For your horse, and for hunting."

"As soon as you've learned to use weapons properly, you will be hunting with our Great King every day," Lawkham informed Keren.

"Every day? But why?"

Lawkham shrugged. "Dear Lady, there are only two reasons our He-Who-Lifts-the-Skies will take anyone hunting: either you are an exceptional hunter, or he intends to 'guide' you until you comply with his wishes." Quizzically birdlike and cheerful, he asked, "Are you an exceptional hunter?"

Frustrated, Keren shook her head. Like most women, she was reasonably adept at fishing, and at netting or snaring small game. Some women enjoyed hunting with their families for larger creatures, but that pastime had never appealed to Keren. Now she was being forced to accept it until she complied with Nimr-Rada's wishes—and that would never happen. She fumed, "So, I'm going to make weapons and follow that Nimr-Rada for the rest of my life!"

Zehker gave her a warning look as Lawkham coughed.

"Lady," Lawkham muttered beneath his breath, "never use such a tone of voice in reference to the Great King. Not with all these strange ears listening."

Keren swallowed and glanced around the open courtyard, realizing that some of her new guardsmen and servants were hovering nearby, occupied with irrelevant tasks. They had heard everything. They would tell Nimr-Rada and Ra-Anan; Keren couldn't stop them. She had no say over anything in her life now, and it infuriated her. For her brothers' sake, however, she had endured all these new, sly-eyed faces, the strictly controlled routines of her days, the strange food, and the new tunics of pale cloth—such as the one she was wearing—which felt so insubstantial compared to the good, long, sturdy fleece and leather tunics and leggings she had worn since childhood.

But now, by one thoughtless comment, she risked subjecting her brothers to further punishments—a threat Ra-

Anan had been using against her these three weeks since her arrival. Aloud, she apologized to Zehker and Lawkham. "You are right to correct me. I was rude to speak of the Great King in such a way. Now, please explain why I need all this gear."

To her dismay, they settled down for the warm, humid afternoon, teaching her how to string her bow stave with cordage. How to smooth the arrow. How to notch the arrow. How to ensure that the arrow flew straight to its target like a bird, with the fletching of resin-and-sinew bound feathers straightening its path. And how to fasten the flint tip of the arrow with resin and sinew, giving it deadly strength.

Keren gritted her teeth through the whole ordeal. She would have preferred to join Tsinnah and Revakhaw in the shaded area of the courtyard and help them to bind their new grass mats. Comfort came when Lawkham and Zehker disagreed on which tip to use for one of the arrows they were making. In the midst of their debate, Lawkham shoved Zehker, who instantly grabbed Law-kham's tightly bound hair at the nape of his neck and wrenched it into disarray.

"Ow! You make me look bad," Lawkham howled. Surrendering at once, he attempted to bring his dark, tousled curls to order. "Savage."

"Pretty boy," Zehker answered, rapidly joining his choice of flint to the notched arrow with a dab of resin, then winding it neatly into place with a piece of sinew. He seemed stoic as ever, but Keren saw him *almost* smile.

The effect was shocking—so unlike Zehker—that she whooped delightedly. At once Lawkham pretended offense, while Tsinnah and the fun-loving Revakhaw emerged from the shade to learn why Keren was laughing. Zehker became remote again.

"Test your bow, Lady," he commanded, keeping all the arrows in his firm grasp.

Unable to be indignant with Zehker's abruptness now, Keren obeyed.

Still struggling with the leather cordage binding his unruly hair, Lawkham offered Keren a profusion of happy instructions as she stood with her new bow. "Stand easily, Lady. Now, lift your right elbow. Higher. No, keep your shoulder lowered. Yes, that way. Push your left arm straight and forward as you pull the bowstring back. Good! Let the hand holding the bowstring rest just beneath and against your jaw, then align the bowstring with your chin and nose. Wait, wait . . . which eye is your sighting eye? Zehker, give her an arrow."

"She might kill someone."

"Not if she aims at the wall." Lawkham called out to everyone in the courtyard. "Move all of you, before you catch an arrow! Zehker, don't be such a coward. Give her an arrow. What's the worst that could happen?"

Radiating disapproval, Zehker handed Keren an arrow, then backed away.

Lawkham resumed his sociable barrage of instructions. "Relax, relax. Stand evenly, Lady, don't lean like that. Rest the notched end of the arrow atop your long finger and secure it with the finger above. Wait, wait, curl your fingers *slightly* around the string. Raise your elbow. Curl your thumb into your palm. Relax your hand. Don't frown at me, Lady, just stare at your prey. Well . . . imagine your prey standing by that wall."

At last, when all the muscles in her hands were cramping and Keren felt she was going to scream, Lawkham said, "Good. Now, *gently*, flexing all your fingers at once—

then pulling your hand away smoothly—allow the string to slip out of your fingers and release the arrow."

Keren released the arrow and was instantly rewarded with a vicious, searing bowstring snap across her tunic-covered left breast. The pain was so intense she couldn't even shriek. Still clutching the bow, she sank to her knees and huddled over, rocking in misery. Tsinnah and Revakhaw hurried to comfort her, making low noises of distress.

"Can you speak?" Revakhaw asked, rubbing Keren's back in anxious sympathy.

"O Lady, that must have hurt beyond anything," Tsinnah mourned.

"By all the heavens, I should have thought of that," Lawkham said, sounding contrite. "You need a protective covering of some sort. You also need leather bands, to protect your forearms."

Both Revakhaw and Tsinnah cried at him to be silent, their usual adoration of his charms obviously dashed.

"Lawkham," Keren said through her teeth, when she could finally speak, "please, go stand against that wall so I can *hurt* you."

He laughed, obviously relieved that she could joke at all. Recovering, Keren sat up, fanning herself with her hands.

As they were talking, Zehker used a flint blade to slice four strips off a large, squared swatch of leather. He then slit a small hole in each corner of the squared leather and threaded a long leather strip through each hole, knotting them firmly. He also cut two small pieces of leather with matching ties. Finished, he dropped his work in front of Keren. "Use the small ones for your arms, Lady. Then try again."

"I'm finished with the bow and arrows," she told him. "I won't use them."

Half kneeling, he leaned toward her, his dark brown eyes hard, the thoroughly formidable commander-horseman. "You will."

He meant it. Keren knew she would never persuade him to give up these weaponry lessons. She could just imagine him sitting in her courtyard all night long, prepared to greet her by the first light of dawn, her bow in his hands. Exasperated, she donned the armbands, snatched the bow, and stood as Revakhaw and Tsinnah adjusted the protective leather chest covering, tying it in an X behind her back. Before taking aim at the wall, Keren eyed Zehker severely. "If your invention doesn't work, O Zehker, then you can just sit here all night, all month, all year. I'll never touch a bow again."

Trying to follow all of Lawkham's intricate instructions, Keren shot a second arrow. Only her fingers hurt this time, and the arrow cracked near the base of the wall, a far better result than from the first arrow, which had landed on the nearby bricks.

"Two more," Zehker insisted, allowing no argument.

To Keren's relief, her lesson was interrupted by a clatter at the gate. One of the new guardsmen, Erek—the sly-faced young man who had spied Zehker on the day of her capture—went to answer the impatient summons. Seeing her unexpected guests, Keren nearly dropped her bow. "Neshar! Bachan! My own brothers!"

Stick thin, their hair still badly shorn, but clean now, and wearing their proud horsemen attire, Neshar and Bachan grinned at her. They were followed by the solemn Mattan and by the two brothers she had not met: Miyka and Kana, who were wide-eyed and obviously reluctant to enter her courtyard. At Lawkham's cheerful urging, the five men filed in to stand before her, bowing their heads respectfully, their hands folded before themselves as if greeting one of higher rank.

Keren detested their formality. She would have preferred to hug them all—an impulse she hastily controlled. She was so happy that she stammered as she spoke. "Pl-please, can you stay for the evening meal? It will be ready soon, and I'm sure we have enough for everyone. Na'ah always cooks too much."

"If you wish, Lady," Neshar answered, still formal, eyeing her new guards.

Lawkham apparently noticed Neshar's open mistrust; he swept an imperious brown hand at Erek and the other new household guards. "Back away. In fact, go do something useful before our Lady *touches* you."

Erek looked irritated, and some of the other guardsmen protested until Keren frowned at them menacingly—an act, but it was effective. They retreated, fearful that she might actually do as Lawkham had threatened. Miyka and Kana also seemed alarmed. To reassure them, Keren smiled, deliberately clasping her hands tightly before herself.

She led them to a row of grass mats—hastily produced by Alatah and the suspicious Gebruwrah, who had emerged from the house and were scrambling to bring cool drinks to welcome their lady's horsemen-brothers. Revakhaw and Tsinnah swiftly arranged a separate mat for Keren, padding it with a heap of gleaming furs, allowing her to kneel comfortably, facing her guests.

Neshar and Bachan removed their rough, short fleece cloaks, spread them over their chosen mats, and sat down. Mattan, Miyka, and Kana followed their example, watching

Keren covertly. Unasked, Zehker brought a longspear and placed it between Keren and her brothers to serve as a visible reminder that her brothers were not exempt from the death order. She stared at the spear, understanding Zehker's gesture, but disheartened by its necessity.

"Why should you be grieved by this?" the observant Neshar asked, suddenly every bit the older brother. "Be thankful, Lady. This death order is like a gift to you. It maintains your status and cultivates respect and obedience from those who would otherwise take advantage of you. Even Ra-Anan is not above this threat."

"I hate it!" Keren told him fiercely. "I'm all the more an oddity—a freak—because of this command." Tears started to her eyes. She had to pause, pressing her hands to her face to maintain her composure. At last, she wiped her eyes and smiled at the still-nervous Miyka and Kana; they seemed so shy. "You two look so much like our father, I'm amazed. I am so glad to see you, believe me."

"We know you've been concerned for us, sister—Lady," Bachan said, hurriedly amending his lapse in manners. "That's why we've come today. We wanted to thank you for interceding on our behalf with Nimr-Rada. He sent for us yesterday and told us that it was only for your sake that we were released from laboring in the clay."

"He decided to grant my pleas."

"No thanks to Ra-Anan," Mattan grumbled.

Keren frowned. "Tell me, please, what did you do to deserve such a terrible punishment?"

"We hid your existence from him, Lady," Bachan told her. "For years."

"Your existence and Sharah's," Mattan added. Fixing his gaze on Keren, he said, "Please forgive me, Lady. I'm the one who actually told Ra-Anan that you and our no-color sister, Sharah, were alive. We were beginning to hear stories of your existence from other people. I knew that Ra-Anan would be even more furious with us—his own brothers—if some traveler told him first. I told him that you and Sharah were alive, and he told the Great King. It's my fault that you were brought here."

"My situation—and Sharah's—is not your fault," said Keren, forgiving him at once. "If others were talking about us, then everything that's happened was inescapable. Sharah always has been eager to come to the Great City, and as covetous as she is, she wanted to become Nimr-Rada's wife. We would have been brought here eventually."

"We have been told to deny any stories that Sharah was married," Mattan informed Keren beneath his breath, watching Keren's attendants, who were retrieving more mats. "If we—or you—affirm that she was married, we'll all be punished."

"Undoubtedly," Neshar agreed. "And I must add, Lady, that I had hoped that Ra-Anan would be loyal to us for the sake of our parents, but I was wrong. Therefore, I no longer consider him to be my brother."

"Nor do I," Bachan muttered, as the others nodded in silent accord. Changing the subject in deference to Keren's new guardsmen, who were now moving to watch them from a more advantageous corner of the courtyard, Bachan smiled at Keren. His face was a masculine reflection of Chaciydah's, slim and expressive. "I'm curious, Lady. Your leather armbands and front piece . . . very strange attire for a woman. Are you learning to use weapons?"

Glancing at Lawkham and Zehker, who had retreated to stand together at a discreet distance, Keren grimaced. "Yes. Orders," she said, imitating Zehker's abrupt explanation.

"I'm told that I'll be hunting with Nimr-Rada. I've also been told that if I obey my 'orders,' you will be treated well."

"Behave then," Mattan begged, his face also a vivid reflection of their mother's. They all laughed together, even Miyka and Kana, who were beginning to relax.

Keren grew somber, looking at her brothers in loving concern. "I will do everything—everything—within my power to be sure you aren't punished again. But there is one thing I won't do: I cannot bow to Nimr-Rada."

"That's because you've listened to the Ancient Ones all your life," Neshar observed. "They believe that no man on earth should have such authority."

"Only the Most High should have such authority in the hearts and minds of mankind," Keren told them. To her dismay, they reacted like everyone else in this Great City at the mere mention of the Most High—they all made faces or looked away, as if in polite distaste. "Why do you despise Him?" Keren asked.

"Perhaps despise is too strong a word," Mattan said. "Rather, we believe there are other ways beneath these heavens."

"Your own ways? Or the ways of Ra-Anan and He-Who-Lifts-the-Skies?" Keren persisted quietly, unwilling to be deceived with light answers.

Neshar lifted a hand to silence Bachan, who was opening his mouth to respond.

"We shouldn't argue tonight, Lady," Neshar said, gentle again. "Why spoil what could be our last visit together? Listen: We are to be separated and sent in different directions at the command of He-Who-Lifts-the-Skies."

"But . . . why?" Keren felt tears starting to her eyes again. "Is it because of me? Are you still being punished?"

"Not punished so much as prevented from creating the potential for a rebellion, Lady," Miyka explained, daring to speak at last. He was indeed a younger image of their father, from the straightness of his black hair and long limbs down to the very turn of his mouth and the tone of his voice. Keren was homesick just listening to him.

Seated beside Miyka, Kana nodded. He could have been Miyka's twin. "There are too many of our own family here, Lady," he told Keren. "We are all sons of the same parents, brothers to the two highest ladies in these lands—and one sister is wife to the Great King himself. Perhaps it's best for us to be separated. Otherwise we would be suspected of plotting against Ra-Anan or the Great King."

But would you truly plot against them? Keren wondered. She dared not ask. They all seemed loyal to Nimr-Rada, though not to Ra-Anan.

Their furtive conversation was cut short by Na'ah, Gebuwrah, and Alatah, who presented beaten copper trays and large wooden dishes of food. Cold spiced-honey roasted quails, lamb stewed with olives and aromatic herbs, salt-toasted nuts, fresh fruit, pungent vegetables preserved in vinegar, chilled fruit juice, and the ever-present heaps of flat bread, baked and softened with oil.

As they ate, Keren noticed that Neshar was frequently glancing just beyond her. Wondering, Keren looked over her shoulder. Revakhaw was there, eyeing Neshar, and she seemed unabashed that Keren had noticed their silent flirtation.

Leaning toward Keren, and shielding her face from Neshar's view, Revakhaw whispered, "Lady, your brother there is as handsome as you are beautiful."

"You insult my brother," Keren said.

Revakhaw laughed and turned away, gathering emptied platters and bowls, while Neshar studied her every move. He *was* handsome, Keren decided, secretly proud of him—of all her brothers. It would please her if Neshar might someday request Revakhaw as his wife, for Revakhaw already seemed like a sister to Keren. But would Nimr-Rada allow Revakhaw—or any of Keren's attendants—to leave her household to be married? Surely Nimr-Rada wouldn't be so cruel as to deny this. She would have to ask Ra-Anan. Politely.

Too soon, the impromptu feast ended. The sun was setting, and Alatah and Tsinnah were bringing out the tallow-filled lamps of clay, trimming the plaited grass wicks, and lighting them carefully. Noticing that her brothers were becoming restless, Keren stood. Her legs and feet tingled uncomfortably, half numb from kneeling for such a long time.

"We leave before dawn, Lady," Neshar said, apologizing for their departure.

"Tell me that I'll see you again," Keren begged, aware of Revakhaw lingering nearby.

"Perhaps you will." Neshar's expression was circumspect now, all thoughts of Revakhaw apparently, necessarily, disregarded. He stepped nearer, an arm's length away. In a barely audible whisper, he said, "We may be parted for years. Listen, my sister: Learn to use your weapons. And judge everything coldly. I know you detest what I'm saying, but for your own sake you must protect yourself. Trust no one. And treasure your isolation. If you manage everything respectfully, I don't believe Nimr-Rada would kill you. However, he and Ra-Anan will have you enmeshed in countless maddening plots."

Suddenly, he looked very much like Eliyshama, young and worried. Keren watched him intently, trying to hear his every word. He hesitated, then said softly, "I don't wish to see you enslaved here forever, but if our father arrives in the Great City, don't let him try to take you away. Quiet as he is, you know he has a temper, and it won't go well with him if he threatens He-Who-Lifts-the-Skies. You must make our father leave you here willingly. For his life, my own sister, I beg you to weigh every word you say in our father's presence."

Keren's mouth went dry. She hadn't considered this possibility. "Do you think our father would actually come here?"

"Yes." Neshar's face hardened, older now. "Remembering our father, he will try to save you from this place. And from He-Who-Lifts-the-Skies. Again, I beg you, if you cherish our father, you must make him leave you here. Reject him."

If Neshar had beaten her, he could not have upset her so badly. She turned away, feeling ill. When her brothers finally left, Keren lingered in the darkening courtyard, desolate as an abandoned child. Reject her father?

"I can't," she whispered to no one. "I can't."

Twelve

"TELL ME WHAT my brothers say of me," Ra-Anan commanded, as Keren knelt before him beneath a shading canopy in his courtyard.

Keren folded her hands in her lap, hoping she appeared tranquil, though she was sweating in the midday heat. Ra-Anan's servants had brought her nothing to drink, which was good; today Ra-Anan would not detain her to point out all her failings in a long lesson of manners. He simply wanted information.

She refused politely. "What can I tell you about our brothers that you do not already know, O Master Ra-Anan?"

"Very little." Ra-Anan leaned forward, aggravated, his deep-set eyes narrowing as he spoke. "And I am sure that is all you intend to tell me: very little."

When she remained silent, merely staring down at her fingers plaited together in her lap, he said, "Neshar and the others have caused you nothing but trouble. Why should you protect them?"

"They are my own brothers—the sons of my father and mother. And whatever troubles they've unintentionally caused, at least I know they care for me."

"Hence all their warnings against me," Ra-Anan observed darkly.

She wondered at his tone. He sounded as if his brothers had—by their warnings—opened a festering wound. "Are you surprised by this?"

"Not at all. I expected that they would disown me. But you, my sister, have you disowned me as well?"

Keren hesitated, then decided to be blunt. "If I disown you as my brother, Ra-Anan, it will be a decision you have made for me by your own actions."

"And, likewise, my sister, if I turn against you, it will be a decision you have made for me by your own actions."

Trading him stare for stare, Keren said, "I don't pretend to understand you, Master Ra-Anan, but I don't consider myself your enemy."

"Indeed?" He was contemptuous, making Keren grit her teeth as he sneered. "You resist my every suggestion. You ignore my advice. You listen to those who hate me. Dear sister, I am *glad* you are not my enemy."

Infuriated, she burst out, "I resist your advice because you give it in your own best interests, not mine! You're just like Sharah!" To her satisfaction, he looked shocked by the comparison. "I wish you would tell me why you've brought me to the Great City. Why should you endure me when I'm unwilling to be here? It's not because you feel any sense of duty or loyalty or love toward me—because I know you don't. So it can only be that I'm useful to you somehow, being such an oddity."

"You are right, of course," he agreed, his face settling into its usual cold mask. "Why else would I trouble myself with such a boring, rebellious *child* such as yourself? Whether you like it or not, you are useful to me, so I will keep you here and you will accept that fact. Sadly, you are not as intelligent as I thought; I am amazed that it took you weeks to reach such an obvious conclusion."

"Weeks? I've known the truth since our first meeting!" She almost screamed the words. She longed to shove him, to beat him. Brother or not, she wanted to repay his insults with her own hands.

A movement to her right caught her attention. Zehker. By his silent approach, he warned her to control her fatal impulse. Curling her hands into hard fists upon her knees, Keren exhaled before trusting herself to speak again. Ra-Anan was watching her carefully, his dark eyes reflecting a secretive enjoyment of the situation.

Keren spoke to Zehker first. "Thank you, Zehker. Please, bring me my bow but not an arrow. I need to hold something to remind myself that I must not touch my brother; he's not immune to the death order."

"Very good," Ra-Anan approved, lowering his voice as Zehker went to get her bow. "I deserved that threat. But if you ever touch me, my sister, I will kill you with my bare hands. I will be put to death, but you will die first—and in great pain."

Calmer now, she endured his warning, but she couldn't help retorting, "A brother and a sister die tragically by an order from He-Who-Lifts-the-Skies—because the sister scorned the Great King. *That* story would be worthy of an endless chant to be composed by one of your devoted pupils."

"Among whom you are numbered."

"Not that it does any good." Keren grimaced, remembering her music lessons. Ra-Anan's ideas of music were droning, monotonous, mournful chants, usually without the softening touch of flutes, chimes, or strings. She couldn't believe that he wanted her to learn such horrible music. Another thought occurred to her then. She lifted her chin, challenging him. "If I am your pupil, Master Ra-Anan, then isn't it your duty to answer my questions?"

"Only if your questions apply to the lesson at hand."

"Because you haven't declared my lesson for the day, then I will ask you an all-encompassing question."

He smiled a thin, waiting smile. "Ask."

Zehker approached, offering Keren a yew bow. She thanked him and set the bow on her knees, smiling grimly because the ever cautious Zehker had cut the bowstring, leaving her only the stave. Did he think she had arrows in her robes?

Looking at Ra-Anan once more, she said, "Master Ra-Anan: During all my weeks in the Great City and among the surrounding tribes, no one has spoken of the Most High. The nearest reference to Him is 'by the heavens,' which isn't a reference to Him at all. And no one offers Him sacrifices. Why does everyone despise Him?"

Inclining his head slightly, his thin smile still evident, Ra-Anan said, "There are other ways of expressing our devotion."

"But not to the Most High," Keren persisted. "You—all of you—express your devotion to the heavens only. You give no reverence toward the Most High."

Ra-Anan's tight smile eased, and he lifted his hands, the sudden embodiment of a reasonable teacher. "Beneath the freedom of these heavens, and ruled by our protector, He-Who-Lifts-the-Skies, how can we not be glad and praise our liberty?"

He had not answered her question directly, and yet he had told her everything. Her heart sank. Slowly, she rephrased his answer aloud, faltering. "You—and everyone in your Great City—perceive the loving care and wisdom of the Most High as oppressive. And the remoteness of these uncaring heavens is . . . a blessing to you."

Still reasonable, he said, "Here on the plains, we have the warmth of our guiding sun. The rains come when our fields must be flooded in the spring, and the cruel storms of winter are withheld from us—unlike those who live in the mountains. How can we consider ourselves anything but blessed if all these good things come to us from the heavens?"

Ignoring his veiled slur against those who lived in the mountains, Keren matched his reasoning tone as she argued, "The gifts of these heavens are provided by the Most High. And He created the sun—*Shemesh*—to be our servant. Shouldn't we worship Him for granting us such undeserved mercy?"

"Mercy in what?" Ra-Anan asked, unusually gentle. "Look around you, my sister. We are not afflicted in any way. Why should we cry for mercy if we are not afflicted?"

"You have truly rejected Him," Keren murmured, clutching the bow stave on her knees. She was frightened by the extent of the spiritual rebellion in this Great City. How could these people not perceive the love of the Most High? How could they reject Him when He simply desired them to live in harmony with Him in expectation of the Promised One? She shook her head. "I'll never understand. . . ."

"When you are older, my sister, when you have seen more of life beneath these heavens, you will understand.

For now, however, don't trouble yourself with these difficult thoughts. Are you not blessed as we are blessed? Be content; enjoy the freedoms that He-Who-Lifts-the-Skies has given us in his Great City."

Freedoms? Keren almost sniffed aloud at the idea. Why couldn't anyone see the restraints Nimr-Rada had cast over all their lives for the sake of his own personal gain, and his insatiable desire for power? How could they possibly believe that they were free?

As she was considering this, Ra-Anan said, "Neshar warned you that our father might attempt to take you from our Great City. Neshar is right to be concerned. What will you tell our father when he comes here?"

Keren stared at Ra-Anan, speechless. How had he heard of Neshar's quiet warning? Had one of the servants or guardsmen been able to listen unnoticed? Or could one of her own attendants be an informant—Gebuwrah, perhaps? Another possibility occurred to her then. She narrowed her eyes at Ra-Anan. "Did you truly release our brothers? Or have you enslaved them again?"

"They are all free and riding off in separate directions," Ra-Anan said, though the smoothness of his voice was not reassuring. "And if you behave yourself, they will continue to enjoy their freedoms. Tell me what you will say to our father."

"You questioned our brothers again before sending them away, didn't you?" Keren accused, refusing to be distracted. "Which brother did you torment into revealing what Neshar said? Kana? Miyka? Or was it Mattan? You're disgusting."

"I am merely careful," Ra-Anan countered. "How can I prevent you from behaving foolishly if I do not know what rebellious ideas have been poured into your receptive little mind? Now tell me: What will you say to our father when he arrives?"

"I don't know what I'll say." Keren rapped the stave against her knees, wishing Ra-Anan would actually become the snake he so strongly resembled. Then she could beat him to death. *No,* she scolded herself. *Not to death.* She prayed she would never become as hardened toward death as He-Who-Lifts-the-Skies. Or Ra-Anan.

Staring at Ra-Anan, she said, "Whatever I say, my brother, I will say it because I care for our father—which is more than you will do, I'm sure."

"Believe me, I don't wish to see our father die. Listen, my sister: Convince He-Who-Lifts-the-Skies of your devotion to him! Convince our father of the same thing. Then he will leave us alone, and our Great King won't harm him."

Keren leaned forward, shaking her head vehemently. "No. You just want me to bow to your Nimr-Rada. You want me to flatter him, praise him, and adore him—to make him my Lord of the Earth. I can't do that, and you know it."

"It would be easier than watching our father die."

"It would be easier for me to die."

"Perhaps it would."

She glared at him. He was so venomous she could no longer endure his presence. "May I leave now, O Master Ra-Anan?"

He smiled again, the thin brittle smile. "I've said all I need to say. You may go."

"Did you tell her all that I commanded you to say?"

182

Nimr-Rada asked, toying with an empty hammered-gold cup as they sat in the dim coolness of his spacious main room. He had just returned from his daily hunt and had sent for Ra-Anan without warning. "Did you tell her that she must behave during her father's impending visit?"

Ra-Anan nodded. The question caught him midsip; he was thirsty, having just arrived. Swallowing neatly, he said, "I told her that for his own safety, she must convince our father of her devotion to you, my Lord."

"And will she?"

Moistening his lips, Ra-Anan set down his black-glazed clay cup, then paused for added effect. "At this time, she says she would rather die. As young and stubborn as she is, I think she believes what she says. When the time comes, however, I am sure she will reconsider."

"There are other ways to achieve the same result," said Nimr-Rada, drawing his full lips together in a thoughtful bow. Raising one dark eyebrow, he asked, "What of her devotion to those Ancient Ones and their beliefs?"

"She is still loyal to them. But she has more to consider now; I pointed out to her that we are blessed, happy, and free here on the plains. Essentially, we do as we please, yet we have not been cursed by her Most High. And life is much easier for those who live here under your rule than it is for those who live in the mountains in the shadow of her Most High. I will allow those thoughts to gnaw into her mind for a while, then talk to her again. Time, separation from those Ancient Ones, and a life of comparative ease will certainly have an effect on her opinions."

"Does she still refuse to wear the ornaments and garments I commanded for her?"

"Again, she is young and stubborn. She doesn't like

calling attention to herself."

"Unlike her sister," Nimr-Rada growled, leaning back and contemplating the dried skins, horns, and other hunting mementos that adorned the walls of his main room. "Let me consider the matter further. I have an idea, but it will take time to arrange everything. Meanwhile, I am counting on you to convince my foolish wife that she must discipline herself. Otherwise she will suffer unwelcome changes."

Hearing this, Ra-Anan relaxed and took another sip of cooling watered wine. The mercenary Sharah would be far easier to deal with than the idealistic Keren. "Command me, my Lord. I will convince her of whatever she must do."

"Why should I need lessons from you?" Sharah demanded, storming into Ra-Anan's dusk- and torchlit courtyard, her lovely, pale face antagonistic. "Is this another one of your little whims, Ra-Anan?"

"No, your lessons were commanded by the Great King, and you know it. Do not try to evade us in this, my sister. These lessons are necessary. And all the tantrums you could possibly subject me to will only heighten the seriousness of your situation."

"You don't command me!" she screeched, waving her gold-decked hands to emphasize her words.

Undisturbed by her fury, Ra-Anan relaxed on his mat and waited. As he expected, it took her more than an instant to perceive the threat he had implied.

At last she halted and frowned. "The seriousness of my situation?"

He nodded, then flicked a hand toward the mat Keren had occupied earlier that afternoon. The canopy that had shaded them was now replaced by a multitude of flaring, crackling torches anchored between the paving bricks. Ra-Anan wanted to see Sharah's every expression, her every move. As she knelt on the mat before him, Ra-Anan said, "Our Great King is bored with you. More than bored. He is completely dissatisfied; he regrets making you his wife."

"What?" She gawked at him, obviously unable to say more than that one word.

Knowing he had her attention now, Ra-Anan listed her faults, sparing her nothing. "Close your mouth and compose yourself; never allow your weakness to show. Obviously, that dignity you pretend to have is useless. Also, you are lazy. You have no discretion. Only trivial matters hold your attention. You have made no attempt to bring yourself into favor with the people of the Great City. You are cruel, untrustworthy, and have tantrums. . . ."

"Never in the presence of the Great King," Sharah interrupted, justifying herself.

"You are evasive," Ra-Anan continued. "And greedy. In short, you are worse than a child and must grow up. If you do not improve your character and make yourself deserving of your position, then the Great King will discard you. Those unique looks you are so proud of are the only praiseworthy trait you possess, and he is used to those now."

"He loathes me?" Sharah shook her head, as if unable to believe what she was hearing. Denying responsibility, she protested in an almost wailing tone, "My looks were the only reason he desired to have me in the first place— he voiced no other expectations of me. For him to demand all this now is completely unfair!"

She was so contemptibly pathetic that Ra-Anan longed to laugh. But the situation was serious: Her downfall might bring about his own disfavor. He had to retrain her completely. "Instead of grasping for all those ornaments you crave, you will work to enrich your mind," he told her. "And it won't be enough to pretend to change. He-Who-Lifts-the-Skies will see through you at once. He is as cunning and cruel as one of his cherished leopards. Never forget that.

"Now, the first thing you must do is to apologize to him for your failings. Then you must discipline yourself to learn new things and to take an interest in others. It would also help your situation if you will bear him a son."

"He's said nothing of wanting a child!" Sharah snapped, abandoning her wailing tone. "And I don't wish to be burdened with a child; they are horrible to bear, not to mention the effect on my looks."

"He does not think of children yet," Ra-Anan conceded. "But if you gave him sons who would follow him and honor him, then He-Who-Lifts-the-Skies would be less likely to abandon you."

Sharah lowered her eyes, smoldering, but not faulting his logic, which pleased Ra-Anan. Even she—dense as she was—could comprehend that a tribe of worshipful sons and daughters might appeal to Nimr-Rada's vanity. As Ra-Anan waited for Sharah to formulate a reply, Ra-Anan's wife, Zeva'ah, emerged from the shadows of the house, bearing a reed tray laden with cups of wine and an appealing assortment of nuts, fruits, cakes, and delicately smoked meats.

Clad in a subtly woven, flowing robe of tawny fabric, Zeva'ah knelt gracefully near Sharah, bowed her sleek dark head, and offered Sharah a red-glazed cup of new wine. Sharah took the cup silently.

"Thank my wife," Ra-Anan prompted Sharah. "Consider this your first lesson, my sister."

"I never see you thanking your servants," Sharah argued, her temper flaring again.

"My wife is not a servant," Ra-Anan pointed out. "She honors you by her actions, therefore you should thank her and ask her if she is well. If you value your place, you will always do this for her and for anyone else who honors you. Do it!"

"Thank you . . ." Sharah hesitated, her expression going blank.

"Zeva'ah," Ra-Anan's wife reminded Sharah softly. "You are welcome, Lady."

"Ask if my wife is well," Ra-Anan prodded.

Sharah flashed him a cold look but complied. "Are you well, Zeva'ah?"

"Oh, very," she answered, smiling and gracious. "Thank you, Lady. If I can help you in any way, do not hesitate to ask." Turning to Ra-Anan, she said, "Do you need me to stay, or should I go?"

"As you please," Ra-Anan told her politely, knowing she would go. Zeva'ah despised Sharah but hid this fact beautifully. She left them, the epitome of a perfect wife.

"She is with child again," Ra-Anan told Sharah when they were alone. "At your next lesson, you will ask her if her pregnancy is faring well."

"You are enjoying this—humiliating me!" Sharah accused.

He was enjoying himself but would never tell her so. Instead, he reminded her, "This is for your own sake. If you do not work to change yourself, then you will be sent away with nothing but your clothes. What will happen to you then, my sister?"

She scowled at him but said nothing. Ra-Anan smiled inwardly, gratified.

❦ ❦

Unable to relax, thinking of her father, Keren walked out into her courtyard and looked up at the stars.

The loyal Revakhaw trailed outside also, lingering just behind her. As if hearing her thoughts, her attendant asked, "What will you say to your father, Lady?"

"I pray I'll know that when I see him," Keren sighed.

Low guardsmen's voices echoed into the courtyard, making them both turn toward the sounds. Lawkham and Zehker were kneeling on the timber, reed, and clay roof of Keren's house, apparently on watch. Moving near, she called to them as loudly as she dared, not wishing to disturb nearby households. "How did you get up there?"

Lawkham leaned over the edge of her roof, shadowed in the moonlight. "We climbed the wall, Lady. We can see most of the surrounding area from here. Do we disturb you?"

"No," she said, intrigued, "but I would like to climb up there myself."

In response, Zehker descended to the top of the courtyard wall, then dropped carefully, easily, into the courtyard. As he approached, Revakhaw retreated; Zehker's stoic ways intimidated her. "A ladder will be safer for you, Lady," he informed Keren. "We will make one later."

"But not tonight?" she asked, hearing his unspoken words.

"Not tonight," he agreed.

Undaunted by his refusal, she studied the hardened, impenetrable outlines of his face, wishing she could see his expression in the darkness. "Why did you cut the string from my bow today? Did you think that I would kill our Master Ra-Anan?"

"A precaution only."

"To protect him?"

"And you. He is also a warrior. A weapon can be made of anything."

"Including the stave," she pointed out. "If Ra-Anan is so dangerous, should you have given me the stave?"

"You requested the stave, Lady. I obeyed." Pausing, he added quietly, "I would have stopped him."

"But you wouldn't have killed him, would you?"

"If need be."

The thought chilled her. "I'll be more careful in the future," she promised.

"Thank you, Lady." He bowed his head and started to turn away, but then he looked back. "Your father must be protected."

"You think Neshar was right? And Ra-Anan too?"

"Yes."

"Thank you, Zehker."

Unhappily, Keren recognized a weakness in Zehker's logic, and in Ra-Anan's, and Neshar's: If she bowed to Nimr-Rada in her father's presence, then her father would certainly grab her and shake her in a fatal reprimand. How could she protect Meshek without bowing to Nimr-Rada? Feeling sick within, Keren looked up at the heavens again and prayed to the Most High for an answer.

Thirteen

KEREN DISMOUNTED in the courtyard, stroking the black mane of her precious new horse, Dobe. Zehker had decided that Dobe should be hers because he was placid, almost sluggish, and safely dull. But Keren didn't care. *You have the most beautiful eyes,* she thought to the patient animal. *If my eyes were as dark as yours, then I wouldn't be here today; I would be free. I would be preparing to wed Yithran.*

With a small pang, she pushed away all thoughts of Yithran and marriage. She had to focus on covering the wearied Dobe with a fleece and rubbing his hide with a soft swatch of leather, then combing him gently. Her early morning rides were the most enjoyable part of her day, despite the weaponry lessons that inevitably accompanied them. And caring for Dobe never seemed like work.

Keren patted the horse's tawny neck, pleased to feel his muscles quiver beneath her hands. As she stepped back, Lawkham approached, bowed his head to Keren, and chirruped merrily, turning Dobe toward the stables, which were separated from her residence to lessen the swarms of flies.

"Thank you, Lawkham," Keren called after him, grateful that he had behaved himself this morning, teasing her less than usual.

"Certainly, Lady." Lawkham paused then, as if remembering some minor detail. "I should tell you that my mother has asked to meet you and present you with some gifts. She should be here just after midday."

Keren stared at him, openmouthed. No wonder he'd been so pleasant this morning. "Your mother?"

"Yes, I do have a mother," said Lawkham, obviously amused by Keren's shock. "Her name is Meherah."

Meherah, Keren thought. *Hurry*. Appropriate. She would have to hurry all the time to keep up with a son like Lawkham.

"How like you," Keren told Lawkham, feigning disgust. "You say nothing of your mother during all these weeks, but this very morning, you tell me that she will visit my household just after midday. When did she arrive in the Great City?"

"Last night—with my father and my younger brother and sisters."

"And you've managed to keep it a secret all this time? Amazing. Well, now that you've told me about my visitor, you have to get the horses out of the courtyard so we can prepare everything to welcome her."

"As you say, Lady. I'll have Erek scrape up the horse dung," Lawkham answered genially. He loved to harass the egotistical Erek, provoking conflicts that upset the entire household.

Keren lifted her hands, halting him. "Don't annoy Erek, Lawkham, please."

"You're saying I should scrape the dung myself?"

"Your mother will be touched by your consideration," Keren said warmly. She hurried inside before he could disagree.

Gebuwrah, Alatah, and Na'ah were in the cool, shadowed main room of Keren's house, crouching on the woven grass mats, paring a large heap of assorted fruits and vegetables for their midday meal. Tsinnah and Revakhaw were there as well, settling in after their ride with Keren, preparing to grind wheat for cakes.

"We are going to have a visitor," Keren told them. "Lawkham's mother, Meherah, is coming to see us early this afternoon."

"Aha! The first woman to officially visit you since we've been here!" Revakhaw exulted, sifting grain through her brown fingers into a broad, hollowed stone mortar. "Truly, we must celebrate."

"We're supposed to finish your new attire today, Lady," Gebuwrah reminded Keren firmly. "And Master Ra-Anan has asked that when you call on him this evening you should bring all the ornaments he selected."

"I think he means that you should wear them, Lady," Na'ah said, cautiously placing her flint knife on a nearby tray. She said no more but watched Keren's reaction.

Keren suppressed a groan of frustration. The symbol-incised gold ornaments and fine materials so highly regarded by Nimr-Rada and Ra-Anan were completely impractical. Until now, she had pretended to forget that she was supposed to wear them.

"The headpiece is too heavy," she complained. "Also, I have to remove the sandals before I can kneel—not to mention that they blister my feet. And we have yet to create a fabric gown that won't split at the seams or flap in the wind when I'm riding. If we can't do better, then I must wear my leather tunics and leggings."

"I have an idea, Lady," Tsinnah began shyly. "We should dress you in layers of fabric rather than one long gown."

"She would swelter in the heat beneath layers of fabric," Gebuwrah argued, reaching for another tuber.

"No, she wouldn't," Tsinnah said, "not as I imagine her attire."

"Gebuwrah's right," Alatah spoke gently, not looking up from the bowl of dried fruit she was seeding. "It's too warm for us to dress her in layers."

"Let Tsinnah describe the gown to us!" Revakhaw brandished her oval grinding stone at Gebuwrah. "Truly, it might be better than you believe."

"Let's forget about my would-be attire until we've prepared food for our guest," Keren urged, waving her hands to catch their attention.

"You're right, Lady," Revakhaw answered obligingly. "We can argue later."

Keren sighed, thankful, and prayed they would forget about her garments altogether. Why should she have to wear such ridiculous clothes? Sharah would enjoy all this fuss over gowns and ornaments. Frowning at the thought of her sister, Keren reached for a grinding stone and measured some wheat into a mortar. Lately, Sharah had taken to riding through the Great City with Nimr-Rada during his frequent inspections, displaying all her fine robes, new ornaments, and impressive retinue of attendants, while actually speaking to the citizens in the streets. Keren, however, rarely spoke to her.

I pray you are satisfied, Keren thought to her sister as she

193

rubbed the heavy stone over the tan-husked grains in her mortar. *Your new happiness was purchased at an appalling cost to your husband and your beautiful infant son. I wonder if you'll ever regret coming here.*

Keren and her household spent the remainder of the morning cooking, cleaning, and preparing an eating area in the courtyard, with thick mats and a temporary leather canopy for shade. At last, pleased with their accomplishments, Keren went inside to wash herself and change into a fresh tunic.

Gebuwrah was there, her jaw set stubbornly. Silently she pointed to a heap of fine pale fabric and to Keren's ornaments, which she had arranged in a lavish display.

"Not now, Gebuwrah, please," Keren begged. "I want to be comfortable while I'm visiting with Lawkham's mother."

"Her visit is not as important as your meeting with our Master Ra-Anan," Gebuwrah insisted. "Why should you make him angry because you wish to eat and gossip instead of tending to his requests?"

"I won't be *gossiping*," Keren said, frustrated. Truly, Gebuwrah was making herself the lead attendant, seeming to expect everyone, including Keren, to follow her dictates.

Gebuwrah opened her mouth, then shut it hard. When she spoke, her bossy tone diminished. "As you say, Lady. But please, at least let us try this new fabric." Tsinnah and the others were filing in from the courtyard now, and Gebuwrah added grudgingly, "Perhaps we could test Tsinnah's theory of the layers."

"It wouldn't be complicated, Lady," Tsinnah assured her eagerly. "And I hope you won't be scandalized, but I think it should begin as if we were clothing you like a man but make the undergarments fuller. Then finish as if

194

you were actually wearing a long, open robe and a belt, which would be more practical for riding than a simple tunic."

Keren listened, shocked but curious. Tsinnah and the others debated the design, while Tsinnah scratched a rough drawing on a clay platter with a piece of red ochre. They took one of Keren's rejected tunics in the same pale fabric, cut off the skirt, then made Keren put on the top over her short undergarments. Without hesitation, Tsinnah took a longer rectangle of fabric and tied one of its narrow finished edges around Keren's waist over the half tunic, knotting it at Keren's back. Then, drawing the excess fabric between and behind Keren's legs, Tsinnah tucked the remaining narrow edge firmly into, and completely around, the waistband formed by the first knot. Finishing, she folded another strip of fabric to form a wide belt, which she wrapped around Keren's waist, tucking in the ends to cover the knots.

The effect was similar to the garb of a man, but much longer, flaring at her calves like a skirt, yet fitting closely to her waist and hips. "*This* will not flap about in the wind, Lady," Tsinnah assured her, looking thoroughly pleased.

"Of course it won't flap about in the wind; I've never worn anything so tight in my life! Tsinnah, this reveals everything."

"Lady, by the heavens, you're almost completely covered," Revakhaw protested enthusiastically, her eyes sparkling. "Only your arms are bare, and from just above your ankles down to your feet. You are more beautiful than ever."

"We'll also make you a long open-fronted robe, Lady," Gebuwrah decided. To Tsinnah, she said, "You were right; this is what she should wear."

"I want clothing like this," Alatah said. Instantly, they all agreed—except Keren.

A piercing whistle sounded in the courtyard. Lawkham.

"Our visitor is here." Keren raised her voice to be heard—they were ignoring her again. "Go greet her while I put on a decent tunic."

"No," Gebuwrah insisted. "Lady, we must ask this Meherah's opinion of your new attire."

Gebuwrah, Revakhaw, and the others dragged Keren into the sunlit courtyard; someone pulled her hair, making her stumble. Recovering her balance, Keren shook off their hands, rubbed her scalp, and glared at them. Then, chin up, she greeted Meherah, who was tiny, lovely, and standing beside the speechless Lawkham.

"Please, Lawkham," Keren prompted, embarrassed, "introduce me to your mother."

Lawkham swallowed. "Lady, this is my own mother, Meherah. Mother, this is our Lady . . . Keren."

"We are pleased to have you visit us today," Keren murmured.

Clasping her hands politely, Meherah bowed her dark, braid-bound head, then sucked in her breath as she looked up at Keren. She was obviously fascinated by Keren's attire. When she spoke, her voice was warm and musical. "Lady, I'm honored that you've agreed to meet me; thank you. I've brought you some gifts, and I won't stay long."

"But you must stay and eat with us," Keren said, liking her at once. Meherah seemed as charming as Lawkham at his best. "As you noticed, we need you to settle a dispute. I disapprove of my new clothes, but my attendants seem to think they're perfect."

Turning to Lawkham and the other guardsmen, who

were all silent and gaping, she said, "Thank you, Law-kham. Now, please leave. All of you. Go eat."

They all filed out meekly. Lawkham and Erek glanced back over their shoulders at her, then paused at the gate to whisper something to the guard on duty, Zehker. When all the guardsmen had departed through the gate, Zehker leaned in, looked around quietly, then gave Keren an enigmatic glance before closing her inside with her attendants.

Discomfited, Keren led Meherah to the shaded canopy and urged her to sit on the fleece-padded mats.

As Keren poured cups of cooled juice for her guest and herself, Meherah said, "You mustn't worry about your appearance, Lady; the garments enhance your looks wonderfully. By the heavens, you will inspire every woman in the city. No doubt they will copy your new clothes as soon as they can lay hands on any sort of fabric. Then you won't feel so conspicuous."

"But I will be conspicuous," Keren protested miserably. "The Great King has sent me a formidable collection of ornaments to wear whenever I step outside my gates. It's bad enough that I'll frighten everyone I meet, but now I'll blind them as well."

Meherah laughed—Lawkham's mischievous laugh—and her eyes glistened. "I think you are simply not used to such attention, child. Please, I would enjoy seeing all these 'formidable' ornaments."

Instantly, Alatah and Revakhaw scrambled up from their mats and ran inside to gather the ornaments.

Keren reluctantly smiled at Meherah. "Mother of Law-kham, it's good to be called *child* again. Sometimes I think there are no true elders in this Great City. If so, then they are too quiet."

Meherah's expression softened. "Lady, forgive me. I should not have called you that. But I know something of your situation, and I wish to help you in whatever way I can. Above all, if I could say anything to you, it would be that you should be at rest in your thoughts. From what I've heard, you are much admired in this Great City—though, if I may say so, your eyes do cause an impulse of fear. You amaze everyone.

"Now, here come your attendants with these ornaments. Please, later, I beg you to try them on for my sake. But first, let me give you these few tokens of regard from my family."

Meherah went to the gate and retrieved a large, heavy basket, refusing assistance from anyone. "Use these as you wish, Lady," she said, kneeling before Keren once more.

Her gift, carelessly presented, was a beautifully matched set of clay serving dishes. Keren lifted one of the pitchers reverently. It revealed an extraordinary mastery of clay—so thin, smooth, and strong that it produced a marvelous ringing tone in her hands. And it was adorned with meticulously incised lines and dots—a more subtle and restful pattern than the heavy, boldly painted black dishes most people used.

"Mother of Lawkham, these are wonderful—thank you! We must use them now, for our little feast."

"No-no-no, why should you give me such an honor?" Meherah protested. But Keren could see that she was justifiably proud of her family's craftsmanship.

Throughout their feast, Meherah talked easily, laughingly, her small work-hardened hands fluttering at the height of every story or joke. She praised the food, the spiced grains, the roasted venison, the vegetables—seasoned with herbs, olive oil, and garlic—accompanied by the usual flat grain cakes, and an immense platter of fresh and dried fruits, artfully arranged by Na'ah.

Meherah told of seeing He-Who-Lifts-the-Skies for the first time at a hunt where he killed his first leopard, and of how he had encouraged the other young men of various tribes to follow him and subdue all the wild creatures that were terrorizing the tribal settlements. Then she described two of the First Fathers—Yepheth and the famed Khawm, who was supposedly the most rebellious son of the patriarch Noakh, but so captivating that the stories of his defiance were difficult to believe. She also told Keren that she had met two of the First Mothers, the revered fabric maker, Ghinnah, and the exquisitely beautiful Tirzah. They both looked so young. How could anyone believe they had lived through the Great Destruction? It was almost too incredible to believe.

The afternoon passed quickly. In Meherah's refreshing company, Keren felt better than she had at any time since her arrival in the Great City.

When she had finished her food, Meherah sighed contentedly. "That was a wonderful meal. Your mothers taught you well. Now, let's persuade our Lady Keren to wear her dreadful ornaments."

They all laughed and relaxed, passing the ornaments one by one to Meherah, who praised them and insisted that Keren must wear each piece. To humor her guest, Keren donned the heavy gold necklace garnished with bloodred stones, the wide symbol-engraved gold cuffs for her wrists, the matching gold cuffs for her ankles, the thick gold rings, and her headpiece—a slender rim of hammered gold, mounted with three small, beautifully fashioned, rippling points of gold. Ra-Anan insisted that these points of gold gave the effect of rays of sunlight—

to honor Keren's name. But Keren didn't see this head-piece as an honor. It was a burden, as were all the other ornaments.

Meherah thought they were delightful. She gazed at Keren, enthralled as a child, clasping her hands beneath her chin. "Who could compare to you?" she asked. Without waiting for an answer, she said, "I know what's need-ed! Listen; I think you should darken your eyes."

"Darken my eyes?" Keren leaned forward, fascinated, wondering if she had heard Meherah clearly—it sounded like a dream. "How could I possibly darken my eyes?"

"Easily, Lady. You won't believe the effect when you see it; your entire face will change." Meherah dispatched Tsinnah and Alatah to retrieve clay and sandstone lamps from inside Keren's house, pleading with them to also bring red ochre and purified oils.

"Now, I'll tell you, Lady, to the south and west of this great city is the tribe of Mitzrayim, an uncle of He-Who-Lifts-the-Skies. The women of Mitzrayim's tribe darken their eyes with lampblack to protect themselves against the glare of the sun. The effect is wonderful. I've seen it done, and I'll show you. First, I must wash my hands and dip them in some oil to make the lampblack like an oint-ment."

Chatting agreeably, Meherah dabbed purified oils on her clean hands, then ran her fingertips over the darkened interiors of the lamps until she had created an impromptu black paste. Then she knelt before Keren. "Look upward, Lady, without moving." Meherah ran her fingertips along the innermost edges of Keren's eyelids, a movement so ef-ficient and quick that Keren was certain Meherah had practiced this before. "Now, some red ochre," Meherah announced. After washing her hands again, she rubbed

Tsinnah's bit of red ochre on the flat, unglazed edge of a clay lamp. The rasping sound made Keren shiver. "Hold still once more, then you may look in your mirror, Lady."

Keren submitted to Meherah's ministrations uneasily now, for Meherah was dabbing a concoction of red ochre and pure, solidified oils on Keren's lips. Gebuwrah, silent and watchful, handed Keren her small, heavy, rough-backed obsidian mirror. Shifting her position to catch the late afternoon sunlight, Keren gazed into the polished surface of the dark mirror. The rims of her eyelids were indeed very black, but this only heightened the startling effect of her pale eyes—not at all what she had anticipated or wanted. And the red ochre paste exaggerated her lips flagrantly, making her seem harder, older, and completely unlike herself.

"You don't like it," Meherah said, exhaling the words in a dramatic, mourning sigh, as Lawkham often did when trying to coax Keren to agree with him.

"I look very different," Keren began, not wishing to offend her guest.

"But, Lady, you look wonderful, not terrible," Reva-khaw added, obviously delighted. "I want to try this on my own eyes."

"If you all darkened your eyes this way—and wore the new attire and ornaments—you would be amazing," Meherah told them. Gebuwrah, Revakhaw, and Tsinnah agreed, but Na'ah and Alatah looked nervous. Before they could argue, the gate opened. Zehker stepped inside, admitting Ra-Anan's rude guard, Perek.

After gawking at Keren, Perek remembered his few manners and bowed his head respectfully. The instant he lifted his head, however, all courtesy was gone. He strode forward, angrily brandishing his longspear. "You've kept our Master Ra-Anan waiting, Lady," he said accusingly. "And He-Who-Lifts-the-Skies is waiting with him—in the company of his lady, your sister. You are commanded to come at once."

"I—have to go to my privy," Keren told him, almost stammering, she was so taken aback. "I can't show myself to them yet."

Swiftly the guard positioned himself between Keren and the doorway to her house. "I don't wish to die, Lady," he said, holding out his longspear to fend her off. "But I must fulfill my orders; you will leave now."

"We are all with you, Lady," Tsinnah promised beneath her breath, though Gebuwrah was shaking her head. "Whatever you say, we will do." Revakhaw and the others were gathering around her now, in a show of silent support.

Keren shook her head, for once agreeing with Gebuwrah. "Let's not invite disaster. I'll walk there right now, barefoot and looking ridiculous."

"I'm sorry to cause you such trouble." Meherah sounded anxious. "I'll go with you and explain that I'm at fault for detaining you."

"Perhaps He-Who-Lifts-the-Skies will be pleased to see you again," Keren agreed. "But I doubt that my brother and my sister will care to know why I'm late."

Led by Zehker, and followed by the obdurate Perek, they walked through the hardened clay streets. Keren braced herself against the feel of the dirt on her bare feet, and against the shocked stares of the citizens who happened to see her pass. She wouldn't have blamed them if they laughed at her outrageous appearance. Perhaps later she might be amused, remembering this scene she was creating. At the moment, however, she was angry. When they reached Ra-Anan's residence, she stalked inside the gate. Instantly, she stopped, all the breath leaving her body.

Her father was seated stiffly on a mat before Nimr-Rada, Sharah, and Ra-Anan. Meshek was flushed, obviously enraged. And Sharah and Ra-Anan were both tightlipped, staring at him. They had been arguing, Keren was sure. Only Nimr-Rada seemed to be self-possessed, occupying the uppermost seat on a makeshift dais, fingering his ever-present flail, the languid Tselem at his feet. When he saw Keren, Nimr-Rada sat back, his endlessly dark eyes gleaming in undisguised pleasure.

"Come, my sister." His deep, rich voice turned everyone in the crowded courtyard toward Keren. "Come visit with your father."

Dazed, Keren slowly wiped her dusty feet on a mat provided by a servant. As she knelt and glimpsed her father's disbelieving face, Keren remembered Neshar's warning. *I beg you, if you cherish our father, you must make him leave you here. Reject him.*

Lifting her eyes upward to the evening skies, Keren prayed.

Make him hate you, her thoughts urged, *more than anyone else on earth. . . .*

Fourteen

"KEREN?" MESHEK asked, staring at her with an expression of horror.

Keren felt ill. Unable to face her father, she lifted her chin and looked away from him, toward the dais. Let him think she didn't care to see him. Let him believe that she preferred to live here with Sharah, who seemed furious with her, and with Ra-Anan, who was studying her as if she were an apparition whose existence he doubted.

Nimr-Rada, however, was smiling. Inclining his dark head, which was crowned by a rim of gold atop his usual horseman's plait, Nimr-Rada spoke to Keren indulgently, almost paternally. "You have forgotten your sandals, my sister."

She forced herself to smile at him, to seem pleased and equally indulgent. "I was commanded to come at once because He-Who-Lifts-the-Skies was waiting. Putting on my sandals would have taken time."

"Then, seeing that you hurried to obey, we forgive you for keeping us waiting," he answered, so amiable that Keren couldn't believe it was the same tyrannical Nimr-Rada she detested.

"What have you done to her?" Meshek demanded, almost snarling.

"All this, she has done for herself," Nimr-Rada said, waving a dark hand toward Keren's attire, "with our full approval and encouragement."

Keren felt her father staring at her, seething. "Look at you! How can you be my daughter? Your sister's attire is actually more appropriate, and her manners more pleasing. You've not even greeted me properly. At least she's asked me if I'm better today. I've been here for two days; didn't you know?"

Two days? Genuinely shocked, Keren had to steady herself before she answered. Half turning, without looking at him, she said, "No, I didn't hear that you were in the Great City; I've been busy. But I'm glad to know you're well, Father. Were you ill?"

"He was exhausted," Sharah told Keren sweetly. "We begged him to rest."

"They've guarded me the entire time—against my will," Meshek said. His discourtesy caused the servants and some of the guards to visibly flinch, evidently fearing Nimr-Rada's reaction. But Meshek didn't appear to notice or care. He rebuked Keren. "It seems that all I've been told is true; you have your own household, your own servants and horses and guards, and you've no wish to return to a simple life in the mountains."

"Life is easier here," she said tersely, fearing she might choke on the words. *I can't do this*, she thought, staring up at the heavens, pretending irritation, but struggling against the tears that could only bring disaster. *O Most High, let him forgive me eventually. He feels so betrayed; I can tell by his voice.*

As if goaded beyond endurance, Meshek cried, "Look me in the eyes as you say these things, Keren!"

Keren noticed Zehker and Lawkham drawing near to restrain her father if the situation became too dangerous. Their actions distracted Meshek, who tensed, scowling at them. The interruption allowed Keren to compose herself, to glance at him, and to answer curtly. "I wish to stay. Tell my mother I'm sorry."

"It would kill your mother to hear those words! And what of Yithran?"

She had to look away from her father then; he was so hurt. She could see that his anger was a shield for his despair. No doubt he believed that only his youngest son, Eliyshama, remained loyal to him and to the Ancient Ones. But Keren felt she could speak of Yithran coldly. "Yithran gave me a small token when I last saw him; I'll send it to you later. Tell him I won't leave this place."

"That's all you have to say?" her father demanded, the words rasping in his throat.

"Yes." If this meeting didn't end soon, Keren knew she would begin to cry. She watched the drowsing leopard, Tselem, focusing on his dazzling speckled hide. As she expected, her father raged at her, at all of them.

"Then my journey to your Great City has been an evil waste of time! Why should I worry about you? Faithless, misbegotten curs!" Meshek stood, furious. "You're no children of mine! Six of my sons and both of my daughters— dead! You're all dead to me!"

Heartsick, Keren lowered her head and cast a sidelong glance at her father. He spat contemptuously on the courtyard paving bricks, then strode out the gate, his gray woolen traveling robe flaring behind him. Nimr-Rada signaled to several of his guards.

"Go with him; provide for all his needs and be sure he reaches his own lodge safely. Do not delay your return from the mountains, or I will send others after you."

As the gate closed behind the guardsmen, Keren shut her eyes and pressed her hands to her face, trying to stifle her sobs. She felt as if she were dying inside. She wished she would die. Didn't her father say she was dead?

"Lady. . . ." Someone was holding her now. Revakhaw. And Meherah. Tsinnah and Alatah, too, moved to comfort her. Their concern crushed her completely. She clung to Revakhaw and cried like a child.

"Did you *see* her?" A guard's conspiratorial, barely audible whisper lifted just beyond the open doorway of Meshek's temporary lodging. Meshek paused amid the task of packing his gear. The guard sounded wickedly pleased. "With the paint on her face and her new garments and all that gold—I didn't recognize her. It was as if heaven and earth had changed places."

Meshek stiffened, listening with all his might. They were talking about Keren, he was sure. No other woman in this accursed Great City wore paint on her face, not even Sharah—which surprised Meshek, now that he considered it.

"Completely," a second guard's lowered voice agreed. "And she was actually polite to He-Who-Lifts-the-Skies. She's never smiled at him before. I—"

A clatter outside put an abrupt end to this furtive conversation, and a third man's voice called angrily from a distance. "Are you a pair of women, whispering with your heads together? One of you help me with these horses! And the other—yes, you!—go open the gate. We have a visitor."

Baring his teeth, Meshek flung the thin leather cords of his traveling pack to the hardened clay floor. "Stupid!" he muttered to himself. He had let his temper rule him again. Of course Keren had been acting. He should have known at once when she was unable to look him in the eyes. Such behavior was totally unlike her. But why had she behaved so? He would go to her now and demand an explanation, then insist that she return with him to the mountains. The sunlight would be gone soon; he had to hurry. Swiftly, Meshek examined his traveling pack's bent-wood frame to be sure it was fastened, then he folded its protective cover in place and snatched the thin leather cords from the floor.

A shadow in the doorway blocked the already dim light. Irritated, he stood and turned to see who was lurking in the doorway. A guard. No, not just any guard but the one he had recognized from Keren's household. The silent, always cautious young man he had sheltered beneath his own roof after Eliyshama's wedding.

"Zehker," he remembered aloud, not bothering to hide his exasperation.

"Yes." Zehker inclined his head with the proper measure of respect but never moved his gaze from Meshek's face. Straightening, he offered Meshek a small, nondescript leather pouch. "She asks that you please return this to Yithran."

Accepting the pouch, Meshek slapped it beside his traveling pack, then eyed Zehker accusingly. "You threatened me today."

"For her sake."

As toneless as those three words were, they made Meshek stare at Keren's disconcertingly self-possessed guard. *For her sake.* Too much could be made of those three words. Or not enough. Could this man be trusted?

Zehker held Meshek's look steadily, quietly. And the longer Meshek stared at this wary guardian of his daughter, the more convinced he was of Zehker's inherent sense of honor. "She was compelled to behave as she did today, wasn't she?" he demanded.

Zehker's careful glance toward the open doorway told Meshek everything. But before Meshek could insist upon being taken to Keren, Zehker said beneath his breath, "You must leave. At once."

Meshek lowered his voice to match Zehker's. "Am I in such danger?"

Zehker replied so quietly that Meshek almost didn't hear. "Yes."

"Is she in danger?" Meshek asked.

"Less if you go."

"Why?"

Zehker shook his head, warning Meshek that this discussion was unsafe. "You'll be protected on your return journey," he said, raising his voice, changing the subject. He hesitated, then asked, "Did you come alone?"

Exhaling heavily, Meshek retied his traveling pouch, cinching the leather cords ferociously. "I may be a fool," he told Zehker, "but I'm not that much of a fool. No, I didn't come alone. Yithran and his friends and . . . another . . . traveled with me along the river to the northern tribes of Asshur. From there I was brought by boat, watched the entire way by relays of that Nimr-Rada's horsemen. They knew who I was, I'm sure."

Zehker nodded and spoke beneath his breath again. "Yithran and the others should return to their tribe."

Yanking at the final cord to be sure it was secure, Meshek said, "I imagine they would be in even more danger here than I am." When Zehker did not reply, Meshek added, "Tell my youngest that I regret losing my temper with her." He longed to say more but found that he couldn't form the words. His throat ached at the realization that he had caused Keren grief. Obviously she had enough to endure without his adding to her burdens. But evidently he had said enough, for Zehker seemed to relax, as if he had heard what he needed to hear. *Does this man love my daughter?* Meshek wondered.

The very idea roused Meshek's protective indignation and, oddly, relief. Meshek almost hoped his suspicion was true. If he had to leave Keren here in this accursed Great City, then it comforted him to know that she had at least one trustworthy ally. Giving Zehker his most fearsome glare, he muttered through his teeth, "Keep her safe."

"That is my duty," Zehker replied. He was cool and formal now, but his eyes flickered, deepening Meshek's suspicion that this man truly loved Keren. As if to prevent any further questions, Zehker bowed and departed. No one had ever bowed to Meshek before. He was discomfited and glad to be discomfited, for only the Most High deserved such obeisance.

Sighing, Meshek passed one hand over his bearded face, then froze. A thought struck him, and he almost reeled at the impact of this new realization. "You didn't bow," he whispered, remembering how Keren had knelt in Ra-Anan's courtyard and lifted her eyes toward the heavens as if in prayer. Everyone else in that courtyard had bowed to their cherished Nimr-Rada. Everyone but himself and Keren. So the whispers of those errant guards were true; Keren had probably never smiled at Nimr-Rada before this day. Undoubtedly, she was more inclined to scorn him. But today she had been ruled by her fears for her foolish, rage-blinded father.

On their journey through the mountains, Bezeq had warned Meshek that Nimr-Rada would not hesitate to put him to death—a fear Keren apparently shared. Was Keren's life in danger as well? If so, then he—Meshek—could do nothing to help her.

His stomach in knots now, Meshek reached for the nondescript leather pouch given to him by Zehker. Inside, reflecting the last glints of daylight, he found a delicate bracelet of pink gold set with a small, smooth oval crystal. Meshek was sure he could easily crush this little bracelet with one hand. He had forgotten that Keren's wrists were so tiny. Now, the fragile ornament glistened at him through the haze of his own tears. In despair, he silently begged the Most High to protect his youngest child.

Zehker retraced his path through the darkening streets of the Great City, returning to Keren's household. All along the way, he went over every detail of his conversation with Keren's father, questioning his own memory.

Had he said too much? Had he betrayed his feelings for Keren? Zehker confessed to himself that he did not mind too much if he had; Meshek's suspicions couldn't harm him from some distant mountain lodge. No, Zehker's utmost fear was that Nimr-Rada's guards might report an unsanctioned, whispered conversation between Zehker and Keren's father. If so, then a merciless interrogation and punishment would come swiftly.

Save me from the results of this most frustrating day, he prayed, even as his mind shied away from acknowledging the dangerous existence of the forbidden Most High. He was suddenly very tired—unusual for him. Somehow he had to find time alone, to rest and reorder his thoughts. He had watch duty early tomorrow morning, but even so, he might find a small space of quiet time before sleep.

He hoped he would sleep. Other aspects of this day were also nagging at him. Nimr-Rada had gained Keren's compliance in everything but her lack of a submissive bow this evening. Her new attire, her ornaments, her smile, the disgusting face paints, the dismissal of her father—all of it was against her will, but in accordance with Nimr-Rada's will, and too perfectly organized to be mere chance.

The whole episode had shattered Keren. She had fought for composure during the unending walk through the streets after meeting with her father—Zehker was still amazed by her restraint. But as soon as she reached the seclusion of her own courtyard, she had collapsed in tears. It had taken some prompting on his part to remind Keren that she must send the bracelet to her father, so he could return it to her once-beloved Yithran. That had upset her all the more. But at least now, he—Zehker—could assure Keren that her father did not hate her; Meshek knew the truth.

Briskly, Zehker approached Keren's residence, waved aside the ferret-faced guard, Erek, and entered the courtyard. Torches had been lit and brazier bowls were set here and there, exuding pungent tendrils of smoke to ward off night-loving insects. In the torchlight, Lawkham was busily finishing a sturdy reed ladder for Keren, which would allow her access to her roof. Perhaps she would be able to use it tonight. That would comfort her.

Lawkham looked up as Zehker moved past him. As bold as ever, Lawkham said, "Did you speak to him?"

"Yes," Zehker growled. *And I'll speak to you later; I'm going to learn everything that you knew about our Meherah's visit today.* Pushing that thought aside, Zehker approached the door to Keren's low pale-walled house. Lamplight wavered softly from the reed-screened windows, and shadows moved through the interior. No doubt they were watching for his return. As he expected, Keren met him at the door, accompanied by the protective Revakhaw. Looking painfully young and afraid, Keren asked in a tremulous whisper, "Did you see him? What did he say?"

Zehker exhaled, relieved that he could honestly give her good news. "Yes, Lady. He said, 'Tell my youngest that I regret losing my temper with her.'"

Lowering her hands into her face, Keren cried. Revakhaw hugged her.

"There, Lady! Truly, didn't I say he would regret his words? He loves you. Shhhh."

Zehker left them hastily and crossed the courtyard to confront Lawkham. As he watched his adoptive brother and debated what to say, Lawkham looked up at him, good-naturedly indignant.

"Now, Zehker, you're blocking my light, as thoughtless as an ox! Do you want this thing finished tonight, or not? If so, then you ought to remember your manners and move. Why are you staring at me? *What?* What did I do?"

"That's what I want to know."

Meherah waited uncomfortably on a mat inside Nimr-Rada's cool and spacious residence. Small lamps, placed at measured intervals, illuminated this huge main room and made it seem mysteriously cavernous.

She had never been inside a home so large. It actually echoed with her footsteps and movements—an unnerving effect. And it was decorated with frightfully gruesome remembrances of successful hunts—vivid dried skins, white grinning horned skulls, assorted tusks, feathers, and claws that had been separated from their original owners. Most oppressive. Meherah shivered at the sight of them. But she had to tolerate these death tokens. Nimr-Rada had sent for her, and he could never be ignored. Hearing brisk, sturdy footsteps, Meherah straightened, fixing a determinedly bright smile on her face.

"You are to be congratulated," Nimr-Rada said, entering the large room, filling it with his presence. As usual, he was imposing to the point of intimidation. Indeed, he was so overwhelming that she could almost forget those terrible death tokens adorning his walls.

Meherah wondered, *If I am so frightened, how has our frail-seeming Keren resisted him at every possible turn for these past few months? Beyond doubt,* she thought to Keren, *you are not as gentle or frail as you seem. Perhaps it's a terrible thing that my sons are in your presence continually—may the heavens protect them.*

Zehker would be careful, she knew. But Lawkham admired Keren tremendously, and that worried Meherah. She did not want her rascal-son to be fascinated with a young woman who continually rebelled against He-Who-Lifts-the-Skies. But surely the fact that Nimr-Rada was congratulating her now might protect Lawkham. Relaxing slightly, she bowed her head to the mat in humble submission.

"Why should you congratulate me, O Great King? I've only done what I could to help the Lady Keren see her duty. And I will continue to do so according to your commands." Moistening her lips, she hastily called his attention to her one distressing failure. "She has yet to bow to you, which I regret completely."

Nimr-Rada sat on his thickly cushioned mat, tapping his ever-present flail in an artful show of idleness. But he was never truly idle, Meherah knew. He was probably allowing her to sweat while he contemplated whether or not she should be reprimanded for her failure. To her relief, he smiled.

"In time, we will persuade the Lady Keren to show reverence for those above her. But as far as her garments and the gold ornaments—they surpassed my expectations. The paint on her eyes and lips was also effective." Grimacing, he added, "Actually, I was amazed enough by her appearance that I did not notice her failure to bow. I have just sent word to her household that she must destroy all her old leather garments; from this day forward, she will present herself only in her new attire. You must convince her to comply."

"I think she might resist, my Lord."

"Not if the comfort of her household is in question." Nimr-Rada had not raised his voice, but his threat was unmistakable.

Meherah shivered, thinking of her sons.

Quietly, Nimr-Rada said, "By the way, I advise you to rein in Lawkham. He is presumptuous and causes unwanted tumult in her household. Tell him that I want the Lady Keren to concentrate on certain tasks that will be expected of her without any distractions. If he cannot control himself, he will be removed from her service."

"He will obey," Meherah assured Nimr-Rada, alarmed. "Forgive him. If he lacks self-discipline, then the fault is mine—is he not my son?"

Nimr-Rada grunted acknowledgement and changed the subject. "To compensate your husband and your family for the need to move to the Great City, I will grant you two measures of land near the river, where you should find suitable materials for your husband's pot making. I expect a set of new dishes to finish the matter. Here."

Reaching into a fold of his pale tunic, he removed a small leather bag and tossed it at her. Meherah caught it—to her profound relief—and he dismissed her for the night.

Outside in the torchlit courtyard, Meherah had to pause and rest. She felt weak. As she rested, she checked the contents of the leather bag. Inside were three small clay tokens. Two had a pattern of lines, apparently signifying two measures of land, and one was rippled, indicating the river. Land along on the river would please her dear husband, Yabal, and soothe his aggravation at being summoned to the Great City so hastily. But was this compensation from Nimr-Rada worth the loss of her family's ability to travel about freely? Was it worth living so near to the formidable He-Who-Lifts-the-Skies? She feared not.

Walking out into her courtyard, Keren sighed shakily —the conclusion, she hoped, to an evening of tears. As she stared up at the stars, Lawkham approached her. He looked grim, not at all like himself. Bowing, he said, "Lady, my mother's actions this day have certainly added to your grief; I beg your forgiveness. Please, do not be angry with her—or with me."

Genuinely perplexed, she said, "How can I be angry with either of you?" She shook her head. "No, I should thank your mother. I see now that the Most High has brought blessings out of the chaos today. My father is still alive, he doesn't hate me, and my appearance was startling enough that He-Who-Lifts-the-Skies won't punish me for failing to bow." Suppressing a mirthless chuckle, she said, "Apparently, he liked my dreadful attire; I've just received word that I must never emerge from my gates unless I'm wearing all my gold and the other foolishness."

"You did not look foolish, Lady," he assured her softly. His tone made Keren stare at him, unsettled. She didn't want him to look at her in such an admiring manner. Turning away swiftly, she changed the subject.

"Is my ladder finished? I'd like to climb up to my roof."

"We will know it is finished if you actually reach the roof without mishap," Lawkham said, teasing now, as if to cover his transgression.

"You test it," she commanded him. "If *you* actually reach the roof without mishap, then I'll use your ladder."

Zehker had apparently been listening; he lifted the ladder from the courtyard pavings and leaned it against the wall of Keren's residence, jostling it back and forth to be sure it was secure. "Revakhaw should accompany you, Lady," he suggested.

Nodding agreement, Keren called inside to Revakhaw. At once, Revakhaw stored her delicate bone needle in the hem of Keren's new outer robe—to Gebuwrah's annoyance—and joined Keren. Together they watched as Lawkham happily climbed the ladder, stamping on each rung, proclaiming its perfection.

"This ladder is beyond extraordinary! Look how amazing it is; every rung, knot, and binding of unrivaled craftsmanship! Who could fear to climb such a wondrous ladder?"

"Stop praising yourself, O wondrous Lawkham," Revakhaw told him in mock irritability, though she was laughing. "We know you built the ladder yourself. Why do you think we sent you up first?"

"You climb next, O disbelieving one," he told Revakhaw as he knelt on the roof and held the uppermost rung. "I'll show you that my marvelous handiwork can withstand a severe shaking."

Hearing this, Zehker gripped the ladder, actually raising his voice. "Don't."

"Bear!" Lawkham retorted cheerfully. "Come up, all of you."

One by one, they climbed the ladder and knelt on the roof—Lawkham and Zehker a careful distance from Keren and Revakhaw. They were silent, staring up at the dark, sparkling heavens. Appreciative, Keren said, "Surely there is no better viewpoint than this in all the city."

Lawkham said, "There will be, Lady, when He-Who-Lifts-the-Skies finishes his tower."

Keren remembered hearing of a particular building important to the Great King; Ra-Anan had been helping to plan it on the night of her arrival in the Great City. "Why should he need a tower?" she demanded. "Isn't the city enough?"

"A tower, reaching to the heavens, unchallenged in height by anything on these plains, would draw all the tribes of the earth here to see it," Lawkham explained. "And who wouldn't be proud to live in the Great City, being able to boast of such a tower?"

"I prefer the mountains," Keren said, unable to hide

her derision. "And why challenge the Most High? Didn't He command the tribes to scatter and fill the earth? Instead, we are gathering in a city."

They were all quiet—a polite, "waiting-for-the-end-of-her-speech" silence. Keren shook her head, surrendering temporarily. It had been too long a day, too difficult a day, to argue her point now. "Tower or no tower, I prefer to study the heavens from my own roof. Thank you for building the ladder, Lawkham."

"Whatever you command, Lady, I will do," Lawkham said softly.

Disturbed, Keren glanced at him. He was gazing upward at the stars. Zehker was studying him intently, and Revakhaw widened her bright eyes at Keren, obviously enjoying her lady's discomfort.

You are imagining things, Keren thought to both Revakhaw and herself. *He meant nothing, I'm sure.*

She shut her eyes, thanking the Most High that this terrible day was finally drawing to an end.

Fifteen

KEREN COAXED DOBE to plod after Lawkham's horse through the streets, while trying to seem unconcerned about her appearance. The citizens of the Great City were staring and gasping at her bizarre attire, her garish face paints, and her excessive gold ornaments. Their shock made Keren squirm. Last night she had threatened never to leave her residence again if Nimr-Rada and Ra-Anan required her to wear this ridiculous apparel. But this morning, Ra-Anan had retaliated with a terse message: *Surely you are concerned for the well-being of your entire household?*

Ra-Anan's messenger—one of his devout pupils, a bald-shaven scrawny youth—had smirked while relaying this taunt. Keren had been sorely tempted to put her face directly in front of his, with only a hair's breadth of space separating him from Nimr-Rada's "do-not-touch" death order. That would have made the scrawny youth sweat, she was sure. But of course she had restrained herself. *O Most High*, she thought, *save me—and everyone around me—from my foolish impulses.*

Her foolish impulse, at this instant, was to tear off all her gold ornaments, rub dirt into her white robes, and then urge Dobe into the river so she could wash the paints off her face. But Nimr-Rada and Ra-Anan would punish her for such behavior. Sighing, Keren forced herself to appear solemn, and at ease—everything she was not. Now, children were thronging the streets ahead, squealing, pointing, and daring each other to look into her pale eyes.

Little mischief makers, how I wish I could play with you, Keren thought, admiring their beautiful brown complexions, bright dark eyes, and musical voices. How she longed to take care of a child again. As if discerning her thoughts, a young braid-decked mother approached Keren, proudly offering her plump, half-asleep infant to be held and admired by the "sister" of the Great King.

Unable to resist, Keren smiled at the young mother, halted Dobe, and reached for the infant. But before she actually touched the baby, a spear was brandished in her face. She drew back, alarmed. Zehker rode up beside her, asking the young mother, "Is your child a son?"

"Yes," the mother said, plainly bewildered by the question.

Zehker shot a warning look at Keren. *The death order.* She sucked in a fearful breath. Recovering, she said to the young mother, "Forgive me; your son is beautiful, truly . . . but I'm only allowed to hold infant girls." She was even more disappointed than the infant's mother, who had obviously been hoping to gain honor for her tiny child. To ease the situation, Keren hastily removed the smallest of her gold rings, her voice breaking. "Here—please—to celebrate your son's birth. I envy you such joy."

The young mother shifted her infant to one arm and accepted the gold ring, smiling, her disappointment forgotten. Lawkham had stopped just ahead, but seeing that Keren was ready to proceed, he chirruped to his horse and started out slowly. Keren knew he was lingering, listening as she turned to Zehker, who was now riding behind her.

"Would Nimr-Rada take her baby's life, simply because I touched him?"

"Yes."

No, Keren thought. Aloud, she said, "That can't be true. How do you know he would actually do such a terrible thing?"

It was the wrong question to ask, she realized. Zehker was staring past her, his lips compressed, his whole attitude strictly controlled. He refused to look at her or to answer her question. *Why?* Keren wondered. Was he angry with her for doubting him?

"Lady, don't take offense at my brother's silence, I beg you," Lawkham said, leaning back on his horse to speak to her—his lighthearted attitude seeming forced. "How can a man of so few words possibly explain anything of importance to anyone?"

Uncomfortably aware of Zehker's stone-faced presence, Keren didn't respond. She trembled, thinking, *I almost touched an infant boy. What if Zehker is right—and he usually is right. What if Nimr-Rada had demanded the life of an innocent child because of my carelessness? I'd want to die too. Save me from such a disaster, O Most High.*

Followed by Zehker and her attendants, Keren rode in silence to their destination—a field adjoining the river to the west, just beyond the northern streets of the Great

222

City. Lawkham halted his horse and with a dramatically exultant gesture, said, "Here, Lady, will be our wonderful tower."

This whole field for just one building? Keren studied the site, incredulous. Men, oxen, and horses swarmed like insects throughout the boundless field, and only the prized horses were idle. A few men were obviously in charge of all the workers, waving measuring cordage and pointing, or shaking their heads emphatically to emphasize their instructions. Under their direction, a number of men were guiding oxen around the far side of a sprawling trench, hauling loads of sunbaked bricks and huge resin-coated baskets filled with a dark, slimy substance. Other men were gathering loose heaps of earth cast up from the trench, which was being dug by crews of laborers wielding hardened-clay scythes, antler picks, or large gourd scoops. Keren could hear some of the men groaning as they worked. Their discomfort was evident, reminding her of what her brothers must have suffered.

"Come, Lady." Lawkham goaded his horse toward a beaten track in the grass. "You must ride around this whole field to truly appreciate how extraordinary this tower will be when it is finished."

"It's going to be foolish, this tower," Keren muttered. But she prodded Dobe into a brisk trot, following Lawkham, who was jubilant as a wild frolicking colt.

"Here's one corner, Lady." Reining his horse to an unsettled halt, Lawkham indicated a large, perfectly squared pile of blackened, fire-baked bricks, which were joined with the dark, slimy-looking substance Keren had noticed earlier. Nudging one leather-clad foot toward the dark slime, Lawkham said, "This we bring from the north by river; it boils up in pools there for us to gather into baskets as we please. Later, you'll see the reed boats at the river—and perhaps travel on one. Surely you'd enjoy a trip up the river. But come; we'll ride past all the corners of the tower!"

Swiftly, Lawkham kicked his horse into a gallop, compelling her to follow. The loathsome decorative gold circlet wobbled on Keren's head as Dobe jogged forward. Keren snatched the circlet off, slung it over her arm, and leaned toward Dobe's neck, pressing the horse to a smooth gallop. The grass blurred beneath her, the resultant breeze lifting her hair, fluttering her robes, and heightening her spirits.

As she rode, Keren heard Na'ah yelping in protest while Gebuwrah cried, "Lady! Make him stop!" But Reva-khaw was laughing, and Tsinnah and Alatah whooped and squealed, obviously pleased to race their fat, cherished, tawny horses at a full gallop. Zehker rode past Keren, apparently determined to catch Lawkham.

Lawkham finally stopped at the next corner of the would-be tower, with Zehker beside him. As she approached, Keren heard Zehker saying, "She could be injured."

"She's perfectly safe," Lawkham answered pleasantly, waving a careless hand. "Look, my brother, that useless horse you gave her doesn't have the spirit to move suddenly enough to shake her off, much less kick her off. And if she does fall—how hard is this field, eh? Not very."

"Don't talk against my poor Dobe," Keren chided as she reined him to a halt.

"He's fit for nothing but stew, Lady." And Lawkham laughed at her screech of horror, saying, "It's true. Actually, you should be riding a mare. Doesn't the death order apply to males of any kind?"

"*Never* say that again," Keren gasped, truly upset now. "If your He-Who-Lifts-the-Skies hears you and kills my Dobe, I'll never forgive you."

"Yes, you would."

"Lawkham!" Aggravated, she brandished her head-dress at him like a weapon. "Give me your word."

At once he raised his hands, laughing, giving up. "Please, don't beat me, Lady! You have my word. We'll protect your dear Dobe with our lives."

"*You* will," Zehker told him. "I'd find her another."

"You're both cruel—no tender sympathies at all," Keren complained.

"But it's quite the opposite, Lady! I have much tenderness within me," Lawkham protested. Mischievous, he clutched his heart, choking out, "I do! I assure you . . . I feel it continually . . . and bitterly. You injure me every day!"

"Liar," she said, biting back a reluctant smile.

Lawkham laughed and straightened. "There, I made you smile—don't deny it. Ah, here are your adorable companions, who also remind me of my tender feelings—they wound me so often."

Alatah rode up happily, followed by Revakhaw and Tsinnah, who glowed, delighted. But Gebuwrah sulked—she was surprisingly awkward on a horse—and Na'ah looked ready to burst into tears. She hated any horseback ride faster than a sedate walk.

"You don't have to race to keep up with me," Keren said, touched by their misery.

Na'ah was silent, but her dimpled chin quivered, and she sniffed moistly.

Gebuwrah grumbled, "Thank you, Lady."

"Lady," Tsinnah sighed, her brown eyes sparkling in

her slender face, "Think how huge and amazing this tower will be!"

"But think of all the time and work that will be spent on it," Keren responded, waving toward the men laboring in the distance. "Wouldn't they rather be plowing their fields and hunting for food?"

"Plowing?" Lawkham looked shocked—as open-mouthed as a little boy whose favorite toys are suddenly snatched away. "But, Lady, who wants to plow a field when they can build a magnificent tower? Why are you so disturbed? I give you my word that every man working on this tower *wants* to work on this tower."

"My brothers didn't," Keren reminded him, unable to stop herself.

"True, Lady, but that was an entirely different situation," Lawkham said. "And a regrettable one," he added hastily, evidently fearing she was offended.

"Yes, catch yourself, O wondrous Lawkham," Revakhaw taunted him in a singsong voice, "before you end up in a regrettable situation—in the mud and slime!"

"If you were with me, I could bear it, O precious Revakhaw."

"Ride," Zehker commanded quietly, ending their banter.

As they rode past the third would-be corner and turned toward their starting place, a horn sounded in the distance. Alatah gasped, her sweet childlike voice scared. "He-Who-Lifts-the-Skies!"

He-Who-Would-Kill-an-Infant, Keren thought bitterly. *I pray it's not true.*

"Lady," Gebuwrah admonished urgently, "your head-piece."

To sooth her nervous attendants, Keren placed the

despised gold circlet on her head, fumbling with it. "Is it straight?"

"You're perfect, Lady," Revakhaw said. "You outshine your Great Lady sister."

"She's coming too?" Keren moaned, longing to ride in the opposite direction.

Sharah, pale and unsmiling, was indeed riding to Nimr-Rada's left. Keren also noticed a man riding to Nimr-Rada's right, who was thinner than Nimr-Rada but strikingly similar in height and arrogance.

Lawkham leaned toward Keren and the others, hushed yet eager. "Lady, you're about meet our Great King's father—who is also a Father of my Fathers—the formidable Kuwsh."

Kuwsh! Keren sucked in her breath, unable to believe that she was about to meet the very Kuwsh who lived in her childhood stories. Kuwsh, charming, wonderfully clever, headstrong, aggressive—yet the same Father-Kuwsh who humbly bowed to his own son, the Great King Nimr-Rada.

I'ma-Naomi and I'ma-Annah often spoke of Kuwsh, longing for the delightful rogue-child he had been and wondering what sort of man he had finally become, that he would serve his own son. Keren studied him now, mesmerized and nervous.

Kuwsh also stared at Keren unwaveringly. He was a prideful man; she could see it in the straightness of his back, the sardonic curve of his full mouth, and the brilliance of his bleached leather wrap and leggings, gold cuffs, and showy leopard-skin cloak. A rectangular gold ornament gleamed at his forehead, held by thin lashings of black leather, which also restrained his thick, shining black waves and curls. He was handsomer than Nimr-Rada, but his smoldering arrogance lessened his appeal.

As Kuwsh, Nimr-Rada, and Sharah stopped before her, Keren inclined her head in a polite gesture of greeting. Lawkham, Zehker, and all her attendants dismounted and bowed. *You wonder why I don't do the same,* Keren thought to Kuwsh, seeing his black eyebrows lift, challenging her.

Nimr-Rada, however, chose to ignore her lack of submission yet again. His voice deep, booming, he said, "Father, this is our Lady Keren."

Kuwsh nodded to Keren coldly. Remembering Shem and Noakh's recitations, Keren said gently, "Kuwsh, father of Nimr-Rada, Sebaw, Khawvilah, Sabtaw, Rahmaw, and Sabtekaw. I am pleased to meet you."

Somehow, her quiet recitation of the names of his sons disturbed Kuwsh. His soot-dark eyes became wary. And perhaps more respectful. Now he spoke, his voice as full and resonant as Nimr-Rada's. "It seems that you've heard more of me than I have of you, Lady."

Keren smiled. "Many stories. All told fondly."

"By whom?" he asked, carefully polite.

"The Father of my Fathers, Shem, and his Ma'adannah. And our I'ma-Naomi and her beloved—the Ancient One, Noakh."

Kuwsh flung an accusing look at Nimr-Rada, and at Sharah, who was staring at Keren as if she wanted to beat her. Inclining his head toward Keren once more, Kuwsh said, "You must visit me while I am in the courts of my son, our Great King. I will hear these stories, Lady, and perhaps correct any errors you have heard."

I've heard no errors, Keren thought to him. But she smiled. "As you say, Father Kuwsh. I will be pleased to speak with you again."

She meant what she said, but Kuwsh studied her

doubtfully. Breaking their silence, Nimr-Rada turned to Sharah. "Will you return to the city with your sister's household, my Sharah, or will you stay here with us this afternoon?"

As if weighing her decision, Sharah glanced from Nimr-Rada to the forbidding Kuwsh. "Perhaps I should return with my sister. I've not visited her for many weeks."

Keren groaned inwardly. But obviously Sharah gave the answer Nimr-Rada desired, for he smiled at her pleasantly, a rarity. "As you wish. I will see you at our evening meal. And you, my sister," he nodded to Keren. "You will take your evening meal with us. Don't be late."

Was he mocking her, reminding her of the grievous meeting with her father yesterday? Keren's throat tightened as she nodded agreement. Nimr-Rada gave her a subtly taunting smile. Keren bit her lip hard. He *did* want to wound her; he was delighting in her unhappiness. She wanted to scream like Sharah in a fit.

"Come," Sharah ordered, as Nimr-Rada waved them off. "We have much to discuss—and I want to meet that Lawkham's mother. I want her to show me how to darken my eyes and paint my lips."

Keren spoke stiffly, swallowing the lump in her throat. "I detest the paints myself, but if that's what you wish, I'll take you to see her. Perhaps your Great King will be pleased to see you adorned this way. I don't understand why he wants me to look so ridiculous—except that it makes me miserable. He must have been pleased yesterday, seeing me cry over Father's departure."

"Oh, he was." Sharah stared at Keren now, her gray eyes hardening as they turned their horses into the streets of the Great City. "You create most of your own grief, you know—as you did just now when you met the father of my husband. Why did you provoke Kuwsh? Naming his sons and reminding him of the Ancient Ones . . . that was frankly stupid of you."

"I wasn't provoking him," Keren protested. "And why should it be stupid of me? I have no reason to hide the fact that I spent my childhood with the Ancient Ones, but Nimr-Rada apparently *did* hide that fact from his own father."

"Then you're more the fool for revealing it."

Scowling, Keren said, "I'm glad you love me so much, my sister. Your concern makes my grief easier to bear. Weren't you upset by our father's departure?"

"I was relieved; he's as rude as ever." Impatiently Sharah called out, "You, Lawkham, show me where your mother lives."

On horseback, Lawkham bowed to Sharah, so exaggeratedly courteous, so overly respectful that she glared at him. "He should be beaten and tossed in the slime pits," she snapped.

Still fuming at Sharah's disrespect for their father, Keren said, "Lawkham serves my household, not yours, my sister. You have no say over his circumstances."

"Oh. Are you fond of him?"

"He's a prankster and a flirt—not the sort of man I'd admire for myself," Keren said. She noticed Sharah's lovely, pale, scheming face and became alarmed. "Leave Lawkham alone, please; don't make trouble for him with your Great King. You'll like his mother," she added, hoping to distract her.

"We'll see," Sharah murmured, looking unconvinced.

Before Keren could persist, a wide-faced, leather-clad woman with a long black hair plait called out, "Lady! Wait, I beg you." She lifted a tiny baby toward Keren, saying,

"You wished to hold a child earlier, but he was not one you could touch. Here, hold my daughter if you wish."

With a cautious glance at the unmoving Zehker, Keren halted Dobe, then slowly reached for the child, asking, "A girl? She's lovely." The infant girl was truly pretty, with soft ringlets, dimpled cheeks, and tiny hands that curled tight like flower buds. Feeling like a starveling suddenly granted a feast, Keren breathed the warm infant scent of the girl-child and rocked her, kissing her tenderly wrinkled forehead, then reluctantly handed her back to her eager mother.

As she thanked the woman, Keren noticed her avid expression and realized what she wanted, apart from the honor of having her child noticed by the "sister" of He-Who-Lifts-the-Skies. Squelching a laugh, Keren gave the woman the thinnest of her remaining gold rings. Perhaps she would end up giving all her gold away—definitely an idea worth considering.

"You're a fool," Sharah sniffed, "giving her one of your own rings just for holding her baby."

"It was worth it," Keren told her, enjoying Sharah's indignation. Another hopeful mother scurried up with her daughter, who was older than the infant Keren had just held, but a baby nonetheless. Keren accepted the girl, smiling. The baby's eyes were huge, and she glanced at her mother for reassurance, whimpering pathetically.

"Poor thing. I'm too frightful for her," Keren said, handing the now-wailing child to her mother. "I don't blame her for crying. Here." She gave the woman a ring, then waved Lawkham onward and gave Dobe a prodding little kick.

"I forbid you to give away any more rings," Sharah told her severely—all thoughts of Lawkham apparently forgotten.

"I challenge you to give away some of your rings, and to at least act as if you enjoy holding babies," Keren answered. "You're the most exalted woman in this Great City. You should try to please its citizens."

Sharah's mouth went down in a hard, sullen curve. "You sound like Ra-Anan. 'Smile.' 'Be gracious.' 'Act as if you care.' 'Have a child.' "

Keren almost dropped Dobe's reins. "Are you going to have a child?"

"No. But Ra-Anan thinks it would please my husband."

"He's not pleased with you?"

Sharah gave her a savage look.

Keren sighed. "I'm sorry you're so unhappy, my sister; I wondered if this would happen. But now you truly have nowhere else to go. What will you do?"

"Perhaps I must pretend to be you," Sharah said coldly, eyeing the growing throng of women and children ahead. "Look at them, just waiting for you! Everyone loves you. And as much as you anger him, my husband is also fascinated by your spirit."

"I don't want him to be fascinated by my spirit."

"I don't believe you."

Keren stared at her sister, appalled. Sharah's face was the face of an enemy: vicious, unforgiving. If Sharah had ever felt any sense of sisterhood between them, those feelings were obviously gone. Keren winced. "You hate me."

"Yes. Completely."

"Send her back to those Ancient Ones," Kuwsh commanded, willing Nimr-Rada to obey. "She's just like them

—I heard the very cadence of that old fool Noakh in her voice. Send her back."

"Why are you so worried?" Nimr-Rada asked. "It is precisely because she is just like them that I want her here. If I can subdue her, convince her of our ways without utterly crushing her, then I can subdue every creature on earth. And you have to admit that she is as amazing in looks as my wife."

"Yes, but your wife wants to please you. This Keren does not. Why do you allow her to defy you?"

"You mean, why do I not force her to bow to me?" Pondering this, Nimr-Rada studied the field before them, obviously not seeing it at all. "She must become like my leopard Tselem. An amazing creature that will choose to obey me, despite herself. Confess, my father, wouldn't it give you joy to have this small revenge—taking something that is precious to the Ancient Ones and turning it against them?"

"I doubt that will happen. She follows their Most High. I can feel it."

"She will be controlled," Nimr-Rada said.

"Or she will control you."

"Never."

"Never?" Kuwsh shook his head, wishing he could be persuaded that Nimr-Rada would win this particular battle. But the young woman, Keren, had been too close to those Ancient Ones for too long. She would be as stubborn as that idiotic old Noakh.

Kuwsh remembered Noakh, his grandfather, with bitterness. The old storytelling fool. Other memories crowded in now: His own father, Noakh's youngest son, Khawm, had usually been joyous and carefree but grew increasingly frustrated with Noakh's endless faultfinding.

Kuwsh's mother, Tirzah, had been angry with Khawm for continually complaining against Noakh. And the uncles, Yepheth and Shem, and their wives, Ghinnah and Ma'adannah, as well as their revered I'ma-Naomi—all were upset by the growing unrest in their family. And that family had finally separated after Khawm's most flagrant display of contempt toward Noakh.

It sobered you, didn't it, old man, Kuwsh thought to Noakh. *You were always so filled with your own goodness. Seeming so benevolent and kind, knowing what was best for us all. But no, let your youngest son laugh at you when you stupidly pass out drunk and naked in your tent . . . then where is your goodness? Instead you curse a son of Khawm—my own brother Kena'an. Then you declare that Kena'an—and by association, all of his brothers and their children—will be less than everyone else on earth. But you're wrong. We'll rule you instead. Perhaps Nimr-Rada is right. We should turn this situation to our advantage. . . .*

Kuwsh was briefly heartened. But then he remembered Keren's strange, captivating eyes and her obvious spirit.

"No," he said aloud. "She's deluded, as they are; her presence will ruin all our plans. You must get rid of her." *And if you don't, I will.*

234

Sixteen

SWEAT SLITHERED down Keren's back as she fit the nock of an arrow into the dye-marked center of her bowstring. Shutting her right eye against the bright midmorning light, she focused her left eye on a portion of her target—a series of reed posts topped with a row of gourds that Lawkham had erected at the opposite end of the small field before her.

Standing to her right, Lawkham lifted his hands in an overwrought pleading gesture. "Lady! Is this how I taught you? No-no-no! Relax and stand easily."

Lowering the bow, Keren gave him the most severe look she could manage—which was not terribly impressive, she was sure. "You relax and stand easily. You're not the one who must strike those gourds."

"Even so, Lady, you cannot—"

"Stop," Zehker commanded Lawkham.

"Augh!" Lawkham tore at his plaited hair—so great was his frenzy. "Do you mean to tell me that I should say nothing, never mind that our He-Who-Lifts-the-Skies will arrive soon and declare that we've taught her badly?"

"Exactly."

"But she's standing wrong, she's nervous, and she's *leaning*; by the heavens, look at her! You're leaning," he told Keren, extending his hands again.

Zehker gave Lawkham an attention-getting shove. "Sit."

"I may as well sit," Lawkham groaned, plopping onto the stubbled, recently grazed grass. "I'm going to be knocked flat anyway when *he* sees her missing one shot after another."

I haven't missed one shot after another, Keren argued silently. But she excused Lawkham's despair. They were all tense; their perfect He-Who-Lifts-the-Skies had announced that he would judge Keren's progress this morning. If she did well, they could celebrate. If she did badly, then Lawkham—and possibly Zehker—would be removed from her household and replaced by other guardsmen who might be more adept at teaching weaponry. The thought made Keren sweat.

Shifting her stance, she rechecked her leather wrist guards, her protective leather chest guard, and her finely carved bone thumb-guard ring, which was new and irritating. She plucked it off and called to Tsinnah, who was waiting with Gebuwrah and the others. "Do you still have my old leather thumb guard?"

Tsinnah beamed at her. "O Lady, of course I saved the old one; I knew you'd want it today."

"You can keep the new ring," Keren said, trading her thankfully. As Tsinnah tested her new ring on finger after finger, Keren lifted her bow again. Zehker was now standing to her right, and she eyed him, pretending defiance. "Do you want to tell me everything I'm doing wrong?"

He shook his head, his dark gaze fixed on the gourds. "No, Lady. Shoot one."

Relaxing, concentrating, she obeyed. As the arrow cracked against one of the gourds, smashing its top to the ground, Lawkham jumped up, yelling and capering like a child. "There! There! That's how I've taught you! Again! Shoot another!"

She missed. Lawkham slumped to the ground once more, his head in his hands, moaning, certain he would be disgraced. As he was lamenting his fate—his future in trampling clay to be used in the tower he had sworn he loved—Keren heard Dobe whicker softly. Turning, she saw guardsmen riding out from the city. Nimr-Rada was coming with his entire household. Including Kuwsh and the paint-adorned Sharah.

Keren grimaced. No doubt Sharah, her declared enemy, was hoping to see her fail. Kuwsh, too, would take pleasure in her humiliation. Despite his courteous words, Kuwsh had said nothing to her after their first conversation at the site of the would-be tower. And Keren had seen him several times during the past three weeks while she was visiting Nimr-Rada and Ra-Anan.

Why do you refuse to speak to me, O Kuwsh? Keren wondered. *Is it so terrible that I love the Ancient Ones?* Uneasy, she glanced from Kuwsh to Lawkham, who scrambled to his feet and folded his hands respectfully, bowing to Nimr-Rada.

Everyone was bowing to Nimr-Rada now, except Keren. He rode over to Keren and looked down at her, his eyes flinty in his broad, high-boned, dark brown face. His air of command, matched with all his gold and the leopard-skin wrap, strongly reminded Keren of the first time she had seen him, in the Lodge of Bezeq. What if she had agreed to marry him when he had first expressed an interest in taking her as his wife? She shivered at the thought but inclined her head toward him politely.

Nimr-Rada gave her a curt nod. "I see you have already taken down one of your targets—unless Lawkham or Zehker did that for show." He tipped his head toward the shattered remains of the gourd in the distance, flanked by its still-upright companions.

"No, Great King," Keren answered clearly enough for her voice to carry. "I hit that one from this very spot."

"After how many tries?" Nimr-Rada asked.

"Three."

"Seeing Lawkham's misery, I thought you would say thirty." Waving his flail, Nimr-Rada said, "Hit two of the next four and I will be satisfied for now. Begin."

Keren shut her eyes, breathing out a silent prayer. *O Most High, my enemies, Nimr-Rada, Sharah, and Kuwsh, long to see me fail. Please, don't let them rejoice.*

Intent upon the remaining gourds, she reached back over her shoulder, slid an arrow out of the leather quiver, fixed it in her bowstring, and relaxed. She could almost hear Lawkham's frantic, silent instructions. Shoulder down. Elbow up. Sight along the arrow. Ease your fingers. . . . She released the arrow, her gaze still upon the gourd. The arrow struck the gourd and stayed. Lawkham celebrated by stomping one leather-clad foot down hard.

Nimr-Rada glanced at him, then said, "Once more."

Keeping her focus on the gourds, her movements smooth, Keren shot another arrow. It sped over a gourd, barely whisking it. From atop his horse, Kuwsh said, "You would not count that for one of your horsemen, O King. Should she be given more than they are given?"

You will not upset me, Keren thought, staring at Kuwsh, then at Sharah, who was gloating quietly—her lampblack darkened eyes and ochre-stained lips stark and shocking in her pale face. Lifting an eyebrow at Nimr-Rada, Keren said, "I have two more tries."

"Proceed," he said, surveying the remaining gourds.

Her hands were clammy, but she refused to allow Kuwsh and Sharah the pleasure of seeing her wipe her palms. Praying silently, she swept another arrow from her quiver and sighted her target. Bowstring aligned with nose and chin. String fingers curled lightly beneath the jaw, easing fingers slowly . . . the arrow struck the base of the same gourd. Lawkham stomped the ground hard. Zehker never moved.

"Once more," Nimr-Rada said, taunting her.

Irritated, Keren took aim and missed.

Nimr-Rada smiled unpleasantly. "Your aim is fair for a beginner, Lady. But a man would be able to outshoot you from a greater distance; you would be dead before your arrow landed at the hooves of his horse."

Keren stared at him, perplexed. "Why should you say such a thing? It's not as if you could put me in your army."

"If I thought your presence would defeat my enemies, Lady, I would indeed put you in my army. But you'd probably kill my own men by mistake." He sounded amused by the idea, but a vengeful, brooding expression crossed his dark face, as if he were contemplating his enemies.

Who were his enemies? Keren wondered. She remembered as a child hearing I'ma-Annah and I'ma Naomi talk about Nimr-Rada's endless harassment of the tribes of

Asshur. And now, the tribes of Asshur were building small cities of their own—a show of defiance against Nimr-Rada. Horrified, Keren blurted out, "You're planning to attack the tribes of Asshur."

His obsidian-dark eyes flickered. She had surprised him, guessing his plans. Her horror grew. He was going to formally attack the tribe of her cousin Metiyl. *Dear Metiyl.*

Before she could protest, Nimr-Rada quelled her with a smoldering look, which swiftly—bewilderingly—changed to an indulgent smile. In a voice as dark, warm, and liquid as the slime coating the bricks of his would-be tower, Nimr-Rada said, "Come, my sister. We will go to the river to rest and celebrate your little victory."

Numb, her thoughts still fixed on the impending attack, Keren slung her bow over her shoulder and returned to her patient horse. Zehker and Lawkham were already ahead of her, holding the long, thick reed that served as Keren's step onto Dobe. Keren mounted the horse without thinking, planting her sandal-shod left foot on the thick reed, then turning to sit lightly on Dobe's fleece-draped back. Nimr-Rada was watching, apparently admiring her horse-mounting technique more than he had admired her skill with a bow. Keren looked away from him, distressed.

She wanted to cry at him, to beg him to be satisfied with his kingdom as it was. But her pleas would only make him sneer. By everything she had heard and seen, Keren knew that Nimr-Rada's pride—and Kuwsh's pride—demanded complete control of all the earth's tribes, particularly those born of the first fathers Shem and Yepheth, whom they scorned. Even so, she had to try to dissuade him.

While she waited for Zehker to strap the reed pole onto a packhorse, Keren confronted Nimr-Rada again. "Why should you turn against the tribes of Asshur? They're weak compared to—"

"Do not provoke me, Lady." His apparent mood of indulgence vanished.

Keren bit down an aggravated response. The others were ready to ride now, but Keren held Dobe back, allowing Kuwsh and Sharah to move ahead of her with Nimr-Rada. She didn't want to see Nimr-Rada's face again until her rage had cooled. Perhaps later she would charge into the river and swim until she was exhausted. Anything to distract herself from thoughts of Nimr-Rada attacking the tribes of Asshur.

While Keren was trying—unsuccessfully—to think of a way to warn Metiyl, Nimr-Rada suddenly drew his horse back, waiting for her. His black eyes gleamed maliciously. "As you are mastering the bow, Lady, you must also learn to ride without using your hands to guide your horse or support yourself. And you will be trained to shoot into the hoofprints of your horse as you ride."

"What? But why?"

"Because from now on, whenever my household resides in the Great City, you will go hunting with me. And you must learn to shoot lions, leopards, men—anything that would stalk you as you ride. Otherwise you will be overtaken and killed."

She stared, incredulous. "Perhaps I should just throw myself into the river now and avoid these bloody deaths you keep planning for me, O King."

"You will also be taught to swim," he said, countering her threat.

"I *know* how to swim," she retorted.

"I am amazed to hear that, since your mouth is always opening at the wrong times. You should have swallowed water and drowned ages ago."

Keren scowled, and Nimr-Rada laughed at her, his teeth white and dazzling, making him almost handsome. Reluctantly, Keren thought, *Why can't you be like other men? It would be easy to admire you if you weren't so determined to rule everyone else—and to destroy anyone who disagrees with you.*

Nimr-Rada's laughter drew disapproving looks from Kuwsh and Sharah, who slowed to join them. Immediately, Nimr-Rada told his father why Keren shouldn't be able to swim. Kuwsh and Nimr-Rada shouted with laughter, then rode on ahead to talk.

Sharah, however, lingered near Keren suspiciously. "Stay away from my husband."

"You keep him away from me, and I will be completely grateful." Changing the subject, she said, "Your eyes are amazingly darkened. Meherah taught you well."

"She's a clever woman," Sharah agreed. "Never at a loss for words, the same as her son."

Speaking carefully, Keren said, "I like Meherah very much; she's kind and loving. I beg you to cause her no trouble."

"Do you love that Lawkham?" Sharah asked, watching Keren hard.

Keren gave her look for look. "He's not what Yithran might have become to me, and you know it. Please, Sharah, you've stolen enough from me. Don't torment my friends and those in my household—they've done nothing wrong."

"Then stay away from my husband."

"Then you come with us when he takes me hunting. I don't want to be near him, ever. You know it's true, Sharah. To keep your husband away from me, you must remain near me. He wants me to learn to hunt. You should accompany us."

Keren could see Sharah's dislike of physical exertion warring with her ambition and her desire to keep Nimr-Rada. Keren persisted. "It might please him if you learn all these things."

"You've made your point; I'll consider what you've said."

"Thank you."

"Don't," Sharah answered viciously. "If I can ever be rid of you, I will."

"And if I can ever escape you, I will," Keren muttered.

They rode on in bitter silence, following Nimr-Rada and Kuwsh to the river at the site of the would-be tower. There, floating near the riverbank, secured with ropes and pegs, was a long, curved, dark-red wooden barge, surmounted by a large, extravagantly painted black-on-red leather canopy, which shaded an assortment of furs, mats, and cushions.

"Tell me you are unimpressed," Nimr-Rada said, pulling back and challenging Keren with a forbidding look.

"But I am impressed." She stared at the barge, amazed. "Who else beneath these blue heavens could command such a vessel to be used for mere pleasure?"

He grunted, and Keren sensed that he was satisfied with her answer. Sharah was fuming—to Keren's dismay. Nimr-Rada dismounted, commanding his servants and Zehker to follow them along the shoreline with all the horses and supplies.

"You," he called to Keren's attendants, and Lawkham and the skulking Erek, "get into the barge."

Keren would have preferred to leave Erek onshore instead of Zehker but decided not to risk another disagreement with Nimr-Rada. Lawkham and Erek waded out to the barge, climbed aboard—with some difficulty—and began to help the reluctant Gebuwrah, Alatah, Na'ah, Revakhaw, and Tsinnah inside.

Lawkham was laughing, teasing them into a better mood. Erek, however, mocked the timorous Na'ah without pity until Revakhaw cried, "Weasel! Shut your stupid mouth and help her up. You're worthless, as always!"

Revakhaw's voice carried clearly. Nimr-Rada heard her and frowned at Erek. Instantly, Erek hushed. His expression darkened as he helped Na'ah scramble up into the barge. Keren laughed to herself but then sobered, contemplating the best way to board the vessel. She wouldn't be able to accept help from any of the men. Instead, she must depend upon her attendants, who were now giddy and laughing at the sensation of being afloat.

To prepare, Keren removed her protective leather chest guard and spread it out on the trampled riverbank. She stripped off her sandals and the loathsome gold headpiece and bundled them inside the leather chest guard. Kneeling, she tied the cords of the chest guard together, struggling to make the edges of the leather meet without crushing any of the gold. A shadow fell across her, and Zehker's voice said, "Here, Lady."

He was offering her a larger piece of leather. A memory arose then, of Zehker handing her a piece of leather when she was a child—when she had fallen off of Neshar's horse and bit her tongue bloody. He had leaned toward her in exactly this same way and spoken to her in exactly this tone, saying, "Here."

You've always been ready to help me. I think you care. . . . A rush of unsettling thoughts filled her mind. She accepted the leather swiftly, hiding her embarrassment and confusion. "Thank you, Zehker."

He bowed in silent agreement, then waited as she tied the sandals and headpiece safely within the piece of leather. When she was finished, Zehker lifted the bundle and secured it on a packhorse. Keren did not dare look at him again. Instead, she scolded herself silently for imagining that he might care for her more than any other dutiful servant in her household. Really, she was being ridiculous. And she could not be ridiculous now; somehow she had to climb into that formidable barge.

Taking a resolute breath, Keren waded into the blue-green river, gasping a little at its chill, then enjoying the sparkling, refreshing flow of the current at her toes, ankles, calves, and knees. She longed to douse herself in the water and swim, but she stifled the impulse. Nimr-Rada was lifting Sharah aboard. Sharah was laughing, but Keren knew that she was uneasy. Sharah detested water. Nimr-Rada half tossed her into the barge, clearly enjoying her discomfort. His smile vanished when he saw Keren.

"Where is your head ornament?"

"Where it will be safe," she answered gently. "I feared I might lose my headpiece as my attendants help me into the barge. Also, my sandals would be ruined by the water, and that would be a terrible waste—they are still in good condition. But see . . ." She showed him her rings, necklace, and cuffs. "I'm wearing the other pieces."

"You have an answer for everything, don't you?" His voice lowered intimately. "Tell me—since you surely need my help now—should I withdraw the death order?"

Keren's heart thudded hard in her chest. Why would he want to lift the death order unless he wanted to take her for himself? To cover her creeping sense of horror, she smiled. "Why should I cause you such trouble, Great King? Truly, I will be able to get into the barge—clumsily, stupidly, but eventually. Thank you for your concern."

"Of course." He drew back, his nostrils flaring, an eyebrow lifted. "Get in."

Trying to ignore him, Keren waded toward the barge, calling out, "Lawkham, Erek, move away, please. Gebuwrah, Revakhaw, Tsinnah, come help me in."

"Give us your hands, Lady," Revakhaw urged, her eyes mischievous.

"Behave," Keren warned her. "If you drop me, you'll splash He-Who-Lifts-the-Skies."

Revakhaw stopped smiling. She and Tsinnah gripped Keren's wrists and elbows, bracing themselves against the side of the barge as they pulled Keren upward. Keren boosted herself as best she could and managed to hook an arm, then an ankle, over the edge of the barge as Gebuwrah grabbed her waist. They all tumbled together inside, to the bottom of the barge.

Keren laughed triumphantly but stopped when she saw Sharah's flushed face. Her sister's eyes glittered angrily, and Keren knew why: Sharah had heard every word Nimr-Rada had said to Keren. And Sharah had given his tone and words the worst possible meaning, which for once was probably accurate.

You can't openly blame him for wanting me, so you'll blame me, Keren thought to Sharah. *Somehow I will convince you that I don't welcome your husband's attentions.*

"Move, all of you!" Nimr-Rada commanded, his booming voice startling everyone. They moved. The Great King hoisted himself aboard unaided, carrying his flail, a longspear, and bow and arrows. His power and grace put them all to shame, though the barge swayed unnervingly with his movements.

Turning, he hauled Kuwsh aboard as easily as if his

father had been a child. Kuwsh thanked him, then gave Keren a scathing look. He, too, was blaming her. Lowering her head politely, she moved forward in the barge, toward the high red prow. She did not want to be near the painted leather canopy that would serve as shelter for Nimr-Rada, Kuwsh, and Sharah. She sat near the front, with Revakhaw to her left and Gebuwrah and the others behind her, carefully spacing themselves here and there for the sake of balance.

Four of Nimr-Rada's guards climbed in then, sturdy and grim. Bowing to Nimr-Rada, each guard picked up a long sturdy pole from inside the barge. One guardsman handed a pole to Lawkham, and another handed a pole to Erek, who looked frankly dismayed. Lawkham, however, was pleased. He stood not far behind Keren, chatting at the sullen guard to his left as they plied the long poles.

Allowing herself to relax, Keren listened to Lawkham's cheerful banter as she leaned over to her right to stare down at the sparkling ripples in the water.

"Listen," Lawkham said, "I see you've got some hooks and gores and nets over there. Later—to amuse the Lady and her companions—we might let them fish, am I right? Look at her companions: how beautiful they are, how sweetly they smile! How can you dare to disappoint them?"

"Put your energy into your work," the guard told him irritably. "If we have leisure time later, you can amuse those girls with your fishing."

"Naturally," Lawkham replied, unperturbed. "But you will want to help us with our fishing, I'm sure. I cannot possibly assist the Lady and her pretty companions by myself—though I do wish I could."

That thought obviously stayed with the guard. Later, after a midday meal of soft flat bread, dates, nuts, dried fish, and cold water, the guard checked the assortment of nets, bone hooks, and cords. Apparently satisfied, he stepped away to request Nimr-Rada's permission to allow "those girls" to fish.

Engrossed in a hunting conversation with Kuwsh and the yawning Sharah, Nimr-Rada waved his flail at the guard, nodding agreement. The guard returned and handed out nets, hooks, and cordage.

Delighted, Lawkham cajoled Gebuwrah, Revakhaw, and Tsinnah. "Watch. Mold a bit of bread on your hooks. And don't throw the cordage over the side—you could drop it too easily. Look, tie it on the end of this pole. See how much easier it is to handle? You won't lose it that way, and it will be stronger if you catch a large fish. Lady"—he smiled at Keren beguilingly—"won't you fish with us?"

"I'm happy to watch you for now," Keren answered, stretching. "I think the food has made me sleepy."

"Later then?"

"Later," Keren promised.

The previously sullen and tight-lipped guard was smiling, handing a cordage-and-hook-bound pole to Alatah, because Na'ah had refused to take it. At least he was being courteous. Keren yawned. She had awakened too early this morning, worried about practicing with the bow and arrows. Lulled, she drifted into a light sleep, interrupted now and then by Revakhaw's laughter, Lawkham's teasing, and Na'ah's faint squeals of nervousness.

All at once, Na'ah's squeals heightened, becoming an outright scream, joined by thuds and shrieks from Alatah. Keren jumped to her feet, blinking and trying to understand what was happening. An eel—huge, long, dark—was thrashing wildly on the bottom of the barge at Na'ah's feet, while the guard beat its head with the thick pole. Na'ah was hopping about, screeching and flapping her hands like a crazed bird, while Alatah cried, "Ugh! Throw it back!"

Keren laughed; how she would tease Alatah and Na'ah later. Now, Revakhaw and the others were scurrying around laughing as they tried and failed to help. The barge rocked with their movements. Someone brushed past Keren, also laughing. Lawkham. Keren gasped quietly. He had touched her. But it was an accident. Surely no one had noticed in all the confusion. Lawkham certainly hadn't noticed. She would behave as if nothing had happened—

A longspear thudded into Lawkham's back, throwing him to the bottom of the boat. If he cried out, Keren didn't hear him. She screamed.

Seventeen

"LAWKHAM!"

Keren knelt beside Lawkham, trembling. He was half turned on his side, his skin ashen, claylike. And he was bleeding, a dark stain slowly creeping downward from the center of his chest. The longspear had pierced him through. His eyelids fluttered open. He seemed bewildered, and in great pain. Keren lowered herself until she could look into his eyes. She heard his breath—weakened, hoarse, and uneven. He was dying. It wouldn't matter if she touched him now. Tentatively, she caressed his clammy cheek as if he were a young child. His eyes met hers in a mute, agonized appeal.

"Lawkham," she begged softly, trying not to cry, praying he could hear. "Call to the Most High. He hears you. Call to Him!"

His eyes were closing. His lips moved without words. Desperate to hear him, Keren whispered, "Lawkham?"

He caught his breath, then was still. Unable to hear his next breath, she touched his face and tried to feel the pulsing of blood in his throat. Nothing. She sobbed. "No, Lawkham . . ."

"He's dead!" Nimr-Rada snarled. Approaching, he braced his bare foot against Lawkham's body and wrenched his longspear free, checking it for damage—spattering Lawkham's blood everywhere with his movements. Behind Nimr-Rada, someone cried out in horror. Revakhaw. And someone else hit the bottom of the barge with a thud. Na'ah. The others were wailing now.

Keren stared at Nimr-Rada, appalled. How could he behave as if Lawkham were just another kill in a hunt? *Monster!*

Before she could scream at him, Nimr-Rada bellowed, "Look what you've done, Lady! You've caused his death! I asked why you were not wearing your gold—did I not? But you rebelled as always! He would have noticed you if you had been wearing your headpiece. He would be alive now!"

Ranting, Nimr-Rada waved the longspear at her, scraping her jaw with it, marking her with the stickiness of Lawkham's blood, making her cringe. "Your first kill, Lady! Perhaps one day you will listen to me. You should have agreed to lift the death order when I offered."

Nimr-Rada was right. She should have agreed. Devastated, covering her face with her hands, Keren cried. *Most High, let me live that instant again! Let Lawkham live!*

"Get rid of the body," Nimr-Rada commanded, so harshly that Keren looked up, still sobbing, her hands to her mouth. "And scrub away this blood."

As commanded, one of the burly guardsmen and Erek —*Erek!*—grabbed the dead Lawkham by the shoulders and ankles and heaved him into the river.

Keren leaped to her feet. "No!"

Before they could stop her, she jumped over the side of the barge into the water.

Keren slipped downward until her toes just brushed against the thickness at the bottom of the river. Pushing hard, holding her breath, she opened her eyes and gazed upward through the clear waters of the current, seeing the blue sky above. Pale, shimmering bubbles of air, expelled from her own garments, rose through the water above her. Keren followed them. She broke the surface, gasping for air, only to be splashed by someone else jumping into the river beside her.

Fearing that someone had been sent to stop her from retrieving Lawkham, Keren started to swim away. Revakhaw's voice echoed to her across the surface of the water. "Lady, please, let me help you! Where is he? There . . ."

They swam together, reaching through the water for Lawkham, catching his tunic, struggling to turn him and to pull his face above the surface. As Revakhaw gazed into Lawkham's sightless, half-opened eyes and blue-tinged face, she began to sob. "Who in this terrible place . . . will make us laugh now?"

"Stop," Keren pleaded, treading water, catching her breath. "Don't cry; save your strength." She was frightened. The river was deeper here, and they were drifting. The shore was farther away than she had thought. And Nimr-Rada's barge was blocking their way, giving them no choice but to swim around it. Keren prayed Nimr-Rada would not stop them from saving Lawkham's body.

All at once she heard screams and cries from Gebuwrah, Alatah, and Tsinnah.

Revakhaw panicked. "He's killing them too!"

Keren almost cried, praying Revakhaw was wrong. But there was nothing they could do from this distance. And neither of them could bear the thought of abandoning Lawkham. They swam awkwardly, pulling him through the water, stopping now and then to tread in place, change their handholds, and encourage each other. Soon, their difficulties were somewhat lessened: Nimr-Rada was directing his barge downriver. But even with the obstacle of the barge removed, Keren and Revakhaw still had to swim across the current, which was stronger than Keren had expected. She had learned to swim in comparatively sedate mountain lakes—this river was completely different. It seemed to fight Keren, willfully dragging at her arms, legs, and garments like a living creature.

As Keren and Revakhaw paused again to shift Lawkham between them, a man's dark head suddenly emerged from beneath the surface of the river, just beside Revakhaw. Shrieking, Revakhaw dodged away.

Keren gasped in fright. "Zehker!"

Wiping the water from his eyes, Zehker took a quick breath and tugged a plaited leather rein from his neck. Silent, he pulled Lawkham from their grasp, staring hard at his adoptive brother's unmoving face as if searching for signs of life. For a brief instant, Zehker turned his head down and away. Then, without looking at them, he looped the rein around Lawkham's chest. "Go. I'll bring him, Lady."

Revakhaw quavered, "We didn't see you coming."

"Get to shore."

They obeyed him, though Keren looked back frequently to monitor Zehker's progress. He was swimming in measured strokes, pulling Lawkham with him. Once, Keren saw him look at Nimr-Rada's barge, which was now far enough away that Nimr-Rada was not an immediate threat.

"There are the others," Revakhaw said, her voice catching. "They're alive." They were indeed alive but dripping wet and huddled together on the riverbank, almost in hysterics. Erek was standing nearby, just as bedraggled as the others, but definitely more composed. Keren glared at him. Conniving, sneaking traitor. She had her footing now in the riverbed. Her legs were shaking, and she felt as if she might collapse. Still, she glared at Erek, thankful to have a reason to push away the worst of her anguish.

"You self-serving wretch! I saw you throw Lawkham into the river. Don't plead to me that you merely obeyed your Great King; you were *eager* to follow that order. If you want to save your miserable life, you'll stay away from me!"

His eyes wide in alarm, Erek scurried toward the horses, shielding himself with their bodies. Keren looked at Gebuwrah now; she seemed more self-possessed than the others, who were crying on the riverbank, holding the dazed Na'ah. "What happened? Why were you screaming?"

"He-Who-Lifts-the-Skies was so angered by your escape; he threw us over the side, Lady," Gebuwrah replied, flinging Keren a look of accusation. "He just tossed us over into the water by turns, starting with Na'ah. She was unconscious; she nearly drowned before we could reach her."

Animal, Keren thought to Nimr-Rada. *But I'm also to blame.* Pushing a hand over her face and back into her tangled, dripping hair, Keren tried to ignore Gebuwrah's rebuke.

"Get a fleece from one of the horses, please, and cover Na'ah. She's shaking."

Gebuwrah hurried to get a fleece, scowling at Erek, who shied away from her like a whipped horse. Keren turned from him, disgusted. Zehker was nearing the riverbank now, and he paused to lift Lawkham over his shoulders before wading to shore. As he laid Lawkham on the riverbank, Tsinnah burst into tears and ran to kneel beside him. Alatah and Revakhaw followed her, sobbing. Gebuwrah silently shoved the fleece at Keren and joined the others.

Desolate, Keren stayed with the shaking Na'ah, wrapping her in the fleece, not daring to look at Zehker. After catching his breath, he left Lawkham, passing Keren without a word. When he returned a short time later, he was carrying a bundle of leather and two of the reed poles Keren used for stepping up onto Dobe's back. Methodically he unfolded the leather, pierced it at measured intervals, and bound it to the poles with a series of leather ties.

Keren watched while he worked, finally realizing that he was creating a makeshift litter to carry his adoptive brother's body. *Lawkham is dead. And it is my fault.* She approached him, ready for his anger, his contempt. How he must hate her for causing Lawkham's death. Bowing her head, she knelt a proper distance away from him and said, "I'm sorry. I'm so sorry!" She began to cry.

Very softly he said, "Don't."

Keren lifted her head, surprised by his tone of reassurance. Meeting her gaze steadily, he said, "Don't accept the blame." He started to bind the leather to the poles. Wanting to do something, anything, Keren moved to help him, but he said, "Erek is watching, Lady. Stay with the others. Please."

Unable to bear the sight of Lawkham's death-stilled face, Keren returned to sit with Na'ah, holding the speechless girl, fearing Na'ah would go mad.

But Na'ah suddenly leaned into Keren, saying, "I'll never forgive myself, Lady. Never. I wish I had your courage. If I hadn't been so stupid, screaming, he'd still be alive. And I . . . I loved him so!" Her tremulous confession broke down into heavy, racking sobs.

"Oh, Na'ah . . ." Keren rested her cheek on Na'ah's dark, wet head, sharing her grief. At last she whispered, "You can't blame yourself. You didn't throw that spear. Listen to me; we have to be brave now. We have to take Lawkham to his family."

"How can we bear to face his mother?"

Thinking of Meherah, Keren swallowed. "I don't know."

Walking slowly, heavily, they carried Lawkham's body through the streets of the Great City, ignoring the stares, gasps, and whispers of the citizens. Before they reached the fields south of the Great City, where Lawkham's parents lived, Keren and the others paused to lower Lawkham's body to the ground so they could rest and change places.

A number of citizens approached them, staring at Lawkham's face, recognizing him and expressing their dismay. Following Zehker's terse instructions, Keren and her attendants said nothing to the citizens. Whatever they said would undoubtedly be conveyed to Ra-Anan and Nimr-Rada. Then their own words might be turned against them, and they would be punished. But Na'ah,

Tsinnah, Revakhaw, and Alatah cried quietly, evoking sympathy from everyone who saw them.

Keren also wept, numb beyond despair. As they approached Meherah and Yabal's modestly squared and plastered brick home near the river, Keren's stomach churned. How could she possibly tell these people why their son was dead?

Meherah was in front of her house, tending a low, domed, earthen oven, accompanied by several of her younger daughters and her youngest son, who was stretched out on a grass mat, playing with a collection of tiny clay toys. The instant she saw Keren and Zehker leading the procession, Meherah screamed. She dropped to her knees, knocked her forehead against the dirt in front of the oven, and wailed. Clawing her black braids down into long, wild curls, she began to fling blind handfuls of dirt into her hair as her youngest children cried in terror.

Hearing the noise, Yabal came running from the side of the house, his hands covered with wet, darkened clay. When he saw the body of his eldest son, Yabal staggered and wept.

As she helped to gently lower Lawkham's body to the ground, Keren looked into his blue-marked face, thinking, *Never again. This must never happen again.*

"Your sister believed you would die in the river," said Zeva'ah.

Keren knelt with Ra-Anan's wife on fleeces and mats in the hushed seclusion of her own residence.

"He-Who-Lifts-the-Skies also said you might not live," Zeva'ah added.

"Does he intend to kill me now that I've survived?" Keren asked, ignoring the reference to Sharah.

"No, Lady," Zeva'ah answered. "I'm sure he wants you to live."

Keren stared at her lovely sister-in-law's rounded, pregnant body and blooming face, wondering why Ra-Anan had sent her. Zeva'ah—faultless as always—was obviously here for a purpose, and it was not to console Keren in her grief over Lawkham's death. Guessing aloud, Keren said, "Ra-Anan is unwilling to welcome me into his presence until I am forgiven by He-Who-Lifts-the-Skies. Am I right?"

Zeva'ah's unmoving silence affirmed Keren's suspicion. Feeling wholly emptied and cold inside, Keren said, "Tell me what Ra-Anan says I should do."

She had practiced her every move, all her attendants' moves, what they would wear, how they would adorn themselves, and how they would paint their faces. They were perfect now, and completely silent as they entered Nimr-Rada's crowded ceremonial courtyard.

Keren kept her face impassive as she approached the majestic gold-and-leopard-skin clad Nimr-Rada, proud and remote on his dais seat. *How I hate you!*

Reaching her designated place, Keren waited while Revakhaw and Tsinnah knelt to untie her ornate gold sandals. When they were finished, Keren stepped out of her sandals, never once looking down. Revakhaw held the elaborate sandals attentively as she stepped behind Keren. Certain that all her attendants were standing exactly where they had been instructed to stand, Keren knelt on her mat, the others kneeling with her. Then, Keren removed her headpiece and set it aside. For a counted instant they paused, then bowed together in a single motion, touching their foreheads to the mats. Still in perfect accord, they sat up. Keren retrieved her headpiece and put it on again. Then she looked at Nimr-Rada.

His dark eyes were gleaming, smug. Beside him, dazzling in her white robes, gold, jeweled ornaments, and intense face paints, Sharah glared at Keren. To their right, Kuwsh was also fuming at her, resplendent in his leopard-skin mantle, pale wrap, and all his gold.

Ignoring her sister and Kuwsh, Keren faced Nimr-Rada, thinking, *I have bowed to you, but I swear in my heart, which worships only the Most High, that I will repay you for Lawkham's death. Even if it means my own life, I will find a way to destroy you. You have not won.*

Eighteen

"IS MEHERAH coming this afternoon?" Keren asked Revakhaw, who was entering the courtyard from the gate.

Revakhaw tossed her gleaming curls, obviously pleased with herself. "Indeed, Lady. I told her that we're going to do nothing but visit and talk and eat and laugh and rest, as we've not done in an age! She gives her word that she will come. Her daughters Hadarah and Chayeh begged to come too. I told them you would love to see them again."

"And so I will," Keren agreed, smiling, going back to her task of cleaning the courtyard with Alatah. She was grateful, as always, for Meherah's continued friendship in the five years since Lawkham's death. And Hadarah and Chayeh were delightful young women, so much like Lawkham that it sometimes hurt Keren to see them.

Shielding herself from thoughts of Lawkham, Keren

rolled up a frayed mat, deciding that it could be mended and saved. Revakhaw knelt beside her now, unusually solemn. Keren lifted an eyebrow at her. "What's wrong?"

"We are still being followed by those strange guardsmen every time we leave the gates," Revakhaw murmured, glancing at the servants listening nearby. "I don't like it. They followed us more closely than usual today, yet I couldn't tell if they belonged to He-Who-Lifts-the-Skies, or Kuwsh, or Ra-Anan, or your Great-Lady sister."

Keren exhaled, disturbed, staring up at the cloud-hazed sky. "I don't like it either. This has been going on for days. Did they say anything?"

"No, Lady. Alatah said they followed her yesterday when she went to barter for fish. They made her nervous."

Gnawing her lower lip, thinking, Keren said, "Alatah told me the same thing. We should follow *them* next time. Who in our household was with you this morning?"

"That new guard, Qaydawr, and our devoted Erek."

"Erek!" Keren sniffed, wishing she could be rid of him. But he was Nimr-Rada's loyal spy—and Kuwsh's. She was sure that Qaydawr was also an informant. Probably Nimr-Rada's. "Tell Zehker what you've told me. We should track these new spies—confront them if necessary. Also, please tell everyone in our household that if they go outside for any reason, they must be accompanied by others."

"I will, Lady."

Revakhaw hurried away. Keren returned to her work, upset. She had already visited Ra-Anan, who denied responsibility for these new spies. She didn't believe him. But then, it might be Kuwsh, stirring up trouble against her out of spite. And Sharah could also be sending spies after Keren's household for the pure joy of intimidating them. Even so, whoever was having her attendants followed was certainly acting with the full knowledge of Nimr-Rada, who knew everything that happened in the Great City.

When will I be rid of you? she wondered to Nimr-Rada.

Nimr-Rada, as usual, had been tormenting her and indulging her by turns. At present, he was angry with her simply because she had trimmed her hair without his permission. *Her* hair. It had been down past her knees, unbearably heavy and always in disarray, so Keren had trimmed it to just below her waist. When he saw her, Nimr-Rada had actually thrown dishes and food at her, chasing her out of his presence while Sharah and Kuwsh laughed. That had been two days ago. Now, remembering the confrontation, Keren's face tingled with anger and humiliation: how Sharah and Kuwsh had enjoyed Nimr-Rada's rage.

So now I must send a gift to you and beg your forgiveness, Keren thought to Nimr-Rada, grimacing. *Then I will ask you to stop these new spies. Perhaps Meherah can advise me on a gift.*

By now, Keren also knew that Meherah was another one of Nimr-Rada's informants—probably against her will. But Meherah was a tender person, as Lawkham had been. And Meherah had forgiven Keren for her part in Lawkham's death.

Have you forgiven Nimr-Rada? Keren wondered to Meherah. *I hope not. Because I haven't. I took the blame openly, but I will never forget who threw that spear.*

Finished rolling and binding the grass mat, Keren frowned at a mess of discarded fruit pits on the mats beneath her just-harvested almond trees. As she gathered the discarded pits, Zehker entered the courtyard, clenching his longspear. He saw her at once and strode toward her, purposeful as always. Bowing his head politely, he knelt and placed his longspear between them. Keren relaxed, watching him overtly, mindful that they were being observed.

"The spies are *his*, Lady," Zehker told Keren quietly. "I saw them turn toward his residence."

"Then he's planning something," Keren decided, accepting Zehker's opinion without question. "And all we can do is wait for him to act. I wish he didn't enjoy these little games—stalking us, frightening us, whipping my entire household into a state of agitation."

"A part of the hunt."

"The hunt has lasted for nearly six years now. I'm ready for it to end—and not as *he* would have it end."

Zehker was silent, lowering his head, studying his spear. Keren could almost read discouragement into his attitude. They had both been trying, without success, to think of a way to escape Nimr-Rada's control without endangering Keren's entire household. The thought of leaving anyone in her household behind to face the Great King's vengeance made Keren ill.

"*He* is patient when hunting, Lady," Zehker said at last. "As we must be."

For the sake of the spies in her household, Keren rolled her eyes toward the swaying, leaf-draped branches above them, tapping her fingertips together as if irritated. But she was consciously extending her time with Zehker. Soon the leaves of this tree would fall, the rains would begin, and they would have fewer chances to be together. She was restless just thinking of the coming rains and the planting season.

"Patience is becoming more and more difficult to cultivate." Very softly she added, "I wish Lawkham were here. Even after all this time, it's still hard to greet Meherah and not feel the guilt, and the loss of his laughter."

"She loves you."

"Partly for your sake; she loves you as her son," Keren answered, staring hard at one particular leaf, which was fading. "At times I fear I will bring her more sorrow. I feel I should remove myself from her life—as I should remove you from mine. If anything happens to you . . ."

"Don't."

"I know. I shouldn't think of these things. I should get busy before our spies wonder what else we might be discussing apart from *his* new spies."

"Be your sister, Lady," he said, reminding her of her role.

In silent agreement, they parted in their usual way; Keren dismissed Zehker with a petulant wave of her hand, as if she couldn't wait to be rid of him. Her best imitation of Sharah.

Sometimes Keren acted as if she were furious with Zehker. But she didn't have the spirit to pretend a temper today. Nor did she have the time; her guests would be arriving in the early afternoon, and everything had to be perfect because Sharah might show up unexpectedly and criticize things. Zeva'ah, too, would be quietly critical if anything was amiss. But Zeva'ah's criticism was softened by her four-year-old daughter, Demamah, who was loveable, gentle, and Keren's particular delight.

"Do you think our Great Lady will appear today?" Alatah asked, her sweet voice full of dread as she joined Keren to clear the fruit pits from beneath the almond trees.

"I pray not," Keren murmured. "I want to rest and enjoy the evening."

Her hands still busy with the cleaning, Alatah said, "Yesterday, while I was being followed by those spies, I found a seller of carved wares and weapons. His work is marvelous, Lady—not like anything we've seen. Forgive me, but I invited him to come this evening, to show you the treasures he has created. If I've been too hasty . . ."

"Alatah." Keren interrupted her nervous apology. "Don't fret. Your taste is always perfect. As is your timing. I need to select a gift for He-Who-Lifts-the-Skies. If this craftsman has some treasure worthy of *him*, then you've saved me a morning of pacing through the streets. Thank you."

Alatah sighed, relieved. Keren smiled, and they continued their work in peace.

Her disgracefully trimmed hair clean and shining beneath her gold headdress, and her garments and face paints impeccable—thanks to Tsinnah—Keren relaxed and watched her guests.

Meherah was talking to Zeva'ah, their quiet conversation brightened by occasional bursts of laughter. Meanwhile, Meherah's radiant, dark-haired daughters, Hadarah and Chayeh, were clapping cadence for Demamah, who was dancing a game song with them, bare brown feet pattering over the clay brick pavings as they sang.

A bird in spring cannot be caught except by hawks or nets—such as the nets I've cast for you!

Demamah squealed and laughed as Hadarah and Chayeh lunged at her, catching her and swinging her around. Keren laughed, enjoying Demamah's wholehearted glee. Usually Demamah was so serious and wide-eyed about everything. But now, safe on the ground again, she ran to Keren, highly excited. "Come dance with us, Lady!"

"I will," Keren promised. "After you've worn out Hada-rah and Chayeh. And after I'm sure that my own sister won't visit and be unhappy with me for ruining my hair and my robes."

"But you won't ruin your hair and robes just dancing," Demamah protested, widening her dark eyes, which were huge and fringed with incredibly long, black lashes. "And you look beautiful anyway."

"You're wonderful to say such things!" Keren hugged Demamah, who suddenly crawled into her lap, giggling as the mischievous Chayeh growled and pretended to claw at Demamah like a monster. Chayeh's sparkling eyes and brilliant smile pained Keren—she looked so much like Lawkham.

"Demamah," Zeva'ah scolded, "your feet are dirty."

Abashed, Demamah scooted off Keren's lap. But Keren patted her back and said, "We'll clean her up, Zeva'ah. Forgive us; we're to blame."

Zeva'ah was satisfied. And Demamah was thrilled to be the center of attention as Keren and her attendants brought water for her face, hands, and feet. "Make me look like you," Demamah begged Keren in a whisper.

"Well, I wish I could look like *you*," Keren answered, staring into Demamah's marvelous black-brown eyes. "You're perfectly lovely."

They scrubbed her clean, then combed her long, straight dark hair, which was certainly like Ra-Anan's would be if he weren't always shaving his head. But Demamah sighed wistfully for curls and waves, so Tsinnah and Reva-khaw dampened her hair and began to braid it artfully.

"Wear your hair this way overnight," Revakhaw told her, "and in the morning when you comb it out, it will be full of waves."

"Like yours?" Demamah asked Keren, hopeful.

"Better than mine," Keren told her ruefully. "Yours will behave and mine won't."

Which was why she had to send a gift to Nimr-Rada. Though Keren knew that Nimr-Rada's tantrum was provoked by more than her unlawfully shorn hair. *What?* Keren wondered to Nimr-Rada. *What have I done now?*

Soon, Gebuwrah and Na'ah presented their food to the accompaniment of a band of musicians—also arranged by Alatah. Delicate notes from harps, flutes, and chimes floated upward as the fragrance of roasted meats, spiced sauces, sweet fruits, crisp breads, and savory vegetables filled the air.

Keren was serving Demamah when the bundle-laden tradesman arrived. He was small, hunched, and dusty, with rough hair, glittering little eyes, and a nervous smile. And he shrank back at the sight of Keren's pale eyes. To put him at ease, Keren asked the tradesman to sit on a mat and offered him some cool honey-sweetened barley water to drink. Obviously afraid to refuse, he drank a sip of water, stared at it, then finished the cup and licked his lips. "May I say that this is very good, Lady?"

"Our Na'ah thanks you," Keren murmured, smiling at Na'ah, who ducked her head, delightfully self-conscious. "Please, let us see what you've brought us."

Eagerly the tradesman untied various bundles of leather. Combs, flasks, slender pins, pendants, and exquisite knives of wonderfully polished pierced and carved woods, ivories, shells, and gems, all flashed and glittered in the sunlight. Keren stared, amazed. "You carved all these things yourself? They look so delicate; I'm afraid to touch them."

"They are truly strong and durable, Lady," the tradesman

267

assured her, unafraid now, defending his remarkable work. "Holding them and using them will only add to their color and beauty. Perhaps the little one will test these works for herself?"

The little one, Demamah, waited for a nod from Zeva-'ah, then crept forward. She accepted a pendant and a knife and brought them to Keren. The knife, from its fine-edged blade to the iridescent shell carvings set in its hilt, was perfect. And Demamah touched the round ivory pendant over and over, plainly enthralled.

Keren couldn't blame her. She studied the craftsman and his wares again. "What's in that large bundle? Your tools?"

Distressed, he said, "No, Lady. It's a sword—not something to attract the eyes of women."

He didn't want her to see it. Keren guessed why. "Is it an offering for the Great King? Please, I am obligated to find a gift for him. And if this sword is acceptable, then I will exchange its fair worth in goods, but . . ."

She allowed her words to trail off, implying—rightfully—that the Great Nimr-Rada wouldn't barter for a sword but take it as his due. Now that Keren had hinted at such a dreadful possibility, the tradesman couldn't open the parcel fast enough.

They all gasped to see the sword. The blade was fashioned of one long, curved piece of bone, perfect and shining from tip to hilt. And the hilt—of ivory—was richly carved in hunting scenes, ornate leopards, lions, and bulls, with fiery red-stoned eyes. Demamah retrieved it for Keren, walking cautiously as if the sword itself were afire and might burn her. Keren smiled at the little girl, loving her tender, sweet-serious face.

Keren studied the sword, feeling its weight, testing its

balance, pondering its craftsmanship. Its edge was surprisingly keen, and everything about it was unparalleled. Keren had seen enough weapons by now to appreciate this sword. But Nimr-Rada, she knew, would use it only for show. Nimr-Rada loved to kill for the sake of killing— he was a vicious, blood-loving hunter—and he could destroy this wonderful sword with one ferocious blow. Even so, useless gold-and-gem laden objects appealed to the Great King. Keren considered herself to be living proof of that appeal. Such objects were tributes to his power, and this sword was exquisite. "What do you ask for this sword?"

The tradesman shook his dusty head as if arguing with himself. Seeing that he was unable to articulate what he wanted, Keren said, "Would you like your own field near the river? With half its harvest from this year—from which you'll have seeds for planting with the coming of the rains. I will give you the tokens before you leave today."

"Lady!" Gebuwrah gasped, horrified. Keren had just offered this humble tradesman a lucrative portion of her many holdings.

Ignoring Gebuwrah, Keren watched the tradesman. Apparently, Keren had just offered him his most cherished dream. Tears filled his eyes.

"Lady . . . let it be as you say."

"What about the knife and this pendant that my dear niece loves?"

"Nothing, Lady," he said, shaking his head. "Take them."

"These carvings were made from days in your life," Keren reminded him gently. "How can you live if you give up your days for nothing? Ask a price."

"The smallest ring from your hands?" he suggested, fearful. Keren laughed. So the man had a wife, and *she* knew that Keren no longer gave her gold rings out as tokens to anyone—the demand had been too great. Looking down at Demamah, Keren winked.

"Do you want that pendant, Demamah-child?"

Demamah nodded quickly, not looking at her mother, who frowned at being ignored. Keren removed her smallest ring, and Demamah hurriedly gave it to the tradesman, while clutching the ivory pendant tight in her tiny brown hand as if she feared Keren would change her mind.

"Why did you do that, Lady?" Gebuwrah scolded as soon as the tradesman departed through the gate, clutching his tokens as Demamah clutched her pendant. "Do you think it will be easy to replace a field near the river? Or another gold ring?"

Wearied by the thought of yet another argument, Keren sighed. "Gebuwrah, the field doesn't matter. Will you take this sword and knife to He-Who-Lifts-the-Skies?"

"I'll go if she doesn't," Revakhaw said stoutly. She and Gebuwrah had been at odds with each other lately. Her offer was a challenge to Gebuwrah, who stiffened.

"*I* will go."

"And I will go," Tsinnah said softly. "How can *he* be angry with you after you've offered him such marvelous gifts?"

"Indeed," Meherah agreed, eyeing the sword, clearly fascinated by its workmanship. "Our Great King will be pleased." She looked at Keren now, her eyes bright. "By the way, Lady, that field you granted the tradesman . . . is it near my own?"

It was. "I've complicated your life," Keren told her, remorseful at her own impulsiveness. "We don't know what that tradesman and his wife will be like as neighbors. Forgive me."

"I want to apprentice my youngest son to your tradesman," Meherah said happily. "I'll befriend him—and his wife."

Relieved that Meherah was pleased, Keren sent Gebuwrah, Revakhaw, and Tsinnah off to Nimr-Rada's residence with the sword and the iridescent knife. And with Zehker to guard them against the spies. Keren watched them leave, suddenly wondering if she should have presented the gifts to Nimr-Rada with her own hands.

It wasn't long before Gebuwrah returned with Tsinnah, who was in tears. Zehker was right behind them, wide-eyed and silent.

Keren stood, alarmed. "What happened? Where's Revakhaw?"

As Gebuwrah stared, Tsinnah dropped in front of Keren, tearing at her garments in agitation. "He took the gifts, Lady. And Revakhaw. He put a rope around her neck! Tomorrow . . ."

When Tsinnah could not continue, Gebuwrah said, "The Great King says that he will send for you tomorrow. If you don't obey, then Revakhaw will die."

"I'm going to him now," Keren said, reaching for her sandals.

Tsinnah stopped Keren, clutching at her robes, horrified. "No, Lady, you must do exactly as he says, please! Otherwise, he might kill Revakhaw."

"He said he *won't* see you until tomorrow. You must obey him," Gebuwrah insisted fiercely. "Otherwise we could all be punished!"

"She's right," Zehker agreed. There was a lost quality in his voice that stilled Keren completely. She shut her eyes to prevent herself from looking at him—her love and concern for him would have been evident to every person in the courtyard.

Meherah sucked in her breath audibly, drawing Keren's gaze to her. "Lady, forgive me, but we must leave." She beckoned Hadarah and Chayeh, pausing just long enough to touch Zehker's arm and make him look her in the eyes. "Do whatever he says, my son," she pleaded. "Don't anger him."

Zehker nodded and clasped her hand. "I will escort you home."

Now Keren stared at her sister-in-law, who seemed too calm; Zeva'ah was standing, holding Demamah's hand. "You know what's happening, don't you?" Keren accused. "Tell me what they're planning! Ra-Anan knows, doesn't he? But you didn't even try to warn me. How dare you!"

Zeva'ah left quickly, pulling the reluctant, tearful Demamah after her.

Zehker commanded Keren to bar the gate after he left with Meherah. But to Keren, the bar was a futile gesture. The damage had been done. She sank to her knees, stunned, feeling as if she had been struck by a club blow to the heart.

❧ ❦

"I should have gone alone, Lady," Zehker told Keren, when he returned at dusk.

Keren paused, her hand on a rung of the ladder to her roof, Alatah standing beside her. "Would it have stopped him from taking Revakhaw?"

"No."

"Then there is nothing we could have done. And now, we can only wait. I knew his tantrum was about more than the length of my hair. But tell me, did he snatch Reva-khaw at random, or had he decided beforehand that she would be his victim?"

"Beforehand, I'm sure."

"He's punishing her for being my true friend," Keren observed bitterly.

"Yes."

"What does he want?"

"Your compliance, Lady."

"My compliance in what? Ra-Anan is involved in this too. Why? And Zeva'ah knew this would happen. She knew! She *ate* in my household—she accepted our hospitality, and she never warned us of any trouble. I could shake her!"

By now, Alatah was crying softly, frightened. Keren looked at her and suddenly felt tired—completely beaten and ill. "Forgive me. I'm sure our spies have heard what I just said. And I suppose we will know everything when he sends for us tomorrow." Desolate, she added, "It seems that his hunter's patience is gone."

Silent, Zehker nodded. Keren dismissed him with a limp imitation of Sharah's petulant wave. Zehker bowed and departed, walking slowly.

Keren climbed to her roof, aggrieved, remembering Lawkham with every step upon every rung of the ladder. Alatah followed her, then knelt beside her, whimpering in terror, "He won't hesitate to kill Revakhaw. Then he will kill us all, one by one."

Resisting the fears wrought by Alatah's premonitions, Keren stared up at the first stars of the night. But Nimr-Rada and Ra-Anan had even spoiled this pleasure for her.

The stars all had patterns and meanings now, with their shiftings in the darkness of the skies. The signs of the sun, the bull, the ruler, the lady, the lion, the child, the balance, the conquered eagle, the bow and arrow, the man within walls, the flowing water pitcher, and the fish.

The movements of these stars marked the passage of time—days, weeks, months of Keren's life—all wasted and lost to Nimr-Rada's endless schemes. And, of course, all these signs pointed to Nimr-Rada and his kingdom, by his will. According to Nimr-Rada, the stars revealed his inevitable dominance of the skies, the earth, and the waters.

Remembering all these things, Keren could no longer consider only the Most High and adore only Him when resting beneath His heavens. She put her hands to her face in frustration, blotting the stars from her sight.

Where are You? she cried to the Most High. *Why don't I feel You anymore? Why are You no longer with me—though I love You and have longed for You? Have I been wrong? Speak to me, and tell me I've been wrong—help me.*

There was no answering comfort. Nothing. Confronted with silence, Keren mourned.

Nineteen

"PERHAPS HE'S KILLED Revakhaw," Tsinnah quavered as they walked toward the gate of Nimr-Rada's sprawling residence.

Keren stopped and stared at Tsinnah. Her sweet oval face was haggard; she hadn't slept last night. Nor had Keren, Alatah, or any of the others. They were all terrified. Pushing away her own fears, Keren confronted her attendants like a stern mother. "Revakhaw is alive. And if she's in danger, I'll do whatever I must do to save her—as I would for each of you."

Her attitude seemed to hearten them, though Alatah was dabbing at tears that threatened to spoil her face paints. And Na'ah was sniffling. Keren gave Na'ah's arm an encouraging squeeze, then patted Alatah's hand as she smiled at the trembling Tsinnah and the hushed Gebuwrah. "You won't die today. Nor tomorrow. Now, think of

Revakhaw and compose yourselves."

As she turned to lead them into Nimr-Rada's ceremonial courtyard, Keren found the new guard, Qaydawr, standing directly in her way. He had been listening. Nimr-Rada's faithful spy. He smiled at Keren politely and bowed with all the grace of a man who realizes he is attractive—tall, handsome, and openly appreciative of the sight of any woman. Resisting him, Keren said, "Tell the Great King everything you've heard—I command you. Tell him *that* too."

"As you say, Lady," he answered smoothly, clearly determined to charm her.

Keren waited, silently compelling him to step aside. He did so, bowing again, fascinating her attendants. Beyond him was Zehker, his dark eyes alert, watching her continually.

You are—in every way—more honorable and more desirable than that Qaydawr will ever be, Keren told Zehker inwardly, careful to keep her admiration hidden. *O Most High,* she prayed, following Zehker to the gate, *though I don't feel Your presence, be with us today.*

They filed into the courtyard and went through their accustomed ritual of bowing and kneeling before Nimr-Rada. He sat on his fleece-draped dais with Revakhaw kneeling at his feet, his powerful right hand curved around the base of her bruised throat. Revakhaw was shaking, not looking at Keren.

"Please," Keren began gently, scared by Revakhaw's bruises and her obvious terror, "tell me what I've done; don't punish Revakhaw."

"She hasn't been punished yet, Lady," he said, smiling. "And she won't be, if you behave." He caressed Revakhaw's cheek and hair now, as a man might caress his wife.

Keren gazed at him, shocked, trying to understand his intentions. "You're keeping her here?"

"Do you not trust me with your little friend?"

Not when you're behaving as if she's your wife. Had he taken Revakhaw as a second "wife"? The thought stunned Keren. No man beneath these blue heavens had taken two wives for himself. Indeed, according to the Ancient Noakh, only evil men who lived in the times before the Great Destruction had taken two wives. But wasn't Nimr-Rada just that sort of man? He looked so self-satisfied, so above ordinary men—and not one person in this courtyard was brave enough to speak against him. *You are evil! I wish I could destroy you. . . .*

"Say what you are thinking, Lady," he said.

Keren forced herself to speak softly. "I am thinking that my dear friend is in pain. I long to help her."

"You long to kill me," he said.

She stiffened and looked him straight in the eyes, knowing he wouldn't believe her if she denied his statement. "Death is a natural thought under these circumstances. If you are offended, Great King, then you may punish *me* for my own stupid impulses."

"You have chosen." He released Revakhaw and stood. Revakhaw sagged like a dying creature, as if she couldn't bear to watch what was about to happen. Pulling the gleaming shell-adorned knife from a fold in his leopard-skin wrap, Nimr-Rada left the dais and planted his dark, gold-cuffed feet directly in front of Keren. "Stand up!"

Keren stood, looking up at him, resigned to whatever punishment she had brought upon herself. To her surprise, he offered her the knife. "Take it, Lady."

Now, she thought, clasping the warm handle. *I could kill him now.* He leaned toward her, seeming to invite the blow.

She would have only one chance, she knew. A vein pulsed in his dark throat; she watched it, contemplating his death. A thought came to her then; she shut her eyes against it, because it wasn't her own thought.

No.

No? Aggrieved, she sensed that the Most High was against her murderous impulse. And truly, she would fail to kill Nimr-Rada—he was ready for her blow. He expected her to turn against him. Indeed, he probably expected everyone to turn against him. How could he trust anyone on this earth? His cruelty and ambition poisoned all his relationships; he was trapped by his own power. As she pondered this, Keren felt reluctant compassion for the undeserving Nimr-Rada—the last thing he would desire. Opening her eyes, she deliberately kissed the stone blade in submission to the will of the Most High. To Nimr-Rada alone, she whispered regretfully, "If only you could be like any other man."

He actually flinched. His reaction, Keren thought, was almost as if she had wounded him. Then he took a breath, and his broad, muscled jaw hardened. Keren held out the knife, and he snatched it away. Before she could so much as twitch, he thrust the blade toward her throat, startling her. Controlling her instinct to retreat, Keren swallowed as Nimr-Rada snarled, "Swear on your life that you will never try to kill me!"

"I swear on your life." *Forgive me this lie, O Most High.*

"Swear on your life that you will submit yourself to my authority!"

"On my life."

"Swear that you will reveal any plots against me."

"I swear."

"Swear as you live that you are my protectoress, who

will live in the temple of my Tower of Shemesh—the Sun."

Keren stared at him, faltering. Live in that monstrous tower he was building? Wasn't she enough of a freak already? And what did he mean—that she would be his protectoress? What would that imply? This was what Ra-Anan had been planning all along, she realized. She was being trained for their precious temple.

Nimr-Rada turned the blade against her throat, stinging her, making every pore of her body prickle with sweat. Someone gasped, then stifled a sob.

Sickened, remembering what she had promised her attendants just before walking through the gate, Keren said, "I swear."

"On your life?"

"On my life."

Lowering the blade, Nimr-Rada said, "On *my* life, if you fail to keep these oaths, I will slit your throat, cut out your heart, and spill your blood down the steps of my tower for all to see. And everyone in your household will follow you in death."

"I will obey you."

But Keren knew he didn't believe her. Drawing himself up proudly, Nimr-Rada said, "Go tell your sister everything you have sworn. Tell her that she, too, is bound by your oaths."

He returned to the dais, still clutching the knife. Keren bowed to him, glancing at Revakhaw, hoping to catch her eye. But Revakhaw remained limp, almost lifeless, her joy replaced by desolation.

And if I do one thing wrong . . . he will kill her. Keren left the courtyard, nauseated, half faint. If only she could have killed Nimr-Rada. When she trusted herself to speak, she asked the others, "Did I make the right decision?"

"You didn't notice his guards, Lady," Gebuwrah told her. "When you took the knife, they all stepped nearer. They had weapons. If you had turned that knife against our Great King, they would have slaughtered us like sheep."

Her voice shaking, her eyes red, Alatah said, "Forgive me for crying out as I did, Lady, but I thought he gave you a fatal wound—your neck is bleeding."

Keren pressed her fingertips to her throat, then pulled them away, staring at the smears of blood in surprise. "I felt only a stinging." Bleakly amused, she added, "Perhaps my sister will be soothed by the sight of my blood."

"Is there no way we can help Revakhaw?" Na'ah pleaded softly, her dimpled chin quivering as she looked around at all of them.

Though she was touched by Na'ah's timorous longing for action, Keren shook her head despondently. "No. There's nothing we can do. I feel as if I've failed her. We can only pray that the Most High will protect her."

While Alatah, Na'ah, and Tsinnah nodded miserable agreement, Gebuwrah shook her head stubbornly. "For all our sakes, Lady, as I've told you all along, you *must* obey him."

～❦ ❦～

"Do you see how I'm treated?" Sharah raged, storming through her own lush, plant-filled courtyard, her fingers all outspread and curving like pale gold-decked talons. "I could kill him!"

"Then he will kill you and your entire household," Keren told her. "You must be calm. . . ."

"Don't you tell me what to do! You're the reason I'm in

this situation."

"And you know that the opposite is true," Keren answered, watching Zehker from the corner of her eye. He was tensed, staring at Sharah as if she were a vulture he intended to ward off if she got too close to Keren. In addition, the women of Sharah's household were smirking, obviously delighted by her mortification. None of them seemed sympathetic or loyal to Sharah. Now, as always, Sharah was heedless of everyone but herself; she continued to rave and claw at the air.

"I've done everything for him—and this is how I'm repaid! I've taken all of Ra-Anan's advice, attended his stupid lessons, played loving mother to his stupid citizens, given in to all his idiotic whims. As for having a child, my husband has never expressed an interest in being a father, so how can he hold that lack against me? Now he takes this Revakhaw-creature for his own. I could kill her!"

"If you kill her, my sister, then I'll repay you and no one will stop me; I give you my word! Revakhaw is half dead already." As she spoke of Revakhaw, Keren could feel the tears burning in her eyes. "She doesn't deserve your hatred."

Sharah lifted her chin, scornful. "You always were a fool for others. I see you've earned a wound—probably for her sake."

Keren sniffed back her tears, angry with herself for appearing weak in front of Sharah. "He-Who-Lifts-the-Skies inflicted this wound on me while making me swear never to plot against his life. I will also submit to his authority and reveal any other plots against him."

"You would!" Sharah snapped. "Well, if my *dear* husband hears anything that makes him believe I've plotted against him, then I'll be sure your life is endangered with my own. I'll tell him that you're desperate to save your precious Revakhaw. I'll—"

"Then he will slit our throats, cut out our hearts, and pour our blood down the steps of his tower," Keren interrupted, raising her voice to force Sharah to listen. "He gave me his word that's how he'd kill us. And our households will follow us in death."

Everyone in the courtyard gasped or cringed or went ashen. Keren half regretted frightening them.

Glancing around suspiciously, Sharah said loudly, "Forgive me. I'm overcome with despair that my husband has taken another wife. Yet I love him; he is more than the Sun to me." Leaning toward Keren, her pale eyes full of malice, Sharah whispered, "Let his stupid spies tell him *that!* How I wish he'd been killed while driving the tribes of Asshur from his lands!"

Keren pressed a hand to her throbbing forehead. Nimr-Rada's brutal conquest of the tribes of Asshur was still a source of pain to her. Nimr-Rada had celebrated his victory by declaring that he could see a sign in the stars— a man riding an eagle as if it were a horse. The eagle was Father Asshur's favored creature, his personal symbol. "Let's not speak of the tribes of Asshur," she begged softly, eager to be done with her errand. "I was also supposed to tell you . . . He-Who-Lifts-the-Skies has declared that you are bound by these oaths—he also made me swear that I will be protectoress of his Tower of Shemesh."

"Protectoress of Shemesh?" Sharah looked at her, darkly amused, ignoring the fact that she too was bound by Keren's vows. "Oh, but what will the Most High do without you, His most faithful follower? Or do you no longer believe that foolishness? Never mind. I don't want you preaching at me like the Father of my Fathers."

"I won't," Keren sighed. "I've told you everything I was commanded to tell you, so I'll depart. Enjoy your day, my sister."

"You should bow to me," Sharah pointed out as Keren turned to leave.

Keren inclined her head politely, hoping she sounded more confident than she felt. "No, my own sister, I should not. And don't challenge me; you won't win."

They stared at one another. Sharah straightened, suddenly furious. "Get out!"

Keren left her sister's courtyard, relieved to be away from her. Now she could wait for an almost-certain summons from Ra-Anan.

~⊕ ⊛~

Ra-Anan faced Keren, his thin mouth drawn into a disdainful curl. "Again, you have done what you should not do."

As you have done, Keren answered silently. Aloud, she said, "Tell me, O wise one, what I should do."

His eyes flashed, and Keren looked away, regretting her sarcasm. She wasn't helping herself or Revakhaw by insulting Ra-Anan, though he had apparently planned the whole situation. A breeze gusted into the courtyard then, making a tiny nearby whirlwind of dry, rustling, dead leaves. Keren felt as if she were those leaves, useless and caught in a storm she had no power to resist. Exhausted, she said, "Forgive me."

"You berated my wife while she was your guest."

"I will ask Zeva'ah's forgiveness," Keren agreed, toneless. "I know she couldn't have warned me. She's loyal to you above all."

"And who claims *your* loyalty?" Ra-Anan demanded, staring at her hard. "Your Most High?"

Unable to speak, Keren simply looked at her brother. How could Ra-Anan live without the Most High? How could she herself live without honor, righteousness, or love? All these things were being stolen from her. Now, would Nimr-Rada and Ra-Anan officially force her to denounce the Most High?

Ra-Anan knelt, leaning toward her, his hooded eyes fierce. "Give Him up! What has He done for you? Nothing! If you resist, then those you love will die one by one, victims of your devotion to those old storytellers."

Aching, Keren thought of Noakh, I'ma-Naomi, Shem, and I'ma-Annah. Then she thought of Revakhaw. The ache intensified. *O Most High, help me. How can I save her without turning against You? That would be like death to me.*

Unexpectedly, she remembered her brother Neshar's words when they had parted. *Learn to use your weapons. Trust no one. Judge everything coldly.* Neshar would be appalled to know what had happened to Revakhaw. What would Neshar do in this situation, if he loved the Most High? He would trust no one and learn everything he could, then try to find a way to turn his knowledge against Nimr-Rada and Ra-Anan. That was apparently what Keren would have to do. Then, surely, the Most High would intercede for her at His appropriate time. Until then, Keren would have to be like Neshar.

Quietly, she said, "I will do whatever I must do to help Revakhaw—short of killing anyone else. Now, my own brother, what does He-Who-Lifts-the-Skies intend when he commands me to become his protectoress of Shemesh?"

"He intends you to become his most honored servant."

I don't want to become his most honored servant.

Ra-Anan—how he loved to hear himself talk—continued in his reasonable teaching voice. "All your lessons have been a prelude to everything you must learn between now and the highest day of our benevolent Sun. Every tribal leader under the command of He-Who-Lifts-the-Skies will be amazed by your presence." Whispering eagerly now, he said, "You will hold great power, which will strengthen our grip on this kingdom—if you are willing to truly listen and learn, my sister."

Pompous serpent, she thought. *How can you be my own brother?* Keeping her voice tranquil, her expression accepting and attentive, she said, "I'm listening."

The rains had ended temporarily, just before the midday meal, and Nimr-Rada sent word that Keren was to present herself at his gates immediately, prepared to hunt. A general moan arose from her household, but Keren lifted her hands to silence everyone. "Not a word of complaint! He-Who-Lifts-the-Skies is waiting. Hurry as if your lives depend on it."

She joined them in the rush to collect her gear, to inspect her attire and to throw on a half-sleeved, open-fronted outer robe and bind it together with a wide linen sash. She paused to help Na'ah and Gebuwrah bank their cooking fire and pile all their pots of food into large baskets to be strapped onto fleece-draped packhorses.

Dobe was now one of these packhorses, scorned by Nimr-Rada. Keren's new horse was a muscular brute that endured her as badly as she endured him. But he was a gift from Nimr-Rada and had to be accepted.

As Keren went toward Shaw-Kak, she patted her faithful Dobe to let him know she was near. She was thankful, as always, that Nimr-Rada had not sent Dobe to the stew pots—like the ones Dobe now carried so calmly. *I could take lessons in patience from you,* Keren told Dobe in unspoken affection.

Zehker and Qaydawr were waiting, holding the thick reed that served as her step-up to Shaw-Kak's fleece-draped back. "Thank you," Keren murmured.

Qaydawr gave Keren an intense, admiring smile that made her skin crawl. Zehker handed Keren her quiver of arrows, then her bow. She accepted her weapons, pretending to be indifferent, but longing to touch Zehker's hardened hands and coax a genuine smile onto his imposing features. She suspected he had dimples, but until he laughed, or revealed some true expression, she could prove nothing.

Shaw-Kak shifted beneath her abruptly, saving her from the temptation of staring at Zehker. Qaydawr handed Keren her reins, leaning too close for comfort. Incredulous, she drew back.

"Do you want to die, Qaydawr? Please, don't lean so near me."

"Are you worried, Lady?" he asked softly, looking up at her from beneath eyelashes that any woman would envy.

"Of course; please, be careful."

He smiled at her caressingly; Keren almost rolled her eyes. He had taken her warning as an expression of affection. *Wonderful,* she thought darkly. *He's deluded.* She had to find some way to be rid of him.

Keren rode through her courtyard gate, reining in the restless Shaw-Kak long enough to allow her guards and attendants to mount their horses and take their places in front of her and behind her. All the way to Nimr-Rada's wall-enclosed residence, Shaw-Kak skittered, bounded, pranced, and snorted his impatience. Exasperated, Keren wound the reins tight in one fist and gave Shaw-Kak a resounding whack on the neck with the feathered end of one of her arrows. "No! And don't you put your ears back at me—no tantrums!"

To her disgust Shaw-Kak stopped altogether. She had to kick him viciously to make him proceed. By the time she rode up to Nimr-Rada's gate, she was fuming. Her headgear was askew, and she was ready to eat Shaw-Kak for her evening meal.

Nimr-Rada was already mounted and waiting just inside his gate. He looked irritated.

Keren bowed her head formally, then glared, pointing at Shaw-Kak. "I'm ready to stew this one, O King!"

Nimr-Rada laughed at her, his irritation vanishing like a mist. "He is good for you, Lady. He challenges you."

"As you told him to, I'm sure," Keren grumbled, turning Shaw-Kak to ride just to Nimr-Rada's left.

Nimr-Rada's attendants were gathering now, and Keren had to hide her dismay as Kuwsh rode up, eyeing her coldly. But then her dismay turned to soaring hope. For the first time in many weeks, she saw Revakhaw ride out of Nimr-Rada's gate and take her old accustomed place among Keren's attendants. Nimr-Rada prodded Keren with his flail, demanding her attention.

"Do not think that her presence here changes anything, Lady," he warned.

"As you say, O King," Keren reassured him hastily. "I'm just glad to see her. Please, *please*, may I visit with her as we ride?"

"That was my intention," he answered, his voice unusually low.

"Thank you, Great King."

He grunted and waved her off with his flail, nodding to Kuwsh, who waited at his right. Keren pulled Shaw-Kak back to ride with Revakhaw. But her joy vanished when Revakhaw leaned toward Keren and whispered sadly, "I am with child."

As Keren gasped, Revakhaw lamented beneath her breath, "I long to die! What am I, Lady? Every day he taunts me, saying that I am not his wife and he will kill me if I defy him. But then he declares that I am his, and my child is his, yet I'm nothing to him. I don't know what to think...."

Furiously protective, Keren hissed, "Tell no one I said this: As I live, Revakhaw, before the Most High, you are Nimr-Rada's true wife. Sharah was married to another man, whom she abandoned for Nimr-Rada—their marriage is a mockery!" For safety's sake, Keren said nothing more. But she glared at Nimr-Rada's leopard-skin draped back. *Animal!*

Twenty

"TWO WIVES FOR one man invites nothing but dis-aster," Kuwsh said, unable to prevent himself from lectur-ing his son as they rode out of the Great City. "And to ignore these two wives in favor of a third woman—who is also the sister of your first wife—is worse than disaster. It's—"

"I know what I am doing," Nimr-Rada answered, un-perturbed.

"But do your people know what you are doing?" Kuwsh demanded. "Will they still follow you when they become aware of your growing household?"

"They are free to do as I do. I have not forbidden men to take more than one woman. Such restrictive marriage bonds are remnants from the beliefs of those Ancient Ones in the mountains; if I encourage this new freedom, most men won't argue." Nimr-Rada glanced over his shoulder now at Keren.

Kuwsh fumed, watching his son study the obstinate female. "At least you didn't marry *her*. Listen, my son: You are still angry that she refused you as a husband. You're doing all this to repay her, but it will do you no good. Be satisfied with the promise of a son from your Revakhaw. Forget that Keren! She won't give you the devotion you crave."

"Do you speak from your own experience, my father?" Nimr-Rada taunted Kuwsh, because Kuwsh's first love, Bekiyrah, daughter of Yepheth, had shunned Kuwsh in favor of Asshur, son of Shem. Kuwsh seethed, regretting that he had ever spoken of Bekiyrah to his son. He also regretted Nimr-Rada's physical prowess; he longed to thrash some respect into this "Great King" he had helped to create. But he was no match for Nimr-Rada.

Attempting to be reasonable, he said, "A large portion of your power is due to my own homage to you, my son. By bowing to you, I gave you the loyalty of all the tribes of my sons, and most of my brothers' tribes. You owe me at least the freedom to speak without enduring your mockery."

"If any other man said such things to me as I allow from you, my father, that man would be dead within a breath."

"I believe you," Kuwsh replied, controlling his temper. "But because I *am* your father, I'll be blunt: Your prized Keren won't accept you."

"You are wrong. I will become everything to her. She longs for me to be like other men." Nimr-Rada lowered his voice. "She told me so."

"She was tormenting you."

"She was not," Nimr-Rada growled, causing Tselem—

leashed by a keeper nearby—to watch him attentively. "If you could have seen the look on her face, you would have known the truth. Even so, I will never allow her to become a mere wife to me, or to anyone. And I will never allow myself to be a mere man to her."

"Then why do you pursue her?"

"I have my reasons."

Kuwsh could imagine his reasons. Aggravated, he muttered, "She has never given up her loyalties to those Ancient Ones."

"She will forget them," Nimr-Rada said confidently. "Come now. Let's go down to the river and wait. No doubt our prey is there."

Kuwsh turned his horse to follow after Nimr-Rada, wondering if—during the hunt—he might be able to "misguide" an arrow toward Keren.

⌁◉⌁

Keren glanced up at the gray sky, dreading another downpour. She was wet, tired, and hungry, but she dared not complain. For much of the afternoon, they had hidden in the flooded reeds at the river and had netted a raft of ducks and several elegant birds: glossy, reddish-brown and purple-plumed ibis. But this was a yawn-worthy pastime for Nimr-Rada. He wanted larger prey and planned to have Tselem pursue a gazelle. The thought filled Keren with a wearied dread.

She detested Nimr-Rada's kills. Plain arrows or spears weren't enough: Nimr-Rada loved to physically attack his prey, grabbing their horns, twisting and breaking their necks. Worse, he expected Keren to follow him in the chase as an enthusiastic witness to his cruelty and strength.

Therefore, her heart sank as a herd of ibex approached to drink at the river. Tawny and sure-footed, with graceful, back-curving V-shaped serrated horns, the ibex were like goats but larger than gazelles, which obviously pleased Nimr-Rada. He signaled everyone to be still.

Obediently Keren aligned herself to Shaw-Kak's neck, gripping her bow and praying the wretched horse would not stir suddenly and frighten the ibex too soon. As some of the herd lowered their heads to drink, Nimr-Rada rode at them, his spear ready. They scattered, bounding in different directions. Nimr-Rada followed the largest ibex away from the river. Keren didn't have to urge Shaw-Kak to the chase; the brute bolted behind Nimr-Rada, eager to escape his forced stillness in the reeds.

"Go-go-go!" someone cried from behind Keren.

Nimr-Rada's guardsmen and Keren's guardsmen were surrounding her, their horses galloping with their long necks lowered and outstretched as they had been trained, to avoid being shot in the head by their riders.

Keren disliked having others ride so close to her. She always feared that one of the young men would be tossed from his horse and accidentally strike her, causing his own death. She was about to wave them off when the ibex and Nimr-Rada changed direction, suddenly veering to the right. As they turned, so did Shaw-Kak, but not the horse directly to Shaw-Kak's right. The horses collided, tossing Keren to the left. Astonished, Keren watched the earth rush toward her. Falling never seemed real. But landing was too painful to be doubted.

She struck the damp earth, rolling helplessly, crying out as another horse trampled over her, inflicting torturous snapping blows on her legs. Facedown, still clutching her bow, she sucked in a breath and fought back tears.

She hurt everywhere. Others were calling to her. Frightened, Keren lifted a hand to fend them off. "Stop!"

"Lady!" Tsinnah's breathless voice eased Keren's terror that some young guardsman might forget himself and try to help her. "Alatah is with me. And Gebuwrah. No one else will touch you, truly. Can you turn yourself? Can you walk?"

"Wait." Slowly, Keren turned and gasped. Both her legs hurt, the right worse than the left, and they felt oddly cold. She tried to press her left foot onto the ground, but the effort brought vicious stabs of pain. And even the thought of moving her right leg provoked a chill of sweat. Worse, there was a rapidly swelling lump on her right shin.

"You've really injured yourself this time, Lady," Tsinnah told her, studying Keren's legs. "These are broken bones—no little sprains or bruises and scrapes. And I think you knocked your bow into your face when you fell— your right eye is swelling."

"You look terrible, Lady," Revakhaw said tremulously, kneeling beside Keren. "I was sure you'd be killed when that horse ran over you."

"Well, it didn't kick her in the head," Gebuwrah muttered. She sounded almost disappointed.

Keren frowned. *You're becoming suspicious of everyone*, she chided herself. She was in such pain that she probably wasn't thinking clearly. But the unnerving thought remained: if she had a fatal accident, a number of people would be pleased. Among them Kuwsh, who approached her now, his handsome face inscrutable.

Just as Kuwsh started to speak, Gebuwrah prodded Keren's injured left leg with excruciating accuracy. Keren yelped, and the world dimmed; an ominous humming noise filled her head. To avoid fainting, she lay back on the wet ground and shut her eyes. Yes, that was better. If misery could be called better than agony. As she lay there, eyes closed, a stealthy, heavy-scented creature padded up to her, hesitated, and glided on carelessly, uninterested in her prostrate form. *Tselem*, Keren thought. Nimr-Rada was approaching.

"Who did this?" Nimr-Rada's deep, authoritative voice demanded, furious.

Keren opened her eyes and answered before anyone else could speak. "I did this to myself, O King. Please . . . don't blame or punish the innocent."

Relief swept across several faces; Qaydawr's, Erek's, and one of Nimr-Rada's own guardsmen. Nimr-Rada did not see them; he was glaring at his father and at Zehker, who now stood just behind Kuwsh. "Tell me the truth!"

Kuwsh waved toward Qaydawr and the guardsman, distinctly irritated. "Those two. One horse collided with hers, and another horse trampled her. They were riding too close. As was that one." He pointed to Erek, who quaked visibly but recovered when Kuwsh said, "However, his horse did not collide with hers—therefore he is not to blame."

Instantly, Nimr-Rada cuffed his guilty guardsman, knocking him to the ground. Qaydawr dropped to his knees and bowed, seeming ready for punishment.

Keren hastily lifted a hand, begging, "Don't kill them, Great King! Banish them if it pleases you, but let others praise you openly for the mercy you show them!"

"You'd save your own murderer," Nimr-Rada told Keren, grimly amused. "Very well. If you survive this fall with no lasting injuries, they will live. If your injuries are permanent, I will kill them."

Feeling faint again, Keren relaxed in the grass and shut her eyes. "I will recover. Thank you."

"Don't return to the city until after sunset," Nimr-Rada commanded her. "Look at me. Did you hear what I said, Lady?"

Opening her eyes—the right one now painful—Keren said, "I won't return to the city until after sunset, as you have said, O King." Chuckling mirthlessly, aware of her muddied clothes and her missing headpiece, she added, "I must look truly horrible if you want to keep me hidden."

"You do," he agreed. He turned to leave them, frowning at Revakhaw, who bowed humbly at his feet. Coldly, Nimr-Rada said, "Stay here and be useful. But return to me tonight, or I will come after you myself."

"As you say, my Lord," Revakhaw answered, so frightened that Keren hated Nimr-Rada all the more.

Satisfied, he left, accompanied by his father and his household.

Gently, Alatah covered Keren with damp, musky fleeces, tucking them beneath her as much as possible, saying, "I'm sorry you're in such pain, Lady. And we'll have to wait here for such a long time. . . ."

"Then we should try to build a fire so Na'ah can finish her cooking," Keren murmured, exhausted, the stabbing in her legs worsening.

Pleased by the thought of food, everyone scattered to create a hearth and to unload food from the packhorses. Everyone but Zehker. He knelt as close to her as he dared. Keren longed to reach for his hand and to cling to him; her pain was so great. She curled her hands into fists.

"I'll be sure that your attendants brace your injuries properly," he said quietly. "We'll carry you into the city after dark." Then he muttered through his teeth, "Never ride ahead of Kuwsh again, Lady. I thought I would have to strike him down. He was aiming for you."

Keren stared, unable to respond. By the time she could think clearly again, Zehker had departed to assemble a makeshift litter like the one he had made for Lawkham. Keren pushed away all thoughts of Lawkham, too weakened to endure her memories of his death. *O Most High,* she thought, *by this "accident," You saved my life from Kuwsh. I thank You—though I wish it didn't have to be so painful. What are You planning?* Shivering, she closed her eyes and prayed.

Revakhaw knelt beside Keren, holding a cup of steaming liquid. "Zehker won't allow us to give you solid food until after your legs are braced," she said. "I think he fears you'll heave everything up again."

"He's right as usual," Keren agreed. Her pain was nauseating. To distract herself, she concentrated on Revakhaw. Softly she asked, "Is anyone else nearby?"

"No, Lady." Leaning down on her elbow, Revakhaw faced Keren. "What do you want to say?"

Keren whispered, "You can't tell anyone what I've told you today. But do you feel better, knowing that *you* are Nimr-Rada's true wife and that my sister is not?"

Hanging her head remorsefully, Revakhaw nodded. "I wish it weren't so but yes. Until I knew this, I wanted to die; I was so ashamed."

"Why?" Keren challenged her, whispering. "If Nimr-Rada saw no evil in taking you for his own—being the perfect He-Who-Lifts-the-Skies—then you should have been proud. Instead you were ashamed. Why?"

Revakhaw shrugged, bewildered. "I don't know, Lady,

truly. I thought that if I wasn't his wife . . . then it wasn't right that he should take me. And it would be a shame indeed that I carry his child."

"Because his ways are not honorable; you know it."

Hesitant, Revakhaw nodded. "It's true; he's not honorable. Nor is he the Promised One as he implies. He's nothing but a greedy man. And after being with him for all these weeks, I see that he loves no one. Yet if he could love anyone, Lady, it would be you. No other woman on this earth speaks to him as boldly as you do. And you amuse him. Few people can make him laugh."

"When I don't make him angry enough to kill me." Keren closed her eyes again. "I pray he would become bored with me and free us . . . let us return to our families."

"Truly he won't, Lady. Even so, I pray the same things."

"Do you pray to the Most High, or to Nimr-Rada and his Shemesh?"

"You never give up with your Most High," Revakhaw muttered good-naturedly.

Moistening her dry lips, Keren said, "Don't you give up, Revakhaw. These next few months are going to be difficult. Think of the Most High. Call to Him."

"Do you want to drink this broth now?" Revakhaw asked, changing the subject.

A little disheartened, Keren slowly propped herself up on her elbow and drank the hot, salty, herb-scented broth. Then she gave the cup to Revakhaw and said, "Don't worry. I'm done preaching for now."

"Don't worry, Lady," Revakhaw answered, some of her sparkle returning. She clasped Keren's hand fondly. "I enjoy being with you, even if you are preaching at me. I know you're concerned."

"You're the sister I wish I could have had at birth. If Sharah had been like you, my life would have been so much better." Keren settled down again miserably. Just as she was beginning to relax, she was roused by approaching hoofbeats. Curious, she looked up.

Three riders were approaching from the Great City. Two of the riders were Nimr-Rada's guardsmen, and the third was . . . Meherah. Nimr-Rada had apparently sent her to supervise Keren's household.

Keren watched as Revakhaw stood and hurried with Tsinnah to meet Meherah. Zehker also hurried to meet his adoptive mother. He reached up to Meherah and lifted her off the horse, setting her on her feet, solemnly kissing her cheek.

How I wish he could greet me and kiss me in such a way, Keren thought enviously. She stared as Zehker, Tsinnah, and Revakhaw conferred with Meherah, their heads lowered, their expressions grim.

One of Nimr-Rada's guards interrupted them, giving Meherah a sealed clay flask and another small bundle. Revakhaw promptly took these to Na'ah, who was tending a smoking makeshift hearth. Now Meherah approached Keren, clearly worried.

After examining Keren's legs, Meherah looked Keren straight in the eyes and sighed mournfully. "Lady, I'm so sorry to see you in this terrible condition. Listen, we're going to straighten and brace your legs now, and I must tell you that it will hurt beyond anything you've ever known. I'm going to give you some wine and remedies, but it would be best if you could simply faint altogether."

Swallowing, dreading the pain to come, Keren said, "Thank you. I think I will."

Keren looked up to the clear blue morning sky, unable to believe it was finally spring. Tiny pools of water lingered in her courtyard, and the slender branches of her almond trees were budding with the promise of delicate pink flowers. Touching one of the buds, Keren sighed, feeling rested and whole for the first time in months.

"Lady." Tsinnah beckoned to Keren, indicating that her guardsmen were nearing the gates with her horses. Smiling, Keren met Tsinnah and waited, enjoying the freedom of walking without the cumbersome reed splints, fleece paddings, and makeshift crutches she had endured throughout her recovery. Alatah joined Tsinnah, patting Keren's arm delightedly.

"You look wonderful, Lady," Alatah said, her childish voice almost singsong.

The horses clattered into the courtyard, and everyone watched as Keren approached Shaw-Kak. Keren still detested the beast, but the thought of a morning ride eased the irritation of his presence. Carefully, she planted one sandal-adorned foot on the thick reed held by Zehker and the humbled Erek, then hoisted herself onto Shaw-Kak. This now-unaccustomed movement made her leg muscles pull and ache. Even so, she wouldn't admit to feeling pain. Nimr-Rada still insisted that if she did not make a complete recovery, then his own guilty guardsman and that foolish Qaydawr—both now tending horses in Sharah's stables—would forfeit their lives.

Your penalty is always death, Keren thought to Nimr-Rada, frustrated. At least Revakhaw was still alive, though Keren had heard she was dejected, hidden inside Nimr-Rada's heavily guarded residence, awaiting the birth of

Nimr-Rada's child. Few people were allowed to see her now, not even Keren.

"Do we go to our Master Ra-Anan's household today?" Gebuwrah asked, drawing her horse up beside Keren's as they turned out of her gate to ride through the city.

Keren shook her head. "No, though it would be a pleasure to see my little Demamah again." Demamah had been her most sympathetic visitor during the past few months, but those visits had been brief, rushed by the dutifully polite Zeva'ah. "Today our Master Ra-Anan waits for us at the tower."

"More preparations for his grand ceremony on the highest day of our Sun," Gebuwrah said. "Not that I'm complaining, Lady. Our Master Ra-Anan only seeks perfection."

"Of course." She dared not say more, or less; the self-serving Gebuwrah might decide to inform Ra-Anan if Keren became critical of their Shemesh. And that could endanger Revakhaw. Sighing, Keren looked about the streets eagerly now. Some children whooped at the sight of her, and she laughed at them, pleased to be outside her walls at last.

Hearing the shouts of the children, other citizens came out into the streets, calling to Keren enthusiastically as young mothers brought their daughters to see her and be held by her. Though no more gold rings were forthcoming, the young mothers of the Great City still vied for Keren's attention, deeming it a point of pride if she admired their babies. Keren simply enjoyed holding the infant girls and praising the antics of their brothers.

"Lady, are they going to let us through?" Na'ah called, obviously scared by the growing throng of citizens.

"Eventually, perhaps," Keren answered over her shoulder,

aware of Erek's discomfort as he whistled sharply and pleaded for the citizens to allow the procession to pass. Erek, surprisingly, had behaved these past few months and showed admirable restraint.

But the crowd was slow to respond to his pleas. Instead of dispersing, many followed Keren's household on foot, out of the streets of the Great City toward the sprawling grounds of Nimr-Rada's Tower of Shemesh.

"You managed everything well, Erek," Keren called out loudly enough for everyone to hear, deciding that he deserved open praise. "And you were most courteous. Thank you."

Erek looked bewildered, then straightened proudly. "Thank you, Lady."

"He's just relieved that you're fully recovered and he's not been punished for causing your accident," Gebuwrah grumbled to Keren. "Now that you're better, I'd wager all my rings that he will return to his usual sneaking ways within a month."

"It can't hurt to praise him," Keren pointed out. "Perhaps he will find that he prefers our praise to our scorn."

Gebuwrah sniffed, unconvinced. "As you say, Lady."

At the base of the tower, the crowd surged around Keren while she stared, amazed. Much had been accomplished during her seclusion. A neatly squared and corrugated temple of fire-darkened clay bricks now crowned the present summit of the massive square tower. And the stairs that angled precariously up the sides of the tower now boasted decoratively perforated balusters of the same fire-darkened clay bricks. Keren did not admire Nimr-Rada's ambitions, or her brother's deceitful rationale for building this Tower of Shemesh, but she had to admit that their work was awe inspiring, though less than half finished.

"We're expected to go up the stairs, Lady," Tsinnah called out over the chatter of the crowd around them. She indicated a waiting line of horses. "Look, He-Who-Lifts-the-Skies and your Lady-Sister must be inside the tower."

Keren dismounted, eyeing the stairs unhappily. Her legs were going to ache miserably tonight after all that climbing. She was spared the stairs for a time, however, as a crowd of jubilant women and young girls surrounded her. They evidently felt that she belonged to them and no one else. Glad for the delay, Keren visited and laughed with the women of the Great City. Let Nimr-Rada wait.

"She's entirely too popular," Sharah complained to Kuwsh and Ra-Anan as they descended the long bricked tower stairs, distantly followed by Keren and her attendants. "You saw her; she kept us waiting just to prove how much she's loved by everyone. I think we should correct her. She detracts too much attention from my husband's efforts to please his people."

"And from your efforts," Ra-Anan observed acidly, disgusted with Sharah's persistent complaints. Sharah threw him a spiteful look. Ra-Anan longed to give her a shove; she was the one who needed correction. But he restrained himself, saying, "It's useful that Keren is popular and has been missed during her absence."

"I disagree," Kuwsh muttered, glancing toward Nimr-Rada, who was ahead of them, marching proudly down the stairs of his Great Tower, surrounded by his guardsmen. "She could become a focal point for some future rebellion. She needs to be stopped."

Ra-Anan nearly halted midstep, hearing the threat in

Kuwsh's voice. But then Ra-Anan continued, keeping his face a smooth mask of civility. He would have to decide soon if the stubborn Keren was actually useful to his own plans—never mind Nimr-Rada's fixation on Keren's intended role in the tower. If Keren's growing influence needed to be eliminated, then Kuwsh was the best person to handle that task.

Better to be inside this conspiracy than outside. That way I can thwart his plans if I must, to protect myself, Ra-Anan thought. Turning to Kuwsh, he spoke in his most soothing, reverent manner, giving Kuwsh a title he didn't actually possess. "You are worried, my Lord, and I don't blame you. She does occupy too much of our Great King's attention. Tell me . . . how would you deal with this situation?"

I hate it, Keren thought, shivering as she left the gloomy, dark interior of the temple. Did that Nimr-Rada truly want her to live there? She would feel buried alive.

Save me from such a fate, O Most High.

Twenty-One

ASTRIDE THE RESTLESS Shaw-Kak, Keren concentrated on her target—a single gourd mounted on a reed
post, halfway across the trampled field. A sharp whistle
cut through the morning air, making Keren look up. Nimr-
Rada waved his flail impatiently. She lifted her bow to acknowledge him, then pressed her knees into Shaw-Kak's
sides, urging the capering horse into a gallop.

As Shaw-Kak reached full speed, Keren swept an arrow from the quiver on her back and took aim, turning
herself as she rode past the target, releasing the arrow in
an over-the-shoulder posture. The arrow struck the gourd
low, with a quiet thump.

"You gut wounded your enemy," Nimr-Rada told her,
his black eyes gleaming in his broad, high-boned face.
"He will die a painful death as his family grieves."

Keren winced at Nimr-Rada's graphic imagining of

this would-be death. He took a perverse pleasure in trying to upset her. During these practices, he never said, "You felled a lion," or "You wounded a gazelle." Her victims were always humans. She had to clench her teeth hard to keep from screaming at him. Or from using him as her target—a tactic she had rejected, knowing that she and her entire household would be slaughtered instantly.

Changing the subject, she said, "Please tell me that you are satisfied by my full recovery, O King."

"You are persistent, Lady." He narrowed his eyes. "Are you fond of those two fools?"

The "two fools," Qaydawr and Nimr-Rada's former guard—whom she now recognized as Ethniy—were present this morning, tending the bored Sharah. Determined to absolve them, Keren eyed Nimr-Rada, calm and straightforward. "I can tell you almost nothing about them, O King, except that it would be a shame to waste their lives —or to distress them for months when it's obvious that I'm fully recovered. I beg you to be merciful; set their minds at ease."

"An endless sense of mercy makes one weak," Nimr-Rada told her. "Someday you will agree with me." But he shrugged and beckoned the two young guardsmen, who rode forward, dismounted, then folded their hands properly before themselves and bowed to Nimr-Rada.

Coldly dignified, he said, "The Lady Keren has recovered from the injuries she suffered by your carelessness. For her sake only, I excuse your crimes."

Both young men maintained their composure; Keren was secretly proud of them. Even the audacious, enticing Qaydawr was dignified. They thanked Nimr-Rada, then bowed to him again, and to Keren—which made her uncomfortable. Nearby, Sharah watched jealously, clearly hating this little ceremony. Kuwsh, too, seemed disgruntled by the attention Keren was receiving.

Kuwsh rode up in time to hear Nimr-Rada tell Keren, "You will take your evening meal with me tonight, Lady."

"Am I uninvited then, my son?" Kuwsh asked, obviously reminding Nimr-Rada that they had already made plans.

"Do you think I have forgotten you, my father?" Nimr-Rada asked, trading him look for look. "Certainly you will eat with us."

Keren listened, dismayed. The thought of sharing an evening meal with Nimr-Rada, Kuwsh, and probably Sharah was enough to make her lose her appetite. She wished Kuwsh would—for once—include his wife, Achlai, in their plans. Kuwsh and Nimr-Rada neglected Achlai terribly and rarely mentioned her. In fact, Keren had met her only three times in the past five years.

A quiet woman with the same high cheekbones and full mouth as Nimr-Rada, Achlai apparently embarrassed her husband and her Great King son with her yearning glances. Therefore, Achlai spent her time with her youngest daughters in pointed isolation. Keren sympathized with her deeply.

Keren glanced at Kuwsh, ready to beg him and Nimr-Rada to invite Achlai to share their evening meal. But Kuwsh stiffened, clearly forbidding Keren to address him.

I wish you didn't hate me, she thought to Kuwsh, discouraged. *I wish I could tell you how much I'ma-Naomi and I'ma-Annah have always loved you. How I long to honor you. But you've never given me the chance. Instead, you want to destroy me to protect your "Great King" son and all your schemes—though you know you're wrong to do so. I'ma-Naomi and I'ma-Annah would despair if they could see the man you have become.*

She inclined her head, then pressed Shaw-Kak to trot in a brisk half circle around Kuwsh, remembering Zehker's instructions. *Never ride ahead of Kuwsh again.*

Kuwsh turned, glaring at her steadily. Keren shivered. He truly wanted her to die.

Impudent child, Kuwsh thought, glaring over his shoulder at Keren. *What is that sad, put-upon look for? Are you trying to make me feel guilty for wanting to be rid of you?*

But her sadness did weigh upon him like a heavy burden. More often than he cared to admit, Kuwsh felt the genuine kindness and honor within this young woman. She affected him as gravely any of those Ancient Ones; she made him feel shamefully guilty, more than he had felt in years upon years. How he hated her for provoking that most deep-seated guilt—he almost hated himself.

But why should I feel guilty? Kuwsh wondered, justifying his contempt toward Keren. *That misguided girl is a dangerous distraction to my son, and therefore an enemy—as much as if we were in battle. And as a threat, she must become a casualty of battle. If I must choose between a foolish girl and my son, then of course I'll choose my son.* Once again, Kuwsh mentally outlined his plans, seeking flaws and finding none. The next time he took steps to be rid of the Lady Keren, there would be no sudden fall to save her. Keren would do the deed herself.

Sobs and jostling hands shook Keren from a heavy sleep. "Please, wake up!"

"Revakhaw?" Keren thought she was still dreaming.

But Revakhaw *was* here, in Keren's own residence, among the stirring shadows created by Gebuwrah, Tsinnah, Alatah, and Na'ah. Wide-awake now, Keren sat up on her fleece-draped pallet, her heart thudding in alarm. "What's happened? Revakhaw, how did you get here?"

Crying, hugging herself, and rocking back and forth, Revakhaw choked out, "I've been chased into the streets, Lady. Without my baby . . . Your sister took him."

"Sharah?" Keren groaned. "Oh, Revakhaw. You've had your baby? When?"

"Two days past," Revakhaw whispered. "He-Who-Lifts-the-Skies sent me to your sister's household as soon as my pains began." Sobbing again, as if the memory were too much to endure, Revakhaw gulped audibly. "She mocked me! She said I was nothing to him—which is true. And that my son is hers." Revakhaw wiped her face, a quick, agitated movement in the darkness. "As soon as she found a woman to nurse my son, she put me out into the streets."

Thrusting her fingers into her hair, longing to tear her cruel, vengeful sister apart, Keren shut her eyes hard. Hot color filled her mind. *Be calm,* she told herself sternly. *Revakhaw needs you to be calm.*

Finished with sleep for the night, Keren hugged her friend. "I'm so sorry! I feel as if I've been nothing but a curse to you. I'll beg Sharah to return your son. Does He-Who-Lifts-the-Skies know that Sharah sent you away?"

"What doesn't he know, Lady?" Revakhaw asked, desolate.

Tsinnah, Alatah, and Na'ah comforted Revakhaw as Gebuwrah lit a grass-wicked clay lamp. Revakhaw's face was haggard in the wavering light, and wet with tears. "Help me, Lady. I just want my son. . . ."

Keren studied the tiny, chubby, dark-curled infant in her sister's arms. The newborn was unmistakably a miniature of Nimr-Rada.

"You can't have him," Sharah told Keren, smugly triumphant. "He's mine, and no one will take him from me."

Sharah was truly exquisite this morning, her pale hair in thick, gleaming braids crowned with gold, her face paints emphasizing her full lips and remarkable eyes as her light robes and gold adornments called attention to her perfect figure. But more than that, she was truly happy. Anyone seeing her for the first time would have been dazzled and deceived. Sharah's joy made her seem incomparable and worthy of adoration.

"I'll be the perfect mother," Sharah said, smiling, caught up in her own delightful reverie. "Won't my husband's dear citizens be thrilled to see his child in my arms?"

Nauseated, Keren bit down a grimace. "Claim as much of the glory as you please, my sister. But will you at least allow Revakhaw to nurse her own child?"

"And give her a place in his life? Never! I'm his mother now; he will adore me."

"Unlike your own Gibbawr? I should tell everyone of him!" Keren whispered.

Sharah stiffened. "If you say another word, I'll have that Revakhaw chased out to the steppes to face the wild animals. Don't think I won't!"

Keren withdrew from Sharah's household, heartsick. *How can you be my sister? You don't care that you've ruined a woman's life. Revakhaw, I'm so sorry!*

Sharah entered Ra-Anan's courtyard unannounced, too angry to be intimidated. As she had suspected, Kuwsh was visiting Ra-Anan, both of them scheming over their precious temple ceremony. They stared as she waved her attendants off and knelt on the mats near Ra-Anan. Leaning forward, she said to Kuwsh, "We must be rid of her! I don't care what we have to do—I want her gone before she destroys my life!"

Kuwsh studied her silently, then relaxed, as if satisfied. Sharah admired his handsome face, regretting endlessly that Nimr-Rada hadn't inherited his father's looks. Instead she had to be satisfied with her husband's power and wealth—and with as much of those attributes as Nimr-Rada chose to share with her.

"I want her gone," Sharah repeated fiercely, challenging both men. "Whatever you're planning, let me help you!"

Ra-Anan hesitated, but Kuwsh smiled invitingly. "As you say, daughter."

Na'ah crept into the eerily shadowed temple, hating everything about this tower and this Great City. She longed to return to her parents and to the pleasant dullness of her childhood. But her parents had gladly given her up and would be humiliated if she returned to them without Nimr-Rada's permission. Her one comfort was that the Lady Keren appreciated her, though no one else did.

Na'ah watched now as the Lady Keren—accompanied by the hateful Lady Sharah—listened to Master Ra-Anan's tense instructions. The ceremony tonight must be extremely important to Master Ra-Anan; he was snapping at everyone, particularly the Lady Keren, who was holding a large gold cup and frowning at Master Ra-Anan's commands.

A rustle sounded behind Na'ah, and she nearly screeched as a man murmured into her ear, "Little dove . . ." Na'ah felt faint, recognizing the voice as Qaydawr's, the most handsome of the Lady Sharah's servants. He was talking to *her*, and she was scared as a stupid child.

"Listen," he urged in a caressing whisper, "they're plotting against your lady. Tonight she will drink from that cup, but it'll contain worse than wine. Somehow you must save her."

Before Na'ah could recover, Qaydawr had slipped away. Was he telling the truth? No, he had to be teasing her. Yet she knew he was grateful to the Lady Keren for saving him from Nimr-Rada, therefore he would certainly try to protect her. As Na'ah studied the spiteful Lady Sharah and Master Ra-Anan, she realized Qaydawr was right; the Lady Keren's enemies were plotting against her. *But what can I do?*

Terrified, she glanced around. She wanted to ask Alatah or Tsinnah for help, but they'd never believe that the charming Qaydawr had trusted silly, cowardly *her* of all people. *Think,* she told herself fiercely. *For once in your life, be brave.*

"Are you ill?" Keren asked Na'ah as they finished their evening meal.

"No, Lady," Na'ah squeaked, looking ashen. "I'm well."

Unconvinced, Keren said gently, "If you're worried about the ceremony, you don't have to attend; I'll think up some excuse for you."

"No-no, I'm going," Na'ah insisted. "Forgive me, Lady!" She fled outside before Keren could ask anything more.

Gebuwrah sniffed, contemptuous. "She's probably broken a dish and is afraid to confess it. But forget her, Lady; we need to prepare for tonight."

"From what I've heard, most of the tribal leaders will come to the temple to honor He-Who-Lifts-the-Skies," Alatah told Keren eagerly. "Some of the Lady Sharah's servants were talking—though they hushed when I approached them."

"You didn't want to talk to them anyway," Tsinnah said, joining them. "They didn't help our Revakhaw in her misery."

"Where is Revakhaw?" Keren asked, looking around. Revakhaw had refused her evening meal and wandered away.

"She's climbed to the roof, Lady," Gebuwrah said. "I hope she won't throw herself off."

Keren rushed outside and clambered up the ladder to the roof. Revakhaw was kneeling at the far corner of the roof, her head lowered, her dark curls veiling her face.

"Revakhaw." Keren went to her and knelt, frightened by the woman's stillness. "Give me your word that you won't harm yourself!"

Revakhaw shook her head, then leaned against Keren and wept. Her throat aching, Keren hugged her friend. "I'll talk to He-Who-Lifts-the-Skies tonight. I'll beg him to let you care for your son. Whatever he asks . . ." She couldn't finish.

"Silly," Alatah teased Na'ah. "Why are you carrying that?"

Unnerved, Na'ah clutched her sealed flask, determinedly forcing words from her dry throat. "It's for the ceremony—I-I'm just holding it . . . keeping it safe."

Alatah shook her head, smiling, unconcerned. "You worry too much."

Do I? Na'ah wondered. *Am I being a fool? I wish I knew what to do.*

⮜❦ ❦⮞

"Be careful, Lady," Zehker warned softly as he brought Shaw-Kak to a standstill beneath the night-darkened skies near the tower.

Meeting his gaze in the torchlight, Keren saw that he was deeply concerned about something. He didn't want her to participate in this ceremony any more than she did. Keren nodded. She would be cautious, but she longed to hold him and to cry out all her distress and rage. If she behaved tonight, it would only be for Revakhaw's sake. Otherwise, she wished Nimr-Rada's accursed tower would crumble into the river, taking him with it.

Warning Zehker in turn, she breathed, "Whatever happens tonight, *don't* touch me. He-Who-Lifts-the-Skies has planned something unexpected, I'm sure." Reverting to her usual imperious Sharah imitation, Keren waved Zehker away. He obeyed reluctantly.

"We are the last to enter the tower, Lady, am I right?" Tsinnah asked uncertainly.

Keren nodded silently. She had been severely admonished to hide herself from Nimr-Rada's tribal-leader guests until the ceremony.

Now the leaders were gathering at the tower steps. Giddy with wine, and awed by Nimr-Rada and the beginnings of his marvelous tower, they loudly proclaimed that this ceremony would surpass all previous ceremonies beneath these heavens.

Studying their swaying, weaving behavior, Keren realized that the tribal leaders were susceptible to whatever Nimr-Rada had planned for them. And she was a part of that plan.

"I despise this," she whispered to the Most High. She felt ill.

"Lady," Gebuwrah beckoned. They rode nearer the tower, dismounting apart from the others to avoid being noticed by the guests. Keren allowed Tsinnah and Alatah to adjust her heavy gold headdress and check her garish face paints, while Gebuwrah refastened Keren's gold sandals and smoothed her linen robes.

One by one, the celebrants climbed the tower steps. Ra-Anan led everyone, bearing a smoking, fragrant brazier. He was followed by Nimr-Rada, resplendent in all his gold and a magnificent leopard-skin cloak, tended by a trusted servant holding a bundled fleece. Kuwsh ascended next, coldly dignified. Then each of the tribal leaders, accompanied by musicians, climbed the balustraded steps, carrying flaring torches and tiny ornate flasks.

Sharah was conspicuously absent, but Keren soon forgot her, for the musicians were exhaling long, eerie, hypnotic notes on flutes and drones, making Keren's skin crawl. She wanted to run away. *Behave,* she reminded herself. *For Revakhaw.* Slowly she climbed the steps with her attendants and entered the temple above.

As rehearsed, Keren halted before a waist-high raised brick hearth, which Ra-Anan had lit from his fragrant brazier. Gebuwrah stepped forward now, so haughty that Keren longed to shake her. Instead, she raised an eyebrow at Gebuwrah, then accepted a deep, symbol-engraved gold cup from her attendant's hands. The musicians reached an echoing crescendo, making Keren shiver, but she lifted the gold cup as she had been instructed. This was the signal for the tribal leaders to come forward.

They approached by turns: Sons of Tarshish, Mitz-rayim, Put, Rifat, Kena'an, and Aram all poured liquid tributes into Keren's gold cup. As instructed, Keren stared each leader in the face, enduring their reactions to her shockingly pale eyes. The leaders trembled and nearly spilled their tributes, making Keren steady her cup uneasily. Some of the liquid tributes, less than a swallow each, didn't look like wine. Soon, a pungent aroma wafted from the cup. *And I'm to drink this stinking stuff?*

Doubtful, Keren turned, glancing at the resplendent Nimr-Rada, who waited on the opposite side of the raised hearth. Silently Nimr-Rada's dark eyes coerced her to drink the tributes. As Keren hesitated, Na'ah sidled up timidly and began to pour the contents of a decorative flask into her cup. Keren blinked, perplexed. She didn't remember Na'ah having any part in this ceremony. Na'ah's flask contained more liquid than any of the others, filling Keren's huge cup almost to the brim.

Before Na'ah had emptied her flask completely, Ra-Anan tugged her away, his eyes glinting dangerously. Cowed, Na'ah retreated, shaking visibly. Nimr-Rada stared hard at Keren, inducing her to drink. Remembering Reva-khaw, Keren obeyed.

The gold cup was heavy and so full that Keren had to drink slowly. At first the liquid tasted sweet, but then her mouth began to tingle; the liquid turned acrid. She drank as much as she could, then placed the cup on the raised edge of the hearth. Satisfied, Nimr-Rada lifted his hands and invoked a resonant, lengthy course of praises. "All that is above, receive our thanks! From the heavens, Shemesh, you give us blessings. . . ."

His voice was mesmerizing, rich, hypnotic as the music, the darkness, and the wine. Keren felt herself swaying; she concentrated hard on Nimr-Rada, but the whole temple seemed to shift and move around her, making her dizzy. Then her mouth went oddly dry. Her heart fluttered unevenly, and she gripped a corner of the hearth for balance. Shutting her eyes, she opened them again and realized that the hearth flames were unnaturally blurred; she couldn't trust what she was seeing. Her senses twisted.

" . . . and for life and our losses, yet we are blessed," Nimr-Rada intoned.

Losses? Keren tried to comprehend his meaning. She was aware of a servant stepping forward, opening a fleece. Nimr-Rada removed an oiled-linen bundle from the fleece and placed it in the lowering hearth flames. The bundle blurred as it caught fire.

I can't see! Panicked, Keren tried to focus on Nimr-Rada's face. Useless. Her terror grew as a stench permeated her nostrils. She was going to be sick. Wildly she lunged for the doorway, gasps and shrieks filling her ears. Hands restrained her. She fought them off like a madwoman until she dropped into darkness.

She became conscious of screaming. Sharah. "This is your fault!" Sharah accused, shaking Keren where she lay. "You've made my husband hate me!"

Keren opened her eyes, confused, trying to see. A pale blurred face filled her sight, gasped, then vanished.

"Her eyes . . ." Sharah's voice faltered. "Her eyes are *black*."

"They've been black since we brought her home." Alatah's voice sounded thin to Keren.

"She was raving," someone whimpered. Na'ah. "She's dying."

"I'll die with her," Revakhaw said.

Keren tried to speak. Darkness stopped her.

They covered her completely with linen, then carried her into the predawn streets. Her sight was returning, but it was difficult to breathe or speak, and her heart was beating too swiftly. Her muscles twitched involuntarily and ached from violent spasms of nausea and prolonged digestive torments. She didn't know where they were carrying her, but she was too exhausted to care.

After lapsing into a stupor, she awoke when cool air touched her face. Tsinnah, Na'ah, and Alatah were lifting the covering from her face. Their eyes were swollen, and they wept softly when they realized she was watching them.

"You're still alive," Tsinnah whispered, shocked. Zehker appeared behind them, shadowed in torchlight, cautiously studying Keren.

You're alive, Keren thought to him, relieved. She vaguely remembered hands restraining her in the temple and was now alert enough to be thankful that Zehker had obviously not touched her. But her fear grew. She motioned to Alatah, who leaned close to listen. "No one died?" Keren pleaded.

"No man touched you, Lady," Alatah promised. A noise distracted her, and she hastily knelt, staring past Keren, then bowing abjectly with the others. Turning her head, Keren perceived that they were in the main room of Nimr-Rada's residence. And Nimr-Rada was entering the room. Kuwsh, Ra-Anan, and several of Ra-Anan's acolytes followed soon after, all of them uneasy.

Nimr-Rada stared at Na'ah and pulled a decorative flask from beneath his mantle. "You! This was yours?"

Na'ah managed a timid nod. Nimr-Rada thrust the flask at her. "Drink it!" As the girl hesitated, Nimr-Rada growled, "It's just as you left it; I've guarded it myself. Drink!"

Na'ah drained her flask.

As she drank, Nimr-Rada paced back and forth, glaring at Ra-Anan before pointing at Na'ah. "Do you know what this cowardly girl did, Master Ra-Anan?"

"No, Great King," Ra-Anan murmured, subdued.

"She diluted the tributes with fruit juice and saved your sister's life! Thank her!"

"Thank you." Ra-Anan inclined his head to Na'ah without looking at her.

"How did you know?" Nimr-Rada demanded of Na'ah. "Who warned you?"

"I . . . saw no one," Na'ah quavered. "I heard a whisper in the temple."

Accepting Na'ah's excuse, Nimr-Rada berated Ra-Anan. "I have decided that you stupidly misjudged those tributes, *Master* Ra-Anan! I should make you drink them!" Ra-Anan flinched. Nimr-Rada faced Kuwsh. "Tell me you had nothing to do with this."

Kuwsh remained proudly silent. Nimr-Rada turned from him and lashed out at Ra-Anan's trembling acolytes. "You three prepared those tribute offerings! To whom do you owe your loyalty? To me! Remember that while you suffer in the mud. And before you leave, I want to know everything you put into those flasks!"

So you can kill someone else, Keren thought wearily.

Nimr-Rada cursed the acolytes, dismissing everyone. Kuwsh stormed from the room, followed by Ra-Anan.

Now, Nimr-Rada leaned toward Keren, staring hard. "Your eyes are almost their usual pale again. You will live." Ominously he added, "I have dealt with your sister."

─◈ ◈─

Sharah visited Keren the next evening; her face was swollen and bruised. She scowled at Revakhaw, who sat beside Keren's pallet, keeping Keren company. Keren expected Sharah to order Revakhaw away, but Sharah looked at Keren instead.

"He beat me because of you, *sister.* And he smothered the child and put its body to the flames rather than have me as its mother; he hates me so. Because of you!"

Keren gasped, dimly recalling the oiled-linen bundle Nimr-Rada had burned in the temple fire. Revakhaw wailed.

─◈ ◈─

Alone, staring up at the stars, Keren rested against the wall of her house, too weak to climb to the roof and pray. *Let it be enough,* she implored the Most High. *Hasn't Nimr-Rada caused enough destruction? Use me, I beg You, whatever the cost. I'm even ready to die, if that's Your will. Anything to stop Nimr-Rada.*

Revakhaw was almost unconscious from grief; Keren

was frightened for her sake. And she longed for revenge. For Revakhaw. For the infant. For Lawkham. For everyone Nimr-Rada had destroyed.

I am Your servant, Keren promised the Most High.

Zehker approached her from the shadowed gate, watched by Erek. She could feel his distress, his longing for her to recover. "Be well, Lady," he urged, his voice dangerously close to tenderness. To love.

At peace now, Keren smiled.

Twenty-Two

SUPPRESSING HIS agitation, Zehker stood inside the gate, watching Keren. She wasn't recovering. She had crept into the courtyard, then suddenly doubled over, coughing so violently that she hugged her sides and dropped to her knees on the paving bricks. Zehker winced inwardly, watching Alatah and Tsinnah lift Keren to her feet and help her inside. She didn't protest; she seemed resigned, ready to die. Her lack of spirit terrified him. He longed to steal her away and hide her in a safe place—a place that didn't exist in Nimr-Rada's kingdom.

"She's not getting better," Erek said, leaning inside the gate, his narrow ferret face actually puckered in concern.

"She's dying," Zehker replied, amazed at his own calm voice. Wholeheartedly, he wished endless death upon Nimr-Rada and the others for reducing Keren to such a state.

"Perhaps you should bring your mother to tend her," Erek said.

Zehker flashed Erek a dark look. It irritated him that he and this Ferret-Erek should have the same thought: Meherah might be able to advise Keren's attendants on some treatment. She might also help Zehker to free Keren from Nimr-Rada's grasp.

"I will," he told Erek quietly, planning Keren's escape.

Meherah knelt before Nimr-Rada in his courtyard, deeply distressed. "She struggles to breathe, O King. She can't eat or walk. She has a fever, and her eyes are sunken. None of my remedies has helped. If you know of any other woman in your Great City who might offer some cure . . ." Meherah stopped, to cry and humbly apologize as Zehker had instructed. It wasn't hard to cry; she was genuinely scared.

Clearly frustrated, Nimr-Rada pushed one dark foot at the lolling, speckled Tselem and tapped his flail against his own leopard-skin-draped thigh. At last, he reluctantly said what Zehker had hoped to hear. "I will send my own mother to speak to her attendants and to see her. Be waiting."

Almost collapsing, Meherah bowed. "Thank you, my Lord."

Erek bowed to Kuwsh, performing as his paid spy. "She is worse, perhaps dying."

Now we can be rid of her, Kuwsh thought, smiling. *I have to persuade my son in a way that he won't suspect further evil from me. Or perhaps he should suspect evil. . . .*

~◆ ◆~

Keren drank some broth to please Na'ah but shunned Gebuwrah's bread, fruit, and meat.

Gebuwrah leaned forward, insistent. "Lady, you must eat! How can you recover if you refuse food?"

I won't eat again in this Great City, Keren told Gebuwrah silently, shivering with fever. *I no longer care what happens to me.* She was unimportant. What was important was stopping Nimr-Rada—a man who had willingly murdered his precious infant son and destroyed the lives of so many others.

Yet her household was endangered if she actively resisted Nimr-Rada. Wasn't weakness her alternative? *Reveal Your will, Most High,* she implored. *Whatever pleases You . . .*

Gebuwrah snorted in disgust and stomped away. Now Revakhaw knelt beside Keren, still mourning but obviously concerned. Keren clasped Revakhaw's hand, sharing her speechless grief.

Sharp voices and a clamor outside warned them of visitors. Fatigued, Keren shut her eyes. *Let me die in peace.*

"Lady," Meherah murmured, her sturdy clothes rustling as she knelt beside Keren. "He-Who-Lifts-the-Skies has sent his own mother to inquire. . . ."

Keren felt Revakhaw's hand slip away and heard her retreating. Someone else took her place. Reluctantly, Keren opened her eyes, then stared. Achlai, mother of Nimr-Rada, neglected wife of Kuwsh, was truly here. Touching Keren's face with one broad, cool hand, Achlai said, "Your breathing is harsh, child."

Child. Hearing this tender word, Keren almost wept. How could Nimr-Rada not adore his mother? She was so kind; her dark eyes shone gently in her calm, wide face. "You make me miss my I'ma," Keren said. The effort provoked painful, violent coughing and left her shaking miserably.

"Will seeing her give you the strength to recover?" Achlai inquired.

Keren gasped at the thought and instantly coughed again. As she tried to catch her breath, Keren felt Achlai's cool fingertips checking the pulse in her throat. For a long time Achlai sat quietly, then lifted her hand from Keren's throat. Keren shivered.

Achlai tilted her dark, braid-bound head toward Meherah courteously. "Will you go tell the others that I'll leave at once? I must speak to my son." Then, before anyone else approached them, Achlai leaned down and whispered to Keren, "For the Most High!"

Stunned, Keren watched Achlai depart, now fully understanding why Achlai was neglected by her husband and son. *For the Most High.*

"You have been told the truth," Achlai said calmly, standing in Nimr-Rada's gloomy main residence, facing her Great King son, her husband, and the sadly bruised Sharah. "She is half dead. Her heartbeat fades. Lack of appetite, a fever, and the cough are killing her. Moreover, she doesn't want to live. You must give her hope; send her to her mother. Perhaps she will recover then. If not, at least she will die in peace amid her family."

"Her *mother?*" Nimr-Rada sneered. Achlai grieved at

his contempt.

Sharah frowned. "It would be just like Keren to die for no reason."

Nimr-Rada glared at Sharah, making her cringe but earning her Achlai's pity.

"The journey might kill her," Nimr-Rada observed, disgruntled.

Kuwsh said, "She's certain to die here, my son. Send her away."

Nimr-Rada contemplated Kuwsh. "Yes, she is certain to die here, my father, surrounded by her enemies."

"Give her hope," Achlai repeated. Sighing, she looked from her husband whom she honored sadly, to her son whom she loved in despair. "Without hope, she dies."

"You're leaving me," sobbed the child, piteous as she knelt beside Keren's pallet. "My I'ma told me you're ill and have to go, but I need you to stay!"

"Hush," Zeva'ah scolded softly, shaking Demamah's shoulder while preventing her from hugging Keren.

Her eyes filling with tears, Keren said, "Demamah-child, remember always . . . I love you. Don't forget me." She tugged a bracelet from her wrist and set it near her little niece. Zeva'ah snatched it, nodding stiffly toward Keren. Distressed by Zeva'ah's coldness, Keren longed to protest. Instead, she coughed violently. When she opened her eyes, Zeva'ah had vanished, taking Demamah with her.

Meherah hugged Keren, unafraid of her illness. "Be well, Lady," she urged. Beneath her breath, she added, "Remember my Lawkham; he loved you."

Dear Lawkham. Keren grieved silently, clutching Meherah's arm.

Nimr-Rada was wearing the gift Keren had given him: the blade fashioned of bone, rich in hunting scenes, ornate leopards, lions, and bulls with fiery red-stoned eyes. Imperious, he stood in her courtyard, watching as her retainers lifted her pallet to carry her away. Sharah wasn't with him, but no doubt Sharah was glad to be rid of her—and Revakhaw. To Keren's surprise, Nimr-Rada had given Revakhaw permission to leave with her.

Now he frowned at them, making Revakhaw bow her head fearfully. "You will return to the Great City within the year," he commanded.

I would rather die, Keren thought feebly. She was relieved when her attendants covered her face to hide her from the curious stares of the citizens outside. She hoped never to see Nimr-Rada again.

This was too easy, Zehker thought as they walked through fields, away from the Great City. Surely Nimr-Rada would change his mind and send messengers to retrieve Keren and her household. Yet the simplest plans were often the most successful. And this plan had been wonderfully simple—using the heartfelt pleas of the two women Nimr-Rada trusted: Meherah, who had adored Nimr-Rada in their youth, and Achlai, Nimr-Rada's sadly devoted mother. Zehker silently blessed both women but grieved that Meherah and his adoptive family had to remain in the Great City.

Slowing his pace, Zehker walked alongside Keren's pallet, which was carried by Erek and three other horsemen-guards designated by Nimr-Rada. One of these guards was Ethniy, whom Keren had saved from Nimr-Rada. The other two were Becay—an arrogant young man—and Abdiy, who was suspicious and tight-lipped. These four guardsmen disliked each other and hated Zehker, who was their superior. Ignoring them, Zehker studied Keren, whose face was now uncovered.

Her skin was gray, her lips chapped by illness, and her eyelids were closed in her hollowed face. But she was alive. Satisfied, Zehker coldly outstared her four guards, then strode ahead to think. He wanted Keren to recover before the end of their journey and to ride and use her weapons to defend herself if necessary.

Let her be well, Zehker begged Him, whose Presence lingered in Zehker's soul.

Forget Him, Nimr-Rada and Ra-Anan had commanded Zehker as a boy.

How? He had tried. And thankfully, he had failed.

A week into their journey, Keren walked unsteadily through her household encampment, supported by Revakhaw. They stopped to rest and gaze at the red-violet sunset. Disconsolate, Revakhaw said, "If you live, Lady, then I will live."

Keren sighed. "If we live, I pray you laugh again

someday."

"How can you pray such a thing? In fact, how can you still pray?" Revakhaw asked, sounding wounded.

"If I do not pray, I die."

Revakhaw helped Keren back to her pallet near the evening fire. As Keren sank gratefully onto her fleece coverlets, Revakhaw whispered, "How can I ever laugh again?"

Squeezing her friend's hand, Keren whispered back, "If you don't laugh someday, then He-Who-Lifts-the-Skies has killed your soul. He's won."

Revakhaw stiffened, her dark eyes glittering hard in the firelight.

Exhausted, but pleased by Revakhaw's show of spirit, Keren shut her eyes.

In the long weeks following, as they neared the mountains, Keren forced herself to eat. She was determined to walk, to ride, and to not burden others with caring for her. Zehker encouraged her, each day challenging her to do a little more.

Finally, the evening before they were to enter the mountains—now tantalizingly close—he placed her bow and arrows at her feet and spoke tersely, before everyone. "You are still weak, Lady."

He seemed impatient with her, but Keren knew he was pretending. Affecting equal rudeness with her Sharah imitation, she waved him off. "That's not for you to say."

Zehker inclined his head and departed to tend the horses. He was pleased; she could tell by his walk. Gladly, she picked up her bow and arrows.

"Of course you've lost no time putting us back into leather garments," Gebuwrah complained, ruthlessly outlining a fleece with her flint knife.

"Why are you so upset?" Keren stopped working on her tunic, frowning at Gebuwrah. "Cloth is less practical here; you know it's true. And you'll be warmer."

"We'll look like mere hunters' kin," Gebuwrah sniffed.

"There's nothing dishonorable about being hunters' kin." Teasing, Keren added, "Anyway, you have the same status you've enjoyed for years; you can still boss everyone around, so be happy."

Gebuwrah looked offended. She had been spoiled by too many years in the Great City, and by her own self-indulgent nature, Keren decided. Finishing her sleeve, Keren donned her new leather overtunic, then bound all her linen robes into a protective leather hide. She would need them in a few days. But she would continue to wear her gold to remind her guardsmen of the death order.

Relaxing now, Keren gazed up at the rough-barked birches and listened to the birds calling within their branches. It was good to be in the mountains again, though she dreaded the conflicts ahead. *You could become one of those conflicts,* Keren thought to Gebuwrah. *You'll certainly hinder my plans if you learn of them. How can I be rid of you?*

A worse conflict would come when she had to face her parents and the Ancient Ones and see their eyes fill with disgust, anger, and pain. *Forgive me,* she pleaded with them. *You will hate what I must say.*

329

You're planning something, Zehker decided, watching Keren sort through her belongings, packing them. Most telling to Zehker was that she had shunned Shaw-Kak in favor of Dobe. She was using the dull little horse exclusively to carry her personal gear. As Keren finished tying a bundle onto Dobe's back, she turned and caught Zehker staring at her. She swiftly looked away.

Zehker returned to his own horse, thinking, *Obviously you don't want to include me in your plans. Unfortunately, I won't give you that choice. If you run away, I'll track you until your precious Dobe drops like a stone.* Shutting his eyes briefly, he warned himself. *Be careful.*

I can't put you in danger, Keren thought, avoiding Zehker's gaze. *But I'm sure you'll follow me. I won't be able to stop you. What can I do?* She reconsidered her plans. Evidently, solitary escape wasn't an option. But she didn't want her guardsmen following her. Then she smiled. She would make them want to leave her—at least for a while.

Eliyshama's wife, Tsereth, saw Keren first and dropped her grinding stone, astonished, her dark brown eyes widening as she stood. "Keren-child!"

Hearing her, Tsereth's youngest children scampered out of the stone-and-timber lodge, shrieking and laughing. Keren's mother, Chaciydah, followed the children, burst into tears, and ran to her daughter.

Dismounting, Keren hugged her gratefully, crying, "I'ma! How I've missed you!"

Chaciydah wept, refusing to release Keren. "Tell me you won't leave me again."

"Pray!" Keren whispered, wiping her mother's tears and kissing her again.

Nine-year-old Yelalah squealed, "Keren! Let Nekokhah and Achyow see your eyes; I've told them about you, and they don't believe me."

"How can you even remember me?" Keren demanded, laughing at Yelalah, who was a wide-eyed mixture of Eliyshama and Tsereth. "You were a toddler when I left."

"I remember everything," Yelalah said indignantly.

"You only remember all the stories we've told you, O Lady-of-Endless-Wisdom," Tsereth chided. "Now, you and your brother and sister step back. I'ma-Chaciydah, let me hug Keren. You look terrible, Keren-child. But never mind, we'll fatten you up."

Keren hugged her sister-in-law, warning softly, "There are spies in my household; they will report everything to Nimr-Rada. So your sons and my father and Eliyshama shouldn't touch me—I don't dare risk their lives."

"Even here?" Tsereth asked, shocked.

"Even here. I'll keep my household separate from yours to be safe."

"I'll go warn Eliyshama and our Meshek," Tsereth murmured. Turning, she called, "Achyow! Come with me, my son. Let's find your father and brothers. And we should tell Father Meshek that our Keren is here."

"I haven't seen her eyes," Achyow pouted, shaking his dark-waved head. Keren studied Eliyshama and Tsereth's youngest son, guessing he was five years old—and probably spoiled by Chaciydah.

"Look at me," Keren commanded in her best Sharah voice. "Obey your mother!"

Seeing Keren's eyes, Achyow gasped aloud and backed off, clutching Tsereth's tunic. Tsereth winked at Keren approvingly, then led Achyow away. Yelalah twittered.

"You've scared him! He won't come near you for a year; he's such a baby."

"Don't tease him, my Yelalah. Come give me a hug and show your sister that I'm not a monster."

Delighted, Yelalah skipped into Keren's arms, kissed her, and demanded to play with Keren's gold ornaments. Not to be left out, seven-year-old Nekokhah—whom Tsereth had been pregnant with when Keren left the mountains—approached Keren shyly, clasping her hands beneath her chin. She had the same straight dark hair and ruddy-brown skin as Yelalah, but less of her vivacity. Keren smiled at her and patted her mother, who hugged Keren again.

"I'm so glad you're home—we speak of you continually!" Chaciydah wept. "Your brother Neshar is here too; he escaped that Nimr-Rada months ago."

Keren froze, then hushed her mother quickly. "Don't let anyone in my household hear that! Half of them are spies for Nimr-Rada; they'd betray Neshar."

How did you escape? she wondered to Neshar. She was thrilled. And terrified.

Yelalah tugged insistently at Keren's sleeve. "I *do* remember your eyes!"

Keren's fears faded as she laughed, enjoying Yelalah's sincerity. "I believe you."

Tsereth returned as Keren unpacked and tended Dobe. "The men are coming," Tsereth said loudly. Lowering her voice, she added, "I've warned them as you said. Meysha and Darak are going to the Lodge of the Ancient Ones. They will take Achyow along."

Keren sighed, relieved, though she longed to see her nephews, Meysha and Darak, now young men of nineteen and seventeen. "What about Neshar?" Keren whispered.

"I'ma-Chaciydah told you he's here?"

"Yes, and I've warned her to say nothing; we must keep Neshar hidden."

"Neshar will also hide with the Ancient Ones. Thankfully, he rode his horse to the herds this morning." Ever busy, Tsereth lifted Keren's bundled ceremonial garments.

Thinking swiftly, Keren whispered, "Can you hide that bundle in your stable? And is there room for my horse?"

"Of course, now that Neshar's horse isn't there; I'm sure my milk goats won't mind the change." Tsereth smiled. "Keep your guardsmen-spies busy, and I'll hide these— though later I'll want to know why."

As Tsereth departed, Keren approached her guardsmen, Erek, Becay, Ethniy, Abdiy, and Zehker, who was watching her closely. She smiled. "My father will certainly harvest a lamb or a goat for us to feast on tonight, but we'll need more meat later. Would any of you like to go hunting?"

"We'd need to hunt for more than one day to harvest enough meat, Lady," Becay answered, condescending.

"Of course," Keren agreed humbly.

"But for no more than seven days," Zehker commanded them.

Erek narrowed his eyes at Zehker. "What are *you* going to do while we're gone?"

"He will be chopping wood," Keren interposed coolly.

"And he could use help."

The guardsmen bowed and retreated, eager to leave. Zehker also bowed to her. A corner of his mouth twitched, covering a smile.

Hiding her glee, Keren went to help Revakhaw and the others set up their tent.

⁓⊕ ⊕⁓

Keren's eyes filled with tears, watching as her father and Eliyshama penned their sheep before their lodge.

Eliyshama waved his herding staff at her, grinning. "You look awful! Have you been starving yourself?"

"I was near death, which is why He-Who-Lifts-the-Skies sent me here," Keren said, smiling through her tears. "Eliyshama, please, hug Father for me as if you've not seen him for years!"

Instantly Eliyshama dropped his staff and gave his father a crushing embrace, kissing Meshek's cheek, then pounding his back happily. "She's missed you, Father!"

His dark eyes brimming, reddening, Meshek stared over Eliyshama's shoulder at Keren. When he was able to speak, Meshek said, "I wish you the same embrace, my Keren-child. Now tell me everything."

⁓⊕ ⊕⁓

Meshek handed Zehker a copper-bladed ax of marvelous quality. "I'm told you'll need this for a week."

"Yes. Thank you." Zehker appraised the shining, cold-hammered ax. "Who made this?"

"Metiyl of the tribe of Asshur. He brought his family to the mountains after that Nimr-Rada attacked his tribe.

They live within a day's walk of here."

"Good," Zehker said beneath his breath. To have a skilled metalworker nearby was a blessing. His own father had carried such an ax. Zehker swiftly pushed thoughts of his father away and glanced at Meshek, who was watching him steadily.

"Thank you," Meshek said, clearly referring to Zehker's role in Keren's return.

Embarrassed, Zehker changed the subject. "She plans to visit the Ancient Ones?"

"Before dawn," Meshek told him. "Sleep in my stable tonight if you wish to follow her. We'll detain her attendants here, except for Nimr-Rada's wife, Revakhaw." Meshek spoke harshly, not looking at Zehker. "What Sharah did to her . . . !"

Meshek stopped, too angry to finish. He was clearly ashamed of Sharah, knowing now that nothing was beyond her. Zehker shared his opinion. He intended to keep Keren from ever seeing her sister again. Otherwise, Sharah would eventually destroy Keren. Or Keren would destroy Sharah.

"We'll leave before sunrise," Keren whispered to Revakhaw as they tied the lashings of their leather tent. "I'll need your help. And your presence will protect Zehker—I'm sure he will follow us."

"That's his duty, Lady," Revakhaw said. "But must I see the Ancient Ones?"

"They'll love you. And they need to hear your story."

"Why?" Revakhaw dropped a tie.

Keren wrenched a knot ferociously. "Because they need

to know why I long to kill that Nimr-Rada."

"Will you?"

"I long to. Whether I can or not . . . we'll know soon enough."

As instructed, Revakhaw crept out of Keren's tent into the darkness, toward Meshek's stable. Keren waited briefly, then followed her. Tsinnah turned in her sleep. Gebuwrah burrowed deeper into her fleeces but didn't wake.

Sleep until dawn, Keren silently urged her remaining attendants. *Give us enough time to get away.*

Keren approached her father's stone-and-thatch stable. As she expected, Zehker emerged from the shadows. "Revakhaw is waiting inside. I'll lead the horses around; they are ready."

Inside the stable, Revakhaw was trembling, but she had managed to open Keren's bundle of ceremonial robes. Keren dressed rapidly, shivering in the cool air. She threw on her overtunic for warmth, tied her sandals, and hurried outside.

Zehker had halted Dobe beside an old stump, which Keren gratefully used to mount the horse. Revakhaw climbed on behind her, clutching Keren's despised face paints in a pouch. Swiftly, Zehker handed Keren her bow and arrows, then mounted his own horse.

"You're still shaking," Keren whispered to Revakhaw.

"I'm scared."

"Don't be," Keren said. "This will be easy. When we face Nimr-Rada again, then you can be scared."

Revakhaw groaned faintly. Zehker nodded to Keren, and she led them away from the Lodge of Meshek.

Twenty-Three

HUMMING, ANNAH knelt to weed Naomi's prized herb garden. Birdsong and sunlight brightened the morning mist as she worked. This would be a lovely day; soon Shem would return from checking the herds, and together they would walk to the Lodge of Meshek to welcome their dear Karan. Annah smiled, remembering how frightened Tsereth's little Achyow had been the night before. He had described Karan's "terrible" eyes, then asked, "She can't truly see . . . can she?"

Noakh and Naomi had laughed at him as Shem said, "She saw right through *you*, son-of-my-sons."

Annah had soothed the little boy with happy childhood stories of Karan, while teaching him to sort lentils. Achyow's two older brothers, Meysha and Darak, had gladly abandoned him to Annah's care in favor of their Uncle Neshar's company. Now, as she weeded, Annah saw

Achyow wander from the lodge, sleep tousled, his dusky little face creased with imprints from his pillow.

Annah sat back. "Achyow-child! Come to I'ma-Annah."

The little boy stumbled into Annah's arms, still half asleep. As Annah kissed his dark hair, Naomi leaned outside the doorway and pretended indignation, shaking her silvery head.

"Huh! He walked right past me, daughter. Achyow-child, when I catch you, I'll make you sorry you ignored me!"

Naomi stopped, openmouthed, staring past Annah. Puzzled, Annah turned. Two horses with three riders were emerging from the morning mists below. Annah vaguely recognized the young man on the first horse. As for the two young women sharing the second, one was unknown to Annah, while the other young woman was like an apparition—eerie, yet familiar. Annah blinked, astonished by the apparition's dreadful weapons, her three-pronged gold headpiece, form-fitting linen garments, lavish gold ornaments, and gold sandals. Most shocking of all were the apparition's intensely painted lips and eyes—those unforgettable eyes.

Annah gasped, "Karan-child?"

Achyow whimpered and fled from Annah's lap, past Naomi, into the lodge. Annah stood, unable to believe that this cold, shocking apparition—now dismounting from her horse—was Karan. But within a breath, the shock vanished; Karan dropped her weapons, raked off the gold headpiece, and flung it to the ground at Annah's feet. Glittering tears filled her pale eyes.

"See what I've become?" she cried to Annah. "A non-woman!"

"Not in your heart," Annah said, grieved. "Come here,

Karan-child."

Karan crept into Annah's embrace, seeming as young as Achyow. Karan's shame and frailty were obvious. Infuriated, Annah thought, *Kuwsh, Nimr-Rada, Sharah, Ra-Anan—look what you've done to my Karan-child!*

"You'll be well now, daughter," she told Karan protectively.

Naomi approached and hugged Karan tight. "Look at you—wretched and stick thin! This is Nimr-Rada's doing —don't deny it! I long to shake him and his father!"

"Karan-child," Annah murmured, glancing at the young man who was covering their horses with fleeces and tying them to the battered stump near the doorway. "Come into the lodge—you and your companions. Have something to eat and drink; we will hear your story when my Shem and our Noakh have returned from the herds."

In brisk agreement, Naomi nodded to the second young woman, who retrieved Karan's headpiece. "Now, who is this?"

"I'ma-Naomi, I'ma-Annah," Karan said, "this is my dear friend Revakhaw."

Annah studied Revakhaw, liking her immediately, but wondering at the deep sadness in her sweet brown face and shadowed eyes. *What had happened to this child, who lowered her head as if humiliated by my gaze?*

To Annah's horror, Karan said, "Revakhaw is Nimr-Rada's true wife—against her will."

"Against her will?" Realizing Karan's meaning, Annah shut her eyes hard. *How dare you!* she screamed silently at Nimr-Rada. *How dare you shame this sweet girl and my Karan-child!*

When Annah opened her eyes, Revakhaw was crying. Naomi clasped Revakhaw's hands kindly, welcoming her, and Annah gently hugged the unhappy girl. "Come, all of you. We will eat, then you'll tell us everything."

"You'll hate what we have to say," Karan whispered, tears smudging the black paint at the corners of her eyes.

Her words filled Annah with dread.

Neshar sat inside the lodge with Shem, Annah, Naomi, Achyow, and Noakh, listening as Revakhaw told her story. She seemed too ashamed to even lift her gaze. And when she told of Sharah taunting her, taking her newborn son, then turning her out into the streets of the Great City, Neshar shuddered. He was sickened, remembering the one time he had seen Revakhaw in Keren's courtyard. She had been altogether more delightful than any girl alive. Neshar had thought of her often since that day, as one would desire a perfect unattainable dream. And now the same Revakhaw was crying before him, wholly devastated by Nimr-Rada and Sharah's self-serving schemes.

I will kill you, Neshar thought, covering his face with one cold hand, astonished by the depths of his rage. *Nimr-Rada, whatever I must do, you will be destroyed.*

Composing himself, Neshar lowered his hand. Revakhaw hushed, obviously too wounded to speak of her infant son in Sharah's arms. Beside her, Keren was crying again, clenching her hands tight. She looked at Neshar, terrified, seeming to beg him for courage. Neshar stared at his sister, fearing what she was about to say.

Annah almost wept aloud, hearing Karan tell of another god now worshiped beneath these blue heavens at the urging of that Nimr-Rada. His name should have been Nu-Marad, man of rebellion. How could the citizens of the Great City deny the love of the Most High? How could they scorn His wisdom, unless they truly believed that Nimr-Rada was the Promised One?

Karan faltered, speaking of the ceremony in Nimr-Rada's Temple of Shemesh. Of poison. Of fire. Of the death of Revakhaw's child. Listening, Annah was stabbed by a long-ago pain, remembering the stillborn form of her youngest brother. She had tried to bury the memory, telling herself that such evil would never happen again in this new earth. But Nimr-Rada had enacted this same evil. Why? *Why does our Adversary—that Serpent—crave the blood of defense- less little ones?* The thought tormented her.

Nearby, Noakh's voice rose in a mourning whisper. "I've failed. . . ."

Unexpectedly, Neshar bolted from the lodge, followed by the young guardsman, Zehker, who had been waiting near the door. Their grimness alarmed Annah.

"That Nimr-Rada is a madman!" Naomi cried, clutching Achyow in her lap. She turned to Noakh as if to demand the chance to rebuke Nimr-Rada herself. But seeing her husband's anguish, her anger faded and she moaned, "Why did we live to see the children of our children turn against the Most High?"

Now Shem exhaled; Annah could almost feel his inner turmoil. Karan turned to Shem, raising her hands in a fierce appeal. "Father of my Fathers, Nimr-Rada must be stopped! No one should suffer as Revakhaw has suffered. I *have* to —"

"Listen to me," Shem interrupted quietly, halting Karan's tirade. "You bound yourself to Nimr-Rada with your oaths.

Let your word stand."

"What?" Karan gaped at him, clearly shaken. And Naomi stared at Shem as if he had lost his mind.

But Noakh straightened, grieving yet watchful. "Tell us your thoughts, my son."

"She should honor her oaths," Shem said, "until those oaths are openly judged to be against the will of the Most High."

"And when might this 'judging' be?" Naomi demanded, releasing the squirming Achyow, who instantly darted outside.

"Midsummer, next year." Shem held Karan with a steady gaze. "You should confront Nimr-Rada openly, honorably, on a day he surely considers most favorable—the longest day of Shemesh, his Sun. We will summon the leaders of all the tribes to hear your testimony. And we will hear his testimony, then judge the truth."

Karan looked ill. Moved by her misery, Annah touched Shem's arm. He looked at Annah, his eyes as dark and wonderful as when they first met. *I love you,* Annah thought.

Quietly she asked, "Shouldn't our Karan-child stay with us until this judging?"

"She should stay with her mother, to honor her word," Shem murmured. Smiling, he added, "But she should visit us whenever possible, as she has done today." Then his smile disappeared as he spoke to Karan. "Remember your name, *Karan.* Push Nimr-Rada to confront you. Use your testimony to gore his soul until he cannot escape the truth."

Weakly, Karan nodded. Annah wondered if she was about to faint, but Karan excused herself quietly and left the lodge, followed by Revakhaw, who seemed a mere shadow in Karan's footsteps. Shutting her eyes, Annah prayed for both women.

Aloud, Noakh said, "We should offer prayers and sacrifices to the Most High. For their protection, and for ours."

Shem nodded, then paused. Very softly, he spoke to Annah. "Beloved, the children of our children are older than we were at these same ages. . . ."

Unwilling to hear what he was about to say, Annah raised a hand, shaking her head. *Don't say it*, she pleaded in her thoughts. *It's not true. They cannot be older than we were.*

Shem kissed her upraised hand quietly. Annah bit down her tears.

Keren felt the same quivering weakness she had felt when wading from the river after retrieving Lawkham's body. Confront Nimr-Rada? How? He would kill her. He would kill them all. This tribal gathering and judging was not what she had anticipated from Shem. But what had she anticipated? Had she expected Shem or Noakh to say, "Certainly, Karan-child, go kill that Nimr-Rada"?

No. Being the elders, they wanted to negotiate with Nimr-Rada, bringing him peaceably to reason. But Nimr-Rada would never be peaceable. And he held such contempt for the Ancient Ones.

Beside her, Revakhaw said, "*Karan* suits you. After all, you've been pushing Nimr-Rada since the first day I met you. Truly, the Ancient Ones are right; you're the only person alive capable of pushing him."

Keren grimaced, feeling incapable of pushing Nimr-Rada into anything just now, particularly a tribal meeting intended to strip him of his spiritual pretensions. Quietly, she said, "Look. My brother is talking with Zehker."

Like two guilty boys, Neshar and Zehker stepped apart as Keren and Revakhaw approached. Keren's distress eased as she greeted Neshar. "How did you escape?"

"I'm dead," he answered calmly, his face lean and handsome. "I went hunting alone, made a kill, then tore my garments, bloodied them, and scattered them about with some of my weapons. If the Most High blesses us, our Nimr-Rada will believe I'm in some predator's gut."

"Ugh." Revakhaw winced.

Neshar stared at her. "Lady," he said gently, formally acknowledging her as Nimr-Rada's wife, "if I could do anything to compensate you for the sorrows Sharah and the others have inflicted upon you, I would."

Revakhaw nodded and ducked her head, almost in tears. Grieving, Keren glanced from Revakhaw to Neshar, who seemed infinitely saddened . . . and infatuated.

Despondent, Keren thought, *They might have been happy together.*

Meeting Keren's gaze, Neshar changed the subject. "I have returned to the Most High. I believe that our brothers—excluding Ra-Anan—will return to Him eventually. They realize Nimr-Rada is not the Promised One."

Before Keren could exclaim her delight, Neshar nudged the silent Zehker. "We should wash. I'm sure the Ancient Ones will offer a sacrifice this evening—for all of us."

Zehker nodded agreement, eyeing Keren. She gasped, suddenly realizing that he had joined Neshar in returning to the Most High. Exhilarated, she restrained herself from hugging Zehker. Instead she laughed at him, almost dancing.

He grinned, the first genuine smile he had dared to reveal; the sight of his wonderful dimples took her breath away.

She stepped back, sorely tempted by that grin. "Go,

before I touch you," she warned him.

Zehker bowed almost jauntily and went with Neshar to the stream that flowed down the lower hills near the lodge. Keren watched them go, sighing, enthralled.

A hand gripped her arm. Keren jumped, remembering Revakhaw. "You *love* him," Revakhaw gasped, clearly stunned. "And he loves you. . . ."

"Yes," Keren agreed simply. "Forgive us; we forgot ourselves. Now our lives depend upon your silence."

"As if I would say anything to anyone," Revakhaw protested indignantly, showing some of her former spirit.

Keren smiled, then sighed again, wishing Revakhaw were free to marry; she would have encouraged her to escape with Neshar.

"It was kind of your brother to speak to me," Revakhaw said, mournful now.

Carefully neutral, Keren murmured, "He longs to protect you."

"Oh." Revakhaw hesitated, then shook her head. "No one can protect me."

"Only the Most High."

"Your Most High . . ."

"And Neshar's Most High."

Revakhaw stared at Keren, silent.

Sacrificial smoke drifted over them all as Noakh raised his hands in praise to the Most High. Keren watched Revakhaw carefully. She was crying again, no doubt remembering that her infant son's body had been consumed in such a fire. But to a nonexistent god. Keren resolved to talk to her friend later, when Revakhaw was ready to listen. Calm now, Keren lowered her face into her hands and closed her eyes, cherishing her time with the Most High. She felt forgiven. And loved.

When they had offered their last prayers, and the fire was dwindling, Shem approached Keren. "I know you are worried about this midsummer gathering, daughter. But don't be afraid. The Most High guards you in this—as He has protected you thus far. As for Nimr-Rada, you must convince him to accept our summons."

"How can I convince him from a distance?" Keren wondered aloud. Pondering this, she looked down at her bare feet, stripped of her scorned ceremonial sandals. Humbly bared feet were the only way to approach the Most High on His holy ground before His altar. A thought occurred to her, and she smiled, making Shem raise a dark eyebrow.

Answering his unspoken question, Keren said, "He will be convinced."

Meysha and Darak, Eliyshama's two older sons, agreed to act as messengers for the Ancient Ones. To verify that Noakh and Shem had truly instigated this formal mid-summer gathering, Meysha wore Noakh's distinctive gold-leaf pendant, while Shem had given Darak a gold medallion embossed with a tapering branch—the handiwork of An-nah's father before the Great Destruction.

"One more thing," Annah murmured, before the two young men departed. She removed her cherished shell carving—made by Shem—and placed its dark cord around Meysha's neck. "Take this to Yeiysh, son of your cousin Metiyl. Ask Yeiysh to accompany you and to wear this. If the three of you must separate to notify all the tribes, then each of you will wear one of our tokens."

"I'ma-Annah," Meysha protested, stricken. "How can you give up your wonderful carving?"

"This is important," Annah said gently, blinking down her tears. "Everyone will recognize it, and we know you will bring these things back to us again."

"We will, Ma'adannah," Darak promised, hugging her earnestly, then embracing Noakh and Shem.

As they watched the two young men leave, burdened with traveling packs and weapons, Noakh teased Annah. "They love you more!"

She laughed, fondly denying his words.

The two young men paused at the bottom of the slope, waved them a cheerful farewell, and headed off to the nearest tribe, the sprawling family of Metiyl.

"Most High, protect them," Noakh sighed aloud.

"Metiyl will be visiting us soon," Annah announced, delighted.

Returned from their successful hunting trip, Erek, Becay, Ethniy, and Abdiy all expected praise from Keren. They had brought her two deer, plus partridges, hares, and fox furs. Keren thanked them politely and said, "Now, you'll need some of this meat for a journey: I must send a message to He-Who-Lifts-the-Skies."

"But someone should stay to guard you, Lady," Ethniy objected, frowning.

"My father is as strict as Zehker," Keren pointed out. "And Zehker is staying. Though you may stay too, Ethniy. Three men traveling together will be safe enough."

Ethniy clearly regretted his impulsiveness; he eyed

Zehker, who was stacking chopped wood near Meshek's stable adjoining the lodge. Keren smiled, certain that Ethniy was correctly imagining that he would be chopping wood for the rest of the summer, into autumn. He would also be building two small lodges: one for Keren and her attendants, and another for himself and Zehker.

"Let it be as you say, Lady," Becay said impatiently. "Tell us your message for He-Who-Lifts-the-Skies."

"Tell him I will be fully recovered at the end of the year, as he said. Also tell him that the Ancient Ones wish to speak to him personally at a midsummer gathering of all the tribal leaders at the source of the eastern river. Here . . ." Keren handed her right ceremonial sandal to the bewildered Erek. Carefully expressionless, she said, "He-Who-Lifts-the-Skies will understand why I have sent him this."

The guardsmen frowned, doubtful. Keren met their gazes steadily, knowing she looked frail because she had deliberately shunned meals in their absence. "Thank you," she said. "I realize this is a burden for you."

Becay nodded, but Abdiy grunted irritably. "At least we won't have to spend the winter in these mountains," he muttered to Becay as soon as Keren dismissed them.

Yes, Keren thought gratefully. *At least you three will be gone for the winter.*

Erek, however, lingered nearby, holding Keren's sandal as if it might poison him. "Ah, Lady." He hesitated, cautiously keeping his distance. "You're sure that you've nothing else to say to our He-Who-Lifts-the-Skies?"

Keren sighed and knelt, suddenly very tired. "Give him the sandal, Erek. Truly, he is wise and will understand."

Relaxing in the crisp autumn air, Keren watched as her wild-haired cousin Metiyl and his son Khawrawsh worked at the deep hearth near the Ancient Ones' lodge. Khawrawsh was plying a pair of leather foot bellows, heating the stout clay firing pot that contained Meshek and Shem's mangled copper ax heads.

As he worked, Khawrawsh furtively watched Tsinnah, who had accompanied Keren and Revakhaw today. Metiyl looked up from his side of the hearth and frowned.

"Khawrawsh!" he roared. "You'll get burned, and you'll deserve it too! Ignore that pretty girl and stomp those bellows." Turning to Neshar and Zehker now, Metiyl sneered, "You've beaten those ax heads to shavings; I'd almost think you've been working like ordinary men."

Keren suppressed a smile. Metiyl detested Neshar and Zehker for being horsemen-guards to Nimr-Rada.

Now that Metiyl had deigned to acknowledge him, Zehker approached him. "Your axes are exceptional."

Metiyl grunted and shoved some thick clay molds into the outermost coals. "What do you want, horseman? I came to work for the Ancient Ones, not for you."

"You have the wrong opinion of us, cousin," Neshar said. He crouched at Metiyl's right, while Zehker leaned toward Metiyl on the left.

Instantly Metiyl's thick brows rushed together in a frown, and his broad nostrils flared. "Horsemen or not, I can crush you both!"

"Good," Zehker replied quietly. "But first, we'll talk."

"Let's leave them to argue," Keren murmured to Revakhaw and Tsinnah, not wanting them to hear Zehker and Neshar's plans—though Keren resolved to question Zehker later. As they went toward the lodge, she noticed that both young women cast backward glances toward the men at the hearth—Revakhaw sadly, Tsinnah smiling.

Before Keren could enter the lodge, her small nephew Achyow darted out, skittering away from Keren to sit near Metiyl's son Khawrawsh. Now Zehker, Neshar, and Metiyl stepped away from the hearth, talking quietly. Metiyl was listening intently, eyebrows raised, pleased.

You are discussing weapons, Keren decided. *And the death of Nimr-Rada.*

Kneeling beside Keren's I'ma-Annah, Revakhaw moistened her lips. "Ma'adannah . . . our Keren—I mean Karan—told me that you survived the loss of your family before the Great Destruction. How? I feel such grief for my son, I long to die. . . ."

Ma'adannah smiled at Revakhaw, her lovely, dark-lashed eyes warm and understanding. "You will grieve for years, child. But you are cherished by many people, including me. Survival . . ." She sighed, as if remembering ageless sorrows. "For me, knowing that just one person truly loved me and wanted me to live . . . it was enough. My Shem's love—and the love of the Most High—persuaded me to survive."

Their words always return to You! Revakhaw cried silently to the Most High, rebellious, shutting her eyes hard. *But why do You want me to live with such pain?*

In the midst of her unspoken outcry, Revakhaw felt Ma'adannah's arms go around her comfortingly. "Our Revakhaw . . . never forget the child who was stolen from you by Nimr-Rada's schemes and hatred! But remember that the Most High longs to console you; He grieves for you, child . . . as you grieve for your son."

Broken, Revakhaw wept.

Wrapped in the ceremonial splendor of his gold, linens, and a new fleece mantle, Kuwsh shivered in Nimr-Rada's courtyard. He stared at the cause of his discomfort—a slender, sparkling golden sandal, which rested on the pavings where the Lady Keren once knelt.

Also fixated on the lovely sandal, Nimr-Rada waved his flail at everyone in the courtyard, from Keren's wearied guardsmen to Kuwsh and the pale Sharah. "Leave!"

At once everyone began to file out, silent and afraid. Leaning toward Nimr-Rada, Kuwsh begged hoarsely, "Don't go after her! She doesn't love you! That sandal is meant to befuddle your reasoning, my son—not to convey any true message. Those Ancient Ones are using her to entrap you."

Nimr-Rada straightened proudly. "You sound like a fearful child, my father. What are those Ancient Ones to me? Nothing! I will go to their midsummer gathering, listen to their foolish speeches, denounce their stupidity, then retrieve her. She promised me her devotion, and she will fulfill her promises."

"Don't go!" Kuwsh warned again.

"I can defeat any man who stands against me, and my guards can easily overcome their weak rebellion. Why are you so afraid?"

In despair, Kuwsh shook his head.

Nimr-Rada was still staring at the sandal as Sharah left

the courtyard.

Humiliated, she looked around, wondering if her servants were daring to gloat. Her gaze settled upon one of her horsemen, Qaydawr—an amazingly handsome man. He alone was watching her. She held his look deliberately, then lowered her lashes, suddenly pleased.

In her quiet home, Achlai looked at her husband sadly, knowing that Kuwsh was telling her of their son's plans only because he could not speak so freely to anyone else. Achlai always kept her husband's words close. And his fears. But he never admitted that he feared the Most High.

Achlai silently admitted her fear, then thought, *It is a terrible thing to have such a son as Nimr-Rada, while loving You, O Most High. . . .*

Twenty-Four

KNEELING BEFORE the crackling fire in Keren's lodge, Tsereth's youngest daughter, Nekokhah, shyly plucked at the sleeve of Keren's leather tunic.

Keren paused in stitching a soft leather boot. "Yes, my Nekokhah?"

Casting a wary look at Yelahlah, who was kneading dough with Alatah, Nekokhah cupped a small hand to Keren's ear, whispering, "Gebuwrah hates you."

Keren nodded, watching Gebuwrah, who sat with Revakhaw and Tsinnah, sharpening bone needles against a filing stone. Gebuwrah's hostility had grown with the deepening winter cold. And now that spring was almost here, her contempt was in full bloom, every word dripping with sarcasm, every glance suspecting mischief. She was thoroughly aggrieved at being removed from the Great City; she hated the mountains and seemed to hate her mistress as well. Keren dreaded their daily confrontations.

Leaning over, Keren cupped a hand to her niece's ear. "Don't worry about her; let's just enjoy our visit." Aloud, she said, "Shall we go help Na'ah and Alatah with our food?"

Cautiously the little girl nodded and scooted toward Na'ah, whom she liked.

Keren took a dish of dried fruit. "Do you want us to sort these, Na'ah?"

"If you could, Lady," Na'ah said, her eyes shining. "Ethniy said that he and Zehker are making stew for their meal today, but I think we'll have enough fruitcakes to send some to them."

"That's the last of our dried fruit," Gebuwrah said darkly.

Na'ah widened her gentle eyes, indignant. "Don't you think I know it? But we can share, Gebuwrah. Do you think we would have stayed warm this past winter without all the firewood Ethniy and Zehker provided for us?"

"We won't starve," Keren told Gebuwrah, keeping her voice kind. "We'll be able to gather new greens and shoots soon; until then, we have dried meat and grains."

Gebuwrah opened and closed her mouth sulkily. "As you say. Forgive me."

Yelahlah spoke now, waving a dough-coated finger at Na'ah. "You like Ethniy and he likes you. Are you going to marry him?"

While everyone gasped or laughed, Na'ah blushed. Keren smiled, delighted to have her suspicions confirmed; Gebuwrah's hostility wasn't the only emotion to blossom these past few months.

"Ethniy is a good man," Keren told Na'ah. "But He-Who-Lifts-the-Skies will decide our futures this summer."

Her stomach tightened at the thought.

***

Gebuwrah slipped around the corner of the stable and paused beneath the dripping, rain-soaked eaves, peering inside. A pile of fresh wood shavings and some leather scraps had been left on the earthen floor near the shabby horse stall. That arrogant Zehker had been in here all morning, working with that Metiyl.

You're making new axes, Gebuwrah thought angrily. *And I'm sure it's because you're plotting against our He-Who-Lifts-the-Skies.* She frowned, thinking hard. Whatever they were planning, that Metiyl and Zehker would never defeat the Great King. And Gebuwrah had no intention of being seen as a traitor alongside them. Was the Lady Keren involved in this plot?

I won't die with you; you'll bear your own punishment, she told Keren silently. *If you had listened to me, and if you'd been more agreeable all along, I wouldn't be in this miserable situation now.*

***

Keren raised her new shortened decorative bow, masterfully carved by Zehker.

"Your stance is sloppy," Neshar teased, watching.

"Your beard is worse," Keren said sweetly, wrinkling her nose at him. "Now go help Zehker and our Ancient Ones in the fields and leave me alone."

"I tremble."

"Liar," Keren retorted mildly, eyeing her target—a scrap of birch bark, mounted on a swaying deerskin slung from the branches of I'ma-Annah's favorite willow tree, her second Tree of Havah. Relaxing, Keren remembered Lawkham's long-ago weaponry lessons.

Push your left arm straight and forward. . . . Pull the bowstring back. Let the hand holding the bowstring rest just beneath and against your jaw. . . .

A stinging swat frightened Keren badly, making her miss her target. Neshar laughed and taunted her with an unfinished arrow. "See! Your aim is—"

"Rat!" Keren struck his arm with her bow, making him jump.

He swatted her repeatedly with the arrow, grinning. "What'll you do now, *little* sister, eh? I dare you to—"

She swiped him again. He grabbed the end of her bow and they jostled each other.

"Skinny girl! Give up!"

"Big mouth!" Worried about damaging her new bow, Keren snatched an arrow from her quiver and jabbed it toward him. He danced back a few steps, released her bow, then charged at her again. Keren darted across the clearing toward Noakh's lodge, shrieking with laughter as Neshar chased her. Others were laughing with her now—Tsinnah, Alatah, and . . . Revakhaw.

Their laughter stopped Neshar in his tracks. Bowing to Keren mockingly, he said, "Peace, *Lady*." He glanced toward Revakhaw and the others, bowing his head, acknowledging their cheers. "Admit it; I've won."

"*No!*" Swiftly Keren slapped his rump with an arrow and dashed inside the lodge, where she would be safe. Outside, the others howled with delight.

"Hush," I'ma-Naomi scolded fondly, busily winding a spindle of thread. "Achyow is napping." Beside her, combing a fine tuft of light wool, I'ma-Annah smiled.

"What are you doing, Karan-child?"

"Making Revakhaw laugh," Keren said, pleased. She had feared that Nimr-Rada had destroyed Revakhaw's laughter forever. But he had failed.

Don't let him triumph at the midsummer gathering, Keren implored the Most High. *Show He-Who-Lifts-the-Skies the will of his own Creator.*

❦ ❦

Beneath the first misty-gray traces of dawn, Gebuwrah crept through the dew-dampened grass toward the rough-stone stable to check it again—as she had been doing for weeks. They would leave this morning, but she would be sure that the overbearing Zehker would leave without his new weapons. She was going to burn them to ashes and blackened metal. How dare he plot against the Great King and endanger *her!* Well, she'd be sure He-Who-Lifts-the-Skies heard of Zehker's rebellion. *And I will be rewarded.*

Imagining Nimr-Rada's gratitude, Gebuwrah eagerly crept into the stables. Rummaging through the straw, she scowled. Where were those axes? She was sure Zehker had left them here last night. Irritated, she passed Keren's stupid horse, Dobe, and checked Tsereth's milk goats in their little enclosure, then inspected the other side of the feed trough. Nothing. And the dim corners appeared to be empty. After poking through the straw again, Gebuwrah straightened, frustrated.

As she turned, Zehker appeared in the doorway, eyeing her calmly, Dobe's bridle and lead reins in his hands.

"Move," she commanded, her heart thudding hard.

He shook his head. "No."

"Where's Gebuwrah?" Keren asked, looking around the clearing before the Lodge of Meshek.

"She won't be coming," Zehker answered, fashioning a makeshift rein for Dobe.

Keren frowned at him suspiciously; Gebuwrah had been eagerly anticipating their return to the Great City, so it was unlikely that she would refuse to leave. "Is she ill?"

"No, Lady." He bound a leather strap to a toughened leather bit and worked it into Dobe's mouth. "But it's best for her to stay."

"Who tied these here?" Tsereth called from the front of the lodge; her milk goats were conveniently tethered just outside the doorway.

Zehker hurried toward her. Keren followed him, her suspicions growing.

Seeing them, Tsereth smiled. "Did you bring the goats to me, Zehker? Thank you. It's a pity you're leaving, now that I've got you trained."

"Eliyshama should put them in the stable tonight," Zehker informed her grimly. "There's another loud, stinking goat in there who shouldn't be released until then. Keep your children away too; she will be angry."

"You didn't!" Keren gasped, horrified.

Zehker inclined his head toward the amused Tsereth. "Forgive me."

Keren pushed another dried stick into the fire, watching uneasily as sparks snapped upward into the darkness, swayed by a chilling breeze from the huge salt lake nearby. Shem, Meshek, Zehker, the bearded Neshar, Metiyl, his son Khawrawsh, and the guardsman Ethniy were having a loud discussion on the other side of the hearth. After days of travel, Ethniy was finally questioning their new weapons, Neshar's presence, and Gebuwrah's surprising absence from this journey.

"Whatever you're planning, you've involved me against my will!" Ethniy fumed at Zehker and Neshar. "He-Who-Lifts-the-Skies won't believe me if I say I had nothing to do with this. And do you really think you can overcome him and all his guards?"

"Those weapons are for our protection," Metiyl argued. "That king of yours stole my father's lands, and mine. We'd be foolish to go there unprotected."

"We will not provoke a fight at this gathering," Shem said firmly. "I will hear what Nimr-Rada has to say for himself, and everyone's complaints will be heard. Things will be decided justly."

"But will those decisions be obeyed?" Meshek asked, almost challenging Shem—which distressed Keren; her father usually revered Shem without question. "What if that Nimr-Rada decides to take my daughter with him again? She despises him. And I'll refuse to let him take her!"

They all looked at Keren. She felt obligated to speak. "I am unimportant. But Nimr-Rada has committed crimes against all the tribes, and against the Most High. He has destroyed lives—I will testify to that. He should pay with his own life."

"How can you say that without an open rebellion?" Ethniy demanded. "And if there's a rebellion, I'll be considered guilty simply by being here with you now."

"I won't stop you if you wish to leave," Keren said, aware of Na'ah's miserable gaze flicking from her to Ethniy.

"No, I don't wish to leave," Ethniy said reluctantly, glancing at Na'ah. "But I also don't wish to throw away my life for nothing."

"There are things worth dying for," Neshar said quietly, as Khawrawsh grunted and Zehker nodded in agreement, staring hard at the flames.

"There are also justice and order and reason," Shem admonished. "We will conduct this gathering properly. We will hear everyone, including Nimr-Rada. And if he must be punished, then he *will* be punished."

"How, Father of my Father?" Metiyl leaned forward, his big fists clenched on his knees. "His men outnumber our own!"

"Do they?" Shem asked, his dark eyes flaring in the firelight. "Let the Most High deal with his men."

Keren shivered.

Seated nearby, I'ma-Annah said softly, "I'm glad our Noakh and Naomi did not come with us."

Or my I'ma, Keren thought, remembering Chaciydah's fears at their parting. *She should not have to see her husband and children die.*

Later, as the others prepared their sleeping places near the fire, Meshek approached Keren. She waited, certain he wanted to talk about Nimr-Rada.

"Daughter," he said uncomfortably, looking up at the stars. "Before you left the mountains, years ago, to visit the tribe of Bezeq, I asked you to request my approval in a certain matter. Do you remember?"

Surprised, Keren recalled his demand that she seek his approval for her marriage. "Yes, I remember—though that hope is dead for as long as Nimr-Rada lives."

He looked her in the eyes now. "I approve."

He walked off. As Keren stared, astonished, he gave the unsuspecting Zehker a solid thump on the shoulder before preparing for the night.

Zehker lay awake, fatigued, staring up at the glittering stars. Sleep would bring physical rest for him but stir emotional chaos. The nightmares of his childhood had returned in fragments throughout the winter, growing now as this journey progressed.

You destroyed everything I loved, he thought to Nimr-Rada. *But the Most High has given me hope again. This past winter, I actually lived a normal life, which I treasured. And I've remembered peace. Now, I would rather die than return to your service.*

As Keren would rather die—though Zehker wanted her to live.

Turning on his side, Zehker watched Keren sleeping on the opposite side of the hearth. Her face was averted from the flames, and the smooth line of her cheek looked terrifyingly vulnerable. *Protect her,* he prayed. He dared not think beyond those words. Shutting his eyes, exhausted, he prepared to face his nightmares.

Accompanied by Revakhaw, Keren walked along the rushing torrent that led to the main river, which eventually flowed through the eastern territories now claimed by Nimr-Rada. Tents of wool and leather were scattered all along the banks of this torrent. Horses flanked some tents, but many of the leaders had apparently traveled to these low, grassy hills on foot.

"Your nephews and their fellow messengers must have invited the whole earth," Revakhaw told Keren. "But even with all these people, I'm afraid. Are you ready to face Nimr-Rada?"

"I will never be ready to face him," Keren said, sickened by the thought.

Revakhaw sighed, not looking at Keren. "He will demand that I return to him. And I fear that if I bear him another child, he will kill it as he did his firstborn. I've been praying that the Most High will save me from that . . . or . . ."

"Or from death with me?" Keren asked, hugging herself.

Nodding reluctantly, Revakhaw said, "Something I've never told you . . . I heard talk while I was in his household. . . . When his tower is finished, He-Who-Lifts-the-Skies will declare himself to be more than a man—he will be like a god."

"And I will be his most revered servant," Keren agreed bitterly.

"I think he will make you his next wife . . . in his Tower of Shemesh."

Keren shook her head at the thought, speechless.

"I don't want us to die," Revakhaw said, her voice breaking.

"Unless he lives." They gripped hands for consolation; their fingers were cold.

As they returned to the women's tent, Keren looked around, wondering if she would see her once-beloved Yithran, or his father, Ramah. Or worse, Bezeq himself. Thus far, she hadn't seen them, and she was grateful for this; it was safer for them to stay away. Nimr-Rada would almost certainly kill them. *Protect them,* she prayed to the Most High. *Please, protect us all.*

The huge, gauzy woven women's tent was crowded and warm with laughter and chatter. To Keren, it seemed that every woman entering the tent immediately looked for I'ma-Annah, who kept Keren close at her side. I'ma-Annah happily introduced Keren to her daughters by marriage, daughters by blood, daughters of sons and of daughters: Chashum, Sansannah, Tekhinnah, Yishrah, Khemdaw . . . Their names blurred in Keren's mind.

Suddenly I'ma-Annah cried, "Bekiyrah!"

A lovely woman with exquisite dark eyes and a sweetly curved mouth paused at the entrance of the tent, smiling at I'ma-Annah.

"Yes, Bekiyrah! And I'ma-Ghinnah, and I'ma-Tirtsah. . . ."

"Oh, Bekiyrah, move!" someone called behind the lovely Bekiyrah. "Ma'adannah, are you here?"

"Ghinnah!" I'ma-Annah jumped up and ran to hug a rosy, laughing woman swathed in a curiously fringed and beaded pale-blue headscarf that fluttered with her movements.

"Now, *you* move," another woman said from the entrance, her voice husky and warm. "Ma'adannah, tell our selfish Ghinnah that she must make a scarf like this for me."

"Tirtsah. . . ." I'ma-Annah embraced the complainer, who was tall and strikingly beautiful. As the three women laughed together and wiped each other's tears, Keren realized she was seeing the other two First Mothers, Ghinnah and Tirtsah.

"Come." I'ma-Annah took I'ma-Ghinnah and I'ma-Tirtsah's hands. "Meet the cause of our gathering. Karan, these are my sisters by marriage, Ghinnah and Tirtsah."

The other women hushed and moved about silently, offering food and drinks as the three First Mothers knelt with Keren.

"I've heard about you," Ghinnah said, leaning forward eagerly, the blue fringes dancing around her cheeks and throat. "You're my granddaughter Chaciydah's child. Look at your eyes!"

"They are amazing," Tirtsah agreed, raising her perfectly arched eyebrows and staring at Keren.

"I wish they weren't, I'ma-Tirtsah," Keren murmured. "My freakish eyes have caused me such grief."

"Tell us about your grief," Tirtsah commanded, kind and imperious.

Keren looked over at Revakhaw, who took a deep, visible breath, and nodded.

⁓❧ ❦⁓

As they were preparing for sleep that night, I'ma-Ghinnah approached Keren, quiet, unsmiling, but tender. "Karan-child, I don't want to distress you, but . . . I have news from the tribe of Bezeq, and of his father, Ramah."

Bezeq? Apprehensive, Keren whispered, "What is it?"

Softly, I'ma-Ghinnah explained, "Ramah and Bezeq are sons of my sons, and so we stayed with them during our journey. They did not dare come with us; Nimr-Rada would surely kill them. . . . But Bezeq's mother, Nihyah, asked me to bring you word of her regard, and of her son

Yithran. You were almost betrothed to him, weren't you?"

"Yes." Keren felt a stab of fear. Had Nimr-Rada killed Yithran after all? "What of Yithran? Is he well?"

Gently I'ma-Ghinnah said, "Yithran has married some-one else. I saw her; she's a lovely young girl from another tribe; they have a daughter."

Keren sighed. "He's alive then. I'm glad, I'ma-Ghinnah, truly. It's for the best that I didn't marry Yithran. If you see Nihyah again, please tell her I wish them blessings, with all my heart."

I'ma-Ghinnah echoed Keren's sigh, then laughed and gave her a warm hug. "I dreaded telling you this—I didn't want to upset you. But I also wish you blessings, Karan-child!"

If I live . . . "Thank you, I'ma-Ghinnah."

Tsinnah's hands were shaking as she tried to apply Keren's face paints. Alatah had to take the paints from her. Self-conscious, Keren wiped her hands over and over on her fabric-draped knees, wishing the First Mothers and the other women weren't staring. While Revakhaw combed Keren's freshly scrubbed hair, Na'ah coaxed Tsin-nah to help with Keren's gold ornaments.

Tsinnah burst into tears. "He's going to kill us!"

Murmurs of sympathy arose from the watching women. A man's voice called into the tent's entrance. "Where is the Lady Keren?"

Keren shut her eyes, recognizing her guardsman Erek's voice. He had obviously arrived last night with Nimr-Rada and his household.

"I must speak to her personally," Erek insisted, "for

He-Who-Lifts-the-Skies."

Exhaling, Keren stood and crossed the woven grass mats to the entrance.

The instant he saw her, Erek bowed and presented Keren's golden ceremonial sandal. "Lady, I return this to you from the Great King's own hand."

"Thank you, Erek." Carefully polite, she took the gleaming sandal from his warily outstretched fingertips.

"He says that you and your household will leave with him today."

Keren nodded toward him, courteous. Then, before Erek could say or notice anything else, she swiftly retreated into the tent, longing to throw the sandal away. He-Who-Lifts-the-Skies had touched it. Revolted, Keren gave the sandal to Na'ah, who dropped it as if it were poisoned.

While her attendants tied her gold-adorned leather chest covering, Keren looked over at I'ma-Annah, who was watching everything quietly, flanked by the equally somber I'ma-Ghinnah and I'ma-Tirtsah.

Controlling her fear, Keren said, "I'ma-Annah, please, if I die today, tell our I'ma-Naomi and my I'ma-Chaciydah that I love them."

"Surely that won't be necessary, Karan-child," I'ma-Annah responded. But she sounded anxious.

Keren wiped her hands again, her terror rising.

Carrying her decorative bow and wearing its matching quiver of arrows across her back, Keren walked to the main gathering area. A series of leather canopies and tents had been erected in the largest field nearby and were furnished with fine mats, thick furs, cushions, and trays and baskets of fruits, cakes, meats, juices, and watered wines. As she reached the gathering area, Keren slowed her pace, trying to compose herself.

Nimr-Rada's guardsmen lingered here and there, disdainfully proud. The tribal leaders, meanwhile, were crowded beneath the open-fronted main tent, some jovial, but most tense, and all of them focused on Nimr-Rada.

He sat, arrogant and gold covered, on a leopard-skin-draped mat in the center of the tent, surrounded by the leaders and watched by Shem and two men who resembled him so strongly that she knew they must be his brothers. Shem saw Keren first and nodded to her, indicating a vacant fleece-covered mat.

Keren looked over her shoulder at her nervous attendants and the other women. "Stay here, please; it's less crowded." They all looked relieved, except Revakhaw, who would stay with Keren during their testimony.

Slowly, following I'ma-Annah, I'ma-Ghinnah, and I'ma-Tirtsah, Keren advanced to her designated place, making sure that not even the edges of her ceremonial robes brushed anyone. Whispers and muttered comments arose in her wake.

While the First Mothers went to sit beside their husbands, Keren hesitated at the edge of her mat. Revakhaw knelt to unfasten Keren's ceremonial sandals, then scooted away, holding them carefully. Keren knelt, facing Nimr-Rada, her decorative bow resting in her lap. He studied the bow and lifted a dark eyebrow.

"A new toy, Lady?"

She compelled herself to smile, noticing that he was wearing the ornately carved bone-and-ivory sword she had given him. Had he worn it to please her? He stared at her now as if he would memorize every detail of her face, her hair, her eyes. . . . She felt blood rise to her cheeks.

He smiled. "You have recovered from your illness."

She had to clear her throat. "Yes."

"Welcome," Shem said, raising his voice, making everyone turn to him. He introduced his brothers, the solemn Yepheth and the vividly expressive Khawm, who blinked when Keren looked at him.

Shem lifted his hands, praying, "O Most High, be with us today. . . ."

Keren noticed Nimr-Rada shifting impatiently. She glanced at him; he was watching her closely, his eyes impenetrable. She felt like prey. Was he wondering why she hadn't bowed? Or if she had returned to the ways of the Most High? Well, let him wonder. Throughout the prayers, she watched him steadily, quietly, thinking, *Lawkham . . . Meherah . . . Yabal . . . Revakhaw . . . her son . . .*

He continued to stare. When Shem's prayer ended, Nimr-Rada said, "No one has declared the purpose of this gathering. I ask that it be declared now."

"Above all, this is a peaceful gathering," Yepheth said firmly. "Everyone who speaks will be heard. No one will be denied."

Disdainful, Nimr-Rada looked around. "Then let all my enemies speak, and I will answer them." He waited, clearly enjoying the silence.

At last, Shem spoke calmly. "Whom do you consider to be an enemy? My son, your Uncle Asshur, here?" Shem indicated a handsome, solidly muscled man clad in plain gray wool and a wide fringe-tied leather belt. "What did he do to offend you?"

Another man—fine skinned with a long, thin beard said, "Asshur refused to pay tributes."

"Do you say this for me or against me, O Mitzrayim, brother of my own father?" Nimr-Rada asked testily.

Mitzrayim raised a thin eyebrow at him. "It's the truth, nephew. Nothing more. That's why you took his lands."

"Look to your own lands," Nimr-Rada warned.

"Why should you threaten Mitzrayim?" the First Father Khawm asked Nimr-Rada, incredulous. "If it's the truth, then let him speak. It's well known that you've demanded tributes from all the other tribes—and punished them for refusing." As Nimr-Rada stared coldly, Khawm said, "You are entirely too proud, son of my son."

Stolidly Yepheth asked, "What other truths do you hate, O Nimr-Rada?"

"The Most High," Keren answered.

Instantly, Nimr-Rada turned on her. "*You* pledged your loyalty to me—with your life!"

"And you extracted my pledge with your knife," Keren said, gripping her decorative bow. "This scar is proof of that!" She touched the ridge of paled flesh on her throat.

"You threatened this young woman's life?" Yepheth sounded shocked. "You cut at her throat?"

"She is a rebellious woman." Nimr-Rada lowered his chin at Keren menacingly.

"Tell everyone why I rebelled," Keren insisted. "Tell everyone how you've tried to turn me from loving the Most High to make me worship your god, Shemesh."

Nimr-Rada glared at her, his obsidian-dark eyes unblinking.

He's deciding how he will kill me, Keren thought, sweat prickling over her body. She forced herself to return his stare. "Tell them how you killed your own son."

Now Nimr-Rada eyed Revakhaw, who burst into frightened tears.

"You don't deny these things?" Shem asked quietly.

Nimr-Rada ignored him.

Keren persisted, trembling. "Tell them how you murdered Lawkham—one of your near kinsmen—for accidentally touching me as he went to help someone else."

"That was no murder; he disobeyed my orders." Nimr-Rada was tensed, gripping his ornate sword.

"What of your newborn son, whose body I saw you burn on your altar of Shemesh!"

"Did you see me kill him?" Nimr-Rada sneered. "No."

"But I saw you kill my father," another man said, furious. Zehker emerged from the crowd, weaponless.

Keren shivered at his words and his rage. As Nimr-Rada turned, she slipped an arrow from her quiver, praying she could protect Zehker.

He confronted Nimr-Rada. "You had no reason to kill my father."

"He threatened me with his ax," Nimr-Rada said. "You were a boy. You remember nothing."

"He never lifted his ax against you—he only rejected your demand for a tribute!" Zehker cried. "You killed him for the joy of killing—then you wounded my mother, though I begged you for mercy! You left her on the steppes to die with my little sisters."

"I spared you."

"You took me as a tribute—a remembrance of your first murders! *Zehker*—a memento." Zehker spat toward Nimr-Rada. "That's for the name you gave me!"

Wielding the bone sword, Nimr-Rada leaped to his feet.

Keren raised her bow and cried, "Nimr-Rada!" He flashed a look at her, then froze. Keren aimed for his heart.

"Lower your weapons!" Shem commanded. "Karan, put down the bow."

"No," Keren said through clenched teeth, aware of Metiyl to Nimr-Rada's left, raising an ax.

"Metiyl, sit down. Lower your weapons," Shem repeated. "Nimr-Rada, give me your sword. Karan, put down your bow."

"No." Sweat glided down her cheeks like tears. She held her aim.

Softly persuasive, he urged, "Metiyl, Zehker, sit down."

They retreated reluctantly.

Again Shem said, "Nimr-Rada, give me your sword so Karan will put down her weapon."

Nimr-Rada scornfully handed his sword to Shem, then sat down again, sliding his hand into his leopard-skin wrap —*for a knife*, Keren thought, still aiming her bow and arrow.

Contemptuous, Nimr-Rada sneered, "You have made yourself my enemy, *woman*. Pray your Most High protects you."

"Unlike your Shemesh," Keren replied, holding his gaze. She focused on him completely now—as he had trained her to kill.

Before she could release the arrow, a blade slashed Nimr-Rada's throat, erupting in blood. Nimr-Rada's eyes widened, disbelieving, as he lifted his hands to his throat in a futile effort to save himself from his own sword. He toppled.

Amid sudden screams, curses, and the chaos of others fleeing, Keren lowered her bow and stared at Nimr-Rada's executioner: Shem.

Twenty-Five

UNABLE TO BELIEVE what she had seen, Keren said, "Father of my Fathers . . ."

Shem shook his head at her gently and said, "Child, you didn't obey me. But I forgive you. . . ."

Forcefully he pulled out Nimr-Rada's bloodied sword. His brothers joined him, standing guard over Nimr-Rada's bleeding corpse, watching his guardsmen flee in panic. Behind Shem, I'ma-Annah burst into tears, while I'ma-Ghinnah and I'ma-Tirtsah reached for her, dazed.

"Lady!" Her guardsman Ethniy rushed toward Keren; his eyes almost rolled in alarm. "Where are Na'ah and the others?"

Metiyl's son Khawrawsh joined them swiftly, his new ax flashing as he motioned Keren and the weeping Reva-khaw outside. "My father says you must leave the meeting area. I'll guard you. Where are your attendants?"

"Outside; we'll find them." Gripping her bow, Keren stood, looking across the mats at Zehker.

He brandished an ax, calling urgently, "Go! Keep watch; let us know if his guardsmen return."

His guardsmen. Keren glanced at Nimr-Rada's body, disbelieving. His eyes stared at nothingness. He-Who-Lifts-the-Skies had truly rejoined the dust of the earth.

Neshar emerged from his hiding place behind the tent, carrying an ax.

"Get her out of here," he begged Keren, nodding toward Revakhaw, who stood tearfully clutching Keren's sandals.

Keren led Revakhaw from the meeting area. Outside, she scanned the encampment for Tsinnah and her other attendants. She didn't see them. But Nimr-Rada's guardsmen were scattering, mounting their horses, leaving their tents and many of their weapons. Apparently they feared retribution from the tribes they had oppressed for so long.

"Could Tsinnah be in the women's tent?" Khawrawsh wondered aloud, sounding agitated. Eyeing him, Keren realized that his winter-long flirtation with Tsinnah had been serious; he was desperate to find her.

Keren hurried toward the tent; shaded figures lingered inside. Clutching her bow and arrow, she charged through the entrance, looked around, and sighed her relief. Alatah, Tsinnah, and Na'ah were huddled on a mat with Bekiyrah, all of them wet eyed and frightened.

Bekiyrah stood swiftly, crying, "Is my husband dead?"

"No," Keren said. "Asshur is with the other men." Reluctantly she added, "The Father of my Fathers put Nimr-Rada to death."

"Shem . . . ?" Bekiyrah faltered, stunned.

Still half shocked herself, Keren nodded.

Beside her now, Revakhaw tossed Keren's sandals away, yelling, "He's dead! He's truly dead. And we're alive!"

Annah lay in the women's tent, praying she had finished weeping for a while. She hadn't been this upset since the Great Destruction. Nimr-Rada was actually dead, and Shem—her own dear Shem—had struck him down. Annah shut her eyes against the horrible image. She pleaded with the Most High. *Take this memory from me, of my beloved shedding another man's blood.*

Someone pressed a wet cloth to her face. Looking up, Annah saw Tirtsah and Ghinnah leaning over her. Tirtsah knelt.

"Ma'adannah, Shem had no choice. Nimr-Rada was corrupted; he would have destroyed us all."

"He was your grandson," Annah said brokenly. "I'm sorry."

Tirtsah's eyes brimmed. "I wish he hadn't been. . . ." She wept as Ghinnah hugged her, silent and swollen faced.

Grieving, Annah pulled the wet cloth over her eyes.

Still holding her bow, Keren watched with Khawrawsh and Ethniy from their place before the women's tent. A hush had settled over everything; men were quietly shifting their tents and gear and dividing the belongings of Nimr-Rada and his men.

Now Ashkenaz, her mother's brother, approached, brawny and full bearded. Keren hadn't seen him in years.

He beamed at her, his voice raspy but friendly. "The horsemen have all fled. I don't believe they'll come back. But I've told everyone here to bring their tents close in; we'll keep watch tonight."

They're gone, Keren thought. It seemed so unreal. She stared at her uncle blankly, too dazed to acknowledge him properly.

He frowned. "Have you forgotten me, Karan-child? I'm hurt."

"Forgive me, Uncle Ashkenaz. I haven't forgotten you; I'm just a little . . . scared." Keren smiled now, trusting him. He looked half wild, like one who had lived his entire life in the highlands.

Her uncle's brown eyes crinkled at the corners. "Well, don't worry. When you've married that guardsman of yours, you should come live in my tribe. We're close to the Ancient Ones, but far enough from those horsemen; if they want revenge, you'd be safe with us."

"Thank you. I'll remember your invitation." Alerted by his reference to Zehker, Keren looked around, concerned. She hadn't seen him yet. "Are the First Fathers still in their meeting place?"

Ashkenaz straightened, sober now. "Yes. And I think you should know: They've cut Nimr-Rada's body into pieces—to be sent to the Great City and to other tribes as a warning. Nimr-Rada should never have rebelled against the Most High."

Keren quelled her squeamishness, imagining Nimr-Rada hacked apart like some slaughtered bull. And Zehker, Metiyl, and Neshar all had axes. . . . She lowered her head. "I'm glad you told me, Uncle. Thank you."

"Certainly." He marched away, whistling and giving orders to others—a man in benevolent control of his tribe.

Feeling safer, Keren thanked Khawrawsh and the wary Ethniy, then entered the women's tent and went to her pallet. She stored her weapons and stripped off all her gold ornaments, dumping them in a glittering heap on her gray coverlet. By the time she had finished, she realized that the other women were looking at her. Smiling determinedly at the mournful I'ma-Annah, she said, "I'm going to find my father and Zehker. Then I'll come back and help with the evening meal—if anyone can eat."

They were quiet. Alatah pointed out timidly, "You have blood on you."

Keren looked down and noticed a darkening spatter over her chest guard and skirts. Nimr-Rada's blood. Swallowing, she stammered, "I-I'll . . . go wash."

"We'll prepare the food," Na'ah said.

Nodding, Keren hurried outside to the meeting area. Shem and his brothers were standing before the main tent, talking quietly with her father. Meshek held out his arms, smiling. "Daughter, come here."

Keren approached him, suddenly feeling like a lost child, found again.

Meshek hugged her tight and kissed her cheek, muttering fiercely, "I'm proud of you!"

She buried her face against his overtunic and cried, unable to believe that she could actually hug him. He was so warm. And happy. He kissed her again, patting her comfortably. "All's well; you're safe, and that's what matters."

Finally he released her, and she wiped her eyes, sniffling, wishing she could blow her nose.

Shem greeted her formally. "Karan, you've fulfilled your duties as the Most High intended. Thank you."

"But Ra-Anan and Sharah still rule the Great City. . . ."

"Let the Most High deal with them," Shem murmured, subdued. He held out his arms. She hugged him gladly, and he kissed her forehead. "Go wash now; we should all wash ourselves."

Meshek cleared his throat. "Zehker—if he is still named Zehker—is at the river. That way."

Before Keren could leave, the First Father Khawm stopped her. "What of my son Kuwsh?"

Kuwsh. Keren felt ill. What could she say about Kuwsh that wouldn't make his father miserable? She sighed. "Your Kuwsh was proud of Nimr-Rada and loves his status in the Great City. He . . . rebels against the will of the Most High."

"I blame myself," Khawm said, not looking at her. "This is all from my own rebellion."

"You shouldn't blame yourself for everything, Father Khawm," Keren replied. "Kuwsh and Nimr-Rada chose a way they could have easily rejected—as my brother and sister have chosen. They love themselves above all."

"Listen to her," Yepheth told Khawm. "Forgive yourself. Then come with us to visit Father and I'ma."

Sensing the start of an intense family discussion, Keren excused herself, smiled at her father, and hurried toward the river. She met Metiyl, Shem's son Asshur, and her brother Neshar as they strode up the riverbank, all three dripping wet and clean.

Asshur inclined his head toward her, then hesitated, seeming anxious. "Have you seen my Bekiyrah?"

Keren was touched by his concern. "She's in the women's tent, fretting for you."

He grinned, suddenly looking like Shem. Beside him, Metiyl said, "Well done, Karan-child. By the way, your beloved is there." He jerked his thumb toward the river.

Keren thanked him and made a face at Neshar, who bowed mockingly. "I honor you, Lady!"

"Please, never call me by that title again."

He laughed and waved her off.

She found Zehker sitting on the riverbank, staring at the torrent. His hands and arms were clean, but his face was smudged with blood. He looked up at her, clearly exhausted.

Keren unwound her linen belt and partially dipped it in the cold water. Then she knelt before Zehker, suddenly shy. "Here."

"He's dead."

"Yes. We're free."

Zehker shut his eyes. "It doesn't seem real. He ruled us for so long."

She changed the subject, unwilling to think of Nimr-Rada. "I wish I could have met your parents and your sisters."

"They would have loved you." Composed now, he looked around warily. They were alone. He faced her, grim. "Do you *want* to marry me?"

"Only if you want me."

A slow, dawning smile lit his stern eyes and revealed his dimples. Encouraged, Keren scrubbed his face with the wet portion of linen, then with the dried portion. She could truly touch him . . . as she had longed to do for years . . . amazing. She caressed his clean face. Then he seized her, swiftly pulling her into his lap, kissing her mouth, her throat, her cheeks, holding her tight as if he feared she would escape.

Laughing, she hugged him, exhilarated by his new spontaneity and warmed by his ardor. At last he simply held her, sighing, and she snuggled against him. Then she swatted his shoulder. "You terrified me this morning! Why did you challenge Nimr-Rada unarmed?"

He stared, obviously perplexed by her sudden shift in mood. "That foolish Ethniy sat on my mat and fleeces where I'd hidden my ax. I couldn't get him to move." Quietly he added, "I also realized, by the look on your face, that if I could make Nimr-Rada turn from you long enough, you'd draw your bow."

"Even so, you frightened me."

"Forgive me."

Nodding, she paused, curious. "What was your name before you were Zehker?"

"Zekaryah."

Zekaryah—*God has remembered.* Absorbing this meaning, Keren smiled. Truly, the Most High had remembered His small child, stolen by Nimr-Rada. "Zekaryah." Contented, she nestled against him. "I love you."

To her delight, he nuzzled her throat, kissing her again. "But I loved you first."

"See what happens when you bring all these pretty girls into the mountains?" Metiyl grumbled unconvincingly, waving a hand at the crowded clearing before the Lodge of Noakh. "My Khawrawsh loses his wits altogether. I told him he had to marry your little Tsinnah; she'll keep him sensible."

"I'm glad," Keren said, watching Khawrawsh and Tsinnah standing together with Ethniy and Na'ah, jubilant, waiting for their wedding blessings. "Tsinnah will be safe in your tribe."

"Of course she will. But what are you going to do with

her?" Metiyl demanded, jerking his chin toward the sullen Gebuwrah, who irritated him immensely.

Keren almost laughed. "Didn't you know? She and Alatah are traveling with you to rejoin their families when your Father Asshur reclaims your lands on the plains."

"What?"

Zekaryah approached Keren now, frowning at Metiyl. "Don't steal my bride; your wife will beat you."

Instantly, Metiyl glanced at his wife, the hearty, charming Tebuwnaw, whom he adored and feared. Bright as a bird in red wool, Tebuwnaw saw him, put her plump hands on her hips, and called out, "What are you doing?"

"Coming to kiss you."

"Wise answer." They laughed and kissed each other, then went arm in arm to stand near Khawrawsh and Tsinnah, who welcomed them happily.

"Lady—I mean, Keren." Alatah offered Keren a large square of felted gray wool—a shawl Alatah had made this past winter. "I wanted to give you this; I thought you could wear it today, then use it later to wrap your firstborn. It's not much, but . . ."

Keren unfolded the shawl, which now bore red beads on its fringed corners. Keren recognized the beads from a necklace she had given to Alatah after Nimr-Rada's death. "It's wonderful! But, Alatah, I gave you that necklace so you could barter it."

"I still have the gold," Alatah replied. "It's enough. But I wanted you to remember me. I'm going to miss you—though I'll be so glad to return to my family!"

"May the Most High bless them, and you."

"May He bless you," Alatah responded shyly, daring to smile at Zekaryah.

He smiled in return. "Thank you, Alatah."

Noakh and Naomi emerged from the lodge, followed by the First Fathers and the First Mothers, and Meshek and Chaciydah. Alatah gave Keren a quick hug, then draped the shawl over her shoulders, rearranging her hair. Stepping back, Alatah nodded approvingly, unable to speak.

Equally emotional, Chaciydah met Keren and Zekaryah in front of the lodge, hugging them tearfully. "I can't believe this day has arrived. You and Neshar—both married!"

Meshek interposed, taking Chaciydah's hand. "Everyone's waiting, beloved."

Everyone. Noakh, I'ma-Naomi, Shem, I'ma-Annah, Yepheth, I'ma-Ghinnah, Khawm, and I'ma-Tirtsah. Keren was glad that they were finally reunited and amazed at how young the First Fathers and First Mothers all seemed. They had been through so much that surely they ought to look as old as their cherished Noakh and I'ma-Naomi.

Someone nudged Keren gently: Revakhaw. Standing with Neshar, she lifted her eyebrows at Keren. In awe she whispered, "I never dreamed I would meet all the Ancient Ones together, much less receive all their blessings!"

Noakh hushed everyone, lifting his hands, his expression deeply moved. "I am truly delighted to be surrounded by those I love—and to be asked to give the first blessing to these young ones." He indicated all four couples. Bemused, he shook his silvery head. "It's a good thing you've all agreed to be married at the same time; otherwise I'd be exhausted with too much talking."

As everyone laughed, he said, "Please, each of you, take your beloved by the hand."

Zekaryah's hands were warm. Keren looked up at him. He was smiling; she wanted to never look away from his face. All that He-Who-Lifts-the-Skies had been, with all his strength and power and gold . . . he was nothing compared to her husband. *Thank You,* Keren thought, *He-Who-Created-These-Skies, O Most High, thank You!*

Annah knelt beside Shem during the wedding feast, remembering their own wedding day. It seemed only a week ago, yet ages past. *Impossible. But truly, I would have been dead long before now if not for You, O Most High. . . .*

She leaned against Shem, sighing. He bent toward her tenderly. He was so loving; how could he have put Nimr-Rada to death? Another impossibility. At least Khawm and Tirtsah supported his verdict; they had mourned for their grandson, but not for the vicious, unrighteous man he had become.

"Look at them," Shem murmured, smiling at Eliyshama and Tsereth's youngest children, who were capering after their older brothers, Meysha and Darak, delighted to see them after the yearlong separation.

Meysha, Darak, and Metiyl's oldest, Yeiysh, had proudly returned Noakh's gold leaf pendant, Shem's gold medallion, and Annah's treasured shell carving, all virtually unscathed. But the three young men had matured during their journeys.

The children of our children are older than we were at these same ages. . . .

Annah cringed at the thought. But it was true: the younger generations were aging more rapidly. Shem had been trying to warn her of this for years. Even their dear Karan-child . . . *No.* Annah forced the thought away. She couldn't endure it. Particularly not on this day, when

Karan looked so beautiful and happy, preparing to dance with her new husband. To distract herself, Annah took Shem's hand.

"Let's go dance with our children." *And celebrate before the Most High.*

Drowsily, Keren peeked out of her tent. A misty dawn, but she was certain it would clear soon. Shaking herself awake, she knelt and worked her unruly hair into a thick braid, binding it with a leather cord. Behind her, Zekaryah finished cinching his foot coverings. As she wound the braid around her head and fastened it with slender wooden pins, Zekaryah kissed the back of her neck, making her shiver deliciously. He stood.

"I'm going to help your father and Shem. What are you doing today?"

She stood, wrapping her arms around him. "Harvesting, preserving, cleaning, cooking, sewing, chasing Yelalah, Nekokhah, and Achyow . . . and purifying my gold."

"What's left of it," he muttered wryly. To his disgust, she had given a gold cuff and some rings to Gebuwrah.

Keren shook her head at him, stern. "I had to repay Gebuwrah for her time in the goat's pen; you were terrible."

"I considered the dung heap."

Despite herself, Keren laughed. "We'll be rid of her today. Give me a kiss."

He gave her several kisses, lingering warmly, tempting her to forget work. In many ways, it seemed they had been married for years instead of days—but being able to kiss and touch him would always seem new.

An ebullient, high-pitched little voice outside warned them Achyow was near. Zekaryah released her unwillingly. "At least he's not afraid of you anymore."

As Zekaryah left the tent, Keren heard Achyow's piping voice. "Is she ready?"

"Go see," Zekaryah told him. Keren hurriedly gathered her gold as Achyow scrambled into the tent, bright eyed and disheveled.

"I have my hammer," he chirped, waving a wooden mallet.

"Don't hit anyone with it." Keren scooped her mending into a basket with the gold, then rumpled his thick dark hair. "That's everything; let's go. Out-out!"

"You told me I could beat your gold."

"With I'ma-Annah's help," Keren reminded him. Glancing around the clearing before the Ancient One's lodge, she saw Alatah and Gebuwrah preparing to leave with Metiyl's family.

Gebuwrah deliberately looked away.

Keren approached her, hoping to part cordially. "Gebuwrah, I wish you blessings."

"Do you?" Gebuwrah tied a rolled grass mat onto her horse's back. Finished, she threw Keren an unforgiving scowl. "You think you've won, but they'll come after you."

Keren met her glare calmly. "I know. And you're wrong; I don't think I've won. I'll never have a normal life. Nimr-Rada destroyed that hope for me." Keren hesitated. "I don't understand how you can be so angry. You were with us all these years; you know everything that's happened. And you know that if your He-Who-Lifts-the-Skies had lived, others would have died. All I can conclude is that you truly care more about yourself and the honors you've lost. Even so, Gebuwrah, may the Most High bless you."

Gebuwrah looked away, stone-faced. Keren left her without another word.

Before they fell asleep that night, Zekaryah murmured into Keren's ear, "Ashkenaz insists we should live with his people, though Neshar and Ethniy plan to move into the western mountain tribes with my First Father, Yepheth and his Ghinnah; they believe they'll be safer there."

You think you've won, but they'll come after you. Remembering Gebuwrah's hatred, Keren opened her eyes, suddenly wide-awake. "Perhaps Uncle Ashkenaz is right. If his people are willing to risk our presence . . ."

Ra-Anan looked from Kuwsh's dignified brother Mitzrayim to the dark bundle Mitzrayim had just placed on Ra-Anan's courtyard pavings. *His head? Nimr-Rada's head?* Beside Ra-Anan, Kuwsh sucked in a hoarse, raging breath.

"It's enough to know he's dead! What are you trying to do to me, my own brother, by bringing me *that?* Do you want to kill me?"

Mitzrayim lifted his thinly bearded chin. "Would you rather I leave it to be picked apart like carrion? It was all I could preserve of your son's body. If you had seen—"

Kuwsh flung his hands upward, stopping Mitzrayim's words. And before Ra-Anan could say anything, Kuwsh bounded off his mat and fled the courtyard. Mitzrayim followed him quickly.

Good. Ra-Anan relaxed. He would talk to Kuwsh later and help him to see what must be done to preserve Nimr-

Rada's kingdom. But first, he would deal with Sharah. Marching to the gate, Ra-Anan snapped at the shock-silenced Perek. "Go tell the Lady Sharah that I must speak to her alone. Immediately. It's worth her life."

Perek's mouth worked soundlessly, like a fish's. Then he asked, "He-Who-Lifts-the-Skies . . . is truly dead?"

"Yes. Now, tell the Lady Sharah the truth if you must, but bring her to me."

Returning to his emptied courtyard, Ra-Anan opened the dark leather bundle.

Nimr-Rada's dried head gaped at him from within the leather folds—insignificant now. Satisfied, Ra-Anan re-tied the bundle and set it aside.

~·❦ ❦·~

Sharah knelt before Ra-Anan, too excited to be indignant at being summoned like a mere servant. Leaning forward, she hissed, "Is it true he's dead?"

"Completely true. You need to act like a grieving wife."

"Of course." But she was thrilled, thinking, *Now I can marry Qaydawr!* He was the most handsome, most perfect man in the world—the only one she had ever loved—though she had first tempted him to be revenged against Nimr-Rada for his cruelty. It had been so easy to send most of her clever, hostile servants away on prolonged visits to their families, then to meet Qaydawr in Nimr-Rada's abandoned rooms. She weakened, remembering Qaydawr kisses and how much he adored her. She had dreaded Nimr-Rada's return. But now, she would never see Nimr-Rada again. Unable to contain her joy, she smiled at Ra-Anan. "I'm with child."

His eyes widened. "Have you just realized this?"

"Yes."

"Sharah. . . ." Ra-Anan sighed as if disgusted. "Don't tell me that Nimr-Rada is the father of your child. I'm not some ignorant man from the streets: I calculate days, weeks, and months, so I know it's not his—he's been gone too long. Who is the father?"

"It doesn't matter; I'm going to marry him," Sharah answered, gleeful.

"Not if you want to keep Nimr-Rada's kingdom."

Sharah's delight faded. "What do you mean?"

Ra-Anan leaned forward, glaring. "Think! If the citizens believe that you carry Nimr-Rada's child, then they'll pour all their hopes into that child. You'll rule them! But let them realize that you've taken a lover and are bearing *his* child, and you'll be chased from the Great City like the faithless creature you are—if they let you live!"

Sharah shook her head. "They'd kill me?"

"If they don't, Kuwsh will. Whoever your beloved is, you'll have to give him up."

"But . . . I can't. I love him."

"A perfect time for you to fall in love. You'll lose your chance to rule this kingdom for your child. For *his* child."

Sharah tried to think of another way; she wanted everything—the kingdom and Qaydawr. "I could marry him later, after everyone thinks this child is Nimr-Rada's."

"That's an idea worth considering," Ra-Anan said, straightening. "But what man deserves such glory? Whom are we talking about?"

"Qaydawr," she admitted reluctantly. Ra-Anan would find out soon enough.

Ra-Anan grimaced. "I suppose he can be trusted. Obviously you were discreet enough to avoid my spies. Stay for the evening meal. We'll talk again later. But not a word of your Qaydawr to anyone. Not even to my Zeva'ah."

As soon as he was alone, Ra-Anan went to the gate, startling Perek and his relief guard, Abdiy. He had caught them gossiping. "Perek, do you remember Qaydawr, that guardsman who followed Nimr-Rada two years ago but is now banished to the stables?"

Perek snorted. "That long-lashed boy with the oily manners?"

"Yes. He betrayed Nimr-Rada. Bring me some token of his death. But hide his body well. Abdiy, forget you heard this."

Bowing, Perek vanished into the looming darkness. Ra-Anan closed the gate on the dazed Abdiy, then stared up at the emerging stars, for once not seeing them. *He-Who-Lifts-the-Skies . . . you were not our Promised One. No matter. We can create another.* He smiled.

Epilogue

KEREN LED DOBE after Zekaryah, Ashkenaz, his men, and Zekaryah's packhorses, through the damp green valley to Ashkenaz's settlement. She prayed that the women and children of his tribe would not be frightened by her eyes.

"There we are," Ashkenaz rumbled. Waving his long-spear toward a cluster of timber-and-stone lodges, he greeted a rugged leather-clad youth. "Uzziel! Everything's still standing. Is everyone well?"

"Everyone, Father?" Uzziel grinned. "You mean my Ritspah and the baby? Yes, they're well—we have a girl!"

Ashkenaz punched his shoulder lightly. "Good. I hope she doesn't look like you!"

Uzziel laughed.

Ashkenaz nodded to Keren. "The women are probably in the main lodge, Keren. Some of them are shy. Particularly his Ritspah."

By Uzziel's wry face, Keren understood that Ritspah was anything but shy. Zekaryah pulled Dobe's reins from Keren's cold hands and patted her in a temporary farewell. Ashkenaz urged her toward the main lodge.

"Go! They'll be glad to see you. And tell my wife—er, your Aunt Laheh'beth—that I'm here."

Keren approached the main lodge, hugging herself nervously. Her new gold cuffs—made by I'ma-Annah—pressed into her forearms. She paused in the doorway.

Immediately, a woman called from inside, "Well, who are you? Where's your family?"

"I'm Keren. My husband is outside with my Uncle Ashkenaz. I'm looking for my Aunt Laheh'beth and Ritspah."

"I'm Ritspah," the woman said genially. She was tall, keen eyed, and attractive, with flushed brown skin and a ruddy, nursing infant in one arm. "I haven't met you before, have I? How long are you staying?"

"As long as you'll endure me."

Ritspah chortled. "You'll have to endure *me*. Come in, Keren; the others are all here. Laheh'beth, one of your nieces is visiting. Look, everyone—her eyes are wonderful!"

Laheh'beth hurried forward, tall, brown, and brisk, wiping her hands on a rough swatch of cloth. "Now, aren't you Chaciydah's youngest daughter?" She hesitated. "You didn't bring your pale sister, did you?"

Smiling, Keren shook her head. "No, she wants nothing to do with me."

Laheh'beth sighed, obviously relieved. A number of women—about half, Keren recognized as cousins—abandoned various tasks throughout the lodge; Ritspah rattled off their names, which escaped Keren altogether. They greeted her eagerly and sat down near a smoldering hearth, plying her with bread, dried fruit, and a bitter-sweet brewed drink, while small children played throughout the lodge. The women were attractive like Ritspah, all with dark hair and eyes. But Keren gasped to see their children. Some had light skin, others had greenish eyes, and two had copper-red curls such as Keren had never seen. Keren felt dizzied—and not from the strong-brewed drink. She was no longer unique! The realization made her want to dance like a child.

One toddler approached Keren jauntily. He was a handsome, husky baby with glowing tawny skin, clear green-brown eyes, fluttering plumes of dark hair, and a remarkable dimpled chin. But his fine looks were nothing beside his charm. He confidently settled into Keren's lap, inspected her gold cuffs, then showed his approval by cheerfully raising his eyebrows and mouthing an O of mock surprise. Keren laughed.

"Little man! Who are you?"

"He's my youngest, Kaleb," one woman confessed, embarrassed. "Don't let him persuade you to spoil him."

"Kal," the toddler said brightly. Then he spied the leather cord around Keren's neck, which held a new gold pendant created by I'ma-Annah. She let him play with the pendant while she talked with the women. Kal's older brothers, and his mother, Pakhdaw, couldn't lure the little boy from Keren's lap.

At last, as Laheh'beth stood to go outside, Keren said, "If you don't mind, Pakhdaw, I'll tend Kal for a while." Pakhdaw smiled gratefully.

Outside, the men were inspecting the horses and Zekaryah's weapons.

Zekaryah grinned as Keren approached. "You stole someone's baby."

"He stole me." As Keren spoke, Kal pointed to the horses, making Keren hold him toward Dobe.

While Kal happily patted Dobe, Zekaryah said, "Beloved, they'll build us a dwelling if we'll share our horses and teach them to hunt with our weapons."

"Oh." Keren wasn't sure that she wanted to teach anyone to use weapons. However, if the tribe of Ashkenaz was going to shelter her, then it might be best for them to be able to defend themselves against Nimr-Rada's followers. The thought made Keren ill.

Zekaryah distracted her by tousling the toddler Kaleb's dark, red-tinged hair. "He chewed your pendant," Zekaryah observed.

Keren laughed, seeing small tooth marks in the new gold disc.

"Rascal. It doesn't matter; our children will add their marks to his."

Clearly pleased by the thought of children, Zekaryah kissed her, unabashed by everyone's hoots and laughter.

Their teasing made Keren feel completely accepted. She kissed Zekaryah tenderly, then said, "Come, Kal. If your mother agrees, you'll be the first in your tribe to ride a horse."

Triumphant, Sharah rode with her cherished, perfect toddler-son through the streets of the Great City, followed by her servants and guards and Nimr-Rada's prized leopards—reminders of the Great King's power. The citizens' adoration had eased Sharah's violent grief at Qaydawr's death—grief everyone had wrongly attributed to her mourning Nimr-Rada.

Never in her life would she forget the instant when Ra-Anan had placed Qaydawr's unmistakable, long-lashed severed eyelids before her, announcing his death. She had screamed, wept, and raved for days.

I haven't forgiven you, Ra-Anan, Sharah thought. *But you are necessary for me to finish my tower and rule my kingdom. One day I'll tell my son the truth, and then you'll die. Perhaps I'll even be rid of Kuwsh. . . .*

"Little Son of Heaven!" a woman cried to Sharah's child.

Elated, Sharah held her son high. He delighted everyone by laughing and raising his small fists to the skies.

Glossary

Abdiy (Ab-<u>dee</u>) Servicable.

Achlai (Akh-<u>lah</u>-ee) Wishful.

Achyow (Akh-<u>yo</u>) Brotherly.

Alatah (Al-aw-<u>taw</u>) To cover; dusk.

Annah (<u>Awn</u>-naw) A plea: "I beseech thee" or "Oh now!"

Arawm (Ar<u>awm</u>) Highland.

Ashkenaz (Ash-ken-<u>az</u>) ? Meaning unknown.

Asshur (Ash-<u>shoor</u>) To guide. To be level.

Azaz (Aw-<u>zawz</u>) Strong.

Bachan (Baw-<u>khan</u>) To test (especially metals).

Becay (Bes-<u>ah</u>-ee) Domineering.

Bekiyrah (Bek-ee-<u>raw</u>) Eldest daughter. Firstborn.

Chaciydah (Khas-ee-<u>daw</u>) Kind (maternal) Bird, i.e., a stork.

Chashum (Khaw-<u>shoom</u>) Enriched.

Chayeh (Khaw-<u>yeh</u>) Vigorous: lively.

Darak (Daw-<u>rak</u>) To tread.

Demamah (Dem-aw-<u>maw</u>) Quiet.

Dobe (<u>Do</u>-beh) To be sluggish, i.e. restful.

Eliyshama (El-ee-shaw-<u>maw</u>) God of hearing.

Erek (<u>Eh</u>-rek) Length.

Ethniy (Eth-<u>nee</u>) Munificence.

Gebuwrah (Gheb-oo-<u>raw</u>) Force. (By implication, "victory.")

Ghinnah (Ghin-<u>naw</u>) Garden.

Gibbawr (Gib-<u>bawr</u>) Valiant.

Hadarah (Had-aw-<u>raw</u>) Decoration: beauty, honor.

I'ma (<u>Ame</u>-aw) Derived from "Im" or "Em" and the syllable "Ma." Mother. Bond of the family.

Kaleb (Kaw-<u>labe</u>) Forcible.

Kana (Kaw-<u>nah</u>) To bend the knee.

Karan (Kaw-<u>ran</u>) To push or gore.

Kebuwddah (Keb-ood-<u>daw</u>) Weightiness, as in "glorious."

Keren (<u>Keh</u>-ren) A ray of light.

Kharawsh (Khaw-<u>rawsh</u>) Craftsman.

Khawm (Khawm) Heat, i.e., a tropical climate.

Khawvilah (Khav-ee-<u>law</u>) Name of lands in the preflood world. "Circular." Son of Kuwsh.

Khemdaw (Khem-<u>daw</u>) Goodly; precious.

Khuldah (Khool-<u>daw</u>) A weasel (from its gliding motion).

Kuwsh (Koosh) Possible meanings: To scatter. Confusion. Chaos.

Laheh'beth (Lah-<u>eh</u>-beth) To gleam. A flame. Or the point of a weapon.

Lawkham (Law-<u>kham</u>) To feed on or (figuratively) consume.

Ma'adannah (Mah-ad-an-<u>aw</u>) Pleasure. Dainty. Delight. Also, A bond or Influence.

Mattan (Mat-<u>awn</u>) A present. Gift.

Meherah (Me-hay-<u>raw</u>) Hurry.

Meleah (Mel-ay-<u>aw</u>) Fulfilled, i.e., abundance (of produce or fruit).

Merowm (May-<u>rome</u>) Height.

Meshek (<u>Meh</u>-shek) Sowing; also, a possession: precious.

Metiyl (Met-<u>eel</u>) Bar. In the sense of hammering out or as forged.

Meysha (May-<u>shah</u>) Safety.

Mitzrayim (Mits-<u>rah</u>-yim) Derived from Matsowr (Maw-tsore.) A limit. Fortified. Egypt.

Miyka (Mee-<u>khaw</u>) Abbreviated from "Who is like God." Miykayah.

Na'ah (Na-<u>ah</u>) To be at home: i.e., beautiful.

Naomi (No-om-<u>ee</u>) Pleasant.

Nekokhah (Nek-o-<u>khaw</u>) Straightforward. Integrity.

Neshar (Nesh-<u>ar</u>) Eagle.

Nihyah (nih-<u>yaw</u>) Doleful.

Nimr-Rada (Nem-<u>ar</u>-raw-<u>daw</u>) From Nimar—Leopard and Radah—To tread down. Subjugate.

Noakh (<u>No</u>-akh) Rest.

Pakhdaw (Pakh-<u>daw</u>) Fear.

Perek (<u>Peh</u>-rek) To break apart. Severity. Cruelty.

Qaydawr (Kay-<u>dawr</u>) Dusky.

Ra-Anan (Ra-an-<u>awn</u>) Prosperous: green, flourishing.

Rahmaw (Rah-<u>maw</u>) The mane of a horse—as in "quivering in the wind." Son of Kuwsh.

Ramah (Raw-<u>maw</u>) To delude or betray.

Revakhaw (Rev-aw-<u>khaw</u>) Relief; breathing. Respite.

Ritspah (Rits-<u>paw</u>) Hot stone.

Sabtaw (Sab-<u>taw</u>) ? Unknown meaning. Compare to Sebaw. Son of Kuwsh.

Sabtekaw (Sab-tek-<u>aw</u>) ? Unknown meaning. Compare to Sebaw. Son of Kuwsh.

Sansannah (San-san-<u>naw</u>) A bough.

Sebaw (Seb-<u>aw</u>) ? Unknown meaning. Similar to Saw-baw: To become tipsy. Son of Kuwsh.

Sharah (Shaw-<u>raw</u>) A fortification. Wall.

Shaw-Kak (Shaw-<u>Kak</u>) Rush. To be eager. Greedy.

Shem (Shame) Denotes honor. Literally means "Name." Also, Appointed One, and To desolate.

Shemesh (<u>Sheh</u>-mesh) The sun.

Tebuwnaw (Teb-oo-<u>naw</u>) Intelligence.

Tekhinnah (Tekh-in-<u>naw</u>) Entreaty; favor.

Tirtsah (Teer-<u>tsaw</u>) Delightsomeness.

Tselem (<u>Tseh</u>-lem) To shade; a phantom. Illusion.

Tsereth (<u>Tseh</u>-reth) Splendor.

Tsinnah (Tsin-<u>naw</u>) A hook. Also, a large shield.

Uzziel (Ooz-zee-<u>ale</u>) Strength of God.

Yabal (Yaw-<u>bawl</u>) A stream.

Yeiysh (Yeh-<u>eesh</u>) Hasty.

Yelalah (Yel-aw-<u>law</u>) Howling.

Yepheth (<u>Yeh</u>-feth) Expansion.

Yishrah (Yish-<u>raw</u>) Uprightness.

Yithran (Yith-<u>rawn</u>) Excellence.

Zehker (<u>Zeh</u>-ker) A memento.

Zekaryah (Zek-ar-<u>yaw</u>) God has remembered.

Zeva'ah (Zev-aw-<u>aw</u>) Agitation, fear.

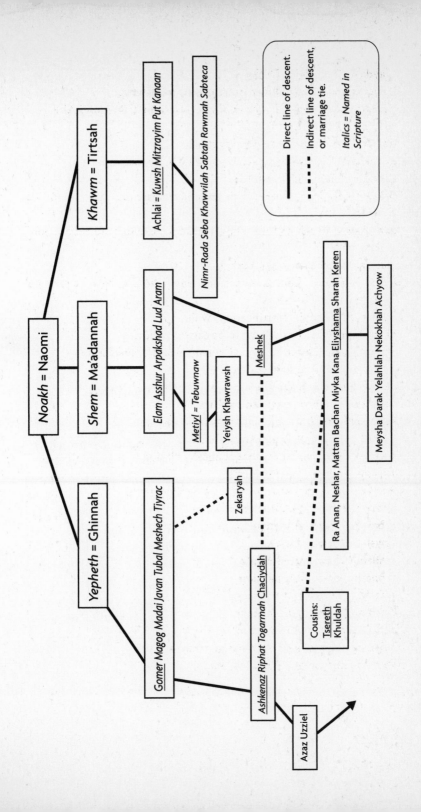

The Heavens Before

ISBN: 0-8024-1363-3

A human! A woman! A nothing!

Annah has not spoken a word in the years since she witnessed her father's brutal murder. Now a young woman, she is desperate to escape the cut-throat society that considers her mad. Then she has an unexpected encounter with a young man who is different from the rest. His name is Shem, son of Noakh.

The Heavens Before retells the enthralling biblical account of the Great Flood—as seen through the eyes of a courageous woman. Brought face to face with an ancient evil, Annah dares to believe in the Most High, the God who is nothing more than foolish legend to the people of her settlement. In a world of astonishing beauty and appalling violence, a world unknowingly speeding toward disaster, Annah's choice will have unforeseen consequences.

MOODY
PUBLISHERS

THE NAME YOU CAN TRUST®

1-800-678-6928 www.MoodyPublishers.org

S<small>INCE</small> 1894, Moody Publishers has been dedicated to equip and motivate people to advance the cause of Christ by publishing evangelical Christian literature and other media for all ages, around the world. Because we are a ministry of the Moody Bible Institute of Chicago, a portion of the proceeds from the sale of this book go to train the next generation of Christian leaders.

If we may serve you in any way in your spiritual journey toward understanding Christ and the Christian life, please contact us at www.moodypublishers.com.

"All Scripture is God-breathed and is useful for teaching, rebuking, correcting and training in righteousness, so that the man of God may be thoroughly equipped for every good work."
—2 T<small>IMOTHY</small> 3:16, 17

MOODY
PUBLISHERS

THE NAME YOU CAN TRUST®

HE WHO LIFTS THE SKIES TEAM

ACQUIRING EDITOR
Michele Straubel

COPY EDITOR
LB Norton

BACK COVER COPY
Julie-Allyson Ieron, Joy Media

COVER DESIGN
Barb Fisher, LeVan Fisher Design

COVER PHOTO
Kamil Vojnar/Photonica and Paul Burley
Photography/Photonica

INTERIOR DESIGN
Ragont Design

PRINTING AND BINDING
Bethany Press International

The typeface for the text of this book is
Weiss